The Royal Regiment

I0681838

Santosh Kalwar

UNELMA PUBLISHERS

Published by:

Unelma Publishers
Nuijavuori 1
02630 Espoo, Finland
email: unelmapublishers@gmail.com

UNELMA PUBLISHERS

The Royal Regiment

ISBN 978-952-65358-1-4 (softcover)
ISBN 978-952-65358-2-1 (hardcover)
ISBN 978-952-65358-3-8 (PDF)
ISBN 978-952-65358-4-5 (EPUB)

Disclaimer

This is a work of fiction. Names, characters, places, events and incidents are either the products of the author's imagination or used in a fictitious manner. Any resemblance to actual persons, living or dead, or actual events is purely coincidental.

Synopsis / Book description

The Royal Regiment is a British India story that occurs shortly after the First World War. It revolves around a British Battalion serving in India and chronicles the lives of people who have lived there for most of their lives or are relocating by sea for the first time. The characters include Emily Sheffield, a doctor involved in running a mission hospital on the North-West Frontier, Robin Cuimein, a man born in India returning from war in France to begin an appointment with the Indian Civil Service, and Lily Richmond, a teenage girl who experiences high drama marked with cruelties but also finds genuine love from a young soldier. While exploring these characters' journeys, the story predominantly focuses on the British Battalion's experiences serving "East of Suez".

Content

CHAPTER 1

There's little in my lifetime left,
In the race I'm well behind.
Still the memory of my younger days,
So strong, so sweet, so kind.
-David Kerr

Scant attention was paid to the two elderly men as they slowly made their way up from the depths of the Waterloo underground system to the train platforms above. They were largely overlooked because they were just two aging individuals, like thousands of others in the twilight years of their lives. The younger London travellers around them didn't give them a second glance - they were just two old men. However, if any sharp-eyed observer had lingered a few seconds longer, they might have noticed that both men wore their age with dignified pride, as if it were a distinguished dress. A few might have even discerned a military air in their posture and manner. And they wouldn't have been wrong; both were ex-army, having served over sixty years with the Colours.

Joey Payne, the younger but taller of the two, was seventy-eight years old, with silver-white hair and a matching, neatly trimmed moustache. Clad in a thick, sand-coloured camel-hair coat, he used a walking stick in his right hand to ease the stride of his right leg, which had been injured years ago by a Japanese bayonet thrust and was now affected by arthritis. His companion, Benedict Lyall, eighty years old, walked with a slight sag in his shoulders, amplified by hands buried in his overcoat pocket, but his back remained straight. Hidden beneath a grey plaid trilby was the evidence of the years - his once coal-black hair was gone, with only a speckled, granite-toned lower fringe remaining.

It was nearly ten o'clock on a mild Saturday evening in October 1982. The two gentlemen were returning from a memorable occasion - the sixtieth anniversary of the 2nd Battalion, the Queen's Light Infantry's departure for India. This was a significant event as it was the last such reunion. Every two or three years for the last twenty, Lieutenant-General Sir Kyle Bate had arranged for a formal regimental reunion dinner at one of the messes at the Duke of York's Territorial Army Centre in London. Now, this tradition was coming to an end for the most natural of reasons. Sixty years on, only seventeen of the two thousand men who served with the 2nd QLI in India during the mid-1920s were present at that night's dinner. Many of their comrades had been claimed by sickness contracted during Indian service, Pathan bullets, or later by Hitler's and Hirohito's bullets, mines, and shells. Therefore, the reunion was held as much in memory of those who had passed as it was for those still living. At the close of the meal, when General Bate called everyone to their feet for the three loyal toasts: to Queen, Regiment, and absent friends, it was the last one that brought back memories of distantly remembered young, smiling faces, set against the backdrop of hot, dusty, sun-blinding plains. Among the two, Joey had the longest tenure in the Army: thirty-seven years, four of which he spent fighting the Japanese, initially in Burma, then with the 14th Army. He retired in 1957, holding a quartermaster's commission as a lieutenant colonel. Shortly after his retirement, during the Ministry of Defence economy cutbacks, the Regiment was amalgamated, then in the 1960s, amalgamated again. Today, the remnants can be found within the framework of what is now the Light Division.

Benedict left the Army much earlier, in 1946. At the onset of World War II, he was the Regimental Sergeant Major of the 1st Battalion, which was deployed to France during the war's deceptive first nine months. After being wounded during the retreat to Dunkirk and subsequently recovering, he was appointed RSM of the depot, where his age kept him for the duration of the war. The two old soldiers took the tube from Sloan Square and left Chelsea for Waterloo, where they were to board the last train to Edenbridge, Kent. Joey had a bungalow there where he lived alone. A widower for the past seven years, he had shared many pleasant days there with his wife. He stayed active in his community as a local councillor.

Accepting Joey's invitation to spend the night, Benedict planned to travel back to the Midlands on Sunday afternoon. After setting up a garage and taxi business in 1948, he retired and now lived outside of Derby with his granddaughter and her widowed husband. While in the narrow tunnel leading to the escalators that would take them to the station above, the two men had a casual conversation, uninterrupted by the dull echoes of their footsteps. This tranquillity was disrupted by the sound of thunderous running and vulgar swearing. A group of rowdy football supporters, mostly skinheads donning braces, short jeans, football club caps, scarves, and rugged boots, rushed towards them.

Benedict, who was on the outside, tried to drop back behind Joey to allow the youths to pass. However, the inconsiderate mob, bolstered by alcohol and their numbers, brushed past Benedict, one of them even pushing him aside. Not one to tolerate violence, Benedict responded with a swift backhand, catching the youth on the ear with the heel of his hand.

"Imbecilic yob", dismissed Lyall, placing his hand back in his coat pocket to continue walking. The skinhead who had received the cuff spun about, holding his ear. Then, judging not the justification of the old man's retaliation or the cowardliness of his actions, the young thug charged at Benedict with kicks and punches, screaming abuse.

"See ya, ya decrepit old fart!" The first blow struck Lyall on the back of the neck. Then, turning, the second smashed his eyeglasses, embedding splinters in his right eye first. Then, with kicks aimed at his crotch, the old soldier stayed on his feet, doggedly but feebly returning punch for punch; then, with the courage of the pack, he was set upon and beaten to the ground by four or five gleeful skin-headed creatures screaming foul abuse.

The speed of the action caught Joey totally unprepared. One moment his companion dropped back behind him; the next, he turned to face a howling mob set on kicking his friend, now at his feet, to death. With an anguished bellow, he lunged forward, striking blows with his cane, beating back the mob to stand legs astride his fallen mate. Momentarily they recoiled, as much in shock at Payne's crazed appearance as from the sting of his stick. For crazed Joey was, so sudden and atrocious was the assault and so like a past attack on them that he, in a raging trauma, was in mind and vision sped back in time, fighting that enemy and not these modern street savages around him.

Dusk on a Frontier hillside – Benedict down this time – he defends him. The tribesmen in their ragged, grime-grey soiled dresses were on them, jabbing and cutting with their curved bladed talwars (swords). Scraggy men with beak noses, unkempt beards, and dirt-tarnished turbans, they closed in. Again, Payne smelled the stomach-turning defilement of decayed, layered, unwashed body stench, amassed from goat droppings, wood and dung smoke, camel urine and a hundred other excreted wastes picked up while asleep on village earth. Wild-eyed, he stood swinging his walking stick as if a rifle butt, his burning vow: they would not take his mate alive. Screaming almost forgotten eastern curses, "Bhag Jao! Behenchod! Bhag jao!" They, in his delusion, were also howling a Pathan battle cry: "Halla ho! Halla ho!" Defending to his front, Payne never saw the brute who stepped up behind to plunge the blade of a knife into the base of his back. Sagging, he dropped his guard and was punched in the mouth. A razor carpet knife sliced a thin, deep, instantly bloody line from the left forehead to the jawbone as his knees gave way. Collapsed on top of Benedict Lyall, a further attack with boots was delivered to his face and head. Then for several seconds, the tunnel vibrated with victory whoops, cries, and the echoing of fleeing boot steps.

Breaking the silence that followed came the click-clicking of a woman's high-heeled shoes approaching from the tunnel's rail end. At first, she believed them to be just a couple of passed-out drunks. Then she saw the blood, the little rivulets that joined to search for a way down over the dirty cement floor and with a choked inwards gasp, she stepped back, the sight of Joey Payne's gouged face almost causing her to faint.

--oOo-

The nearby St Thomas's hospital was where the two battered old gentlemen were taken to repair and recover, just another couple of victims thrown up on an average Saturday night in central London. Dealt with first by casualty reception, they were X-rayed, operated on for glass splinters in an eye, the knife wound, and cuts stitched. In Joey Payne's case, this meant thirty-seven to his facial slash alone. They were kept in intensive care under sedation for the next four days to spare them the pain accompanying consciousness.

On the fifth morning, Payne, recovering from a second operation to ascertain mending to a kidney and intestines, stared at the ceiling with one eye, the one nearest the stitched slash. The other, swollen closed from repeated kicks, was an ugly distortion of dark purple and red flesh. He spent over an hour that way, repeatedly closing the eye to rest it, slowly getting to grips with his memory as the effects of the operations anaesthetic wore off.

"How is Benedict?" were the first words from Joey Payne's lips on hearing someone walk past the foot of his bed.

"Oh, so we have decided to come back to the land of the living!" replied the black ward sister, who, when asked, stopped to peer inquisitively into Joey's one good eye.

"I asked, how is Benedict?" repeated Payne.

"Now, would that be Mister Lyall, Mister Payne?" answered the sister in a Caribbean accent, her voice a lilt going up and down as if on musical scales, presenting Joey with a question of her own.

"Yes, Benedict Lyall, how is he?" pressed the old man again.

"In better shape than you, Mister Payne", was the woman's quick return, "Now rest, keep quiet; the Doctor will be around soon".

As the ward sister took his wrist for a pulse check, Joey again fell asleep.

By the end of the week, both men were moved to a ward, confined to bed, unable to make contact and still far too ill to be allowed even to sit up. But, here, at least, they were able to have visitors. Benedict Lyall's granddaughter and her husband spent half an hour with him, but she ultimately left in tears. Payne's granddaughter, his second eldest, came alone one evening, but on seeing him, she collapsed on his chest to sob for most of her stay. Nevertheless, she was his favourite because she reminded him of his wife. Joey did his best to joke and comfort her, stroking her hair.

"Nine days after the assault, in the early hours of Monday morning, Joey Payne slowly pushed his bedclothes back, laboriously sitting up in bed. He paused to let his head stop spinning before he studied the glass-panelled cubicle three beds away. The young duty night nurse was engrossed in writing a letter to her boyfriend. Preparing for his next move, Joey held the drip tube connected to the needle fixed into his vein and taped to his left forearm. With a swift pull, he disconnected it and, clutching his bed, placed his feet on the floor to navigate around it. His neighbour, who moved around the ward with the help of aluminium crutches, left them resting against a chair each night. Payne took one to use as a prop and painfully made his way down the ward. First, he clung to a chair, then pivoted on the crutch to grasp a table end. He slowly, with frequent stops for breath, made his way from bed to bed. At each bed, he studied the occupant's face with his one good eye until he was certain it wasn't the person he was seeking. Then, with a whispered sigh of recognition, he maneuvered his body towards a bedside chair, guiding himself on shaky legs into its rest. His forehead was dotted with tiny beads of sweat. He slouched for a full minute to let his mind clear and his heart

9

rate slow. Reaching out to hold one of Benedict Lyall's hands, he looked at his friend's stubbly, unshaven face. From what he could see, which was only the lower half, Lyall was in bad shape, his face swollen and scabbed. Payne didn't know that under the bandages, Lyall had a fractured skull, one eye blinded from glass splinters, and the other swollen shut. Beneath the bed linen, Lyall's organs were ruptured. Adjusting his grip on Lyall's hand, Payne settled back in the chair, preparing for a vigil with a friend he valued more than his own life. Unexpectedly, the hand he held gave his own a slight squeeze."

"Is... is that you, Joey?" Lyall's voice came slowly and artificially through a broken, wired-shut jaw.

"Yes, it's me," answered Payne just above a whisper, not wanting to alert the night nurse that he had gone for a walk.

"Are you alright?" asked Benedict, his head motionless, only his lips moving.

"Like a Hindu temple gong," growled Payne dryly, "the only thing easing the pain is seeing you and knowing you must be hurting more." This brought a gurgled chuckle followed by a pledge from the man in the bed.

"Last time I get you into a fight, I promise."

"When did I last hear that?" replied Payne with a half-smile, his eyes remaining closed.

"You remember the All-India Football Cup?" Lyall's humour bubbled up with the question.

"I remember the All-India Football Cup,"
answered Payne in a deliberate tone, "why is it
you always pick fights with ten-to-one odds?"
Both men laughed to themselves for a moment,
squeezing each other's hands.
"Do you remember that march back through
that bloody monsoon?" prompted Payne,
guiding their conversation back to their youthful
days.
"And that bloody CO on his bloody horse,"
Benedict confirmed. A pause followed as
memories wandered, the silence broken first by
the older man.

"Joey, do you remember Sheela?"
"Of course," Payne answered affectionately.
Softly, Lyall added, with palpable emotion, "I
loved her, Joey; I loved her so much." Despite
their injuries, even though they were wasting
vital strength even as they strove to knit muscle
fibres and hold together tissues which, with the
ease of parting cobwebs, could begin to
haemorrhage, they continued to jog each other's
memories. They recalled people and events, but
above all, places.
The names of the cities were once as familiar to
every English schoolboy as his own town streets:
Lucknow, Meerut, Poona, Peshawar, Khyber,
Waziristan. Others, like Bannu, Landi Kotal,
Landi Khana, Wana, Rasmak, required close
examination of large-scale maps. These all held

11

significance for those who once governed India and even more so for those who defended it. These frontier outposts of the British Empire were still living history, locked in the memories of overlooked veterans like Joey Payne and Benedict Lyall.

Gradually their reminiscences dwindled, as did the speed of reply. Lyall's voice weakened, the pauses between speeches grew longer until it was only Payne setting the questions. "That loose-wallah shot in the lines at Firozpur, who shot him, Paani Waters or Bert Colling?" There was no response from the man in bed; he lay silent and serene. Payne gave the hand he held a gentle squeeze. Tense with foreboding, he waited for the faintest of acknowledgements, but none came. With his head bowed and eyes closed, Payne sank into his chair. As tears he wasn't aware of trickled from his good eye, his fingers tightened around Lyall's hand.

His mind was at peace, teetering on the edge of enchanted oblivion. Payne willingly let himself fall into its abyss, flying to a land that had once forced him to plead and cry for release from its heat and depravities. But it was also a land that captured a man's soul with a silken cord, wrapping each new sight and sound in retention, remaining as vivid as the first day of experience in later years. Willingly enslaved, these hostages would, in the stillness of a summer evening or the warmth of a winter room, hear the rhythmic grind of the bullock cart again, smell the sweetness of wild jasmine, and see the kite hawks circle in lazy loops above a furnace-dry plain.

He soared high over a jewel-blue ocean, passing the sentinel swallows stationed well seaward. As he approached the land, its tart, pungent scent was a forewarning of its closeness, and he drew in the familiar aroma.

"I've returned," he nearly cried out. "I've returned."

Upon reaching the palm-fringed shore, he climbed above the coastal Ghats, over the cane and millet crop fields of the Deccan plateau, to reach green wooded hills and the thick, foreshadowing jungle. This eventually gave way to mile upon mile of withered land, once lush and fertile, now dry, and desperately awaiting the monsoon rains. Soon, a border of green appeared along the banks of the Ganges, the lifeblood and mother of India. The land began to rise again, signalling the proximity of the mighty Himalayas and, for Payne, his destination.

To his right were the tea plantations of Darjeeling, perched on terraced meadows on the hilly slopes. Before him, a pine-shaded foothill ridge scattered with bungalows and a larger mission hospital. He followed the miniature rail line to its western terminus, where the tracks began their zigzag descent to the plain. He descended from his flight below the trees, meeting a young girl with straight blonde hair, wearing a pale dress patterned with tiny lilac flowers.

"A kiss?" she asked, "A kiss for saving my life? I won't pay a penalty for that." She then danced away to the edge of a sloping glade before turning back. Beyond her was a broad valley that dropped five thousand feet to a river below, appearing as a silver thread from this height. Far off in the distance were purple mountains, their peaks obscured by grey banks of rain-filled clouds, except for one that stood out, bathing in the sun's full blaze. Its snowy majesty floated like an island on a bed of white cotton clouds, detached from everything else. This was the grandeur of Mount Everest. Flanking the glade were evergreen rhododendrons, blooming in reds and pinks, their fragrance mingling with the scent of pine and wild roses, adding to the delight of the moment.

Standing with her arms at her sides, the girl, with a challenging smile, set her terms:

"A kiss as a forfeit I'll not give you, Joey Payne. What I will do is give it as a gift in gratitude. But you will have to come and claim it!" As her arms swung out from her body, palms opening to beckon, the smile faded to one of languor, filled with enticement.

"Come, Joey, claim your reward." This time he did not rush, unlike the first time – there was no need. They were together once again, and they would not part this time. Spreading his arms with an unhurried lightness of pace, he began to approach.
"I'm coming, Lily, I'm coming."

CHAPTER 2

The adventurer is an outlaw.
Adventure must start with running away from
home.
-William Bolitho

The last item Joey Payne packed into his small
hand-case was his father's gift, which had been
given to him the previous evening. He lifted the
shiny brass safety razor from its petite wooden
box, admiring the novelty of the instrument,
before replacing it and securing the lock. The
gift served a dual purpose: to commemorate his
eighteenth birthday and his impending departure
from home. Joey was set to join the army. Born
and raised in the same house on his father's
four-hundred-acre tenant farm, he was now
leaving it behind. The home and farm, owned by
a Lord whose family lineage traced back to
William the Conqueror, was only one of several
such properties on the estate. The farm had been
established over a century ago, primarily
cultivating root and cereal crops. Over time, the
surrounding county of Kent had seen an
increase in fruit orchards and hops, given their
guaranteed profitability. However, Joey's father

held a different view. As a young tenant farmer and newly married man, he refrained from adding more trees or high-poled frameworks to his land. Like his ancestors, he saw himself as a custodian of the soil and focused on farming rye, barley, wheat, vetches, swedes, and turnips, rotating each field through a four-year cycle to maintain soil fertility.

Exiting his bedroom, Joey walked downstairs to bid his first farewell. His mother was in the laundry yard behind the kitchen, removing a freshly hand-washed linen sheet from a large, soap-filled copper basin. She passed it through a hand mangle with wooden rollers before rinsing it in cold water.

"Are we ready to go?" she asked, hearing the scrape of his metal-heeled boots on the flagstones.

"In a moment," Joey replied uneasily, finding the formality of a goodbye discomforting.

His mother, aware of this, immediately diffused the tension with a smile. She dried her hands on her apron, used for household chores, and swept a lock of speckled grey hair back into place. Taking his arm, she guided him through the house, reminding him to write a letter from time to time. At the gate, they said their goodbyes with a hug and kisses on the cheeks, doing their best to hold back tears. His mother, a farmer's wife with her daily chores, did not linger over his departure. After taking a minute to wave him down the farm lane, she returned to her household duties.

By nine o'clock in the morning, having had breakfast at six, she had already remade the beds, swept, and tidied all the rooms, and cleaned and rekindled two fire grates. Then, after the washing, Mrs. Hilton, the carter's wife, had a week-old baby to visit and bread to bake, all before midday. The third time Joey turned to wave; his mother was gone.

To his left, within the large brick and timbered barn with its weathered grey thatched roof, was where Joey first realized he would have to find a life outside the farm. It was at the annual harvest supper held each September; a banquet given by his father to thank the farm's workforce for their service throughout the past year. With the barn cleared, tables were laid, and oil lamps hung from beams to light the windowless room. At the head table, his father sat with George Peters, his foreman, and James, his older brother. Down the sides of the U-shaped table, feasting on ham, beef, pork, and lamb, were the rest of the farm staff: carters, dairymen, water-keepers, gardeners, farm hands, gamekeepers, underkeeper's who managed the ferrets, and young boys who worked on the farm under their fathers' supervision.

When the foreman rose to respond to his father's seasonal speech, Joey first discerned a fact that would directly impact his future. In previous years, the foreman would have begun by thanking his father, the 'governor', on behalf of all farm workers. This time, however, he also included 'young master James'. James was twenty and had attended agricultural school. At first, this simple act of politeness seemed insignificant to Joey. But in the following days, it kept coming back to him until he grasped its true meaning. James was to be the heir, and when his father gave up the tenancy of the farm, it would most likely be offered to him first. By Michaelmas, the farmers' New Year, Joey had made up his mind. His life's purpose could not be tied to this farm, and he decided his fate; he would leave before the spring.

The dairy cow sheds were a short distance away, where the leafless plum trees that lined the farm lane ended. In the yard, the head dairyman, old Tom Fern, loaded the farm's horse-drawn wagon with the previous evening's and that morning's milk. From the cool dairy room, he and two of his milkers were lifting the silver metal churns from the loading platform into the well of the wagon. Nelson and Wellington, the team, stood still and silently, only occasionally dipping their heads, or glancing around with a bored resignation. Seven days a week, these two trudged down to the train station with their cargo for shipment to London. The dairy was the one area on the farm that Joey's father had expanded. Even before the war, milk was profitable; it provided income when some field crops did not.

Raising an arm, Joey called out to the grey-bearded man as he neatly arranged his milk containers. "Tom! I'm just on my way to the West Hill rick to say goodbye to the Governor. But I won't keep you," he said, thus confirming his ride to the train station. "There's no need to rush, Master Joey. I'll be waiting at the gate when you're finished," answered the dairyman, punctuating his reply with a wave of his bony hand.

A ten-minute hike brought Joey to the farm's primary work centre for the day. At the peak of a round-topped field, a group of men under his father's watchful eye were threshing a corn rick of barley. The thresher was powered by a steam engine, and the two men who operated it had risen at four that morning to ensure the engine was ready for work at seven. It was a cold, dry morning in early March 1922, late for threshing. However, with the sudden increase in the price of feedstocks, Joey's father intended to use the grain to supplement the dairy's cow feed, rather than sell it.

Threshing was a team task that once started, needed to proceed with the rhythm of a carousel for labour economics. As the sheaves were passed up to a man on the thresher, their binding string was cut, and the headed stalks were fed into the machine. Below, others collected the grain and built a separate rick from the rebounding chaff. Joey chose this time to visit - it was now half past nine, and the team was just breaking for their lunch. For five minutes, this group of comrades, with whom he had shared their work since he was a boy, engaged him with good-natured teasing and well wishes. Their faces and clothes were coated in grain dust, as threshing was a filthy task, requiring constant work in its powdery soot. "Give no back lip to the NCOs!" "And just heed their words. You don't want the trouble they'll cause you if you don't." The advice was from two smiling ex-soldiers, survivors of the Great War."

Before mounting the pony-drawn trap he used to tour the farm, his father took Joey's hand, wishing him God's good fortune with the army. Then, with a click of his tongue to the horse, he sped off to fulfil an inspection appointment, accompanying his head water-keeper over one of the downriver meadows.

Just like with his mother, their parting was not laden with emotion. His absence would be felt by them, as he would miss them, but his parents were seasoned farmers and understood the logic behind Joey's departure. A tenant farm could not be split, nor did his father have the power to do so. Joey was simply following a path well-travelled by countless younger sons in past centuries. Turning his face away from the receding outline of the pony and trap as his father trotted the rig into the first dip of the field, he waved a final goodbye to the team of threshers eating their cold lunch.

For a few moments, the young man struggled with understanding his action as he walked away. However, seeing Tom Fern hunched on the dairy wagon waiting at the farm's boundary gate, he broke into a trot, and all doubt disappeared. Joey Payne had never been to London before, so he had decided several months earlier to enlist there. Thus, with an open and expectant mind, he exited a South London station and stood to one side of the entrance, observing the sights and sounds. The broad street before him bustled with contrasting movements. Motor cars and lorries hurriedly weaved around slower, horse-drawn hansom cabs, and teams of tall, noble shires hitched to brewers' drays. Brightly painted motor-powered omnibuses competed with brown and white track-bound trolley buses for the passengers waiting at the curb side. Despite being engrossed in the bustling activity, the grime struck Payne most vividly.

Coal, in unlimited abundance, had been the country's primary source of fuel for numerous decades. Regrettably, its widespread use came at a cost. The day, which was dull and cool in the farmlands of Kent, was filled with an artificial haze in London. The air was so rife with acrid fumes that Payne could taste the atmosphere as much as he could smell it, which, surprisingly, did not bother him as a visitor. He was surrounded by streets lined with tall buildings, both commercial and residential. They should have stood out in rusty, house-brick red, edged with pleasant, light-coloured sandstone or ash-white marble facing. Instead, every surface was coated in black soot, like a funeral shroud draping the entire city. The cause was no mystery. Rising above every rooftop were countless chimneys, each capped with tall, slender decorative pots that constantly emitted ribbons of blue-grey smoke.

Fetching a leaf of paper from his coat pocket, Joey studied a rough street sketch given to him by one of the farmhands who knew where the nearest army recruiting office was. At his elbow, a man in his late twenties, one-armed and with an eye patch, sold papers. The headlines all proclaimed the previous day's joyous event of the royal wedding between Princess Mary and Viscount Lascelles. Joey briefly considered confirming his direction with this man but then thought better of it. This man, obviously marked by disfiguring signs from the Kaiser's War, was not a person from whom to request information about joining the army.

Setting off, he walked along the main street. On the walls of some buildings were advertising billboards touting the attractions of teas, whiskeys, tobaccos, gravy stocks, and many other commodities. Stopping on one corner, he checked his sketch again. Down the cobbled side street, a horse-drawn coal wagon was being slowly led by a young boy. A man, his clothes, face, and hands stained with coal dust, paced slow steps while calling up at the tall tenements: "Coal! Coal!" As Joey watched, a woman appeared, pushing a coin into his hand. Tipping his cap to her, the man hoisted a coal bag from the wagon onto his back before following the woman into one of the buildings.

Payne found the recruitment office twenty minutes after interrupting his search to have a light lunch at a tea shop. The cost: tuppence for a hot bun and a penny for tea. Next to a branch office of the Abbey Wood Building Society, he spied a soldier standing on the steps of a doorway. Beside the steps was a framed poster extolling the joys of enlistment. "I've come to join," announced Payne politely. "Who do I see?" "Army's full up. Try the navy, Portsmouth; I suggest you take the train," replied the soldier, sharp and crisp, looking high over Payne's head. Joey, shocked and speechless, could only gawk. In black boots, high puttees, khaki trousers, a jacket, a peaked cap, and a red sash angled across his chest, the soldier stood behind him, rocking on his heels, eyes engrossed in something across the street. Joey's heart sunk to his feet, and he froze with indecision on the spot while the soldier, with a waxed moustache and hair so short that none was visible below the cap, totally ignored him. Finally, with his plans in ruins, Joey turned about, his shoulders sagging, to walk away.

"Here now, lad, let's not be too hasty with the feet. Perhaps we can find something to suit your talent," said the soldier. "You weren't planning on being a jockey, were you?"

"Jockey?" echoed Payne, confused.

"Cavalry, my lad, Cavalry," the man in uniform clarified.

"No, sir! I had my heart set on my county Regiment, The Queen's Own Royal West Kent's," replied Payne, his hopes rising.

"It's sergeant, not sir," the recruiter corrected him, bringing his hands forward to point at the three stripes on his sleeve. In his other hand, he held a board with a sheet of paper clipped to it, which he began to study.

"Let's see now," he said, running his finger down the paper. "Kents? Kents? No luck, lad. No one required. You'll have to go to the Queen's Light Infantry. How does that sound?"

"Yes, that'll be fine," Joey agreed, his despair suddenly lifting.

"Well, then, come in and we'll deal with the formalities," suggested the sergeant. Inside, a broad hallway contained two desks at the far end. Office doors were spaced along one side, and a row of chairs lined the other. After being asked his age and a few other simple questions,

Joey was handed a shilling and instructed to sign his name and then sit and wait. He chose an unoccupied chair next to a square-shouldered man in a rolled woollen cap and a heavy sea jacket. Despite his weather-beaten face, Joey guessed the man wasn't much older than himself.

"Smoke?" The stranger offered, holding out a packet of Churchman's Tenor cigarettes.
"Benedict Lyall," he introduced himself after lighting one. Payne declined while introducing himself in return.
"What mob are you in?" He asked, exhaling his first breath of smoke.
"Oh... Queen's..." Joey struggled, unable to remember.
"Queen's Light Infantry," Lyall helped with a smile. "Yeah, me too. I asked for my old regiment but let them convince me I'd be better off signing up for the Queen's." Joey, cheering up at hearing Lyall say he had done previous service, was interrupted in learning more by calling over a tall, skinny, red-haired youth. He was leaving one of the desks, looking downhearted.
"What's wrong, Bluey? Did you get turned down?"
"Yes! Rightly so," replied the youth bitterly.
"Why, what's your issue?" asked Benedict.

"Age," the youth confessed sheepishly, "I was caught off guard when the man asked me how old I was and I told him the truth, I'm 15." Benedict, forearms resting on his knees, hands cradling his cigarette, his voice low but firm, gave a gentle order, "Get up, go straight back to the same guy and tell him you're 18." The red-haired youth didn't move, still unsure.

"No hesitation," encouraged Lyall, "Besides, what do you have to lose? Now, go back."

With a half sigh, the young man raised his head, turned around and presented himself at the same desk.

The sergeant sat there, a different man from the one who had enrolled Payne, watching his second approach.

"Well, what is it this time, lad?"

"Please, sir, I'm 18," lied the youth unconvincingly.

"Well stated, my boy. Here's your King's shilling; sign your name," the sergeant congratulated, extending both arms, a coin in one hand and an ink pen in the other. Shortly after, the three newly enlisted recruits were approached by a third sergeant who informed them that they would now be escorted to another part of the city for a medical exam and, if passed, be sworn in. Joey, following Lyall, who was carrying a drawstring kit bag over one shoulder, out of the main door, tripped suddenly on the first step upon overhearing the conversation between a youth on the street and his recruiting sergeant, who was again observing the shops across the street.

"Looking to join the Queen's Light Infantry," the youth said.

"You have no chance there, my dear friend. How about the Royal West Kent's? We have a few vacancies with them," said a recruiting sergeant, finding a way to spice up the monotony of his daily task.

They boarded a tram, which took them to a tube station. For Joey Payne, the underground rail system that sprawled like a gigantic rabbit warren beneath one of the world's largest cities was a remarkable revelation. The steep descent, the crowded platforms, the gust of air that preceded the tube train's arrival making both men and women steady their hats, and the speed of the journey left him absorbing only half of what was happening. Emerging again into the muted city light, their party arrived at their destination: the Whitehall recruitment centre near New Scotland Yard. Along with other groups that kept replenishing the persistent queues, they spent the next two hours waiting. They waited naked on benches, clutching their clothes in their laps, waiting to be medically examined. They waited to pledge allegiance to the King and country, four at a time, with a Bible. And then, they waited some more.

While waiting, they overheard a conversation about people like Payne and Lyall who had completed their final joining procedure. Then, with about thirty others, all sitting on benches on either side of a corridor, an officer, his high boots shining, holding leather gloves and a leather-bound swagger stick, announced that it was time for their departure. "Sergeant-Major," he addressed another upright, moustached soldier who accompanied him into the hallway, "We should try to get these people off before teatime." "Very good, sir," responded the sergeant-major, "I'll group them into railway station parties and send them off." Soon after, the Sergeant-Major returned with a few sergeants.

"Now listen carefully, all of you. It's time for you gentlemen to move on," the sergeant-major's voice escalated, capturing everyone's attention. "When you hear your name, stand up and be ready to follow one of my sergeants." From a sheet of paper, he called out five names before handing it over to a sergeant, with a brief instruction: "Royal Regiment of Fusiliers, Hounslow and East Surrey, Kingston."

He started calling names again while waiting for that party to leave, finishing with another paper handover to a second sergeant. "King's Royal Rifles Corps, Winchester."

"On Payne and Lyall, along with two others, were called to their feet. The sergeant-major's directive to their sergeant escort was: "QLI, Harwich." After a tram ride to Liverpool Street station, the four were guided to a second-class compartment on a London North-eastern train. Under the watchful eye of the sergeant and at his insistence, the train guard locked the compartment. With his duty done and their arrival at Harwich assured, he left them to their confined journey. Amid neighbouring whistle toots, the hissing of steam like witches, and the grinding of metal wheels, their train, its carriages jerking impatiently, began its scheduled journey to the Essex port.

Just like any travellers embarking on a journey of discovery, their close association loosened their tongues. After exchanging names, questions were asked by and of all four. Payne summarized his life history in a few sentences. Farming was not a topic that invited probing. Similarly, Tommy Gilbert, a short, slightly built lad who is yet to turn eighteen and looks much younger, did not pique much curiosity. Gilbert, pallid with weak blond hair the colour of ripened wheat, grew up in Peckham. At twelve years of age, he took the labour education test, passed it, and secured a job at Hamilton Gardens as a junior groundsman. After six years, he'd had enough and enlisted at the Whitechapel Road recruiting office three days prior. Yet, after failing his first medical for being underweight, he was kept at the upstairs Whitehall sleeping quarters, where he was fed sausages, bread, and milk to gain weight.

Sid Frith, an eighteen-year-old with a stocky build and dark hair combed straight back, had a broad neck and a thick waist. His face bore blemishes and pits from a childhood illness. He kept his life history brief. From Bethnal Green, he had been employed by a firm of furniture repairers for the past two years. However, he didn't mention that his alcoholic father had remarried following his mother's death. His stepmother, a widow with her own family, was a burden he bore until he finally decided to get away.

Fortunately, after sharing their mundane journeys to adulthood, they could enjoy Benedict Lyall's exciting adventures. At fourteen, he tricked his way into the army and spent nearly two years in the trenches. Upon demobilization, he took to the sea as a deckhand, only to leave his ship in Australia. There, he spent three years as a stockman on a cattle station. His return to his home country was prompted by a gun-wielding husband whose wife had been overly generous with her affections. While working his way to Liverpool on a wool cargo steamer, Benedict managed to hitch a ride to the Thames. He arrived in the Pool of London that morning and received his pay. The decision to join the army a few hours later was an impulsive one, driven by the need for immediate lodgings. Benedict found it easy to recount this period of his life in open conversation. However, he kept his dark childhood a secret, only allowing a few people to know about it throughout his life. Born in a Manchester slum to a fatherless family, his mother earned money by working in a textile mill and accepting whatever her revolving door of male friends could provide. From this, she managed to feed, clothe, and pay rent for a single room for herself and her three children. One night, she went out to indulge her fondness for gin and a new man and never returned. Faced with starvation and eviction, the eldest sister, then fifteen, turned to prostitution to provide food and keep the roof over their heads. Benedict, who was only ten at the time, never forgot those months. His six-year-old younger sister huddled in the hall landing, while the eldest sister accommodated men, she had picked up at pub doorways. This life, which saw him and the youngest child begging on the street, ended with the arrest of the now pregnant eldest daughter." Separated from his sisters, Benedict lived in a harshly run orphanage until he was twelve. When the war began and drew men away from semi-skilled jobs, he was finally released. For two years, he worked as a butcher's assistant. His meagre wages were so heavily diminished by payments for his meals and lodgings, a small, dim, stuffy room above the butcher's shop, that he scarcely had enough for a hot currant bun at night. Eventually, tired of the long working hours, wearing cast-off clothes, and the ill-tempered behaviour of his employer, he decided to run off and join the army after a bitterly cold December night in 1916 kept him awake.

At Harwich Station, patience was required. When the guard finally arrived to unlock the gates, he was accompanied by a stout, khaki-uniformed private soldier in a leather jerkin. "There we are, all present and correct," the guard confirmed. "My, don't these new recruits ever look different? - same innocent faces." Not expecting an answer, he turned away, motioning for them to follow. His comment did, however, elicit a response from Benedict Lyall: "Alright, lads, pick up your gear and follow that fellow with the big belly and the mouth to match." The stout soldier heard this but only half-looked over his shoulder before pointing at a cluster of crates and jute gunny bags. "Right, grab hold of them here, quartermaster's stores, and load them onto the transport." Following the soldier's nod, Benedict saw what he recognized as an army GS wagon hitched to a team of horses. After three trips of manhandling the goods, they were stowed in the cargo well. Then, with the four new arrivals sitting on top, they set off, the wagon's steel-rimmed wheels grating on the cobblestones and the horses' shoes tapping out a metallic rhythm.

Because of the overcast, the evening twilight was racing towards complete darkness, but not so much that Benedict didn't realize where they were headed. They were well outside the town, on what used to be a broad rolling pasture, where a large, hutted encampment stood. He remembered it as the camp where he returned from France for de-mobilisation in 1919. Back then, it held several thousand men eager to discard their uniforms and return home. Unfortunately, de-mobilisation took time, which led to turmoil in the camp. After four years of war and obeying life-or-death orders, basic discipline was contemptuously flouted. Gangs of men roamed the camp causing havoc and complying with no demands other than to collect their de-mobilisation suit, rail fare home, and sign-off.

At the same time, small batches of young recruits were also arriving. These recruits, who were the targets for the mobs that would charge drunkenly into their accommodations, flipping beds over and threatening them, were so desperately needed for the army of occupation in Germany. The training staff would fit them out with uniforms, take them for a stroll around the local lanes, and then without so much as firing a rifle, ship them off to police the occupied Hun.

Upon entering the main gate, a painted sign with a regimental crest could be read in the fading light: Training Depot, the Queen's Light Infantry. After unloading the freight at the quartermaster's stores, a corporal took charge of them, issuing bedding, eating utensils, and an enamel mug and plate. They were led to one of the huts which housed twenty beds and ten other men, some of whom, like themselves, were in civilian dress. As they all ate off tables, one of the uniformed eaters told them to claim a bed. He, without a jacket, showing braces over a collarless grey shirt, introduced himself as the hut lance-corporal. He also sent a man off to collect a late helping of food and tea, both arriving in pails.

After eating and washing their plates and mugs in a washroom sparsely equipped with tin wash bowls on slate slab decking, water from cold taps, and open drains, the corporal gave the late arrivals their introductory chat. He warned that their civilian clothes would be taken from them the following day and a standard army kit would be issued. Everything was to be cleaned, hung on pegs above their beds, and placed on display or out of sight in a kit box. Lastly, he quickly demonstrated how to arrange the bed for sleeping.

This was in two halves, an iron frame with interwoven metal struts that could be pushed

into each other to save space during the day.
Once assembled, the mattress was laid out,
consisting of three coconut-hair-filled hassock-
type cushion pads called biscuits. The sheets
were a yellowish hue and starch stiff, creating the
sensation of sleeping in a paper bag when used.
Simultaneously, the blankets emitted a musky
smell due to their neglect in storage. After the
'bedding in' was complete, the lance-corporal left
these latest additions to the Regiment to
entertain themselves, giving them a light warning
for when they would be needed next.

"Make sure you sleep like angels tonight;
tomorrow will be busy," he advised. "Here, Joey,
let's you and I have a look around," suggested
Lyall, springing off the bed he had just made.
Outside, Benedict moved through the camp area
as if searching for something. The huts, made of
wood with slate roofs, were connected by
wooden duckboards. Where these were absent, a
combination of walking boots and winter rain
left mud, but only in the occupied portion of the
camp, which made up about a tenth of the
buildings. Once housing a horde of troops, the
remaining structures lay abandoned and
neglected, with the oncoming knee-high spring
grass turning each hut into an island.

"Yup, here's the one," said Benedict, bringing
both to a halt.

Walking between the abandoned ghostly
buildings, Joey saw nothing more significant in

the evening dark than two rows of concrete foundation support interspaced among half-overgrown blackened timbers.

"Here's what?" he asked.

"Headquarters hut," answered Benedict, grinning. "Or what's left of it. I turned it down in '19. Well, me and about two hundred others. We had just returned from France, and the camp RSM instructed us to get ready for a route march. Felony bent, the boys and I quickly informed him that wasn't going to happen. Didn't have an office quick after that!" His nostalgia satisfied; Benedict now set his sights on finding a drink. He would have preferred a pint of brown ale but had to settle for a mug of tea and a cake at the Church of England Institute hut.

Returning to their billet, the night air turned chilly, prompting them both to huddle around the central iron coal stove. Activity elsewhere in the room was primarily focused on brushing, polishing, or squaring up by those who had received their kit. At one end of the hut, a card game was in progress, being played on top of a wooden soldier box near their beds. With nothing else to do, both Joey and Benedict sat back and watched the hands being played. The game was poker and there were five participants, one of them, Tommy Gilbert, needed more luck. He had never gambled before and had only reluctantly joined in at the insistence of the winning men. Tommy started the game with all his money and eight shillings and five pence. All that remained in front of him on the box lid was two and nine.

"That's another for me," said a well-built, pale-skinned youth triumphantly, as he laid down his winning hand and raked the small cluster of coins towards himself, leaving a single penny behind. "That's me in there. Come along now! Dub up! Dub up!" The others each added their own penny to the centre of the box, staking their claim to cards for the next hand, except for Gilbert, who hesitated.

"Come on, pal," another player urged. This man was a friend of the first, tall with long arms, rust-blonde hair, and a square-jawed face. These two were the ones winning consistently.

"I don't know," Tommy pondered, "I think I've had enough."

"Come on, pal, you don't want to do that," the darker one advised, flashing a smile that didn't reach his eyes. "Luck has a funny way of turning things around; pull out now and you might miss a couple of winning hands. That's the way it works. So, keep your seat and make a fortune," added the tall one.

Not enthusiastically, Gilbert played the next hand and lost again. Then, unwilling to risk more of his meagre wealth, he started picking up his few remaining coins, apologizing for not understanding the game and having to withdraw.

"No, no, you're being hasty, pal," the darker player said, putting a hand on Gilbert's shoulder to keep him seated. "No, no, I can't afford any more losses," Tommy pleaded in response. "Look, I can feel it; you're about to start a winning streak. Now take a seat." The hand pushed Gilbert back onto the bedside.

"The lad said he's had enough," an authoritative voice chimed in, clear and raw. All heads turned to Benedict Lyall, who was lying on his bed, propped up on one elbow with his hands clasped.

"Who the hell asked you to stick your paddle in?" the dark youth questioned, his tone sour.

"It's not good practice to start out in army life by fleecing blokes at cards who may well be watching your back in a scrap where bayonets are flashing about."

"Fleecing?" The word was spoken by the card player as if it were a quick question.

"That's a fact. I haven't seen a hand go to anyone but you and your mate since I've been sitting here," Benedict pointed out dryly. The dark player rose, challenging, "I don't much like being called a cheat."

Seemingly delighted, Lyall jumped to his feet and drew an imaginary line across the hut floor with one toe. "If that's a serious accusation, mate, step across this line, and we'll resolve the misunderstanding."

At this, the taller of the two also stood up. "Let's just let him have his turn, Danny."

"So, we want to play in pairs, do we?" Benedict responded with a wolfish grin and a voice that sounded almost joyful, "Well, if that's the game, then my old mate here will be more than happy to fill the empty corner." Joey Payne, who had been watching the drama unfold, found Lyall's hand pointing at his chest. Shocked and speechless, the Kent farming lad didn't respond, but his mind raced. He had only known this young man with the northern accent and Australian slang for eight hours. Now he was being invited to a fight. Without replying, he stood up and turned away to remove his blazer, swallowing the lump in his throat and steeling his expression. Then he turned back, hoping he looked determined, and removed his tie. In a business-like manner, he rolled up his sleeves, imitating the volunteers he had seen at the boxing booths at country fairs.

"Come on, champ; put your toe on the line," Benedict, standing on his line, ran a hand through his black wavy hair before spitting into both hands, and waited, his fists circling at his waist.

"Go on, Danny, teach him a lesson," the tall card player encouraged.

Danny stepped forward, assuming a boxing stance as he faced Lyall. For several seconds, neither of them made a move. Then, Danny lashed out with a solid swing. Benedict, sitting back, waited for the moment to recover. He launched two low punches: a left in the ribs and a right in the solar plexus. As arms instinctively dropped, he delivered a powerful straight right into Danny's jaw. Danny's head snapped back, and he sprawled sideways and down, unconscious.

"Okay, pal, your turn next. What's your name?" Lyall asked without taking a breath, beckoning the tall, rust-blond youth forward.

"Been answering to Gynger most of my life," the youth replied gruffly, his look smouldering with thoughts of revenge after observing his unconscious partner.

"Well, this here is Joey Payne," Lyall introduced, slapping Joey on the shoulder as he stepped up. Payne had never engaged in a real fistfight in his life. He and his brother often practiced shadow boxing in the hayloft, but a bare-knuckle brawl was unfamiliar to him. Facing each other, Joey held his fists high in traditional style, while Gynger's swung at his waist. Both waited for the other to make the first move. Payne was the first to act, his face firm but his sky-grey eyes betraying his fear. His swing to Gynger's head fell short of its target. Gynger jerked his upper body back and instinctively countered with a punch to Joey's head. Landing on the bare boarding floor between two cots, Joey felt the pain and a nauseous sickness that he didn't like.

He was on his knees regaining his bearings when he tossed his head to clear the blond hair from his eyes. He looked up to see his opponent strutting confidently, like a rooster in a farmyard. Jumping up, Payne lunged at Gynger, throwing wild punches. The fight had devolved from a dispute-settling boxing match to a melee of flying fists and tangled arms.

At five foot eleven, Joey was still the shorter man compared to Gynger, who was two or three inches taller and had a longer reach. However, Payne was the more substantial of the two and he was angry. Punches landed and were received, each taking their turn on the floor, sometimes both at once. The rest was brief, as a crowd had gathered, cheering, and encouraging, helping both fighters back to their feet. The conclusion, when it came, was swift and immediate."

"Jesus Christ! Hell's pit, you lot!" The lance-corporal from the hut, who had been off for a short visit to a pub below the camp, had returned. His shout brought stillness to the room.

"Leave you unwatched for a few minutes, and you're knocking the starch out of each other."

"No, not at all, Corporal," declared Benedict Lyall with earnest conviction. "Just a simple exhibition of boxing prowess. It's just that Joey and Gynger here, being a bit weak on the fundamental skills, looked a bit un-gentlemanly."

"Is that a fact?" The lance-corporal doubted, spotting loose cards on the floor. "Well, just in case the urge manifests next time, we will do it like gentlemen, down at the gymnasium, with proper gloves on." Then, instructing Payne and Gynger to shake hands, he hurried them off to the ablutions to wash away the blood.

"Now, every one of you," he commanded, turning on the room, "get tidied up and into your beds. The duty bugler will be blowing lights out shortly and tomorrow morning I expect you all up before bird twitch."

Long after the bugler's notes had faded and the room darkened, Joey Payne lay awake reflecting on the day and its bruising conclusion. If at home, he would have ended the day, climbing the stairs to his room with an evening glass of the farm's dairy milk, heated by his mother. Instead, here he lay, carefully resting the back of his head on a hard sack pillow, his face discoloured and throbbing with pain.

CHAPTER 3

Beware of all enterprises That require new clothes.
-Henry David Thoreau

"Battalion, attention!" Regimental Sergeant
Major Jake Richmond stood rigidly at attention;
his eyes concealed beneath the broad brim of his
Wolseley topee. He surveyed the scene from left
to right, searching for any sign of movement
among the nine hundred men, organized by
companies, lined up before him. Seeing no
flicker of activity, he turned abruptly to inform
the adjutant that the Battalion was present and
correct. Upon doing this, he was told,
"Excellent, Mr. Richmond. The battalion may
stand easy." Once again, he pivoted his upper
body without deviating even slightly from his
vertical posture.
"Battalion, stand at ease." Then, the clatter of
nine hundred iron-clad boots rang out in unison,
reverberating off the ship's sides and echoing
back from the interior of the sheds. Stiff limbs
responded to a second command to relax.
Joey Payne, positioned in the front rank of 6
Platoon, B Company, stretched his back and
turned his head, observing his surroundings. It
was nearing noon on a sombre October day. He
was standing in front of a drab, rust-speckled
troop ship on a Southampton wharf. The 2nd

Battalion of the Queen's Light Infantry was about to set sail for India. During their six months of training, there had been no ambiguity about the fact that every member of Payne's recruit platoon was destined for the 1st Battalion stationed at Jersey in the Channel Isles, soon to return to Catterick Camp. However, their destination was abruptly changed to the 2nd Battalion at Aldershot, which had been given orders to go to India, only after they had returned from their ten-day leave to complete recruit training.

The Queen's Light Infantry was established in 1759 as the Queen's Regiment of Volunteers. It was formed in county towns and villages south of King's Lynn by a local squire. The reason for its creation was yet another war with France. The unit gained their first battle honour by capturing the island of Belleisle from the French, a feat that earned them the distinction of incorporating a fleur de lys into their regimental cap badge.

At the conclusion of the Great War, there was a mass disbandment. The QLI, like the rest of the army, erased most of their emergency-formed battalions from their rolls, although not as many as the government would have preferred. The end of hostilities with the Central European powers, the containment of Bolshevik Russia, the occupation of conquered areas, and the troubles in Ireland all demanded substantial

drafts of soldiers. The Queen's regiment
supplied a battalion for occupational duties in
Turkey and another to combat the Reds on the
Russo-Persian border before being withdrawn to
Egypt. The 2nd Battalion was based at Dublin
Castle, confronting the IRA. After four years of
fill-in roles, the army was finally slimming down
to a lean post-war state with two battalions in
each infantry regiment, one stationed at home.
The second was posted somewhere among
Britain's worldwide Colonial Empire. For the
QLI, this meant more reductions and
retirements. Once Ireland won self-rule from
Britain, the 2nd Battalion returned to Aldershot
to await reinforcement drafts before being
posted to India. Consequently, Joey Payne found
himself waiting at a Southampton dock,
preparing to board a troopship. When the order
came, the band and bugles, dressed in green with
black plumed shakos and black belts, began to
play military tunes. Accompanied by the harsh
cries of swooping seagulls, nine hundred men
shouldered their gear, slung rifles, and boarded
the ship.

In the troops' rear half of the ship, six platoons
with nothing better to do watched as the
battalion officers and their dependents boarded
the forward half of the vessel."

"Listen to this, Jeffrey," Nash Slyfield said to his
friend Jeffrey Harrison. Harrison was a scrawny,
loose-limbed man with a narrow face. Both men

were old 2nd Battalion members who had spent the previous two years chasing down the IRA.

"Mr. Philip Bernard Cosgrave, the uncle of the chairman of the Irish Provisional Government, was shot dead in a Dublin bar on Sunday night as he fought with four armed robbers," Slyfield, who had black hair, broad eyebrows, dark skin, and was built like a boxer, quoted from a newspaper he had bought earlier in the day.

"I'm laughing in church," snorted Harrison. "Let's see if they can take it now, the way they've been dishing it out." Joey Payne wasn't listening. He was leaning over the rail, having spotted a teenage girl, slim and blond, boarding the ship. She was assisting an older woman with two young boys while RSM Richmond followed, each carrying a piece of luggage. From Payne's vantage point, he assumed that this was RSM's family, and the girl was his daughter. He was partially correct. The woman was his wife, and the boy was his son, but the girl was his niece, Lily.

Jake Richmond and his brother, both married, had joined the QLI at the outbreak of war in August 1914. As part of Kitchener's new army, they served as sergeants with the 7th Battalion in 1916 and took part in the first day's assault that launched the Battle of the Somme. That evening, as the commanding officer struggled to regroup the few survivors in a sunken, shell-fire-bracketed road, he grabbed Richmond's arm,

shouting, "You are now the battalion RSM."
Richmond's brother died in that tragic battle,
leaving a wife and young daughter. Then, during
the flu epidemic of 1918, his brother's wife also
died, leading to Lily's adoption and their living as
a family for the past four years. Jake Richmond
decided to stay in the army after the Armistice
was declared. However, due to other senior
officers also wanting to stay, he had to drop in
rank, only regaining his promotion to RSM this
year. Now, 16-year-old Lily, with no other
relatives to take her in, was accompanying her
adopted family into an uncertain military
environment in India. She was, however, looking
forward to the new adventure with growing
enthusiasm.

"On the third day of the voyage, Sid Frith gazed
out across a flat, uneventful expanse of ash-
green water and commented, "So, this is the
infamous Bay of Biscay." The stories about the
Bay's temperament had been circulating for days.
Now, as they neared its farthest edge, with
Gibraltar just around the corner, they had
crossed it with hardly a gust of wind to alter their
course."

No reply came from the group of men
surrounding Sid until Jeffrey Harrison, seated on
the deck behind them, removed an unlit pipe
from his mouth and began tapping the bowl on
one of his rubber shoes.

"You should count your blessings," he advised. "In '13, I came across her on the old Astara enroute to Egypt. The sea was so terrifying that four of my old mates were thrown so violently that they had to be evacuated in Malta, bound in rope, and screaming like wild banshees".

The 2nd QLI was moving east, 'trooping', a tradition practiced by the nation's military since the late 17th century and finessed to a smooth drill by this point. From 1st October to 31st March, to avoid traveling and arriving in hot weather, fleets of ships rushed back and forth from Hong Kong, Singapore, Bombay, and Aden, through the Mediterranean, all starting or ending at one of Britain's coastal ports. Unfortunately, they discovered that their journey would not be idle. There were emergency drills with cork life jackets. Plenty of tasks were at hand, such as washing dishes and peeling potatoes in the galley, cleaning the ship for officers' rounds, keeping a fire watch, or even standing guard in dark, narrow corridors and small hidden rooms in the deepest, most cramped areas of the boat. Games were organized: boxing, tug-of-war, or physical training, but the tilt of the deck made most of these activities impractical. The ship, due to a design flaw or a war injury, sailed with a permanent tilt, leaning five degrees to starboard. The midpoint of the 2nd QLI's journey was Port Said, at the northern end of the Suez Canal, as their destination was Bombay. After docking at a wharf piled high with coal, small boats swarmed around the ship, unloading locals selling jewellery, clothes, footwear, fruits, and other items of interest to sea travellers. Boys, some fully nude and others nearly so, also emerged, diving from the ship's deck for coins. If the coin was silver, a boy would leap from the ship's high rigging to retrieve the sinking coin, then swim under the ship to resurface on the opposite side. Trade and sport both ended when families went ashore to shop in town while the soldiers left for a march. Once everyone was gone, the crew sealed all ventilation and entrances in preparation for refuelling. Upon lifting the bunker covers, two gangways were positioned from the wharf, initiating a steady procession of ebony black coolies, both men and women. Ascending one gangway, they'd arrive with a shallow basket of coal balanced on their heads, which they would dump into a hopper before descending the second gangway to collect more. Upon returning, the passengers found the ship covered in coal dust. Despite the uncomfortable heat, they had to remain sealed in for the remainder of the day and night as coaling by hand was a long and dirty task. The next morning, as the ship set off in 'sweet water,' the crew was busy washing the black film off its superstructure. As they entered the sweltering heat of the Red Sea, rumours began to circulate that everyone onboard was to switch ships mid-sea. Dismissed as a joke from a prankster, they rendezvoused with another vessel two days later under a sky that matched the plate smooth, sapphire blue sea. The new ship, featuring four funnels and a more prominent appearance, was overdue for painting. More rust was visible than on their original ship. The name "Green Hunter" was displayed on the bow, but a failed paint job revealed its original German title. This was just one of many ships Britain had seized from Germany as reparation after the war.

Manoeuvring and stopping, gangways were run across and lashed. Passengers, carrying their baggage, rations, and stores, trooped over these for several hours. Their original ship then cut loose, turning about at full speed in response to an emergency call, its five-degree list giving the illusion of a wounded animal. In contrast, their new ship set its course towards the Arabian Sea and Bombay.

Other passengers were already aboard this new transport, advising the newcomers not to occupy the cabins due to a rat infestation. As a result, most passengers lived day and night on the upper decks, seeking shade on the port side during the hottest periods of the sun and sleeping wherever space was available at night. The rat problem led to the dispensing of segregation; families and soldiers intermingled in the evening to secure sleeping spaces. Before sleep, a cabaret singsong took place. A three-piece band, consisting of an accordion, harmonica, and banjo, provided the music. The women danced, and the men sang, each song performed with Dutch lager-fuelled enthusiasm. Peter and Simon Richmond, Jake Richmond's sons, made a small fortune by collecting and returning the empty bottles for a penny each. At one point, as the men sang 'Danny Boy' with gusto, an Irish corporal's wife rushed up. They stopped the band, restarted them, and sang the lyrics in their rapturous lilting form. This performance mesmerised the audience, reducing them to a silently swaying mass.

In conclusion, to lift everyone from their melancholy, Lily Richmond took the stage to sing and dance to ragtime tunes that even her Aunt Harriet didn't know she could perform. The men loved it, cheering her on and joining in the songs.

"We'll be docking tomorrow," Jeffrey Harrison informed Joey Payne the following day.

"How can you tell?" Joey asked with curiosity.

"See those?" Jeffrey had removed his empty pipe from his mouth to point at specks in the sky. "Those are swallows. By this evening they'll be darting around the ship. They nest in India. And tomorrow we'll be there too."

CHAPTER 4

Bombay has a lower death rate than London. If we do not take care, Bombay will outstrip us in the sanitary race. People will be ordered for the benefit of their health to Bombay.
-Florence Nightingale, 1860

On the day the Green Hunter spotted the Indian coastline, another vessel was also preparing to embark on the same journey. A liner belonging to the Peninsular and Oriental Steam Navigation Company had raised steam and was gearing up to depart from Tilbury Docks. Its course was set to sail through the Thames Estuary and into the English Channel.

The ship's steward, clad in white, hurried along the deck, striking a bronze gong to signal that it was time to disembark. Since the ship was moored riverside, few passengers were present to heed the call. Instead, the dockside was a flurry of activity. Travelers bid farewell to their loved ones, tossing paper streamers, and waving goodbye. One man, Robin Cuimein, stood apart from this emotional tableau. He was content to watch Gravesend across the river. From beneath a lifeboat suspended from its davits, he observed the river traffic of steamships, cargo vessels, and crimson-sailed Thames barges, all navigating towards or away from London's commercial docklands.

Robin was a man of over six feet, with black hair, a clean-shaven face, and hazel brown eyes. His height gave him a deceptively slim appearance, a fact that many of his adversaries in school and university rugby games had underestimated, often to their detriment.

At twenty-seven, Robin's somewhat serious demeanour led many to guess he was older by three or four years. This wasn't unique to him. The war had spawned a whole generation of such men. He had enlisted at university as soon as the war broke out, spending four years on the Western Front, ending with the acting rank of major. In the following year, he indulged in parties, women, late nights, and heavy drinking, like so many others seeking to escape their fears and forget the past. Eventually, he came to terms with the senselessness and loss of the preceding four years and resumed his university studies, focusing on India and Indian languages. India was his birthplace, and he wanted to return there to secure a position in the Indian Civil Service. After completing university and passing the ICS exam, Robin used his probation year to pursue further study in Indian languages. With his life's career path clear, he was setting sail for a place he considered home, not just a province of the Empire.

As he settled into a seat at an empty table in the lounge, the ship began to move. The room filled with sea travellers: men in blazers, cravats, plus-fours, and autumn jackets, women in tweed or sleeved chiffon dresses."

Two young army officers, both 2nd lieutenants, stood nearby with eager expressions, searching for an available table on the ship. One of them politely asked Robin if they could share his table. Robin agreed and introduced himself as a member of the Indian Civil Service.

The first officer, Kyle Bate, had straight blond hair and blue eyes, a slightly built frame, a rosy complexion, and a bubbly personality. Both officers were of medium height and in their early twenties, but the second officer, Hugo du Rand, was more decisive with dark eyes and tightly cropped black hair.

All three men were graduates from the Royal Military Academy, Sandhurst, and were on their way to India to join their regiments. As they conversed over drinks, they speculated about the upcoming voyage, what they might expect upon arrival, and discussed the latest news of the day. Topics included Mustapha Kemal's next military move in Turkey and the formal takeover of the Conservative Party by Bonar Law, with the possibility of a general election looming.

A half-hour after departing, Cuimein, who had given control of the bridge to the Thames pilot, noticed a confident-looking woman in her fifties entering the lounge. Her complexion was yellowed from years of sun exposure and her greying hair was styled in a pre-war fashion, matching her attire - a hat, shoes, long dress, and overcoat, all reminiscent of the pre-war era. Even her umbrella and handbag appeared to be from a bygone age. Standing at five-foot-four, she exuded an air of stateliness as she surveyed the room.

A group of men near the bar, jacketless and tieless, with reddened faces, greeted the woman as "Emily!" One of the men stood to offer her a seat, but she declined with a wave of her umbrella. Instead, she asked the three men seated nearby if she could join them. Bate replied, "By all means, please do. Your presence will add charm to the table." All three men stood up as Cuimein quickly extinguished his cigarette in an ashtray.

Emily removed her gloves and introduced herself, shaking hands with each man as they stated their names. She held onto their hands until she had memorized their names. "du Rand? du Rand?" she repeated, "Any relation to Brigadier William du Rand?" Hugo, the blond officer who was formerly a Major-General and now retired, replied, "He's, my father."

When Emily asked Bate if he had any connections to India, he answered with a grin, "None whatsoever. My family is in textiles and incredibly wealthy. I'm escaping east to get away from it all!" Emily then turned her attention to Cuimein, repeating his name as she recognized it. Her eyes suddenly filled with admiration as she asked, "Sir Nathaniel Cuimein, would he be...?" Cuimein interrupted, "My grandfather."

As the four prepared to sit down, du Rand nodded towards the party of red-faced men and asked Cuimein if he had any friends aboard. "Those? Gracious, no," Emily dismissed with a wave of her hand. "They're planters who deal with tea and indigo from Assam and Bengal. And you shouldn't get involved with them unless you drink heavily and can afford a large bar tab at Ballard Pier."

For an hour, the two young officers peppered Emily with questions while refilling her port and lemon. Emily Sheffield had lived in India for thirty years and had good reason to do so. As a young wife, she and her doctor husband left their Dorset village for the turbulence of a mission hospital and school on the North-West Frontier. Despite being penniless, they were in love with each other and their work. They shared the heartache and reward of trying to provide medical care and education for the fiery and temperamental Pathan tribesmen.

Emily quickly broached the subject of her husband's death, which occurred after only five years of marriage, and swiftly moved on to discuss the expansion of their mission. They had established branches throughout northern India, and Emily had struggled to qualify as a doctor. She was returning from a summer in England, where she had given lectures in church halls and spoken at garden parties. She had readily asked those of wealth, and those of lesser means, for donations to support her cause. Their conversation concluded after an hour, signalled by the sounding of the luncheon gong.

Robin had engaged in the conversation, asking Emily simple and natural questions, despite her legendary status in his eyes. Her husband's death was not due to natural causes; he had been ambushed and shot dead one morning by a young Bhittani tribesman while riding on the outskirts of a Tank. Incited by fanatical mullahs promising eternal life in heaven's gardens, the young man murdered this unsuspecting and defenceless Christian. He managed to avoid government punishment and returned to his hometown. However, the doctor who had administered life-saving treatment, without asking for any compensation, was so revered that a tribal jirga seriously considered claiming his life. His life was spared only because his elder brother offered to act as a guardian for the widow. As Cuimein knew, he still lived there, guarding Emily's bedroom door every night. What Cuimein did not know was that Emily was also keeping his history a secret. She had met Charles, Robin's father, and his grandfather, who was in his late eighties and residing in a garden bungalow on the foothill slopes north of Dehra Dun, before the turn of the century. Sir Nathaniel Cuimein was knighted for his lifelong service in India, starting as a young officer with the Honourable Company's army, then transferring to the civil service as a district magistrate, and ultimately becoming a high court judge when the British Government took over the administration of India from the East India Company.

Emily thought to herself, "So, this must be Cuimein's grandson." As she gazed upon Robin's handsome and relaxed face, she wondered if he knew about his family's involvement in the Sepoy Mutiny 65 years ago and how close it had been for him to never exist. The story would have been remarkable in any ordinary period, but after the bloody upheaval of the Indian Mutiny, it was just another tale of the rebellion. Emily was convinced that Robin knew the story.

In May 1857, Nathaniel Cuimein grabbed a Wesson Levatt pistol from his dresser and checked the rounds in its cylinder drum. He then hid it under his waistband and put on his lightweight frock coat. It was almost 7 a.m., and

Cuimein had to go to his courthouse for the morning session. His wife and two eldest children were finishing breakfast on the veranda, while the youngest child, Charles, was inside with their nanny, Bina. Cuimein hugged his children, kissed his wife, and promised to be back for lunch.

As he walked out into the carriageway, Mangat, his servant, held his saddled horse, Khan. Cuimein mounted the horse, waved goodbye to his family, and rode out into the tree-lined Mall of the minor civil lines, enroute to his morning's work. Munnilal, the housekeeper, would soon secure khas-khas tatti reed frames in the open windows and doorways to keep the bungalow's interior at a bearable temperature. During the peak hours, water was splashed on the outer surfaces.

In 1845, Nathaniel arrived in India at the age of eighteen with a commission in a regiment of the Bengal Infantry, which his father had secured for him. After seven years, he left the army to become a magistrate. Before starting his new job, he took leave to return home, where he met and married his wife, Agnes. Together, they embarked on a five-month journey aboard a masted steamship to Calcutta. Agnes was heavily pregnant when they arrived, and they had to travel six hundred miles by bullock cart to Nathaniel's posting in Mauna, a town one hundred miles west of Allahabad.

Mauna was home to a small European cantonment that was made up of retired officers, lower-middle company officials, and ex-employees. In addition, there was a regiment of Bengal native infantry and a squadron of irregular cavalry, whose officers were responsible for organizing the year's social events.

Nathaniel began taking a pistol to work due to the spreading rumours of rebellion and massacre throughout the stations north and along the basin of the Ganges, reaching as far as the gates of Calcutta. Although many of these rumours were exaggerated, both Nathaniel and the British felt apprehensive. However, the British officers who were leading the native troops were confident in their men's loyalty and believed that if a fight did erupt, it would be to suppress other rebellions, not their own.

Unfortunately, this confidence was misplaced. In previous decades, the status of a soldier, or sepoy, from Jake Company's army was highly respected in his village. But unwise government legislation had gradually diminished this status, unbeknownst to many. Rumours circulated about Christians taking control, allowances being reduced when serving away from home provinces, and being shipped across the sea, which incited fears of caste destruction. The most alarming rumour, however, was about the use of pig and cow fat in the new greased rifle cartridge, which would violate their religious customs. Despite the unchanged recipe of beeswax and linseed oil, it was challenging to comfort the anxious sepoys.

Moreover, the land was populated with individuals eager to cause chaos and fuel the sepoys' doubts. After the Afghans' victory over the English fifteen years prior and the recent conclusion of the Crimean War, rumours spread that the British Army had been defeated. The people began to believe that the era of the British ruling India was nearing its end, and soon the rivers would be flowing with their blood. Conspiracy theories thrived and unexplained deliveries of baked chapatis from one village to another added to the sense of impending disaster. Cuimein was oblivious to the fact that the chapati had already circulated through his district, and the rumours persisted: the reign of the saheb, or British ruler, was ending.

Unknown to him, rebellion and massacre were rampant in Bengal. On May 10th, the 11th and 20th Infantry and 3rd Cavalry regiments mutinied at Meerut, killing many white officers and civilians, including children. They rushed to Delhi and were joined by three more regiments, sparking hostilities that would last for three years as others also joined them. News spread throughout northern India, causing native unit after native regiment to mutiny. At Mauna, where there was no railway or telegraph line, word of rebellion had arrived, but not to the British authorities; the first messenger had gone to the sepoy lines that night.

Cuimein cantered to the end of the dirt-surfaced Mall and turned into a street that was the British Raj's administrative centre of the town. Along the Mall, he noted the scarcity of native workers, grounds men employed by the cantonment and sweepers clearing the cow dung. Approaching his court building, the emptiness of the area now gave an air of unease. On any session day, the street outside would be filled with up to a hundred people, witnesses for cases of criminal acts and petty misdemeanours, and petitioners and their witnesses seeking a settlement of a dispute. Today, however, the magistrate's eyes only saw one person across the street, the town postal clerk, a retired British army sergeant married to a Hindu woman, standing bewildered in his office doorway. Even at the jail building next to the court, there was no life, which was worrying, as a jailer usually stood guard in the shade of its veranda.

With a wave of his riding crop to the postal clerk, who responded with a jerky lift of one arm, the magistrate guided his horse to the back of the courthouse where he dismounted. Usually, before Khan halted, two grooms would be on hand to lead him into the open, thatched-roofed stable, but today Cuimein had to tie his own horse. The court building was eerily silent for the first time; only high in the eaves was there any sound, sparrows chirping and darting, seemingly unaffected by the day's advancing heat. Upon entering, his Indian court clerk, sitting stiffly at his desk, rose to his feet, a courtesy he never failed to extend to his magistrate.

Cuimein's comment to his clerk was intended to make light of the strange situation, "It seems like there is a festive holiday I am unaware of." However, the elderly clerk responded in a grave tone, informing Cuimein that there was no festival, and that the people were frightened due to the possibility of trouble and bloodshed. Cuimein dismissed the clerk's concerns as outlandish bazaar gossip and assumed that they were safe with the army nearby.

However, the clerk's ominous warning that all white faces were to die forced Cuimein to recognize the seriousness of the situation. The clerk told him to leave immediately and warned him that even he, as a loyal government employee, was in danger. Cuimein rushed outside only to find the streets deserted, and even the jail was empty, with all cell doors flung open.

Suddenly, gunfire erupted, and Cuimein saw Major Francis, the second-in-command of the native infantry regiment, riding towards him with a blood-streaked sabre. Francis informed Cuimein that the sepoys had risen, and he had to warn everyone to get to the cantonment. Francis was heading towards the cavalry lines and hoped that Stewart's squadron would remain loyal; otherwise, they were all doomed.

Minutes later, with Khan at full gallop up the Mall, passing fleeing, terror-stricken servants, Cuimein saw horsemen racing away. The yellow coats of the riders identified them as belonging to the irregular Cavalry. He brought Khan to a halt at his bungalow, leaping down to rush across to a lifeless body in the carriage drive. "Agnes! Agnes!" he cried, flinging himself to his knees, clutching at his wife's lifeless form. Her face, body and limbs were lacerated with sword cuts; she, first repeatedly raped, had been run through the heart and her stomach cut open before being dragged from the bungalow. Horror-stricken, he wailed, tears of grief running from his eyes. Then leaping up, he frantically rushed into the house in search of his children. Everything that could be smashed or broken, the baby cot empty, but the framework cut to pieces, the bedclothes smeared with blood. The two eldest children he found outside the back garden playhouse he had built for them. On being discovered hiding there, they had been dragged out whimpering and then dismembered with sabre slashes. Shrieking with hysterical anguish, he collapsed, his mind crippled with grief. In this manner, he remained until the nearby sound of musket fire triggered a screaming hunger for revenge. Then, charging to his gateway, pistol in hand, he saw an open carriage thundering towards him driven by a retired major. In the back, his elderly wife comforted another woman in her arms, her clothes bloody.

"Cuimein!" screamed the major, "your family - run, man! Run!"

"They're all dead! They're dead!" screamed back Cuimein. "Into the carriage, man, quickly - we must bolt. It's cut and run or die", the major beseeched Cuimein, clear as their only hope of survival.

"No! No! I'll not leave them," cried Cuimein.

"Then I'll leave you to God or the devil, for you'll see one or the other this day".

With that, the major departed, whipping his team into a gallop.

In moments another rider thundered into view from the town. He, too, reined to a halt.

"Nathaniel," said Lieutenant Hancock, a detached officer on settlement survey duty. "The native troops are everywhere, burning and slaughtering. Get your family and flee. The only hope is to take flight."

Cuimein clenched his teeth and said, "Dead! They're dead!" He saw a ragged body of red-coated men spill into the mall and aimed his pistol at them, advancing towards them. Firing his rounds away, he stood waiting for the musket-armed mutineers to reappear from cover. He was prepared to die fighting bare-handed.

"Mount, Nathaniel! Mount!" said Hancock.
"You won't gain revenge at these odds."
At his side, Khan appeared, holding the reins of
Nathaniel's horse.
The two men climbed into the saddle and raced
away from Mauna, firing their weapons as they
went. They saw slender shafts of smoke from
burning bungalows snaking skywards.

Over the next six months, the white population
was stunned by reports of the mass butchery in
Bengal and elsewhere. The few British troops
and native sepoys remaining loyal spread along
the Ganges and fought back as best they could.
Their one significant and all-important success
was the recapture of Delhi Fort. Not until
reinforcements were sent from England and
other parts of the Empire could the carnage at
places like Allahabad, Meerut, and Cawnpore be
avenged.
During this interim period, Nathaniel Cuimein
threw his lot in with a group of men who
formed a band of moss-troopers. They, like him,
were made redundant by the rebellion. Many
also had scores to settle. Officers of the
mutineers' regiments, white merchants,
government teachers, church clerks, loyal Indian
officers, and sepoys eager to redeem the shame
brought upon their regiments, railway officials,
and telegraph operators, all banded together as a
bush militia. They were mounted on whatever

horses were available, and their weapons were an assortment of carbines, sabres, shotguns, lances, pistols, and whatever they could acquire. Nathaniel armed himself with his pistol and a hog spear, a hunting tool that proved most effective in slaying men from horseback. Forty-three troopers patrolled through the summer and monsoon months in the saddle every day. The warrant given them was to keep the byways south of the Grand Trunk Road free of dacoity and rogue bands of mutineers set on plunder. To fulfil this task, the group of moss-troopers operated from a mobile camp, quarter mastered by a pastor whose family had all been massacred and staffed by a dozen native Christian band boys whose regiment had orphaned them by killing their officers and marching off to Delhi. The camp, set up for a day or a week, would be the central point from whence they patrolled. Any robber bands or mutineers ran to the ground. They were not killed but were taken as prisoners to the nearest army detachment. There they would be tried by an army court-martial, and if found guilty of being a mutineer or plundering the land, they would be hanged or blown from a gun in most instances. With backs to the muzzle, the native's arms would be lashed by ropes secured to the wheels. On the firing of the powder charge, the torso would disintegrate, legs sagging to the ground, arms flying away on their ropes, the head constantly popping in the air like a cork. Action for Cuimein's band was at times furious and deadly, but only in small ways. A sighting sparked breakneck pursuits across dusty plains or rain-flooded jungle trails, ending in the capture, or if their quarry turned to fight, wounds and deaths. Their first significant engagement in which substantial casualties were suffered occurred on a moist morning at a remote village beside a cart track twenty miles east of Banda.

A young Muslim farmer, barefoot and turban-less with only a loin cloth for cover, staggered into the arms of the night. His back was wounded by a sword cut and he was incoherently terrified. The one fact learned from his babbling was that his village seemed to have been attacked. Minutes later, his wound was bandaged, and he was lifted onto the back of one of the troopers' horses. The horsemen rode south at a canter for the first five miles before slowing to a trot. As they came across bodies on the cart track, their pace slowed to a walk. The frequency of the dead bodies caused the farmer to talk loudly out of fear, indicating he was afraid to continue. Thus, having outlived his usefulness, he was pushed from the horse. Light was beginning to break as a village of mud-walled huts emerged from a thick forest. Captain Hobday, who had narrowly escaped with his life from Jhansi when the 14th Cavalry turned against their officers and was now their agreed commander, stopped the cavalry. The village, surrounded by crop fields of root vegetables and barley, was perhaps half a mile away. Narrow irrigation ditches crisscrossed the fields, fed from an earth-banked water tank north of the village. The village consisted of forty huts with several pens and straw-roofed pole frameworks for sheltering livestock. To maintain the cover of the remaining darkness and wait for better light, Hobday led the group around the edge of the forest to the western side of the fields. Even there, they encountered bodies of men, old women, and children, who were apparently killed before reaching the shelter of the forest. Silently, they moved, with only the creaking of leather and the light jingle of saddlery metal breaking the silence. The troopers, formed into a single line, sat facing the village and the whisper of morning light beyond. Without any proof that the raiders were still present in the village, Hobday was unwilling to enter until he had confirmation either way. They sat motionless, listening to the awakening forest around them: a jungle cock, a peafowl and the howl of a jackal disturbed from feasting on a corpse. However, no sound came from the village, an unusual silence since the village's pariah dogs would usually be making noise at this time.

Deciding it was no longer safe to wait since the morning light would soon uncover their presence, Captain Hobday nudged his horse into a walk. On that signal, the whole rank moved with him. Then, having covered a third of the distance to the hutment, somewhere in the village, a horse neighed to be answered by one of their own green mounts. At that, caution was discarded, horses spurred to a canter, trotting across the crop fields and over-irrigation ditches. Swinging around a tall clump of bamboo, Cuimein could see the village layout clearly before him. Surrounding the ashes of fires from the night before, clusters of men lay asleep, until one, on hearing the thudding of a horse's hooves on a hard earth pathway, leapt up to shout a warning. They, in tattered uniforms, were a body of renegade mutineers taken to pillaging. After attacking and butchering the village, they remained to rape the women and drink darro, the village's alcoholic brew.

Awakening to find charging horsemen all but upon them, they either ran or stood. One, before Cuimein, held up a musket with a bayonet sword ready. The magistrate brought his spear down, and with Khan at a dead run, he leaned low over his horse's neck, letting the point drop. In a blink, the native soldier, with a cry, vanished below Khan's hooves. Cuimein swept his spear up behind to recover, aiming forward, the point blooded. Again, he used it, this time into the back of a red-coated figure running between two huts. Then again, into the back of someone trying to reach the cover of a sugar cane patch. Turning his horse, he galloped back into the village to find single combat everywhere.

The mutineers who were asleep in the huts were spilling weapons into the earthen yards, while one trooper stood dismounted at a doorway, sabring all who came out. Another trooper left his horse to hunt in the darkness of a hut with his shotgun. Cuimein rode with the assistance of a railway plate man on the horse but was surrounded by mutineers. He was dragged down and repeatedly bayoneted until he managed to rein his horse and fire his pistol at the group, killing or driving them off. He then raced through the village, spearing as many of them as he could before they reached the forest's edge. Out of the forty-two troopers who charged that morning, one lost a hand, three later succumbed to their wounds, and six were buried before midday. They engaged a force that was over two hundred strong, and succeeded in killing nearly a hundred mutineers, immediately dispatching thirty-one who were wounded. Nineteen mutineers who surrendered were hanged.

A year later, Captain Hobday and his group passed through Mauna, a year after quelling the rebellion. Cuimein went through the town to the cantonment and discovered that the court building was still standing, though derelict. He found his burnt bungalow in the back garden, which had three large and two small graves. He was relieved to know that someone had provided most of his murdered family with the dignity of a burial.

Cuimein returned to the front of the bungalow grounds and sat on the steps of his former home. Khan, still saddled with a water skin slung under his belly, a carbine, bedding, and saddlebags on his flanks, wandered into the shade of a banyan tree. A Hindu woman, barefoot with a year-old baby on one hip, entered the bungalow grounds through the gate. Cuimein, in a soiled dress and worn boots, with a year-old beard and weeks of dirt, initially paid no attention to her until she stopped before him and held out the sun-blackened baby. It was Bina, his ayah, returning his baby son, whom she had managed to keep alive by secretly feeding him with the milk of other native women with young babies. Cuimein reached out to take his son and then pulled him close, weeping with disbelief at his good fortune.

In response to Emily Sheffield's question, Robin Cuimein confirmed that it had indeed been thirteen years since his last visit to India. He elaborated that in 1909, when he was 14, his grandfather passed away, and his father fell ill, forcing him to retire early from service. As a result, they moved back to Surrey.

"Did you find it strange growing up in India?" she asked. "Yes, very," Cuimein replied simply.

"Well, you'll not find India has changed much," the woman assured. "Perhaps there are a few more automobiles on the streets, but the country and its people have hardly advanced much beyond what it was a thousand years ago. So here we still march to the pace of the bullock cart."

It was early morning on the last day of the voyage, and in the distance, just above the horizon, was a grey but visible line of hills. These were the Deccan Ghats, below which, and yet to be seen, were India's coastline and the city of Bombay. Emily and Robin were taking the morning air in their pre-breakfast attire, a kimono, and a dressing gown, moving about the promenade deck, one step ahead of a boatswain's mate supervising a team of deckhands who were hosing down the wooden surface.

What Emily Sheffield said was nearly correct. The only real advancement in population had been estimated in 1920 to be over three hundred million. This was vastly more than there were in the country when English seagoing merchants first arrived to exercise the Honourable East India Company's trade charter, bestowed by Elizabeth the First. It was from this modest concession that Britain could turn India into the jewel of the Empire. Having seen off all other competitors, Dutch, French, and Portuguese, by trade, treaty, and musket, the East India Company, or Jake Company, took three-fifths of the country's commercial, civil, and military control. The remainder, mainly the Princely States, under a watchful eye, was granted freedom to administer their own domestic affairs. This meant that, excluding Burma, a commercial business concern run by a Board of Control headed by a cabinet minister, was in sole charge of the triangular-shaped eastern sub-continent almost fifteen hundred miles in depth from corner to corner.

Of course, in the mid-nineteenth century, following the Sepoy Mutiny, this all changed. The British Government took over responsibility for the country, but more changes were needed during this handover. The systems used to run the country were too successful or traditional to amend; those in office, now earning a government salary, found they had merely swapped coats. Road, rail, and vast irrigation projects continued or were initiated, not just to facilitate the export of goods and speed their movement to ports, but for the overall betterment of the country. As for the average Indian, ninety percent were rural tillers of the soil, and for them, life remained relatively the same. A slave to the monsoon, where its failure could mean famine, or to keep his holding, a lifetime bound to a money lender, they or their families could at any moment fall victim to the plague, cholera, leprosy, or a hundred other fatal or crippling diseases, which served to illustrate that Britain had not taken over a pleasant land of milk and honey. The truth was quite the opposite: India was a multitude of contradictions, most of which pushed her steeply towards base poverty. Late in the afternoon, with the liner's rails thronged with eager spectators, the ship rounded Colaba Point into Bombay Harbour. Du Rand and Cuimein stood with Emily, pointing out the landmarks. "Malabar Hill," she said, pointing to the high ground covered with trees and fine houses beyond the docks. "The Gateway to India is an ugly thing, really." Her unflattering comment was directed at a large, solitary square structure with a massive archway. Despite being built as a notable landmark, its isolation gave it the impression of a castle.

The liner turned inside Oyster Rock and Middle Ground, two small islands with six-inch gun batteries mounted on them and maneuvered to line up alongside Ballard Pier. The decks were now complete, with most people dressed in Indian travelling clothes: topees for the men and lightweight pith helmets or wide-brimmed sun hats for the women, all in delicately coloured and lightweight garments. On the pier, teams of coolies stood ready to move the passengers' luggage: suitcases, wardrobe trunks, and wicker travelling chests. Above them on the ship, a deck officer bellowed orders to the crew through a megaphone.

"God!" said Hugo, sniffing the air. "I had forgotten how the country smells." Although he was born in India, his mother had taken him back to England at the age of five for proper schooling.

Robin Cuimein inhaled the air deeply, a mix of stale urine, animal dung, body sweat, and betel nut juice, and exhaled with a silent sigh of long-awaited ecstasy. "I'm home! I'm home!"

"Oh damn! I forgot it was Friday," Emily remarked, irritated.

"Friday?" asked Hugo.

"The Southampton Mail Boat," the doctor succinctly stated, referring to a smaller ship already docked with teams of coolies unloading mail sacks. These would be taken to a distribution hall overlooking the harbour, where they would be sorted for destinations throughout India by two thousand sorters from various government departments all over Bombay. "The Mail Trains will not depart until the postal workers have finished their tasks, which should be around midnight."

Robin pulled out a pocket watch, opening the cover. It was five o'clock.

The moment of farewell had arrived. Over the past three weeks, the four friends had grown close, despite Kyle's temporary absence due to his infatuation with a young woman from the Fishing Fleet. The women who travelled to India during the winter months were often perceived as seeking husbands due to the gender imbalance. Those who returned without a husband were labelled "returned empties," which was considered unkind.

As Bate left with Hugo to head to their assigned post at Deolali, Kyle's 2nd QLI battalion awaited orders to move to its permanent station. Hugo, who was not a part of the QLI regiment, would serve with the newly formed 13th Frontier Force Rifles. British infantry subalterns assigned to Indian regiments were required to spend a probationary period of one year with a British regiment.

After their friends departed, Robin and Emily were left alone to face their fate. Robin had been eagerly anticipating this moment since he was sixteen and chose to continue his family's tradition of joining the Indian Civil Service. After clearing customs with Emily, he proceeded to the shipping agent's office to collect an expected telegram. Unfortunately, the message only contained three words instructing him to report to Delhi, instead of the villages and communities he had hoped to serve.

Disappointed, Robin cursed, but Emily consoled

him. She suggested they have dinner and enjoy a bottle of Cockburn '97 before taking the Frontier Mail.

CHAPTER 5

Welcome misfortune if thou comest alone.
-Jake Ray

Drowsily, Joey Payne's eyes opened, staring at a wooden beam and roof tiles above his bed. This scene had become as familiar to him as his own fingers. After a moment, he rolled his head sideways to check the time, not with a clock, but by judging the angle of sunlight and the lingering shadows in the room from the gaps around the high, unglazed windows. It was almost time to rise from the enforced afternoon rest, but not quite. Enclosed in his mosquito net, Joey's eyes fell on his possessions at the foot of his bed. His greatcoat was either hung or neatly folded on a wall shelf and peg, accompanied by its black buttons, pack, webbing, haversack, and topees. Joey gave no thought to why he had woken up. It could have been due to any number of causes: the heat, a fly entering his net, the duty bugler sounding a call, or more likely, the irritation from his prickly heat rash. Naked, except for a towel draped over his stomach to prevent a chill from the draft created by the punkah, he swung out from under the mosquito net to dress in a grey shirt, shorts, and sandals. Picking up an enamel mug from his kit box, he headed for the exit onto the bungalow's veranda, taking care to keep his footsteps light.

In India, the soldiers' accommodation was no longer in billets or huts, but bungalows, a term used for almost all living quarters in the country. These bungalows boasted high ceilings for coolness and extended, sloping roofs that led to open verandas, providing maximum shade from the sunlight for the room behind. The bungalows occupied by the 2nd QLI at this camp were all identical. Each platoon of forty men had one, split into two sections, with twenty men in each, and a third room in the middle used jointly for lectures and dining. Built during the reign of young Queen Victoria, the bungalows were spaced widely apart to catch available breezes and to prevent the spread of what was then believed to be clouds of cholera-infected gases.

On the veranda, Joey turned away from the glare reflected off the baked ground. It was late in the mid-afternoon of May, and the power of the sun was only beginning to diminish. He removed the lid of an earthenware chattie and dipped his mug into it, drawing it out filled with cool water. After drinking his fill, he threw the remainder onto the ground, causing a puff of dust. A few minutes later, the wetness was gone. In the shade of the veranda, a native lay with a rope running from one foot up into a hole that led to the bungalow ceiling. This was one of the room's

Punkah-wallahs, employed to propel the large cloth punkah frames that swung back and forth, stirring the inner bungalow's atmosphere with gusts of air.

"Kisch! Punkah-wallah! Kisch!" Payne barked sharply. The native had fallen asleep but was awoken by Payne and jerked his leg twice before settling into a slower rhythm.

"Char-wallah! Come here, you lazy man," Joey called to a white-bearded native sitting in the shade on the veranda.

Payne's voice was not harsh, nor was he cursing the man. He was making a firm but friendly request that was accepted by both parties as the only suitable approach. The native, dressed in a turban and loincloth, approached carrying a copper kettle attached to a metal stand holding smouldering charcoal. He was the bungalow's tea boy, employed by a camp contractor who provided all the battalion's luxuries, from tin whistles to hired cars. A small force was needed to cater to the battalion's needs, each one having his realm.

In addition to the char-wallah, there was the dhobi-wallah, a laundry man who would beat clothes on river stones and iron uniforms by spitting rice starch onto them, so they ended up stiff like cardboard. Their numbers were boosted by the Connor-wallah who sold bread rolls, the under-wallah who sold eggs, the mucking-wallah who sold butter, the cheeni-wallah who sold sweets, among others. One Joey found he could do without was the napi. He would come around before reveille and shave the men before they woke up. Joey thought this was good value for eight annas a week. However, one morning, he woke up to discover the napi was shaving everyone with the same pot of charcoal-heated water.

"Bhag jhow! You old man!" Payne ordered the char-wallah, who had leaned too close while filling his mug, breathing the stink of betel nut juice into his face.

"Yes, Soldier Saheb. Right away, very quickly," chuckled the old man, shuffling back to his shade.

Betel nut was to the natives what tobacco was to Europeans. The smell was bad enough, but what made it worse was how they were forever spitting it onto the ground, leaving foul, purple splats. If a soldier caught them doing this in the lines, it was sure to mean a kick.

As Joey sipped his tea, he squinted his eyes and gazed out beyond the lines to the shimmering plains, flat with scrub bush and scattered trees. In the distance, a ridge of broken hills loomed on the horizon, and just two miles away stood a fort guarded by a section from the battalion. This fort was formerly a Mughal fort, but now, it served as the site of a radio relay link from England to Calcutta and Madras. The battalion found this useful for gathering football scores, which could be radioed in Morse from Aldershot to the fort's duty signaller. On the plains, several circular stone towers could be seen. One Sunday afternoon, Joey, Benedict Lyall, and Sid Frith investigated them, only to discover a corpse being eaten by vultures and kite hawks. This was the local population's unique religious way of disposing the dead; they would leave the larger bones beneath the grill, which were too heavy for the carrion feeders to fly away with.

Upon returning to the bungalow, Payne noticed that some of the figures under their mosquito nets were awake, scratching their prickly heat rash. Tommy Gilbert, the day's bungalow orderly, passed the rifle rack and asked Payne for a sip of his tea. Payne refused jokingly and reminded Gilbert of his duty. His job involved guarding the room's rifles and ammunition for twenty-four hours, as they were highly coveted by India's thieves. To pass the time, Gilbert played endless games of push-ha'penny with other bored men on the board on the lid of the rifle ammunition box.

Joey, sitting on his cot, took another sip of tea. Across the way, a man rolled onto his back. "Hey Benedict, when are you going to come out from under that mosquito net and join us in life's adventures?" asked Joey.

Lyall, who had just woken up, peered through the mesh screening, and replied, "Maybe when some newbie who just joined the army offers me some of that chai he's drinking."

The 2nd battalion of the Queen's Light Infantry had been in India for almost eight months and was starting to feel like seasoned veterans. After leaving Bombay, the battalion travelled through the night, climbing five thousand feet over the ghats to Deolali camp on the Deccan Plain. The camp had a bad reputation for causing men to go mad, as it was where soldiers who had completed their service waited for shipment home. Kyle Bate and Hugo du Rand joined the battalion at Deolali and were given commands in B and D Company respectively.

The next day, the battalion paraded at the rail station for transport to their first posting. Two hundred sullen artillerymen, who had been ignored for over two months, were also waiting for orders to join their regiments. They hijacked the first train arriving in a northerly direction. For two days, the 2nd Queens travelled across India, stopping frequently for no apparent reason due to the low priority of troop trains. Most men aboard simply gazed out at the passing country and its people. Rarely did they appreciate the nation's history, culture, and beauty or the significance of landmarks such as forts or the relationships between mahouts and elephants. Few recognized the devotion between humans and animals or appreciated the beauty of the sari-clad women carrying water pots on their heads.

During autumn, the countryside changed as they travelled further north after the monsoon season. On the second day after crossing a rocky hill range, they travelled thirty miles across a dusty plain to stop next to a small patch of concrete. The men got off the train onto the Railside dirt, as the concrete platform was for unloading officers' horses. This was different from the local rail station, which was located two miles further in town. Here, troops bound for or leaving the garrison lines would board or leave their train.

Jhendara is located in the northern half of the Central Provinces; it was a backwater town with only ten thousand inhabitants. The railroad ended there, as its rails and sleepers were taken up and re-assembled somewhere south of Baghdad during the war. For this reason, it was only considered a third-class station, the lowest category, and was listed as a garrison with a strength of one battalion. Some rumours suggested that it was a punishment posting.

The 2nd Queen's Light Infantry left a baggage party and animal handlers behind to transport their belongings and marched a mile to their positions. Leading the march was the band, followed by the commanding officer, who was the only person mounted. They walked down the road in sync with the music. A battalion of

the Bedfordshire and Hertfordshire Regiment
was assembled on the parade square, which the
2nd Queen's was relieving.

The Queen's stopped to face the Beds and Herts
once the colours were uncased and presented
arms. The Light Infantry turned their eyes right
to acknowledge that regiment's own colours as
they passed. They then turned left twice, and the
Beds and Herts marched away, also turning, and
passing in front of the new battalion as their
band started to play. After forming pairs, it was
the Queen's turn to present arms while the Beds
and Herts acknowledged them with a glance to
the right. The commanding officer of the Beds
and Herts was also mounted, causing his sword
to flash as he brought it down to dip.

The men of the battalion stood at ease, seeking
shelter from the sun under their solar topees
while ordering arms. Meanwhile, the sound of
the other regiment's band gradually faded as they
boarded the train, leaving the 2nd QLI alone.
The men awaited the order to dismiss with
anticipation, as the temperature had reached a
scorching ninety-two degrees, despite it being
late autumn in India.

At Joey Payne's bungalow, everyone was awake
and calling for the char-wallah at four o'clock.
The char-wallah entered barefoot, singing a little
tune as he swiftly moved from bed to bed,
serving tea to the men. Later, the soldiers
occupied themselves with various sports to

alleviate boredom and maintain their physical fitness.

With only half of the battalion at the station due to station commitments, the lines were crowded with men engaged in football, hockey, and other challenging sports. The other half had relocated to a hill station to escape the intolerable summer heat. Nevertheless, the heat remained lethal, leading to depression, suicide, and illness. The 2nd QLI recorded one death per week during the summer, caused by malaria, sand-fly fever, sunstroke, or depression. The band played mournful songs while burying their fallen comrades, including five from B Company in just one month. In addition, two young children of a sergeant passed away, adding new headstones to the century-old church graveyard. Joey Payne and Jeffrey Harrison were taking a break from their football game with the platoon at half-time, sitting on a low mud-brick wall that bordered the playing pitch. As sundown approached, the on-duty drummer at the battalion HQ bungalow prepared to lower the battalion flag, while the duty bugler on the veranda readied to blow retreat. A group of local women, baskets filled with collected cow dung atop their heads, walked back to the village. Joey watched them, his attention shifting when birds suddenly took flight and the wall beneath him trembled. Jeffrey noted the peculiarity of the situation and Joey agreed, but they dismissed it and reclined once more. Shortly thereafter, a sharp shake of the wall startled them into standing. The surrounding trees and bungalows trembled, and tiles cascaded from roofs. Gilbert darted towards the doorway, but his duties as an orderly prevented him from leaving. Others in the platoon also pondered the mysterious shaking, but most of the field games continued. Then, a rumble echoed from the western hills, growing in volume until all motion ceased. A ripple travelled at the speed of sound, knocking men onto their faces, and causing widespread destruction throughout the camp. The wall beside Joey crumbled, and the bungalows collapsed. Men rushed to aid their friends, tearing through rubble in search of survivors. Gilbert was helped to his feet, narrowly escaping being trapped under the collapsing bungalow. "Jesus, Joey! What happened?" He blurted out. Payne couldn't respond and looked around in bewilderment. There wasn't a building left standing in sight. Amidst all the chaos, a saddled but riderless horse charged, neighing, and shaking its head in terror. It belonged to Lieutenant-Colonel Claude Gibson, the battalion commanding officer. The Colonel found himself on foot after he and his horse were knocked to the ground by a roadway that had suddenly risen while they were on their way from his bungalow to the officers' mess.

Just minutes earlier, Kyle Bate and Hugo du Rand were in the middle of a tennis match when, without warning, they found themselves helpless on their backs, being tossed about as if they were on a small boat in a raging sea storm. When they finally managed to get back on their feet, they found the once flat-surfaced clay court raised and broken like a ploughed field. The mess building and all the bachelor bungalows lay in ruins around them. From underneath these ruins and the enveloping clouds of dust, voices in both native and English languages called out for help.

At the battalion headquarters' orderly room, RSM Richmond was desperately removing tiles and timbers from the wreckage. As soon as the first tremor hit, he left his office desk where he had been working with the adjutant in the next office and joined the duty bugler on the veranda. This act of curiosity undoubtedly saved his life, as they were both thrown to the ground when the main surge of the earthquake hit. There was no doubt that it was an earthquake. In a few minutes, an opening was torn apart from the shattered tiles and crossbeams above the adjutant's office. But it was too late for Richmond, the sixteen-year-old bugler, and the fifteen-year-old drummer; Richmond was found dead, pinned under the rubble that had crushed him at his desk.

Only one battalion unit recognized the warning signs of the tremors for what they were: the Vickers Machine Gun Group. Under a new scheme introduced to British Regiments in India, all battalions now included an Indian machine-gun platoon. These men were Dogras, often mistaken for Sikhs, but were Hindu hillmen and shorter in height than most Sikhs. At the first tremble of the ground, they cried out "Earthquake! Earthquake!" which triggered a mass exodus from the bungalows and sent the men running towards the mule stables to lead their beloved animals into the adjoining corral. Now that the sun's harshness had subsided, Lily Richmond rode her bicycle into the bungalow grounds of her only remaining friend on the station, who hadn't yet retreated to the hills. She was also seventeen, the daughter of the District's Sub-Sanitary Commissioner. As she navigated along the driveway, she dismounted at the veranda steps, letting her bicycle fall onto the scorched lawn grass to one side. On the forward edge of the veranda, the gardener, Ravi, was watering a collection of earthenware pots containing plants, the only splash of greenery not wilted by the summer heat.

"Good afternoon, Ravi," Lily called out cheerfully as she ascended the steps. Ravi reciprocated the cheerful greeting with a smile as she crossed the veranda. She halted at the doorway and called out, announcing her arrival. "Miriam!" The bungalow was the grandest in the small civil cantonment. The grounds, now parched and barren, blossomed with vibrantly coloured flowers and lush greenery in the winter. Off to one side sat a tennis court where Miriam and Lily frequently played. Lily had come to bid farewell, as Miriam's family was departing for the hills.

"Here, Lily, come in!" her friend beckoned from the back rooms.

Before Lily could respond, a gentle tremor jolted the house. Perplexed, she glanced around before stepping into the house, half-convinced she had imagined it. Everything seemed normal, except for Ravi who was dashing off across the grounds. Upon entering, Lily sidestepped the wicker furniture and made for a doorway on the far side of the living room. She had barely advanced a step when the house shook violently, knocking a mounted tiger's head from the wall. The tremor subsided within seconds, leaving the two girls terrified and calling out for each other. Rushing to the doorway, Lily saw Miriam emerging from a bedroom into the hallway.

"Lily, what is it? What's happening?" she asked, alarmed. A muffled roar was moving towards them through the early evening air.

Unable to speak, Lily's question was answered by her friend's mother, who appeared at the far end of the hallway. "Earthquake!" she screamed. "Miriam, quickly, get out of the house. Run! Run!" However, even as she shouted, it was already too late. A two-foot ground wave lifted the mother and threw her backward. A fraction of a second later, the same wave carried the daughter upward and a wooden spar dropping from the roof hit her. Lily, watching this as if in a slow-motion dream, was also lifted into the air, then hurled to the rippling floor. She was rocked up and down while bricks and timbers fell against her, encasing her body. When the earthquake finally stopped, Lily was left gasping for breath in a small, confining space filled with brick dust. Frantic and choking for air, she weakly began to call out, "Miriam! Miriam!"

CHAPTER 6

All that is born is doomed to die;
Whatever dies shall live again.
-Krisha (a diety in Hinduism)

Lieutenant Colonel Gabson, a regular army officer since the age of eighteen, is forty-five years old and not the Duke of Wellington. Although he briefly commanded a brigade at the end of World War I, he was demoted to lieutenant colonel due to the surplus of rank. He fully understood that he would not progress beyond the rank of colonel when he was given command of the 2nd battalion and stationed in Jhendara. However, he did not let his rank impact his competence. He faced numerous challenges and disasters during the war and understood the aftermath of these events when he saw the ruins of his lines.

Lieutenant Colonel Gabson, due to his rounded figure and weight, ran awkwardly in his riding boots. He shouted to Kyle, a subaltern, dressed in tennis whites, who was carrying a piece of wooden planking. He instructed Kyle to gather all the officers and bring them to him as he wanted to confer with them. However, Kyle informed him that Major Fletcher was first trapped under a beam before running off.

"Bate!" the colonel barked, causing the young man to stop. "Damn it, youngster. I told you to gather the officers. Do it now." Within ten minutes, seven officers, dirty and sweaty from their rescue attempts, stood before him - most of them wild-eyed and angry. Gabson, who had lost his topee, remained upright, tapping his riding crop against his boot top. He knew that providing his junior commanders with a stable base was his priority.

"Gentlemen, fate has dealt us a catastrophic hand," he began. "Our primary concern is rescuing those who are trapped - but this needs to be done with properly organized rescue parties, not by haphazard individual action." The colonel paused to look at each officer before continuing.

"We have lost the light and it's almost dark. This means that we'll have to work through the night, which will slow down our progress." He then turned to a tall, bare-chested man. "Major Stockmann, take two officers and go down to the men's lines. Parade everyone there and divide them into groups. Keep some for-rescue work and send others into the cantonment and civil line to look for anyone trapped. Deploy armed patrols as quickly as possible around the perimeter and assign one of your officers to that task. As soon as the locals hear about what happened, they'll be down on us like vultures, so arms - every rifle, Lewis's gun, pistol, and round of ammunition - must be recovered and accounted for. Put a guard on the quartermaster's ammunition stores."

The colonel paused again, this time to look for another officer. "Lieutenant Tolhurst, dealing with the dead will be your responsibility. They must be buried as soon as possible. Dig a big pit for them to be buried in and mark it as a graveyard. We'll see that they're properly buried later. Use the GS wagons for transport and find Subedar Nath. He and his machine gunners will provide the haulage animals for them."

The CO stopped again, this time to select an officer who was still unmasked. "Mister du Rand, hurry to the fort. If it hasn't been done already, inform the outside world of our situation. Send a message to Delhi or anyone who can hear us, explaining that we've been hit by a major earthquake and require urgent assistance." He paused to scan the faces before continuing, "Do we know the adjutant's whereabouts?"

"He wasn't in the mess, sir. I believe he went to his office," a junior officer replied.

"Right," the colonel responded, almost shouting. "Mr. Bates," he barked, and Kyle immediately came to attention. "From now on, you will serve as the adjutant. Starting from this moment, this spot right here is my headquarters. Any questions?"

"What about the injured? Where do we send them for treatment?" the Major asked.

"Send them here, to the mess grounds," the colonel responded after some thought. "We have more shade here than anywhere else in the lines, and we'll need that tomorrow." Lastly, he advised, "You may roll up your sleeves, but remember that you're King's Officers. So, carry on and fulfil your duties."

As dawn approached, everyone's tasks became more challenging. Men searched through the rubble for bodies, injuries, and weapons. Frustrated sergeants tried to locate their platoon's soldiers, and officers grappled with limited resources and increasing responsibilities. Every necessity was complicated by the disheartening reality that everything they needed was buried under debris and had to be dug out: tents for wounded soldiers, shovels for burying the dead, and food to feed the exhausted men. Worst of all, the cantonment's wells had collapsed, as du Rand discovered while returning with more bad news. The east battlement of the fort, which housed the radio equipment, had crumbled and fallen forty feet into a dry nullah, killing most of the signal detachment and damaging their equipment. On his own initiative, du Rand headed to the railway and planned to follow it into town. He hoped to send a warning message over the telegraph line from the station.

Since dusk, flames from the direction of the town had lit up the horizon, filling the night air with falling ash and the bitter smell of smoke. As he approached the outskirts, the young officer realized the extent of the damage that had befallen the town. He stuck to the railway line, determined to follow it to the station. The cries and lamentations of the townspeople signalled what lay ahead, and he witnessed the destruction and flames becoming more visible. Despite the people's heartbreak, Du Rand tried to focus on reaching the station, but the despairing populace blocked his path, pleading for help. Despite his best efforts to reason with them in Urdu, he eventually turned back, conceding defeat, and reporting back to his colonel.

After the earthquake, all survivors trapped in the bungalows were successfully rescued, though some were severely injured. The deceased were buried in shallow monsoon ditches and covered with a layer of sand. The injured, with injuries ranging from dislocated bones to crushed limbs, were initially treated at the officers' mess by the battalion medical officer until a small hospital was established at the station to provide emergency medical care. An additional section was added, catering to the wives, children, and Europeans living in the civil cantonment. Fortunately, the small hospital was in ruins, but few patients or personnel were buried alive, and most of the population was in the hills. The same could not be said for the bungalows and homes in the civil cantonment, which were mostly uninhabited, except for a few household servants who had escaped. The fact that fires didn't break out among these remains was pure coincidence, as the town relied on oil and hurricane lamps for lighting, which hadn't been lit during the earthquake. The main cause of the town's conflagration were the cooking fires that the townspeople used inside their homes. As time passed, men laboured under the sweltering sun, sifting through the ruins for bodies and weapons, aiding the injured, and setting up tents as a medical aid station. Meanwhile, others worked tirelessly to restore a functioning water supply to save what was left of the town.

A picket line of sentries was established around the boundary of the cantonment, their primary duty being to prevent potential looters from invading. The guards were selected based on their attire, which had to be proper uniforms, as the commanding officer did not want his men to appear outside the lines in anything less. They were the symbol of Pax Britannica, needing to project an image of dauntless fortitude to the native population, especially during this period. Joey Payne and Benedict Lyall patrolled a section of the civil lines, assigned to guard duty. However, they took a break under the shade of a mango tree in front of a demolished bungalow. Though they appeared properly dressed, nearly everything they wore was salvaged from others. They had spent the night searching for bodies and weapons without proper attire, wearing only football gear with hard leather bars attached to their boots. With morning orders, they used whatever gear they could find and prepared for duty. Benedict believed he had found and was wearing his own puttees and hose tops, while Joey claimed ownership of his heavy Wolseley topee, with the rest of his kit buried under a heap of bricks. The rifles they carried even belonged to another platoon.

Lyall suggested going for a walk, but Payne declined due to the intense heat. Instead, he offered to keep a lookout for any officers snooping around. Joey leaned against a tree trunk, observing the plain and the collapsed buildings around him. He noticed vultures perched in trees, anticipating a meal, half hoping the rubble held something for them. Payne didn't join his friend in exploring the ruins because the air was too hot and heavy. Occasionally, the atmosphere would stir as dust devils swirled around the cantonment's scorching, arid plain.

Unable to resist, Payne's head fell back, and his topee rested against the tree trunk. He was exhausted from working throughout the night without any rest, and it was taking its toll on him. Slowly, his eyelids drooped, but each time he attempted to fall asleep, a faint dream-like cry jolted him back to reality. At first, he thought it was imaginary, but finally, he opened his eyes to look around. The stillness of the air allowed the cry to come unhindered, but it was muffled as if it were coming from a house several rooms away.

Payne stood up and looked around. The voice was repeatedly calling for help, coming from the remains of the bungalow with long pauses in between. Walking forward, he stopped beside a lady's bicycle and cocked one ear to shout, "Who's there? Where are you?" For a few seconds, he listened in silence until the call came again, "Help! Help!"

"I hear you. Where are you?" shouted Payne, moving to the very edge of the damage.

"Oh, please help me! Help me!" cried the voice of a girl.

"Benedict! Benedict! Give us a hand. There's somebody underneath the bungalow," he called out to his companion. Lyall joined him, and Joey began burrowing under part of a tiled roof that allowed him to crawl underneath it. He took off his topee and handed Benedict his rifle, saying, "Keep an eye on my rifle for me; there's an English girl trapped. I'm going to see if I can reach her."

Payne began to sweat profusely as he entered the confined space. The limited visibility and choking dust made every movement a challenge.

"I'm coming to you, miss. Keep calling out to me!" he shouted.

"Oh, thank God! Bless you!" the girl responded. Joey moved forward on his hands and knees, covering about ten feet before being forced to crawl. In the pitch-black darkness, he cautiously felt his way with his fingers, creating a tunnel by removing and setting dozens of bricks aside. Guided by the sound of the girl's voice, he managed to traverse a few more yards and seemed to enter a low chamber. Feeling around, he realized he could lift his head but couldn't get onto his knees. As he moved further in, the girl, no longer needing to shout, could speak to him normally.

Upon reaching the girl, Joey found Lily sobbing. "Oh, thank you, thank you!" she cried. "No problem, love. I'll have you out of here in no time," Joey replied, trying to sound confident. Payne explained that she was trapped under a plank that was pinning down one of her legs and both arms. He would need to remove the bricks beneath her to free her. "What's your name?" Lily inquired. "Private Joseph Payne," he answered. Joey lightened the mood with jokes and formally introduced himself. "What's yours?" he asked Lily. "Lily Richmond," she replied. Joey was taken aback as he knew someone with the same surname. "We have an RSM named Richmond," he remarked. "Yes, I know. He's my uncle," Lily responded cheerfully.

Joey joked about her situation, but Lily started to fear he would abandon her. He reassured her that he was there to help and would not leave her.

Joey tried to soothe Lily by talking about his life and family. He worked meticulously to remove the bricks without stirring up dust, which would cause discomfort for both. It was a long and arduous process, but eventually, they managed to remove the bricks and free Lily from the rubble. Overcome with joy, she crawled out from under the plank, shedding tears of relief. Joey was astounded that she had survived being buried for so many hours in the oppressive heat.

Joey, having been told to keep hold of one of his boots, led the way inch by inch on his belly back up the tunnel he had made. Upon emerging, Benedict greeted him with laughter at his dirty and grimy appearance. Joey then turned to assist the girl out, who collapsed into the two men's arms, unable to suppress her laughter.

"Oh, Joey, do I look as bad as you?" she asked. She looked worse, with her hair caked in dust and grit, her dress filthy and torn, and scratches on her arms and legs, some cuts drawing blood. She was half carried over to the shade of the mango tree, where she momentarily rested before asking for water.

"This stuff is as warm as Hades but better than our canteen pani," apologized Lyall, pushing down the glass marble in the neck of the bottle to free it for drinking before handing it to the girl.

"Joey, you saved my life. But unfortunately, I'll never be able to repay you," she began, several minutes later.

"I know a way," replied Joey, drawing on his second bottle of lemonade.

"How?" Lily quickly asked.

"Teach me some of the rag-time dance moves you did on the ship coming from Blighty," Joey suggested. Despite her dirty and sweaty appearance, Lily's face instantly formed the cutest smile Joey had ever seen.

"Is that all, Private Joseph Payne? Is that all?" she replied, holding the smile for a few moments before being overcome by uncontrollable sobbing.

Later that afternoon, as the sun began to set, signalling its intention to call a truce only to replenish its scorching rays for the next day, Jhendara's first rescuer arrived. Relieved of his adjutant's duties, Kyle Bate was now the officer in charge of the northern perimeter guard. Commanding thirty men who patrolled a two-mile line, he had established his headquarters in an abandoned hut beside a track that ran north across the plain.

"Visitor arriving, sir!" the young officer responded to his corporal's call. Rising from his lone stool, he joined the Non-Commissioned Officer outside the hut. Down the track, a camel rider approached, their figure distorted by the heat haze. A stream of refugees had been leaving the town via this track since midday, but this was the first person coming the other way.

It took ten minutes for the rider and camel to reach Bate's hut. As they halted, a young offspring of the older beast, with a woolly coat, wandered over to a thorny bush by the roadside and began munching its leaves. The rider, dressed in a topee and skirt, sat atop the mount with two leather baggage cases strapped on each side.

Stepping forward in a soiled uniform he had salvaged from his ruined bungalow, Kyle explained to the visitor that entry to the town was restricted.

"If you have business in the town, you may not be allowed to enter. Jhendara has been struck by an earthquake and is currently sealed off."

"Kyle, you cannot bar me from the town just because you think my poodle is young and fake. I have important business there, and that business saves lives," Emily asserted, removing a travel-worn cotton scarf from her face.

"Bate was astounded by the unexpected appearance of his shipboard companion in the middle of India under such dire circumstances.

"Emily Sheffield!" he exclaimed in disbelief. "Where have you come from?"

"I'm from Raurdia, which is about twenty miles north of here. I heard about your tragedy from frightened people who arrived early this morning at one of our Missions," explained Emily, shaking the dust off her scarf.

Kyle was amazed that Emily had ridden through the heat for over twenty miles to get to them. "Emily, you're incredible," he remarked.

Emily asked for information on who was in charge and where he could be found. Kyle directed her towards the colonel, who had moved his headquarters from the officers' mess to the Anglican Church.

Emily thanked Kyle for his help, and with her umbrella as her only source of shade, she urged her camel on to continue her journey with the command "Hoy! Hoy!"

Bate watched Emily depart on her camel and remembered her entertaining performance during the ship's fancy dress evening.

Emily had no trouble finding the church, which stood out above the trees of the cantonment due to its spire. The church was one of only two types of construction that had survived the earthquakes: the other being the wood and wicker huts. As minor tremors were still occurring, causing fears of another major shock, the church was not occupied but provided a central landmark that made it easily recognizable. Lieutenant-Colonel Gabson had moved his headquarters there immediately after dawn.

To one side of the church, an emergency camp had been set up using recovered tents and sheets of canvas. The shelter was providing care for casualties in need of hospital treatment, as well as a hastily rigged kitchen and refuge for homeless survivors from the civilian lines. The camp also served as the centre from which Colonel Gabson was directing all rescue work. Emily ordered her camel to lie down before dismounting and tying the reins to a bush. As she made her way to find someone in authority, the younger camel nuzzled at its mother's belly in search of milk. However, the mother remained squatting in the dirt roadway.

Around the area, men were working in groups on a dozen different jobs, most dressed in a mix of different clothing. At the back of the church, a well was discovered that still provided water. Mules, under the watch of Dogra's machine gunners, were filling containers with water for distribution. Emily asked a soldier about Colonel Gabson's whereabouts and was pointed towards a tree where four men were standing, and another was sitting behind a makeshift desk made of boards balanced on bricks.

"Colonel Gabson?" Emily inquired of the seated man.

"I am Colonel Gabson, madam," replied a heavy-set man with a walrus mustache, who was standing near the tree.

"Very good, Colonel," responded Emily as she moved closer to introduce herself and offer her services. "I am Dr. Sheffield. I've just come down from Raurdia, where I have a mission. I'm here to assist as much as I can with the injured."

"My goodness, madam!" Gabson exclaimed in genuine surprise. "You're the first help we've received from the outside. Do they know out there what's happened here?"

"By now, yes!" Emily assured him. "Early this morning, when I left, the Assistant Magistrate was dispatching a messenger to the telegraph and rail station at Ampur."

"Hmm! Good. Good," the colonel muttered in subdued satisfaction, half-turning to tap his boot with the riding crop he held. He had spent the entire day battling to hide his anger over the complete breakdown of communication. With no radio or telegraph link, his only option was to send a messenger across the plain. After learning that the rail line was heavily damaged and the roadway destroyed, he dismissed it as useless. At dawn, he sent Lieutenant du Rand and a corporal on horseback to seek help beyond the hills. It was from these hills that Jhendara finally received a signal that the outside world was potentially aware of their predicament.

Just before noon, a heliograph message in Morse code flashed, inquiring if everything was alright. Those in the cantonment could only watch helplessly as the message continued to flash for another hour. If their heliograph equipment hadn't been buried deep in the rubble of the signal store, and if the dust and heat haze had subsided for just ten minutes, a reply could have been sent and seen. However, all they could do was assign someone to watch and note down the incoming messages.

"Colonel, could you provide me with a guide to the centre of your operations in the town? I would be most grateful," Gabson said, pulling himself out of his worries and glancing at the woman.

"At present, there is no such thing, madam," he replied.

"Oh God, Colonel Gabson! Are you saying they haven't received any assistance from you?" Emily exclaimed, pointing toward the rising smoke from the town without mincing her words.

"Doctor Sheffield, I am fully aware of what hasn't been done. This is because we are just now starting to get back on our feet," Gabson responded.

"I can see that," Emily snapped back, pointing towards the town. "But that is the point of greater devastation where your rescue attempts should be concentrated."

"It is not as straightforward as that," replied Colonel Gabson, keeping his voice low and level. "Only now have I been able to gather a large enough force to provide any sort of realistic support to the town survivors."

"Fiddlesticks, Colonel Gabson! Sending even one man with a spade would be better than sending none," Emily dismissed.

"Damn it, woman! I will not be rebuked by some female poultice-wallah telling me my priorities. What men I can spare, I will move into the town tomorrow at dawn, and not one dashed moment sooner. If you think one person can do so much, then I suggest, with my full permission, you go and try yourself," Gabson exploded.

"That, Colonel Gabson, is and always has been my sole intention," declared Emily, standing up to her full height before turning about and storming off.

Colonel Gabson paced up and down for a full minute after, repeatedly striking his boot top with his riding crop. Then, he addressed one of the standing officers, "Lieutenant Joyce, track down Major Stockmann. Inform him of our plan for providing rescue assistance in the town. I'm bringing it forward by several hours. Tell him to move his men at dusk."

The colonel had spent most of the day formulating plans and gathering tools for this operation but had set aside a sleep period for his men so they would arrive at the task refreshed. However, Emily Sheffield's snarky comments, laced with points of truth, stung his soldier's pride. They weren't ready, and the move was premature, but the woman was right; swift action was key.

"Hold the basket still, young lady. I don't expect you to look, just don't faint on me," Emily instructed.

Lily Richmond, sucking in a sharp gasp of air, held a wicker basket under a fourteen-year-old Hindu boy's mangled and infected arm. Rendered unconscious with chloroform by Emily Sheffield, the doctor was poised with a scalpel to amputate the limb. Trying to concentrate on the boy's face, Lily caught the red gash of the doctor's bold cutting of the flesh of his upper arm from the corner of her eye. Then reaching for a surgical saw, the grind and scrape of whose blade nearly caused her to pass out. In just seconds, there was a weight in the basket, and Emily told her to hurry out of the horse stable used as their hospital and dispose of the severed arm.

It was the afternoon of the third earthquake day, and Lily was no longer in the cantonment. After being rescued by Payne and Lyall, she joined them in a futile search for Miriam and her mother. Eventually, after an hour, she gave up and went with Benedict to the Anglican Church. When she arrived, pushing her bike, she saw her uncle directing a group of men who were setting up a tent. As she approached him, she said only two words: "Uncle Jake!" Jake Richmond spun around and stared at her in disbelief. He had spent the last two hours searching through the remains of his bungalow, convinced that his niece was buried underneath. He cursed himself for not having made her go with Harriet and his two sons to the hills. In front of him was the girl, covered in dirt and almost unrecognizable, whom he had given up for dead.

"Lily! Oh, Lily, my darling!" The regimental sergeant major almost wept as he embraced her. Lily was given a basin of water to wash and a light meal of corned beef and biscuits before being left alone. After some time, she went into shock. Emily Sheffield found her collapsed against a tree in the early evening heat, shaking uncontrollably.

"What's wrong with you, child?" asked Emily as she returned to her camel after confronting Colonel Gabson.

"I was buried all night," stuttered Lily.

"Really?" replied the doctor, unimpressed. "Well, sitting there with your hands in your armpits isn't doing anyone any good. Come on, girl, I've got work for you."

Lily followed Emily, still shaking, and collected her bike. For half an hour, she struggled behind Emily over the broken road surface that led to the town. At the outskirts, they passed through refugees from the burning ruins who were squatting beneath trees or around shrines and fallen temples. Most were wandering aimlessly or sitting with blank stares, awaiting their fate. Skirting the damage, Emily led Lily along narrow tracks and irrigation stream beds in a half-circle around the town. She understood the native population's fatalistic attitude towards disasters of this size, accepting them as the work of their angry gods. But she also knew that somewhere among the devastation, there would be people fighting against the odds to repair, feed and save lives.

Coming upon the rim of a nullah, the same one that part of the old fort had fallen into, which ran for several miles from south to north, Emily followed it. At the eastern edge of the town, there was an iron bridge that crossed the nullah to a suburb of undamaged houses, shops and parched farmland waiting for the arrival of the monsoon rains. Miraculously, the earthquake's epicentre being to the west, it seemed that the shockwaves had died against the geological fault below the nullah, sparing everything east of it. Crossing the bridge, they joined a small stream of people leaving the town. Some carried the dead and injured on litters or in their arms, while others transported goods on their backs or on oxen carts. Emily suspected these people were likely looters. With her keen instinct for pinpointing such things, Emily maneuvered her mount around the back of a row of buildings. At the rear of one of the houses, she found a low-walled courtyard that evidently enclosed a stable, now devoid of animals. Numerous trees provided shade for the hundreds of people huddled together in the courtyard. They were a sombre assembly of both genders and all ages, waiting in the hope that someone would step forward to offer them a means to rebuild their lives. After dismounting, Emily Sheffield tied her camel to a gate, leaving it and its offspring to look around with the animal's typical vacant expression.

"What's your name, dear?" she asked a girl. Upon hearing the response, she directed, "Well, Lily, leave your bicycle here and come with me." As she entered the courtyard, Emily realized it had become a casualty collection centre. Injured individuals were scattered everywhere, lying on the ground, leaning against the courtyard wall, and squatting in the open. Only a few lucky ones lying down had charpoys, a type of Indian cot, while the rest were fortunate if they had a reed mat beneath them. The courtyard echoed with cries of sorrow and grief from distressed relatives of the injured and the anguished moans of the wounded themselves. Along part of one wall was an open wood-frame stable with a straw roof. Underneath it was what appeared to be a makeshift surgery or aid station dealing with a long line of people seeking medical help. Marching to the front of the line, Emily encountered a Eurasian man in his early forties. Dressed in European attire, he was bandaging a Hindu woman's arm with a strip of bed sheet. Seated on a stool, he had a table next to him cluttered with bottles of pills, ointments, and medicines, and a messy pile of makeshift bandages.

"Doctor, I am Doctor Emily Sheffield of the Livingstone Missions," she introduced herself, offering her assistance. "Can I be of service here?"

The man swiftly released the bandage, leapt to his feet, and grasped Emily's right hand in both of his, shaking it vigorously. "Oh, Doctor, you are the answer to my prayers."

Overjoyed by Emily's arrival, the dark-skinned Anglo-Indian introduced himself:

"Doctor, I am Timothée Hillier, and I am not a doctor, merely a pharmacist, and I am so pleased to see you."

"Mister Hillier, who else is working with you here? How many have had medical training?" Emily asked sternly.

"There is no one else," admitted Hillier. "In the town, we had a modest hospital and clinic, but I've been unable to locate any of the staff. Out of desperation, I began administering basic nursing care here."

"Well, it's a start, and you have done very well," she commended him before authoritatively outlining her immediate plans. "But now you and I must begin turning these grounds into an emergency hospital. I have brought a small number of medical supplies with me, inadequate for our needs here but it will be something with which we will be able to establish ourselves."

"Lily, child," Emily called, anxious to get things moving, "bring in those two small cabin cases from my beast. You'll have to enlist the help of some of the able-bodied individuals around here. Be quick; there's a lot of work to do."

Lily had followed the woman through the yard. Still, unlike Emily, who seemed oblivious to everything around them, she looked and was numbed by the sights and sounds. The heart-rendering cries, the anguished expressions and reaching arms with accompanying grief-stricken pleas in Urdu, Hindi, and broken English. Combined with this was the sickening sight of bloody, crushed limbs and still bodies clouded with swarms of flies. Some of these still forms were clearly dead from the foul stench that wafted around them. Lily, seventeen years of age, her chest tightening like a drum skin, stood frozen by the horror of it all, but her mind was crying: "Run! Run!"

Emily had to repeat her request to the girl before she went to the camel. At the animal, she found un-strapping the cases simple but heavy. Then, approaching a family group under the nearest tree, she had to ask for their help several times before a youth rose from among them to assist her in carrying the cabin cases to Emily.

Throughout the night, she constantly worked to the orders of Emily Sheffield. Finally, she said: "Water, child! We need Water." And Lily went off and found a well, then organised a posse of

116

women to bring it in pots and tins to the hospital. In this same manner, a fire for boiling Water was established in the corner of the yard, a pit was dug for depositing human remains, and bodies were taken out into the fields for Muslim burial and burning of Hindus. Emily had requested the finding of more charpoys for the patients to lie on. Still, Lily was unsuccessful in this, having to make do with reed matting instead.

To get all this done, Lily had begun by asking for help using the limited few words of Urdu she had picked up, then when this produced a scant response, pleading with individuals. Finally, disgusted at the lacklustre attitude of these people towards cooperating in tackling this calamity visited upon them, she began to shout and stamp her feet. This did the trick. After that, all her requests began as arm-waving, shouted commands.

Eighteen hours later, Lily stood over the pit she had dug, tipping the fly-coated arm into it. One of the two Harijans, responsible for the pit's duties, threw a light covering of sandy soil over the mutilated arm. This was the first time Emily had asked for Lily's assistance during operations, primarily using her as an overseer to ensure tasks were completed. The Anglo-Indian pharmacist had fainted from exhaustion, and Emily trusted no one else. Upon entering the stable shelter, the doctor signalled Lily to give the unconscious boy another whiff of chloroform. Lily poured the fluid onto the mask, dropping a few drops at a time to stretch the chloroform as far as possible. As she did this, Jake Richmond entered the stable, his gruff voice calling her name. Jake, having given up on finding his lost niece, was angry and frustrated when he discovered her location after one of his sergeants saw Lily and informed him. Lily was relieved to see her uncle but was interrupted as he demanded explanations for her disappearance. Lily was speechless, but Emily, noticing the crest on Richmond's wrist and feeling guilty for abducting Lily, intervened, and apologized. Jake Richmond didn't reply, instead he looked away to draw in a deep breath of air. "Someone with a reliable mind and a willing pair of hands is priceless in the situation we are facing at this moment," continued Emily, without looking up. "Here in this compound, we have patients who would surely be dead if it wasn't for the work of your niece. As it is, they now have a chance." The RSM remained silent, then asked in a more tempered voice, "Is there anything you need?" He knew this wasn't the time to upset her. "No, nothing," replied Lily, gratefully, relieved to see her uncle's anger had diminished. Wistfully, she added, "Maybe a clean dress?"

"Major Richmond, what news is there of help?" asked Emily, steering the conversation towards a more urgent matter.

"There has been none," was Jake Richmond's deliberately measured reply. "We remain more or less marooned. One of our officers was sent by the colonel along the railway to the west and contacted a civilian reconnaissance party. However, we cannot expect much help from that direction. The hill passes are blocked, and the rail line is buckled."

"The devil has chosen an excellent playground for making mischief!" Emily muttered aloud before stopping her work to look up. She addressed Richmond with a frank request, "RSM, I know there are other emergency centres like ours, but I would greatly appreciate if you could relay my appeal to your colonel for any assistance, he might be able to direct our way. We are desperately short of food and medical supplies."

Jake Richmond's face was stern, but his eyes betrayed a feeling of unease. "Doctor, you are the only one providing medical facilities here."

"But the town has a civil structure, judiciary, public works, police..." Emily began in an astounded, high-pitched voice but was interrupted by the warrant officer.

"Most people are spending the summer in the hills. Those who aren't buried or injured were enjoying an early drink at the Gymkhana Club in the cantonment when it collapsed. Our medical officer is trying to organize an aid post north of the town. But we only have a few hundred troops and a handful of police here. Most of them are deployed in maintaining law and order; less than half are involved in rescue work."

"My gracious," the doctor uttered. "I never realized the situation was so grave."

"Colonel Gabson believes it can only get worse," Richmond added.

"Agreed," Emily nodded as she lowered her head to resume her task of bandaging the amputated limb. She then asked in a matter-of-fact tone, "Now, will you be taking your niece, Doctor Sheffield?"

"Doctor Sheffield!" Lily protested.

Emily praised Lily, saying, "You've done enough, child. Besides, the colonel is right. With so many unburied dead bodies, we will soon be facing epidemics we may not be able to control, such as dysentery, typhoid, and cholera."

"But you'll be staying?" Lily asked the doctor.

"Yes, at least until sufficient help arrives," the doctor replied.

This prompted Lily to announce, "Then I'm staying as well."

"But child, you should see yourself," Emily began, trying to persuade Lily to withdraw to a safer location. "You're exhausted, and you need rest, a good meal, and a clean-up."

Despite Emily and the RSM's suggestions, Lily refused to leave. "I'm needed here, and as long as the injured keep coming, I'm staying," she declared.

Jake Richmond, unsure of what to do, looked to Emily for support, but she was too focused on her bandaging to offer advice. In the end, he simply put his arm around Lily and kissed her cheek before promising to send a change of clothes.

Meanwhile, Emily instructed Lily to put the lid back on the chloroform and signalled for two patients' relatives to carry the injured man to a shaded rest area in the compound.

On the third day, relief supplies arrived in the form of eleven motor lorries from a neighbouring state. They were followed by a mixed party of military and government officials on horseback, and a battalion of the Royal Irish Fusiliers who marched in after midnight. An Indian battalion from the 8th Punjab Regiment acted as an escort to a two-mile-long baggage train. This train consisted of army GS wagons and carts drawn by mules, bullocks, and camels. Over the following week, there was constant activity around Jhendara, with motor and animal traffic turning the town's dirt roads into powdery tracks, inches deep in dust. Temporary villages also sprung up, providing housing for the rescuers and the homeless locals who remained in the vicinity. However, their numbers were dwindling. Most of the town's inhabitants were trapped in the aftermath of the earthquake. The fortunate ones died quickly from being crushed or choking on brick dust. Others died far more painfully, either burned alive or waiting for a rescue that never arrived. Despite this, the community's numbers grew as hundreds of vultures descended upon Jhendara.

As for the Queen's Light Infantry companies, their posting in the backwater of the Central Provinces came to an end. Ten days after the town and station were devastated, Colonel Gabson led the survivors north to join the rest of his battalion. The army had other stations, and it was easy to accommodate these displaced individuals. True to expectation, a new station was found for them in less than a month. The only drawback was that the Queen's new neighbours saw them as easy prey for hunters.

CHAPTER 7

Under the wide and starry sky Dig the grave and let me lie.
-Robin Louis Stevenson

Robin Cuimein carefully placed a sheet of blotting paper over the ink to finish the last memo on his daily correspondence list. He did this to ensure that his hands did not touch the writing, as the sweat from his hands could smudge his work. Above his office desk hung an electric-powered fan intended to cool the room. However, since it was June in Delhi, the peak of summer, the fan could only manage to stir the stifling air, making it more of a hindrance. Every sheet of paper on his desk was weighed down to prevent them from being blown away by the fan's breeze.

Cuimein had been working in semi-darkness since late March with his woven-grass window blinds perpetually down. His office faced south, receiving the sun's full glare throughout the day, making his workspace unbearable during these hot months. To avoid the worst part of the day, Secretariat employees commonly started early and finished around noon. However, Cuimein was working late this day as he had overslept, wrapped in the arms of a woman.

Upon his arrival in Delhi, Cuimein was offered shared accommodation in a chummery, a bachelor's bungalow, with three other young men of the service. Delhi was the administrative headquarters of the Indian Civil Service, with a significant military staff presence and the centre of numerous other government departments. During the winter months, a substantial number of girls from the 'fishing fleet' cast their nets in Delhi. With most doors open to them, their life was a whirlwind of entertainment - sports and gymkhana clubs, tea dances, dinner parties, and balls - hopefully ending the season lucky enough to attend the Viceroy's Ball. The girls either received marriage proposals or sailed back to England as 'returned empties'. Cuimein spent the winter enjoying their company, while also avoiding commitment, as Emily Sheffield had pointed out to him on the ship that he was a member of the Indian Civil Service, the 'heaven born', and to a young bride worth a thousand pounds a year, dead or alive.

The reason for Cuimein's tardiness was British customs in India. During the summer, most Europeans in Delhi relocated to Himalayan hill stations, leaving only a skeleton staff of junior officials to administer the country. Cuimein's roommates had left on vacation, leaving him alone. He met a Eurasian girl who came back to his bungalow for drinks and gramophone music. These girls were usually looking for European husbands, but Cuimein made it clear he was not interested in marriage. Nevertheless, they had romantic encounters during the summer.

As Cuimein was tidying his desk in preparation to leave, he was interrupted by a chaprissi who informed him that Under-Secretary Hunt wanted to see him. Cuimein followed the chaprissi to the building's shaded wing, where the undersecretary's Indian secretary introduced him to the undersecretary.

With the door closing behind him, Robin crossed the spacious, high-ceilinged office and stood before a broad mahogany desk. Seated at it was a man in his late fifties with thinning grey hair and an open-collared white shirt. The under-secretary, who oversaw the department as all the other seniors were summering in the hills, interrupted his writing to look up and welcomed Cuimein with a cordial question, "Ah, Cuimein, good! It was to your advantage not to dally. Tell me, have you found Delhi to be an agreeable posting?"

Cuimein lied, replying, "Yes, Sir. Quite!" He knew better than to voice dissatisfaction to higher-ranking officials. The under-secretary smiled briefly before reaching for a slip of paper on his desk and saying, "Hmmm, really? That doesn't tally with the corridor gossip I've been hearing, but if it's true, I've got bad news for you."

He went on to explain that one of their officials had broken his leg quite badly, and Cuimein was to act as his substitute until he returned. Cuimein was thrilled with the news, but he kept his joy hidden and simply replied, "Excellent, sir."

"The Under-Secretary scoffed sceptically, but then dismissed Cuimein from his office and instructed him to leave for Ranhar that night. He handed him a slip of paper and informed him that the finance department would handle his rail fare and expenses. He would be gone for six weeks, and the Under-Secretary assured him that his pending work would be completed by others. Cuimein didn't ask any questions and hurried back to his own office after leaving the Under-Secretary's presence.

In his office, a map of India hung on the wall, indicating the location of each district in the country. Cuimein traced a finger across the map and found Ranhar, two hundred miles northwest of Delhi in the Punjab Province, bordering the eastern side of the Hissar District.

After gathering some writing tools and stationery from his desk, Cuimein swiftly packed them into a leather briefcase. Without hesitation, he left his office to hand over his slip of paper to the finance clerk. Since his rank didn't warrant official transportation, he hailed a tonga, a two-wheeled horse-drawn carriage, and packed his suitcase and grip for his journey. He then informed Mangat, the house bearer, about his sudden departure and left notes for his roommates. Unfazed by the sweltering afternoon heat, he eagerly headed to the railway station. Once he arrived, Cuimein paced impatiently in front of his luggage while waiting for his train. The platform teemed with travellers and vendors, mostly Indians. When his train finally arrived, he boarded the first-class compartment and purchased a block of ice to combat the heat. Despite the slow and tiring journey, punctuated by lengthy stops at small stations, Cuimein finally reached his destination in Chamblapur. Upon disembarking, he was greeted by a small man wearing an eclectic outfit who introduced himself in a sing-song accent.

"Mr. Cuimein, I am Navin Row Kavi, a town schoolteacher and representative to the District Board. As such, I not only welcome you to Chamblapur but I must also perform a distressing duty," he said, closing the umbrella that he had used to shade himself from the sun. Cuimein noticed that Navin's shirt tail hung out, covering the back of his upper bare legs.

"How do you do?" Cuimein accepted the greeting and extended his hand, which Navin shook before explaining his distressing duty. "It is with a heavy heart, but I must regretfully inform you that Sub-District Officer Peterson has passed away."

"Died?" Cuimein repeated, stunned.

"That is correct. The cause was a fall from a horse. He had complained of headaches which, to everyone's shame, were not taken seriously. He was a much-loved official and will be sorely missed," explained Navin. He finished by holding out a telegram envelope and said, "We have informed Delhi - this is their reply - it is for you."

The message on the Indo-European Telegraph Company headed paper was brief; it read: 'Regret death of Peterson. Assume post. Confirmation will follow. Hunt.'

"I am to take over as Sub-District Officer," announced Cuimein in a cheerless voice. He had desired an independent post, but not at the cost of a man's life.

"Then I will take you to your bungalow now," said Navin apologetically. "There is no other Englishman in town, and Saheb Peterson has yet to be laid to rest. So, sadly, your first duty as Sub-District Officer will be performing a Christian burial."

Cuimein's luggage was taken by a turbaned native who also doubled as the carriage driver. He guided them through the town, across a mile of cultivated farmland, and up onto a low plateau. They turned off the dirt road and entered the gravel driveway of a tile-roofed bungalow. A garden and an expansive grass lawn were on the property, but both had been reduced to dust by the summer's scorching sun. The only greenery and blooming plant life were in earthen pots lining the driveway, a mandatory decoration for all British residences.

Below the veranda stood a line of Indian men. On the veranda, a Hindu woman waited for Cuimein to alight from the carriage before descending the three steps. Navin introduced the woman as Hemlata Chawla, the housekeeper. This puzzled Cuimein, for he knew of no household that employed a native woman as a housekeeper; the manager of the house staff was always a male bearer.

"Welcome, Saheb," the woman greeted him, pressing both her hands together and bowing her head in the Hindu fashion of namaste. Cuimein acknowledged this by removing his hat and nodding, noting the sari-clad woman's attractiveness, and estimating her age to be close to his own.

She securely guided him along the line of men, introducing the bungalow workforce which was paid for by the ICS. Included among them were a Bobajee, the cook, a Mali, the gardener, a Syce, the groom, a Mehtar, or sweeper who handled the unpleasant tasks, and others who each performed their traditional and clearly defined roles. With a brief pause, during which the woman discreetly suggested how Peterson's burial ceremony should be conducted, Hemlata led Cuimein to the back of the bungalow. They followed a path past the stables to a godown, or store shed, where four barefoot men in soiled clothing were waiting. Upon her command, they entered the godown and emerged a few moments later carrying a plain, boxwood coffin. The Indian climate was unforgiving to the deceased. Cuimein, following the procession, recognized a familiar smell emanating from the coffin, reminiscent of a stench he had encountered many times during the war in France. Peterson, who had only been dead for a day, had already begun to decompose. The group made their way to a small cemetery hidden behind the bungalow, where Cuimein discovered graves dating back centuries, including those of two sub-district officers who had preceded Peterson. Hemlata handed Cuimein a Bible with a prayer and burial recital bookmarked. With the coffin lowered into the prepared grave, Cuimein read a passage from the Bible and recited the burial service. He then took a handful of soil to sprinkle onto the coffin as a final gesture. Hemlata, grief-stricken, stood veiled in tears as the rest of the staff watched as witnesses. Cuimein comforted her and led her away from the graveside.

Joey Payne scratched his puttee-wrapped lower legs before joining the rest of the 2nd Queen's Light Infantry on the march to their new station. The battalion had travelled over 200 miles in nine days, marching only at night. Following the tragedy at Jhendara, Lieutenant-Colonel Gabson led the battalion north to the United Provinces to regroup, re-equip, and await further orders. The order came to move to Landi Kotal in the Khyber Pass, one of the most dangerous positions on the North-West Frontier. Families were not permitted to accompany the married members of the battalion, causing displeasure, while the young and single soldiers were excited at the opportunity to fight the notorious Pathan. During the summer months, the British Army would march at night to avoid the harsh heat, a sensible decision since marching during the day could have caused the battalion to collapse. They marched along the Grand Trunk Road, a nearly fifteen-hundred-mile engineering wonder built by the British in the middle of the previous century, following the path of an old Mogul Empire bullock track. Payne, distracted from his thoughts, sought signs of dawn, and commented on them to ignite a conversation. Talking during the march occurred in fits and starts, with no singing or smoking permitted except by pipe. Each night, the battalion would march for up to ten hours, their metal-heeled boots drowning out most other sounds of the countryside with a consistent 'crump, crump' sound. Shortly after sunrise, they would reach a staging camp for the day.

The battalion followed a summer marching routine, where they would sleep or doze uneasily after breakfast due to the heat and flies. They would then be roused in the late afternoon, fed, and the camp would be cleaned in preparation for the next leg of their journey. They would then assemble in their column formation and turn into the setting sun to march west. The architectural style of the historic buildings began to exhibit a predominance of Persian and Mogul influence past Lahore as they crossed into the North-West Frontier Province. Eventually, they halted at Jamrud Fort for forty-eight hours before the final two days of the march, which had to be conducted in daylight since no one dared traverse the Khyber Pass at night. Departing at dawn, the rising sun lit up the hills before them, exposing their prominence and dangers. It was as though the sun was issuing a fair warning that death was an ever-present companion among the rocky crags and cliffs. Armies had perished and garrisons had been massacred in these hills. From Alexander the Great to the present, no force had passed through these hills without suffering deadly attacks. The threat did not stem from a population loyally defending their sovereign domain, for the Pathan tribesman had no national allegiance. His motivation was greed; the Pathan was primarily a robber who killed for plunder.

The infantry could see the road from the plain but couldn't spot an opening that could be referred to as a pass. They began to ascend, winding along the sides of the hill slopes on a road built for motor vehicles. A second road, primarily used by camel caravans transporting trade goods from Persia and Afghanistan into India and back, ran mainly in the lower areas of the pass. There was also a narrow-gauge railway line under construction, although it deviated significantly from their route and was only occasionally visible.

After the first day, the battalion stopped for the night, taking shelter under the protection of Ali Masjid, a fort built high above the road. In the morning, they continued their journey, passing through a narrow gorge that was barely twenty feet wide. Protected by hill pickets and occupied blockhouses along the route, they reached their destination late in the afternoon. Cresting a high saddle, Joey Payne and the rest of the 6th Platoon found the pass widening from three to five miles across. Most of this levelled area was the station, stretching two miles square. The centrepiece was a fort spanning three hundred by one hundred and fifty yards, complete with towers and a main gate.

A mile from the camp, the band at the head of the battalion began to play. Then, with their rifles sloping onto their left shoulder, the men's right arms stiffened, swinging shoulder-high, as they adopted a swaggering stance. After marching almost five hundred miles, they were about to enter their new station, giving the impression they had marched scarcely five. Struggling to alight from the cramped rail carriage with her luggage, Lily Richmond barely had time to draw a breath and look around before she was caught in a hugging embrace from a woman wearing a familiar, jaunty, time-worn topee. "Welcome, Lily! Indeed, welcome," it was Emily Sheffield.

"Oh, Emily, thank you," responded Lily, smiling as she removed her newly purchased ladies' pith helmet to kiss the doctor's sun-weathered cheek. "Train journeys can be such an annoyance. I hope yours wasn't too uncomfortable?" enquired the older woman with concern.

"It did go on for a long time," the girl confessed. "But oh, Emily, I'm so pleased to see you."

A very long time was an understatement. Lily had set out from her Aunt Harriet's hill station quarter two and a half days earlier. She had journeyed by train from Moradabad to Rawalpindi, then on to Mari on the banks of the Indus. She crossed the river by ferry boat to Kalabagh, where she boarded a narrow-gauge rail line. Her journey ended at Gambila, a station twenty-five miles south of Bannu in the North-West Frontier Province.

"Welcome, child. Let's get you to the Mission and into a bath straight away," said Emily with sound sense as she introduced a tall, grey-bearded Pathan gentleman wearing a light, thigh-length coat, baggy trousers, a blue turban, and leather sandals.

"Lily, I want you to meet Zahir Khan. He has been my major-domo for over twenty-five years," she continued.

"Nice to meet you," Lily smiled.

"Salaam Alaikum," replied Zahir, dipping his head to salaam with a hand from chest to forehead before shaking Lily's hand.

She noted that his gesture was not servile or cringing, as it is found in the south, while his dark, steady eyes looked into hers as if those of a tamed beast of prey. Zahir took her luggage and bedding roll to carry it as though his arms were empty, and the two women followed him to the front of the station. There, they found an open-topped pre-war Napier car that was in dire need of paint, maintenance, and above all, youth. Emily took charge of the steering wheel, and Zahir cranked the starting handle to bring the engine to life.

They drove west of the town across a broad valley towards a line of khaki and grey hills shimmering in the afternoon sunlight. It was August and the Frontier was receiving its annual sprinkling of summer rains, but the sun flamed through between the showers that could sometimes last for days. Not with the intensity of the south, though. Lily found it more remarkable. On either side of the rutted and bumpy cart track they were driving on, the country was a plain of yellowish grass. Bearing to the left, the road led them towards a village of towered houses two miles distant at the mouth of a smaller valley that wound into a ridge of hills.

"There we are, my dear!" shouted Emily above the noise of the car's engine. "That's Saysha."
Her heartbeat momentarily increased, and Lily lifted her head to look over the cracked and discoloured glass windshield. This small town of sun-bleached stone houses and whitewashed bungalows was to be the first training centre for her future career. She had set her heart on becoming a nurse.

While working under Emily Sheffield during the disaster in Jhendara, Lily's admiration for the doctor's untiring dedication to the sick and injured took deep root. So much so, that reflecting on her prospects in India, living with her uncle and aunt, she decided she had to part ways with them. Once she made that resolution, she asked Emily for advice on how to get nursing training. The doctor, after an hour-long heart-to-heart conversation, agreed to help her secure a training spot at one of the larger mission hospitals. However, she first had to complete a short apprenticeship with Emily at the Saysha Mission and get permission from her two guardians. When Lily went back to her uncle and aunt, she explained her aspirations and

Emily's conditions to them. Harriet agreed after an hour's discussion and a day's serious consideration, but Jake Richmond threw a tantrum when he found Saysha on the map. A war had been waged just two days' walk from the mission four years earlier. It wasn't until the day before he left with his battalion for the Khyber Pass that Jake, under pressure from the two women, reluctantly gave his blessing to Lily's plans.

Just before reaching the village, Emily turned off the track and onto another road that was in far better condition, lined with young, shady trees. This quarter-mile road was the mission's drive, leading to a cluster of buildings surrounded by tree-filled gardens, fruit orchards, and vegetable plots on three sides. Beyond the buildings, a river flowed at the bottom of a shallow valley. Emily parked her car in front of a bungalow, enclosed by a mud brick wall and a lawn just beginning to green after the summer dryness. A group of children surrounded Emily, excitedly shouting, "Daktar Memsaheb!" (Doctor Miss), but Emily affectionately patted their heads and shooed them into the care of Sarita, a slender Pathan girl in a European dress who was also in the early stages of a nursing career. Emily introduced Sarita to Lily and then led her into the bungalow where Zahir, the servant, had taken her luggage.

"This is my home," Emily said as she led Lily into the bungalow. "The bachelor quarters here are not the best, so please pardon any inconveniences you may encounter. I'll put you in the spare bedroom for your stay. But first, let's get you a bath and then I'll show you around the mission."

After a cup of tea and a change of dress, Lily was given a tour of the mission which proved to be a community. In addition to the hospital, there was an Anglican church, a small orphanage, a school, storage buildings, and huts for the native workers. Lily asked Emily where all the patients came from, as she couldn't believe that the sparse population in the surrounding area warranted such an excellent institute.

"They come from everywhere," Emily replied, opening her hands. "Thirty years ago, my husband and I struggled to establish this clinic, but now people come to us from all parts of the Frontier. We treat patients from all tribes and clans, even those from across the border in Afghanistan. Some travel for days with the most horrendous injuries."

On one of the hospital verandas, Emily stopped to speak to a woman in a tribal dress whose face was bandaged. "Unfortunately, you'll likely see more cases like hers while you're here on the Frontier," Emily warned Lily as they moved away.

"Her husband cut off her nose, believing she had been unfaithful," Emily explained. Lily gasped in horror, and Emily continued. "The husband brought her here. It turns out she was innocent. He begged us to restore her beauty."

After sunset, Emily hosted a small supper party where her two other doctors, a Bengali Muslim, and a Eurasian Christian, both young men, were invited. Along with them, the middle-aged Anglican missionary, and his wife, who managed the church and orphanage, were also present. The casual gathering was intended to give Lily an opportunity to get to know the key members of the mission. Despite Lily's eagerness to hear all the accounts relating to Saysha and her incessant questions, her tiredness was obvious. After Lily's third yawn, Emily took her by the hand and led her off to bed. The journey had been long and exhausting, draining all her resistance to sleep. This early retirement, coupled with the unfamiliar bed and the chill of the Frontier night, caused Lily to awaken in the early hours of the morning. She lay in her bed listening to the barks and howls of prowling night animals for almost an hour before deciding to slip on a robe and step out onto the veranda. As she opened her bedroom door, she did not notice the dark figure resting in Emily's bedroom doorway until Zahir Khan's head and shoulders rocked forward.

"Oh!" gasped Lily, startled. However, her cry was muted. Recognizing the man, she quickly apologized, thinking she had disturbed his sleep. "I'm sorry, Zahir. Please forgive me," she whispered, then hurried, elf-like, through the large archway entrance to the dual parlour dining room and across it, out onto the veranda.

The moon had set, but the stars from a cloud-cleansed dark sky lit the landscape as if from a million candle flames. Lily settled into a wicker chair to savour the charm of this nocturnal plain and ponder the significance of the high-towered village houses, showing slate grey in the starlight. Beguiled by the soft silence, the girl initially did not notice two turbaned figures stealthily approaching the front gate. Startled and apprehensive, not knowing if she was in danger of reacting foolishly to stories of Frontier abduction and murder, Lily was on the point of calling out to the two intruders when she became aware of someone standing beside her. Her surprise turned to relief as she recognized in profile the outline of Zahir Khan's hawk-like face.

Without a word, he left the veranda to walk to the strangers. Then, holding a short conversation with them, he returned in silence and entered the bungalow again. Lily stood now, left to the side-lines in the role of curious spectator. However, this changed as soon as Emily appeared, followed by Zahir.

"Lily, child, get dressed. Then join me at the clinic medical room. You may as well have your Frontier baptism now as later." The doctor had not paused as she, dressing-gown clad hurried past towards the gate.

Entering the clinic, Lily found light given from three lamps that were lit and placed by Zahir. In a chair, a young Pathan tribesman sat being examined by Emily. Stripped of his upper garments, the doctor looked at a gash of cut flesh oozing blood on his right side, then more extensively at a wound midway between his left shoulder and neck. The second Pathan, a much older man, stood back in the room's shadows, watching through a window. All inquiries of the injured man by the doctor were being conducted in the local language, which she also used to give Zahir an order to send him out of the room.

"Lily, take that bowl and fill it with water from a chattie you will find just outside the door," she said. The girl complying returned to be told to put on an apron and stand ready to assist in dressing the wounds.

As Emily added an antiseptic solution to the water Lily had fetched, Zahir returned with a basin of hot water. They worked without pause for over an hour; the flesh of the side wound being stitched into place without putting the patient under chloroform. Lily admired how the man bore this without so much as flinching. As for her, after the horrors of Jhendara, this was tame indeed, but throughout, her stomach periodically heaved, brought on by foul but inescapable whiffs of the man's bodily stench. Finally, with the side wound stitched and dressed and the shoulder wound bandaged with the arm secured across his chest, Lily assumed the young tribesman would settle down in a ward bed. But after being assisted to dress by the second Pathan and apparently under no protest from Emily, the two, delivering short but earnest thank you'd or farewells, slipped out and away into what was left of the night's darkness.

Lily withheld her question as to who the two men were until breakfast.

"Now they are fugitives," replied Emily, placing her teacup in its saucer but keeping hold of the handle. She stared into the cup for a few seconds before looking into the girl's eyes. "They are a father and son who were farmers with an older son, his wife, a sister, and a mother until yesterday morning. This family is involved in Badi, a blood feud with another family from another clan. Yesterday at dawn, the men from the other family attacked their home as the two were driving their sheep out into the hills. Hearing the shooting, they rushed back to find their house taken. They tried to rescue the women but were outnumbered. The younger one managed to kill one of the other sides, but you saw the price he paid for it - a sword cut and a bullet through the shoulder."

"Where is the rest of the family? What happened to them?" asked Lily, awed by the story and the calm way Emily related it.

"The other son is believed to be dead, and the women are expected to accept slavery and servitude. Those who don't comply may face violence, as Emily suggested with her comment about a cut-throat. When Lily asked about the two from last night, Emily revealed that the father is cursed and seeking revenge while the son is severely injured and likely to die due to infection. Lily expressed horror at the situation, but Emily explained that this kind of violence is common on the frontier due to blood feuds between families and clans. Emily then shared the tragic story of Sarita and her brother, who were brought to the orphanage school for protection after their father and uncle were killed in a feud. Despite their mother's employment in a household, the boy was later killed by a man seeking revenge, and the mother ended up killing the murderer and going to prison for it."

"Lily Richmond had asked where the person they were discussing was, and Emily replied that she was serving her sentence in the Port Blair convict settlement on the Andaman & Nicobar Islands. This news caused Lily to feel both sorrow and anger. Emily continued, explaining that Lily would be working with Sarita and that she should not be deterred by her reserved demeanour. She emphasized that Sarita was highly skilled and intelligent. Emily also stressed the importance of learning the local dialect, which Sarita spoke better than anyone else from the tribes in the area. Lily agreed, knowing that it was essential for her success in the position. As she finished her tea, Lily pondered her future on the Frontier, realizing that her eighteenth birthday was only six weeks away."

CHAPTER 8

By the sin of the sack of Chitor.
-Rajput Patriotic

Seated in his saddle, Robin Cuimein rode out of
the streets of Chamblapur and onto the road
that led to his bungalow perched on the town's
high ground. He felt at ease and relaxed. It was a
bright, warm winter's day in February, and the
sub-district officer was on his way home for
lunch. Being in the latter half of his first year
administering his section of the Ranhar District,
Cuimein woke each morning eager to face the
day's work along with the challenges and
happiness it brought. Despite his movements
being confined during the summer monsoon
months, as soon as they ended, he was out
touring. He visited farms and villages, settled
land disputes, checked field boundaries, and
inspected the types of crops sown. He relished
sitting under a village tree, listening to petitions
from landowners and cultivators while
inspecting various government services, schools,
police offices, village sanitation, wells, and
hospitals. Though the work was hard and

required long hours of resolving disputes, settling grievances, and confirming accounts of crop yield and tax collection, Cuimein had never been happier. Compared to the suffocating confinement of a Delhi Secretariat office, this was like a release into paradise- the India of his youth, the India he so passionately loved. As Cuimein cantered down the road, he saw a six-year-old schoolboy on his way home for lunch and pushed his horse to go faster. The boy turned to look and upon recognizing the Englishman, he stopped and gave a broad smile, calling out, "Hello, Mister Cuimein!" while waving his hand.

"Good afternoon, David," Robin replied, pulling his horse to a stop. "What did you learn at school today?"

"I learned a lot, Mister Cuimein," the boy replied with joy. "I learned how to spell different words and how to add numbers."

"Come up here with me, and we will hurry you home to tell your mommy," Cuimein said, reaching down with his right arm. He took hold of the young boy who, clutching the rider's shoulder, allowed himself to be swung up astride the horse behind its saddle.

David looked Indian with his dark skin and jet-black hair, but his eyes were blue. He was Eurasian, or as they were now being called, Anglo-Indian. His mother was Hemlata,

Cuimein's housekeeper, and his father was Harry Peterson, the man he replaced.

On the evening of Peterson's burial, Robin had sat at his predecessor's desk going through the papers to gain some knowledge of his suddenly acquired domain. The desk and its contents were neat and well-ordered, which was not the hallmark of a business desk. To Cuimein, it appeared as if someone had combed through and given everything a good tidying. Nevertheless, he suspected Hemlata; if his suspicion was valid, she had not been through enough.

Removing an entire drawer, a photo fell from behind. The picture showed a young mother holding a baby in her arms. The photo of the mother had been taken in that room, and the woman, smiling with pride, was Hemlata.

The next day, his superior, Neil Hubbard, the district officer, arrived after a twenty-mile ride in the morning heat to welcome him into his new post. After paying his respects at the graveside, they had a lengthy discussion on matters within the sub-district, individuals he would have to deal with, and reports to be forwarded. When Peterson's possessions were brought up, Cuimein suggested purchasing them - the horses, furnishings, etc. - and sending the money to Peterson's next-of-kin. According to Hubbard, Peterson's wife, residing in England, was his next of kin. She had abandoned her husband shortly after their marriage, finding Chamblapur unbearable, and returned to her mother in Berkshire.

Hemlata only brought up Peterson's possessions after Robin expressed his initial satisfaction with the house staff. "Yes, you should have no issues," he confirmed. "Hemlata will keep the boys disciplined and the bungalow tidy." He believed it was only fair to explain her background. "She is an extraordinary woman. Her father sold her into bondage as a child to repay his debt to a moneylender. Despite this, she managed to escape and survive several months in the countryside and town streets. This is nothing short of miraculous for a girl. She was then rescued by an organization of nuns who ran a school for abandoned children. She intended to take vows, but for some reason, this did not happen. Instead, she arrived here ten years ago as a maid for the then-Sub-District Officer's wife. After his death, she returned to England, and Peterson, who was unmarried at the time, took over. Finding her English and household management skills invaluable, he promptly established her as his housekeeper."

Cuimein, keeping his curiosity about the photograph found in the desk to himself, concluded the discussion by expressing his satisfaction with the arrangement and saw no need for a change.

"There was every likelihood that he and this child would never have met, if not for the threat of one of India's fatal virus diseases. However, one month later, while returning to his bungalow amidst a monsoon downpour, he almost ran into Hemlata, who was sprinting towards him. Despite the darkness and the noise of the storm, he recognized her just in time to call out her name before she could run past him.

'Oh, saheb,' the distressed woman pleaded, her hair and clothes thoroughly soaked. 'Please forgive me, but I cannot stop. There is an emergency.'

'What emergency?' Cuimein asked.

"Don't worry, it has nothing to do with the bungalow," Hemlata quickly assured him. "But I must hurry. Your bath water is ready, and so is supper..."

"Hemlata!" Cuimein interrupted her in an authoritative tone. "What emergency?"

"There is a child in the farm village. A messenger just told me that he's been bitten by a dog that might have rabies," Hemlata explained nervously.

"Which child?" Cuimein asked, slightly annoyed that Hemlata hadn't been more forthcoming. Then he remembered the photograph and noticed Hemlata's hesitation to reply.

"Come up," Cuimein ordered, reaching down to offer her a hand.

"No! No, saheb!" Hemlata tried to resist his offer, but Cuimein was too strong and pulled her up behind his saddle.

The village was a mile east of Cuimein's bungalow, just off a main cart track. They rode along the track, with Cuimein urging his horse to a speed that reduced the risk of slipping. Upon reaching the village, Hemlata immediately dismounted and ran into a mud brick house. Cuimein followed her inside, where he exchanged greetings with the household members while Hemlata knelt to examine a dog bite on a young boy's calf and simultaneously console the child. The wound had stopped bleeding but was torn and would require stitches."

"Where is the dog?" Cuimein, the family patriarch and a Hindu with a snow-white beard and mahogany brown skin, inquired.

"It ran off, sir. It was not a village dog," came the reply.

"Rabies?" Cuimein questioned.

The answer came in the form of an uncertain shrug and a slow shake of the head.

As he moved closer to the charpoy where the boy lay, Cuimein gave him a playful wink and a smile before kneeling beside Hemlata to examine the wound. The boy didn't respond but watched the man with an expectant stare.

"The boy will need medical treatment," Cuimein advised.

"Doctors are expensive, sir," Hemlata responded, stating a difficult reality rather than refusing to pay.

"Not a doctor myself, but I believe the boy needs to be treated at a hospital because he could be infected with rabies," Cuimein whispered, careful to keep his voice low so the boy wouldn't hear.

Hemlata was taken aback by the news. "The nearest hospital is in Rathna, which is ten miles away!" she exclaimed in a low voice.

Cuimein tied a handkerchief around the boy's wound and firmly declared, "Then we must go to Rathna."

He asked the boy his name, and Hemlata proudly repeated that it was David. Cuimein gave him a rain cape to wear so that he wouldn't get wet in the rain. The boy seemed unsure about going with Cuimein, but Hemlata reassured him and let Cuimein carry him outside to the horse waiting for them. Cuimein placed the boy in front of him on the horse, encouraging him to hold on tight for "the fastest ride of their lives."

After a month in the hospital under Cuimein's expense, David returned to Chamblapur. However, he didn't return to his village family. Hemlata placed him in her two-room hut among the servants' quarters, mistakenly believing that he would embarrass Cuimein. When they arrived at Cuimein's bungalow, Hemlata helped her son down from the horse and told him to thank Cuimein for the ride. Cuimein promised Hemlata that he would tell David to call him Robin instead of Mr. Cuimein. As the bungalow syce led his horse to the stables, Cuimein climbed the steps to the veranda, leaving Hemlata to follow, shaking her head. He handed his topee to her before she entered the house and sat down at a small wicker table in the shade. Within moments, Hemlata returned carrying a teak platter with the newly delivered mail, and a servant followed her carrying a tumbler of cooled milk. Sipping his pre-meal drink, Cuimein sorted through the letters and opened a personal one that caught his eye first - an invitation from Kyle Bate to be his companion for a few days of entertainment as guests at a Rajput maharaja's princely state.

This was a return invitation from Kyle for the Christmas camp that Cuimein had held. December in Northern India was the coolest part of the year and the best time for camping. Kyle had also convinced Hugo du Rand to take a week off from the Frontier Force Rifles, the Indian regiment he had recently joined. The other guests included four of Cuimein's colleagues from Delhi, who brought three more adventurous girls from the season's fishing fleet. In the letter, Kyle explained that the crown prince of the state had extended the invitation. Kyle and the crown prince had become close friends at a public gathering in England during the war years.

Cuimein had never visited this princely state, but as he read the name, feelings of nostalgia washed over him. Looking up, he gazed south beyond the railway line and saw the Great Indian Desert. It comprised a significant part of the nation of Rajputana. Somewhere within that vast expanse lay Jaswara, a princely kingdom of parched desert, bush-covered hills, and jungle valleys. It was populated by a tall, lean, and fierce-looking warrior race. Cuimein knew about these things; a few years earlier, he had commanded this state's soldiers in battle. On his orders, they held trenches under heavy shellfire, stood their post during freezing, snow-covered nights, and charged through mud and barbed wire to a certain death. For them, this was preferable to dishonour.

Carrying a pack with a bedding valise on his back, 2nd Lieutenant Robin Cuimein navigated through heavy military traffic congestion in a small French town in late October 1914. He was searching for the unit to which he had been seconded. The troops around him weren't British; they belonged to the Ferozepore Brigade of the Lahore Division, one of two divisions that made up the Indian Corps. Dispatched from India only weeks after the outbreak of war, they received light training and were reorganized upon arrival in Marseilles before being dispatched north. As the German army rampaged through Belgium and northern France, both sides suffered heavy losses just shy of Paris and the Channel ports. With the front lines rapidly deteriorating due to repeated German assaults, the Indian Corps was the last reserve left.

Cuimein stopped a captain of the Connaught Rangers, the British battalion of the brigade. He saluted and introduced himself, then asked the captain about the whereabouts of the battalion he was meant to join. He was directed to a girls' school where he found the 9th Bhopal Infantry. A sergeant escorted him into the main building where he met the commanding officer, Lieutenant Colonel Dobbie.

"Welcome, Mr. Cuimein. But we're an infantry regiment. What am I supposed to do with an engineer officer?" asked the colonel.

Cuimein had been asking himself the same question throughout the three-day journey from Chatham to Wizernes. He provided his theory that he was posted where he could use his Urdu, Hindi, and Rajput language skills. Colonel Dobbie agreed this was likely the case and was intrigued that the young officer could speak Rajput. He explained that the Corps had been assigned a company of Imperial Guard soldiers from the Maharaja of Jaswara, who were Rajput and commanded by their own officers. Cuimein was asked to support Lieutenant Parsons as a liaison to this company.

Cuimein was introduced to Major Harmukh Singh, the company commander, and learned about the soldiers' backgrounds and the palaces of the royal family they had guarded. The 9th Bhopals marched out of Wizernes in escort to the brigade baggage train, and Cuimein spent time with the Company Sergeant Major to learn more about the soldiers' lives. The regiment was held back in Divisional reserve for five days before being rushed to Neuve-Chapelle on French buses. After a successful attack, the Germans breached the line, and the regiment struggled to reach the fighting area. Finally, Colonel Dobbie received the order to attack towards Neuve-Chapelle but could not signal the advance until after dark due to the deployment of the companies.

Cuimein was struggling as he made his way through dykes, hedges, and barbed wire, causing him to sweat despite wearing his heavy greatcoat, which was ideal for autumn weather but not for battle. The Indian troops, on the other hand, were more fittingly dressed in light summer khaki drill, a turban, and a polished leather ammunition cross belt. The lead companies encountered pockets of enemy soldiers, but by midnight, the regiment had reached the forward British trenches, where they found elements of the Royal West Kents still holding out. The

Germans mounted several attacks throughout the early morning, with the last one happening at dawn. During the advance, the companies had become mixed up, leaving the Jaswara Company in intact trenches and Harmukh Singh to fight off counterattacks from an advanced trench with half of his company.

Cuimein, at the rear in reserve with the other half of the company, witnessed the Imperial troops scrambling from their forward trench in retreat, not realizing that Julian Parsons had died and Harmukh Singh had just been killed. With no leaders left, the sowars began falling back. However, Cuimein fearlessly ran towards them and commanded them to stop using an old Rajasthan proverb his ayah had taught him: "A wall may give way, but a Rajput stands fast." He pulled his pistol from its holster and led the sowars back to re-occupy the forward trench. Cuimein was introduced to Major Harmukh Singh, the company commander, and learned about the soldiers' backgrounds and the palaces of the royal family they had guarded. The 9th Bhopals marched out of Wizernes in escort to the brigade baggage train, and Cuimein spent time with the Company Sergeant Major to learn more about the soldiers' lives. The regiment was held back in Divisional reserve for five days before being rushed to Neuve-Chapelle on French buses. After a successful attack, the Germans breached the line, and the regiment struggled to reach the fighting area. Finally, Colonel Dobbie received the order to attack towards Neuve-Chapelle but could not signal the advance until after dark due to the deployment of the companies.

Cuimein was struggling as he made his way through dykes, hedges, and barbed wire, causing him to sweat despite wearing his heavy greatcoat, which was ideal for autumn weather but not for battle. The Indian troops, on the other hand, were more fittingly dressed in light summer khaki drill, a turban, and a polished leather ammunition cross belt. The lead companies encountered pockets of enemy soldiers, but by midnight, the regiment had reached the forward British trenches, where they found elements of the Royal West Kents still holding out. The Germans mounted several attacks throughout the early morning, with the last one happening at dawn. During the advance, the companies had become mixed up, leaving the Jaswara Company in intact trenches and Harmukh Singh to fight off counterattacks from an advanced trench with half of his company.

Cuimein, at the rear in reserve with the other half of the company, witnessed the Imperial troops scrambling from their forward trench in retreat, not realizing that Julian Parsons had died and Harmukh Singh had just been killed. With no leaders left, the sowars began falling back. However, Cuimein fearlessly ran towards them and commanded them to stop using an old Rajasthan proverb his ayah had taught him: "A wall may give way, but a Rajput stands fast." He pulled his pistol from its holster and led the sowars back to re-occupy the forward trench.

At noon, the order to attack and capture Neuve-Chapelle came. However, all the other company officers were dead or wounded, leaving nineteen-year-old Cuimein in charge, a task for which he was not qualified. He had only completed his officer's training after joining the local territorial unit as a private soldier during his first year at university. The training covered only the basics, including saluting, marching, and firing a rifle, but not the fundamentals of attacking under modern firepower. The signal to attack was the cessation of the British artillery fire, and Cuimein, armed with a bayonet-tipped rifle, leapt to the top of the trench, raising his rifle in one hand, and shouting the only patriotic Rajasthan oath his ayah had taught him: "By the sin of the sack of Chitor."

From childhood, every Rajput knew the meaning of the monstrous echo that roared back at Cuimein from the throats of his sowars as he turned to lead them. At first, they made good progress sweeping the Germans out of their defences, but they were forced to go to ground by the enemy's artillery and machine guns. Late in the afternoon, the first counterattack was thrown at them and beaten off, as were the second and third. However, with the rest of the regiment to his left and right beginning to fall back and ammunition dwindling, Cuimein had no choice but to order his men to do the same. With darkness closing in, this nearly turned into a rout as the enemy followed closely, only kept at bay by controlled bounds from one defence to the next. Scattered about the ground they retreated over were the regiment's dead and wounded, including Sikhs, Muslims, Brahmins, and Rajputs. Just forward of the trenches they first held that morning, Cuimein came upon Piyan Singh, wounded in the hip and unable to walk. Discarding his rifle, the subaltern lifted the havaldar-major onto his shoulders and began to carry him. In the closing gloom and over this broken ground, control of the retreat was lost to him, his company, and the others, breaking up into small groups. Unaware that except for Lal Singh, who had not been further than ten feet from his office since the battle began, he was alone, Robin struggled to get his havaldar-major to a location of safety. It was not until the servant fired his rifle from behind as he cried a warning, "Saheb! The enemy!" that Robin realized the danger.

They were in an old sunken trench, and turning about, he could see three German soldiers, their spiked helmets outlined in the twilight sky on the trench lip behind. One, shot by Lali, had dropped to his knees, but the other two leapt into the trench to close on his servant. The first fired his rifle on the run then lunged at Lal with his bayonet. The young sowar parried the thrust to fork his own bayonet into the German's chest, but the third German shot him through both thighs as he did so. Lal dropped sideways, trying to extract his bayonet from the second German's chest. Cuimein, who had lost his balance on turning around and collapsed under Piyan Singh, desperately fought to his feet while clawing his 45 Webley pistol from its holster. As the third German drove his bayonet at Lal on the ground, the teenage Rajput deflected the blade by clutching it with his hands. In that instant, Cuimein's first heavy lead bullet struck the German in the chest, the force of it propelling him backwards, the second-round ripping into his throat before he toppled backwards into the oily mud of the trench.

The officer examined the injuries of the second German's servant after dragging his dead body away. He observed that both servant's hands were lacerated and bleeding badly. Additionally, the servant had sustained bullet wounds to his thighs, leaving him unable to walk. However, despite these injuries, the servant displayed bravery and honesty when he suggested that he would crawl while his officer went with the Havaldar-Major. The officer, Cuimein, forbade this action and decided to carry Piyan Singh, the wounded servant, himself.

As Cuimein struggled across the difficult terrain, he stumbled into a group of his regiment's remaining soldiers who were huddled together or collapsed on the ground. After regaining his footing, Cuimein knelt beside Piyan Singh and was relieved to hear that he was still alive. A fellow soldier, Havaldar Jetmal Singh, had been left in charge of the half company.

Cuimein removed his coat and covered Piyan Singh with it before instructing Havaldar Singh to organize the defences, tend to the wounded, and send a message to Regimental Headquarters to request more ammunition. He emphasized that they must defend the road into the night and prepare for a possible attack. Cuimein then ordered the men to spread out along the banking and set out a forward picket to warn of any impending danger.

As Robin paused to catch his breath and frantically searched his mind for battle hints from his vague Territorial Army training, the Havaldar urgently spoke out, pleading with him to remain, as he was the sovereign's palace guard. Barked Cuimein in a flash of anger, asking if he was Rajput. The Havaldar braced to attention as if struck by an electric shock, stung by the officer's questioning of his manhood. Cuimein explained that his servant was wounded on the battlefield, and he would not leave him there, feeling he owed the Havaldar at least that explanation for leaving him with so much to do.

Drawing his Webley pistol and discarding his hat long lost, Cuimein scrambled back up the banking, finding it hard to keep his direction in the dark. Wet and covered with mud, he finally slid down into the old trench, where he called out his servant's name and received a faint reply from further along. Lal Singh was safe, and Cuimein hoisted him up on his back, carrying him through treacherous shell-cratered fields, barbed wire, and ditches. With Lal's legs giving out, Cuimein had to carry him through the obstacles, and every muscle in his body screamed with fatigue. On reaching the company position where Lal was taken from him, Cuimein fell to his hands and knees, unable to speak for many minutes. No attack was mounted against them that night, and the 9th Bhopal Infantry had achieved their goal, stopping an enemy flooding through a breach in the line but losing over three hundred men, a quarter of its fighting strength. The Jaswara Imperial Company alone had begun the battle with one hundred and eighty men, reduced to one hundred and ten by the morning count. The regiment withdrew under Captain Jamieson's command and clung to the track on the outskirts of the hamlet of Pont Logy until relieved, re-grouping after a short rest. The officer casualty rate from this one day of battle was appalling, leaving Captain Jamieson as the most senior officer fit enough to command.

After reorganizing the regiment, Cuimein was given command of the Jaswara Imperial Company, as they refused any other leader. He led them through the winter months, participating in two battles at Festubert and Givenchy amidst shell-fire infernos. However, he was wounded in April at the second battle of Ypres and was carried away by Lal Singh and another sowar with a splinter embedded in his back. This injury marked the end of his association with these fearless Indian warriors from the desert lands, as the Bhopal Infantry left France during his recovery to fight the Turks in Mesopotamia. Cuimein was then reclaimed by the Royal Corps of Engineers, where he spent the next three and a half years of the war repairing trench damage on the front lines with his sappers. His bravery earned him two Mentions in Dispatches and the Military Cross, awarded after he clung to a bridge with his sappers during the German onslaught in March 1918. He was wounded again in the summer and recovered in a hospital on the Sussex coast at the end of the war. At just 23 years old, he was a decorated Major, but his most vivid memory was the responding cry of his comrades as they rushed to his side during battle.

CHAPTER 9

Sweet is revenge — especially to women
-Lord Byron.

Caught up in the carnival-like atmosphere that was a defining characteristic of an Indian railway station, Robin Cuimein scanned the crowded platform for Kyle Bate. He had accepted the young officer's invitation to visit Jaswara. They were supposed to meet here for the final leg of the journey at this station, serving a town in Rajputana, situated just across the border from British India.

"Hi Ho, Bob!" called out a voice. It was Kyle, waving with his upper body protruding from a railway carriage window.

"I hope you've saved a spot for me, Kyle?" Cuimein asked good-naturedly, reaching up to shake the younger man's hand.

"Oceans of room, dear chap, come aboard," Kyle replied nonchalantly.

The train was part of that state's railway service. The first-class carriages were kept in immaculate condition, with its orange, blue, and white livery gleaming as though new. Dismissing the Indian porter who had stowed away his bedding roll and luggage, Cuimein hung his topee on a hat hook and then settled onto the green leather upholstered seating opposite Kyle. Above their heads, two pairs of folded-back bunk cots provided sleeping accommodation for the travellers in the compartment.

"Alright, Kyle," Cuimein began, eagerly awaiting an update on Bate's most recent adventures. "Whose heart have you broken this month?" But, of course, Cuimein was joking, for no European would get within shouting distance of a tribeswoman before finding a Pathan blade at his throat. As it were, he didn't have much to share about Landi Kotal, for their movements there were restricted, and work was routine. Instead, he steered the conversation towards his connection with the royal household of Jaswara. During the war years at Winchester College, Kyle became close friends with Prince Sahil. It was almost impossible to guarantee safe passage due to the submarine threat to and from India, so rather than having his friend spend holiday periods in some dreary official residence, Kyle obtained permission from his family for the prince to stay with them as a house guest on their Lancashire estate. The prince also had a sister, a year younger, who was also receiving a British education. She occasionally spent part of her holidays with the Bates, but not all, as she had a similar arrangement with her own school friends. After Winchester, Sahil attended university at Oxford, while Kyle chose a career in the army at Sandhurst. This was a departure

from his father's wishes, who had hoped that
Kyle would take a leading role in the family
textiles business after university. However, Kyle
was a rebel. In 1915, his favourite teacher had
volunteered to fight in the war and was killed a
year later, which influenced Kyle's decision to
pursue a military career.

Kyle informed Cuimein that Sahil was not the
heir to the throne of Jaswara by birth but was
instead the Maharaja's nephew. The Maharani
did not have any children with Sahil, leaving
them without direct heirs. While the Maharaja
could have taken a second wife to resolve this,
his love for the Maharani was stronger than his
desire to continue his royal line. Sahil's father
was appointed as Dewan, a common
arrangement to ensure the stability of the
monarchy and to prevent those with dubious
claims from taking over the throne. This also
satisfied the British, who had previously annexed
Indian states that could not produce a legitimate
heir.

During their journey, the two men travelled in
comfort, with only four people in their
compartment and a dining car at their disposal.
However, everything changed the next day when
they transferred to a narrow-gauge system. They
were now in Jaswara, not the most modern state
of the Rajputana Agency, due to the legacies of
past rulers. It was only when the current
Maharaja Indar Singh took over from his

deceased father that the state began to adopt modern practices and innovations such as railways, electricity, telephones, irrigation, and well drilling. These practices were particularly important as Jaswara was a land of large desert tracts and arid hills.

The journey quickly became uncomfortable due to the lack of glass in the windows, causing sand and dust to blow in through the reed blinds. Moreover, the expedition lasted all day with stops at every village station they encountered. The only entertainment Cuimein found during these stops was observing the people in detail. These people were of the warrior caste, the Kshattriyas, and claimed to be descendants of Kutcha and Lava, sons of the god Rama. This caste had managed to hold off invaders for centuries, preserving their Hindu religion and Aryan blood, until they suffered defeat at the hands of the Moguls in the 16th century.

As evening approached, the country transformed from a dry desert to fertile land with crops of cotton, bajra millet, maize, wheat, and sugarcane. Upon arrival at Udaigarh, the state capital and winter palace, a court official requested to see Kyle's invitation card before granting them access to a car that would take them to their destination. They soon arrived at a fort nestled on a rock bank, complete with lush gardens, sports fields, and a small village of tents. Access to the fort was through an arched stone gateway where they were greeted by a young Indian man dressed in Western attire, flanked by two sentries of the Imperial Guard.

"Inches, old man! Inches!" he called, smiling broadly.

"Sadder, you beggarman!" howled Kyle, leaping from the car in one bound.

Opening his door, Cuimein joined the two men who were embracing, waiting to be introduced.

"Sahil," said Kyle, extending his arm towards him, "this is Robin Cuimein, a dear friend from the ICS."

After exchanging greetings and shaking hands, Sahil excused himself to prevent the smartly dressed servants from removing their luggage from the car, directing the driver elsewhere.

"The apartments here are reserved for my uncle's more distinguished guests, which means you commoners will be staying in the bazaar."

"Bazaar?" echoed Kyle, puzzled.

"Down by the tents," explained Sahil with a grin. "Come, I'll take you there; it's only a short stroll. You can bathe there, then come up for drinks and dinner."

"This is a delightfully situated winter palace, your Highness," commented Cuimein as they descended the steps overlooking the grounds.

"No, I'm afraid not, Robin. That's not the winter palace, you missed seeing that back in Udaigarh. This is my uncle's hunting lodge," corrected

Sahil, adding politely, "And please, Robin, call me Sahil; I'm not the Maharaja yet."

"Tell me, Sahil," asked Bate cheekily, "when are you going to give up our corrupting habit of shaving and grow a beard like the rest of your countrymen?"

"That, Kyle, my dear friend, will be the day I become the Maharaja," winked Sahil.

"I say, Kyle, what's become of our old friend Fatty Frank?" asked their host as they reached the base of the steps.

"Penrose," replied Kyle, his school day memories jogged. "Blew if I know. His male parentage was a judge, so he must have entered the law. No doubt now spends his time kicking some poor sod of a clerk up the backside."

"School bully," explained Sahil to Robin.

"Yes, but Sahil and I had his measure," proudly boasted Kyle. "The boy was as dumb as an ox. When he came after us, one would kick and punch him from behind. Then when he turned around, the other would leap in and do the same."

Cuimein had expected little of his tented accommodation but misjudged Rajput hospitality. At the entrance of his personal tent waited a servant appointed for the length of his stay. The front half of this spacious lodging was an open lounge, Persian carpeted and furnished with soft chairs and a divan that allowed the occupants to look out over the lake through sheer gauze netting. The other two rooms were a bathroom with a porcelain wash basin and a large bath and a bedroom with a bed of almost double size. Compared to the contents of his sub-district bungalow, this was stately indeed.

The next day, his servant woke him up an hour before sunrise with hot shaving water and tea. Afterward, he, Kyle, and the other guests headed towards the first event. They were driven ten miles through the morning's dawning, dressed in riding togs, to arrive at a cluster of marquees with many horses tethered in stable lines behind where they would participate in a boar hunt for the day.

The guests quickly finished their breakfast and congregated around a raised display board showing their names, their four-person teams, and the ground locations where they would wait for sightings. Bremner, a worker employed by the state to expand its irrigation system, joined them. He was a friendly, overweight man in his fifties, with grey hair and reddish-brown skin, showing the effects of many years spent under the Indian sun. The guests realized they were to form a hunting team, otherwise known as a heat. As they awaited their mounts, they reminisced about past hunting encounters while the new born sun's rays glinted off upheld spear tips. A confident young Indian woman approached Cuimein's heat. She wore a topee, a white silk blouse, riding jodhpurs, and gleaming amber riding boots. Bate greeted her with surprise and admiration upon realizing she was Sahil's sister. She extended a hand towards Kyle, who tipped his topee in response, and apologized for not meeting him the night before.

Kyle introduced her to his friend, Robin Cuimein, who cordially bowed to her. However, she did not return his friendly glance. She immediately turned to Bremner, the oldest member of the party, to request joining them as the fourth spear, for they were short a member according to the position board. She presented her request to Bremner, but her gaze shifted to each man in turn, seemingly providing them with an opportunity to object.

"Hearty reply," said Bremner, "Your Highness." "Splendid, gentlemen," she thanked them, "I'll fetch my mount and join you." "Ah, now, that was quite cunning of the Princess," Bremner commented as she sauntered towards the horse lines. Nodding, he shared his suspicion with the others. "We have been assigned Tree Point, where she narrowly missed capturing a massive black beast last year."

Tree Point was situated on the slope of a hill, providing three advantages against the heat: shade, cover from the scrub bush, and an elevated position from which to observe the terrain. This ground was a vast plain of cacti, desiccated chaparral, and dried watercourses.

Shortly after they established their position, a faint whistle blast echoed through the still morning air, followed by distant shouts and the clanging of metal instruments.

"That's the start of the beat," announced Bremner. "It will be hours before anything is driven our way," Krishna added in a flat tone. Despite this knowledge, the four dutifully remained on their mounts. As the sun rose higher and the horses became restless, the woman was the first to dismount. She leaned her spear against the tree trunk and sat down, back against a small rock, while still holding the reins. Bremner was next to descend, shortly followed by Cuimein. Kyle remained on his horse, eager not to miss a potential hot pursuit. His only experience hunting boar was at Cuimein's Christmas camp. He found it exhilarating but, though a skilled horseman, he had yet to make a kill. Nonetheless, he envisioned presenting a mounted head to his officers' mess for display in the billiards room.

Cuimein casually chose the first shaded rock within reach for his seat, positioning himself tactfully to keep the young woman in his peripheral view without making it apparent. Notably beautiful with her pale brown skin, she sat upright with her legs tucked and crossed. Rather ungallantly, he envisioned her as the goddess Kali, who, adorned with a necklace of skulls, her waist girded by a serpent, and with her many arms, revelled in blood.

"Tell me, Mr. Cuimein, what is your role in the Civil Service?" The woman's question took Robin by surprise, his mind immersed in mischievously altering her appearance. "Oh, the job entails various responsibilities, your Highness," he explained. "I am required to resolve disputes, inspect government facilities and projects, and evaluate crop yields."

"Do you have a title?" Her interruption bordered on rudeness, but with justifiable reason; he was not answering her question. "Sub-District Officer," he responded.

"Ah! You are a Collector!" She exclaimed softly. "Yes, in some districts, that is the term used," Cuimein admitted with suppressed annoyance. He disliked the title.

"And where is this district you oversee?" Krishna asked. "Chamblapur. It's in the Ranhar District," he answered. "And how long have you been stationed there?" She further inquired. "Less than a year," he replied.

"So, I assume India must feel quite foreign to you, especially after England and four years at which university?" She posed another question. "Cambridge," he simply responded. She perceived him as a novice with little experience in the country. He didn't feel obligated to change her view of him with an appeasing explanation of his and his family's background. Instead, he turned the tables: "Yes, they are quite different, but of course, you already know that. You spent several years in England, I've heard."

"My schooling," she confirmed. "Well, if I may say so. It seems you did not squander the opportunity. Your English is flawless," he complimented. Krishna did not respond to this, possibly thinking Cuimein intended it as flattery. "Do you have a wife, Collector?" she asked, using the title he despised. "No! Sub-District Officers are far too poor to wed. And you, may I ask, do you have a husband?" he countered. She almost smiled at this. "No. Two suitors have been proposed, but I rejected both of them." "Your father's selections?" Cuimein assumed. "No!" she replied. "They were my uncle's selections, the Maharaja's," she said, not seeming to mind his curiosity. "I believe you had a good reason to dismiss them?" Robin pressed. "They were box wallahs," her head rose, and her voice hardened. "Rich merchants, but nonetheless, box-wallahs. I am Rajput, Collector of the Kshatriya Caste; we are of a kingly order and soldiers. When I marry, it will be to a warrior." "Pig! Pig!" Kyle alerted from his perch on the saddle, pointing with his hog spear. Jumping to remount, the other three scanned the rapidly heating mid-morning countryside. In the distance, three black dots could be seen running along the edge of a dry nullah. "Sounder!"

Bremner called out. "Sow and two squeakers."
"The boar is smart," Krishna commented. "He is keeping hidden." Then, a more prominent black dot emerged, sprinting after the sounder who had turned into the plain. The heat stationed nearby, seeing the boar appear, for only the male pig was hunted, charged from cover.

The pursuit was hot and gaining on the boar for some distance, which suddenly turned back, causing the horses to jumble about trying to turn. That was the end, the boar escaping into thick cactus, leaving the riders to trot back to their waiting point.

After that brief disturbance, the plain again became lifeless, the riders at Tree Point settling back in their saddles. No one made a move to dismount because the beat was drawing nearer. Still a long way off, it was moving from the left across their front. Annoyingly, there was a wait of another hour before anything else happened. Then it was only a shout and the far-off sighting of a rider at full gallop.

Yet, this was the beginning. As the beat drove all before it, the game was seen fleeing. Two jackals and a cheetah were spotted from Tree Point as heats, stationed to their left, sprinted to the hunt. Seeing a boar out of cover, it was well after midday before a chance came their way. "Ghost alive. Look at the size of that devil!" All eyes turned to where Kyle was staring while, at the same time, crouching in their saddles.

A large black boar had emerged from some nearby bushes and was sticking to the banks as it moved into the ground below them. "He's not in our sector yet, Mister Bremner," Krishna whispered. "He's still in the territory of the heat to our left, but they haven't seen him." Cuimein watched the animal on stumpy legs with a sense of sadness. He often had to cull boars that were damaging crops for farmers, but he admired them for their bravery and tenacity. However, killing them for sport was something he disliked. Bremner muttered, "Keep going, my beauty." Suddenly, the boar entered their area. The sound of hooves on stone and a whinny from Kyle's horse alerted the animal to danger, but it briefly surveyed its surroundings before running across the open ground and turning right. Bremner and Kyle turned their horses in the same direction, anticipating the boar would try to escape from the other side of the bush. Robin followed behind, but the princess took an entirely different direction to the left, surprising him. Recalling Bremner's comment about her from the year before, he followed as she dashed through low brushwood. Falling behind, he watched as she disappeared into a wide, dry watercourse.

Looking down into the nullah, Cuimein saw Krishna in hot pursuit of the boar. Using its knowledge of the local terrain, the boar had first fled in one direction, then another, hoping to confound its pursuers. Despite their bulk, boars are deceptively fast over short distances, matching the speed of a horse. However, they tire quickly and when winded, they are prone to attack. When the boar charged, a woman was prepared, and her horse was not. The mare charged at the boar, but the woman skilfully aimed her spear at the boar's flank, causing it to flee with a broken spear point embedded in its flesh. Upon reaching the scene, Cuimein dismounted and positioned himself between the woman and the wounded boar. Despite his protests, she insisted on finishing off the boar herself and chased after it on horseback. Cuimein noted the woman's fierce determination and saw her as Durga, the goddess of war. The rest of the hunting party eventually caught up and admired the slain boar.

"Your Highness, please forgive my impolite outburst. Regrettably, my concern for your safety overpowered my good manners," Cuimein apologized as he returned Princess Krishna's lost topee. She had earlier criticized his lack of warrior-like conduct during the hunt.

Cuimein knelt to touch the head of the deceased boar, a colossal creature. He asked Krishna if the boar died honourably, to which she responded that it had charged with spirit. The hunt concluded after the boar's demise, and they returned to the marshalling camp with the trophy on a cart pulled by camels.

Later, a havaldar from the court guard approached them to report that the hunt was ending, and the beaters were being dismissed. Cuimein recognized the havaldar, Lal Singh, and congratulated him on his promotion. He returned Lal Singh's regimental badge, which he had held onto for nine years, and offered him his crest of the Jaswara Legion.

"Lal, completely astonished, exclaimed, "Cuimein, saheb!" He jumped off his horse and ran a few steps before stopping to salute. The Englishman touched his topee in response, then extended his hand and gave Lal a handshake while gripping his shoulder. "The years have been too long, my friend," Cuimein said warmly. "Saheb! Saheb! Not a day has passed since we parted that my thoughts weren't with you," Lal responded emotionally. "Your badge," Cuimein extended his hand. "No, saheb," the havaldar declined, "it's a part of me that I want you to keep." "Thank you, Lal Singh," the ex-officer accepted, clutching the crest in his fist. "It's the only memento of the war I cherish." Princess Krishna, preoccupied with loading her prize onto the cart, didn't witness this exchange between Cuimein and one of her uncle's palaces havaldars. Yet, back at the marshalling camp, she noticed something that momentarily puzzled her. As she stood in front of her boar that hung alongside four others, she saw Cuimein conversing with a group of Imperial Guards at one end of the horse lines. Just then, another sowar rode in from the plain, abruptly stopped, creating a cloud of dust, and dismounted to salute the Englishman. Before she could observe more, someone obstructed her view, excitedly asking her to recount the story of her day's significant kill. The evening concluded with a formal dinner in the fortress. The interior was adorned with broadcloth in Rajput colours: white, blue, orange, yellow, and green. In the reception hall, Cuimein and Bate conversed with Bremner and his wife, a forthright Yorkshire woman. "Are either of you going to Meerut for the Kadir Cup?" she asked Robin and Kyle during the discussion about the day's hunt. "Many people in this room are," she informed them when they said they weren't. "This Maharaja's hunt is an annual event, well-known as a precursor to the Meerut meets." This information was confirmed by Sahil, who then arrived looking strikingly handsome in a silk coat and pants, with a pristine white turban covering the tops of his ears. "Will the Maharaja be leading a team from the court this year?" asked Bremner. "Absolutely. He'd rather miss entry to paradise than the hog-hunting at Meerut," the prince responded. "And your sister will be among them?" Cuimein assumed. "I can assure you she won't, Robin," Sahil emphasized. "She is far from being my uncle's favourite child, being

too wilful and full of European habits.
Moreover, she's turned down two of his chosen suitors."

"Ah! Here comes the beautiful huntress of the day," Kyle announced as Krishna approached their small circle through the crowded hall.

"Thank you, Kyle," she responded to his compliment. "Good evening, everyone, Collector."

As she singled out Cuimein for an individual greeting, the princess paused for a moment to examine the miniature medals on his dinner jacket. Then, with a smile, he inclined his head before turning to accept a glass of champagne from a tray held by a waiter, offering it to her. She took the glass by the stem, pressing her fingers hard into his. The conversation then shifted to the dinner arrangements, and Kyle was surprised to discover that, as custom dictated, men and women would be dining separately.

The Maharani lived a somewhat secluded life, shielded from public view. She occupied the women's apartments, the zenana, which were in no way a harem. On occasions such as this, she would entertain the female guests. For example, earlier that day, while the men were out pigsticking, she hosted a morning round of tennis and croquet and, in the afternoon, a game of bridge.

While the conversation revolved around this topic, Cuimein's gaze casually drifted towards the princess. This woman was not the warrior demon he had spent the day with, as Kyle had noted upon her arrival. She was dressed in a crimson sari with silver trim, worn untraditionally draped over her shoulders rather than over her head, allowing her long ebony hair to cascade down her back. Underneath the silk, her shoulders, upper arms, and chest were covered in a silver waist jacket that served as a bodice. The skirt of her sari clung tightly to her waist, hips, and lower limbs. Her face, however, was what captivated Cuimein the most: smooth, flawless skin; dark, spirited eyes; and lips that seemed to beckon to be caressed. Free of makeup, her only added adornment were two small silver earrings. He admired her, seeing her as a golden Aphrodite at his side.

However, this appreciation did not mean that the Englishman had become infatuated; she was a bit too sharp to capture his desire.

Finishing his champagne and not wanting to hold an empty glass, he looked around for a waiter. Finding nonclose by, he walked over to a small flower stand to set his glass down. He was about to re-join the conversation when a faint melody of a song held him back. Intrigued, he traced the source of the melodious Rajasthan tune to a salon off an adjoining hall. The electric lights in the room were concealed, casting only a warm glow behind and to the sides of the musicians.

The singer was a woman in her thirties, sitting with her legs tucked up and her body straight, enveloped in a robe of the finest muslin that flowed around her like a gown. Her high soprano voice resonated as she moved her head from side to side and examined her arms as if they were newborns, extending them out and pulling them back in a fluid motion. She sang a melancholy and romantic song about a prince's love for an ordinary girl, maintaining the melody by elevating multiple tones, stacking one on top of the other in a shrill voice, depleting the surrounding air. Two elderly men with gray beards and turbans provided musical accompaniment, one playing a small drum with two thin sticks, the other on the sitar. The audience was small, consisting of a dozen or so Indian guests, several men in European dinner jackets, and all the women in traditional attire. Cuimein was captivated. He found a cushion near the doorway, the room's only seating, and sat to listen and watch.

During the second ballad, Cuimein's concentration was disrupted when Princess Krishna joined him on a cushion at his side. She whispered to him that it was a village folk song, offering to explain some of the simpler movements the singer was making. Over the course of the next few songs, she enlightened Cuimein about the meanings behind the movements of the head, fingers, and eyes. Their conversation was interrupted when Sahil and Kyle urgently whispered that Robin was needed elsewhere.

Once in the chamber hall, Bate kindly reprimanded Cuimein for not informing them that he was a national hero. Sahil explained that they were summoned by the Maharaja, who had been furious upon discovering that Cuimein had been their guest for 24 hours without his knowledge. The Maharaja entered the chamber hall with his guard colonel, and Sahil hurried Cuimein along by taking his arm.

Dressed in elegant knee-length coat and trousers, embroidered with silver, and adorned with a gemmed aigrette on his turban, Robin Cuimein, determined and at a decent pace, held eye contact with the tall Maharaja, who had a fuller face and a predominantly black beard with streaks of white.

Speaking in Raj, Sahil introduced Cuimein as a former lieutenant who had commanded troops in France during the early stages of the war. The Maharaja recognized him and embraced him in a Rajput hug, welcoming him to Jaswara and inquiring why he had arrived unannounced. Cuimein humbly explained that he saw himself as a young officer doing his best and that leading brave men was not necessary as he only led. The Maharaja commended his bravery and removed the jewelled aigrette from his turban as a recognition of Cuimein's heroic acts that were often talked about around their campfires but never acknowledged.

"Well, by the sons of the gods Kutcha and Lava, you will now receive recognition for it. Therefore, Lieutenant Robin Cuimein, for your deeds of gallantry while in command of my troops detached for service with His Royal Highness the King, I present you with this deserved treasure of the State." Stunned, Cuimein looked down at the diamond and ruby clustered brooch offered to him. He thought it might be an impulsive gesture, but if so, he believed it was one born of national pride and given as a tribute to the soldiers he had led. Robin understood this of the Maharaja, who, despite volunteering his Imperial State troops at the outbreak of war, was forbidden by the Viceroy himself to go in command of them. He had provided each sowar with a flask of holy Ganges water for use as purification against loss of caste after crossing the black water to France. The Englishman knew he had to reject the aigrette. Delhi would never allow him to keep possession, but that was not the basis of his rejection. His refusal to the Maharaja's offer echoed his long-held belief but never expressed: 'Your Highness, I feel I cannot accept your gracious gift. If I take it, I would be doubly rewarded. You see, I have led your Jaswara Legion in battle. That is an honor; there is no greater reward.'"

Now, it was the Maharaja who stood thunderstruck. For a moment, he stared at Cuimein, then turned to the Dewan, and announced a change in the evening's proceedings. 'Brother, during the banquet, state affairs that require your attention will arise. Mister Cuimein will take your place.' With a smile, he stepped forward, wrapping an arm around Cuimein's shoulder. 'Come, Robin, if you will not accept my token of gratitude, then tonight, you will sit beside me as my guest of honour.'

Princess Krishna did not join the others as they left to dine; instead, she and the rest of the women would be attending the Maharani's dinner party in another wing of the fortress. Yet, she did not rush off, choosing to linger and watch the tall, dark Englishman who turned out to be far more than he initially seemed.

With March approaching, the nights were growing warmer. This, coupled with his thoughts of the day's events, contributed to Cuimein's inability to sleep. Instead, he sat slumped on the lounge divan, watching the stars and moonlight reflecting off the lake's water. The banquet was initially a near-career disaster for him. The Maharaja had seated him at the head table to his right, between himself and the Viceroy's appointed Regent. Since the latter was new to the office and only spoke Raj sporadically, the Maharaja introduced Cuimein to the Regent as his brother's stand-in interpreter. This excuse was less than convincing, and he felt like he was holding a very leaky bucket. Many cold glances were directed his way from the lower tables, as table seniority was a valued prestige at an event of this magnitude.

At first, Cuimein found the situation exceedingly embarrassing, sensing that the Regent felt the same. However, after he openly admitted the Maharaja's hastily awarded honour, the Regent relaxed, confiding in a gruff but sensitive voice that he had lost a son at the siege of Kutal-Amara in 1916 while serving as an officer with the 66th Punjabis.

Later, all of his previous stiffness evaporated upon learning that Robin was the grandson of Nathaniel Cuimein, whom he had met when he first came to India forty years ago. For the remainder of the meal, interspersed with translations for the Maharaja, Robin and the Regent engaged in a lively conversation. Most of the discussion revolved around Britain's future role in India, and Cuimein's hopes and intentions were closely tied to that role. After the meal, they and the women reconvened in the main hall, where a band was playing European and American dance music. This allowed Robin to return to his small group for more casual conversation and to relieve the pressure on Kyle, who was repeatedly called upon to satisfy Meg Bremner's insatiable desire for dancing.

During a rest break, Princess Krishna approached Cuimein while he was fetching a glass of punch for Meg. "Collector, would you like to dance with me?" she asked in a voice that was sultry and completely different from the fierce horsewoman he had spent the day with. As they waltzed to the music, she remarked, "I should be dancing on your toes instead of the floor, Collector." Cuimein hid his amusement and asked, "Oh, and why is that?" Princess Krishna retorted, "You are a deceitful rogue. You led me to believe you were not what you truly are - a warrior." The Englishman stressed that he was now a district administrator, but Princess Krishna shot back, accusing him of toying with her by displaying mini military medals on his dinner jacket. "I could have gleefully slapped your face!" she exclaimed. Cuimein responded with a quote from Shakespeare: "If you prick us, do we not bleed? If you tickle us, do we not laugh? If you poison us, do we not die? And if you wrong us, shall we not revenge?" However, this did not placate the princess. "Well, Collector, quoting Shakespeare will not heal my wounds. I warn you, be on your guard," she said without smiling. Cuimein made light of being her prey, but Princess Krishna hinted at a potential hog spear in his back or a knife at his throat while he slept. Cuimein brushed off this threat, trusting in the princess's commitment to the fairness of the hunt.

Nevertheless, this dance kept him awake in the early morning hours as he recalled the warm, velvety texture of the princess's hands and arms, as well as her enticingly moist lower lip.

With a sudden shiver, Cuimein awoke from his doze. Clad only in a bath towel around his waist, he felt the temperature drop that accompanied the small hours. As he was about to rise and return to bed, he froze; his ears had picked up a faint musical sound. A dark figure startled him at first, nimbly moving from the tent shadows to the netting hanging at his lounge entrance. However, in the light of the stars and the waning moon, he recognized it to be a woman dressed in a red sari. As she pushed aside the netting to enter, he recognized the tinkling sound as that of an anklet bell.

"Are you here to place a knife to my throat, Your Highness?" he asked, rising from the divan.

"No, Collector, not a knife," replied Princess Krishna, removing a fold of her sari that she had been using as a headscarf and veil.

"In that case, you have misplaced yourself," cautioned Cuimein.

"Oh no, Collector, I have come out of obligation," assured the woman, her voice heavy with implication. "Earlier, you refused to accept my uncle's gift of gratitude. So now, I present another gift of gratitude on behalf of the Royal

Court and subjects of Jaswara. A gift befitting a warrior."

"A gift at this hour?" questioned Cuimein, his suspicion clear.

"Yes, at this hour, Collector. As a Rajput Princess, I offer you my only possession. I give—myself."

As she spoke, she let the sari's outer garment fall to the ground, revealing that she wore nothing beneath it. Standing naked, her golden body glowing the colour of copper in the moonlight, only two areas on her form did not shimmer: her hair, cascading gracefully down her head and neck, and the small patch of coarse black hair nestled at the junction of her thighs.

Struck speechless by this revelation, Cuimein stood in awe, his admiration palpable as the naked princess stepped away from her discarded wrap. She approached him with the slow, sensuous stride of a beckoned concubine.

"I believe you will not reject this reward so willingly given, will you, Collector?" Her words were sultry pleas as she slipped her arms around his body, pressing her porcelain-firm breasts into his chest, the nipples prodding his flesh like the tips of tiny fingers. Then, six inches separating their height, she rose up on her toes to brush a cheek and an ear with feather-touch kisses.

Cuimein, aware he was a guest of the State and who, as a junior member of the Indian Civil Service, should have avoided any scandal this night might bring by rejecting his visitor's carnal offering, felt his resolve crumbling under the assault from the princess's lips. Lowering his head, he took and held her lips with his own while, with one hand, casting the towel from his waist. For some minutes, they were moulded, locked in a kiss, their arms wrapped, bodies pressed and rotating in a search to fill each other's folds and recesses. Then, breaking from the kiss, he lifted her into his arms to carry the warm, clinging creature of desire to his bed. Laying her beneath the mosquito netting, he crouched above, savouring the sexual aura she emitted with every groan, sigh, and turn of her body. Then, with this kindling, his own uncontrollable lust, he slowly lowered his head to encircle the crown of an apple-hard breast with his lips.

They made love three times during those pre-dawn hours, the first two with unrestrained, frenzied hunger, wildly fulfilling crazed, erotic needs. Between, they kept their passions inflamed by tracing each other's bodies with kisses and incitements of the tongue. Finally, on the third occasion, with their wanton thirst quenched, Cuimein rocked his hips in a slow thrusting rhythm maintaining the pleasure of their mating on clouds of dreamy erotica. Braced above, he studied Krishna's face as she, enraptured in a sexual trance, arched her chin upwards while, with closed eyes, she rocked her head slowly from side to side.

"No, Princess," whispered her lover, wishing she would hear and understand, "you are neither Kali, the eater of human flesh, nor Durga, the fighter of battles. On the contrary, you are Shakti, the custodian of sexuality."

CHAPTER 10

Slowly and sadly we laid him down,
From the field of his fame fresh and gory;
We carved not a line, and we raised not a stone,
But we left him alone with his glory.
-Charles Wolfe

Joey Payne regained his focus on his job after
yawning and adjusting the shoulder of his slung
rifle. He gazed out from the battlements of the
Border fort of Landi Kotal, where he was tasked
with sentry duty. In the dawn light, he could see
as far as the perimeter wire towards Afghanistan,
and a guard could patrol along the wire-bound
trenches and be served tea three times a night.
Joey's wistful thoughts of tea were interrupted by
the duty officer on his nightly visit to the
sentries. He dropped a pebble in warning to the
gate sentry below and waited to see if his silent
alarm had alerted him. Moments later, he heard
Tommy Gilbert's left boot crash to attention and
the slap of hands hitting his rifle stock as he paid
the officer the proper respect.
As the lieutenant retraced his steps, Joey could
make out shapes beyond the shadows. He could
see the two twin peaks of Big and Little Benedict
a mile to the east and the dragon-backed ridge

beyond that ran south to the border crossing at Landi Kana. The garrison was stationed at this crossing, along with the 4th Battalion of the 5th Mahratta Light Infantry.

Bugle calls were sounded, and men emerged to carry out their morning ablutions as the garrison began to awaken. Across the valley, the tribesmen were escorting women to their daily labour in the infertile fields. The British took on the responsibility of providing safe passage through the thirty-three-mile length of the Khyber Valley, which was plagued by ambushes that attacked, robbed, and murdered camel caravans. Twice a week, its entire route was picketed: on Tuesday when the caravans travelled east out of Afghanistan and on Friday when the camel traffic meandered west of India. Joey Payne watched as the battalion briskly marched through the perimeter gate and eastward down the Pass. They were on their way to occupy critical heights on either side of the dual roadways. His guard duty was nearly over.

--oOo-

After breakfast, Kyle Bate left the officers' mess dining room and headed to the lounge for some reading material. He didn't need to work that day, as B Company was providing security for the battalion's camp guards. Meanwhile, the other companies were on defensive picket duty for the traffic kafilah.

Upon entering the lounge, he greeted Captain Russell McQuaid, the quartermaster, who responded warmly. Kyle offered him a cigar, but McQuaid declined, explaining they weren't his preferred brand. Kyle lit one for himself and relaxed in his chair. McQuaid then commented on the smoke, revealing that the secret ingredient was found in the sweat of the large-bodied women who rolled the leaf.

His relaxation was interrupted by the mess steward, who informed Kyle that the adjutant had summoned him. The adjutant informed Kyle that his trip to collect the weekly pay had been cancelled. However, he still needed to drive to Peshawar within the hour. Kyle was pleased with the news, but the adjutant reminded him to ensure his car was in good condition and to return by the afternoon. The next day, they were to picket the road as an arms and ammunition convoy for the Afghan army was passing through.

"From us, sir?" asked Bate.

"No, we didn't make the purchase. The items were bought from the French and arrived just in time," explained the adjutant. He then added, "It seems the Amir is facing a revolt in the Khost Valley. He tried to introduce education for women, and that's just suicide."

Kyle quickly left the battalion headquarters as he saw camels carrying goods and armed men passing by. They were heading towards the plains of India.

"All right, Sergeant Ridley, let's stop here. Dismiss the men and have them follow me," ordered Kyle as he moved towards the edge of the road to select a path uphill.

Sergeant Ridley complied and added his own unique twist to the order, "Move it, you bunch of sun-baked jokers! Follow Mister Bates up that hill, I want to see you jumping and leaping like Douglas Fairbanks from the moving pictures!"

Nash Slyfield whispered to Jeffrey Harrison, "More like Mary Pickford."

Sergeant Ridley overheard the comment and inquired, "What was that, Slyfield?"

"I said, it was a great inspiration, Sergeant," Slyfield shouted back, grinning as he began his ascent up the hill.

The battalion was on another road picketing operation. Each time the head of the column arrived at a picket point, a platoon would peel off and climb up the feature overlooking the road. This was a tactic refined through years of conflict with the renegade Pathan.

6 Platoon had drawn the short straw this time and had to endure a long and challenging climb to reach their vantage point. Once there, they promptly secured the area and remained vigilant as they waited and watched. They were on the shoulder of a spur that extended from a much higher peak and had an unobstructed view of the

surrounding terrain. For those facing upwards, it was a critical area to monitor as any attack would likely come from downhill.

Joey surveyed the barren Afghan Border hillside while the sun blazed down on the broken rocks in front of him. Although he remained alert for any signs of movement, his mind was not on the hill now. He was back home in Kent, helping with the haymaking at the farm's Slow Bell pasture. Having served as a soldier for over two years, mostly in India, his thoughts often wandered to the meadows and crop fields of his family farm, where he used to watch bees collect nectar from the flowers. Even on this barren hillside, he could close his eyes and recall the scent of a freshly ploughed field or visualize the kitchen door rain barrel overflowing after a spring rain.

Despite having a full water bottle on his hip, Joey, like all other soldiers on picket duty, would not drink from it. It was a point of regimental honour to return to camp with the water bottles untouched, no matter how hot or thirsty they became. The 2nd Queen's Light Infantry was close to completing its one-year tour of duty at Landi Kotal, and in a month, they would be moving to a new station. Many soldiers, including Payne, had hoped for more excitement during their stay, but aside from occasional sniping and harmless pot-shots, nothing happened. Even the local tribesmen seemed uninterested in engaging with the British troops. By noon, with no shade except their topees, the sun had taken its toll on the soldiers, who could not escape the heat or find a more comfortable position without burning their bare flesh on the hot rocks. Joey wiped the sweat from his temples and noticed his section commander, Lance-Corporal Benedict Lyall, throwing a small stone his way. Silently pointing across the far hillside half, a mile away, Lyall drew Joey's attention to a hawk climbing toward the hill's peak on busy wing beats. For a full minute, Payne searched among the rocks for any sign of movement or someone hiding, but he found none. He looked back at Lyall and shook his head.

Benedict had held the rank of lance-corporal for a year now, ever since the earthquake at Jhendara. The platoon had dug one of their lance corporals out of the collapsed bungalow with two badly crushed legs. Unfortunately, he died a week later due to his injuries. As a result, Lyall was put forward to fill the vacancy. Mr. Bate, with over two years of war service, had no hesitation in approving the promotion. Benedict accepted the stripe because it meant more money, and he wouldn't have to stand any more sentry duties.

Bate was also promoted, no longer a second lieutenant and now sporting two pips on his shoulders instead of one. Becoming a full lieutenant didn't inflate Kyle's ego as it did for some. He continued to command 6 Platoon, and the money was insignificant to him as he was already a wealthy man thanks to his grandmother's endowment. Therefore, he carried on his career in a relatively flamboyant manner, using the Army to enjoy the hospitality and wonders of India.

"Any sign of them, Bate?" asked Sergeant Ridley. "No, not a trace," replied Kyle, lowering his newly acquired Swiss binoculars. The furthest view he had of the road's Indian approach route remained desolate as ever.

The officers had been briefed the previous evening that the picketing completion was scheduled for this day in the early afternoon; it was now almost three o'clock. Unbeknownst to them, the delay was due to the drivers hired by the French arms firm to deliver their vehicles and cargo to the Afghan Army, who were held up at the border crossing. The Khyber Pass was too formidable a challenge for these drivers, even with protection, and they refused to go beyond Peshawar.

As a contingency plan, Afghan Army drivers were transported by truck from Landi Kana through the Pass to collect the convoy at Peshawar. However, this process was time-consuming and the Afghans, unfamiliar with the vehicles and road, drove at a slow pace. There were also two breakdowns that had to be fixed, as under no circumstances could arms and ammunition be left unattended in Pathan territory.

Wilf Ridley glanced up at the sun to check its position, then reached into his haversack for his lunch. He had refrained from eating his bread and meat sandwich earlier to avoid exacerbating his thirst. However, as the day dragged on, hunger overcame him. The sergeant of 6 Platoon had acquired a unique distinction when the battalion first arrived in India - shortly after reaching Jhendara, he found himself married. While on embarkation leave, he stayed with his sister and her husband. Also residing with them was a sister of the husband, a woman in her mid-twenties, who had been widowed as a bride near the end of the war. As nature would have it, these two struck up more than just a friendly relationship, leading to Ridley receiving a letter from her upon his arrival in India. The letter informed him that, wanted or not, he would become a father by the first week of May. Until then, Wilf had no intention of marrying, content with his single army life. However, he knew his duty. With the letter in hand, he requested his commanding officer's permission to marry. Upon approval, his bride-to-be's passage to India was paid for. In Bombay, she was greeted by Ridley, who hurriedly escorted her to the Anglican Church where they were married on the spot. The ceremony was witnessed by two total strangers, hired by Wilf off the street for five rupees each. It wasn't exactly a dream wedding for a bride, but with only two hours between the ship docking and their train departure for Jhendara, Wilf left no room for the frills of cupids and arrowed hearts. Under orders from Colonel Gabson to report as a married couple, Ridley similarly left no room for such sentimentalities.

At five o'clock, Kyle had become irked by the prolonged time they spent on the hill, with no sign of the convoy. By seven, he was fuming, as he and another officer had been invited to the Mahratta officer's mess for a game of bridge and they were now going to be late. By eight, his mood had completely shifted, as he was now focused only on preparing his platoon to spend the night on the hill. If the convoy didn't pass by dusk, they, along with the rest of the battalion, would be forced to remain static, as moving in the dark in the Khyber was too risky.

Under Sergeant Ridley's guidance, Kyle had his Lewis gun section start building a stone sangar for the platoon to take refuge in if they were stranded for the night. As time was running out, Kyle constantly raised his binoculars to search the road below and finally spotted the slow-moving convoy. He watched as twenty-two lorries and six armoured cars passed by, waiting for a signal to either leave or stay.

When Kyle saw the forward companies marching back towards him, he knew it was just a matter of time before they would be called to re-join the tail of the column. He no longer consulted his pocket watch for the time, instead judging it by looking at the sky. As he waited, Kyle saw the 7th Platoon move down the valley and knew that his platoon would be next. Using his binoculars, Kyle searched for the all-important signaller who would relay the message telling them to move down. As the 7th Platoon reached the road and took over as the rear guard, Kyle spotted a man carrying a red flag denoting the tail of the column. However, the column stopped due to a broken-down lorry, with the commander of the 6th Platoon becoming impatient as seconds turned into minutes. "We're cutting this perishin' fine, sir," commented Wilf Ridley, coming to his side. "Agreed, Kyle, not by bloody half," corrected Kyle. As they finally hit the road, the officer warned them in an anticipatory tone, "Here we go! Here we go!" He kept his binoculars fixed on the strip of road where the rear control would come into view. With darkness gaining the upper hand over daylight, the lower level of the Pass was shrouded in gloom, causing a restriction of sight that increased rapidly with the added cloaking of mountain shadows. Only thanks to Bate's binoculars were the 6th Platoon able to pick out the controlling party, but even then, the flag's colour was indistinct. Kyle's eyes flitted from one figure to the other, expecting to find the signaller pausing to wave his blue and white semaphore flags spelling out three Morse code letters, RTR, return to the road. Instead, following them as they moved further up the valley, his concentration was broken by an amazed curse from Ridley. "Jesus, they've missed us. Look, sir. There's the 5th Platoon lickety-splitting it for the road."

Looking towards where his sergeant was pointing, the officer could just make out in the fading light a line of men dashing from a picket position off a hill half a mile up the valley. "Well, that's damned untidy of them," commented Kyle nonchalantly before dealing with the situation with the seriousness it needed. "We will remain until the 5th Platoon reaches the road. One of us must protect the other. But once they are free of the hill, I want us off here in record time."

"Very good, sir," replied Ridley, turning to alert the section commanders. Responding to Benedict Lyall's call to move, Joey Payne spat the pebble from his mouth with relief. The day had been long, hot, and the waiting galling. Now up and on his feet, the wretchedness of this forgotten, he ran like everyone else. In the lead was Sergeant Ridley with 3 Sections, followed by 1 Section and the Lewis Section. Benedict Lyall's 2 Section with Mister Bate bringing up the rear. There was no hanging about. On the word to leave, 6 Platoon rose as one and raced off. The downhill journey, like the ascent, was where the most danger from attack lay, and the best counter to this was speed. Tactics disappeared; all that mattered was that no one should lag or injure themselves in a fall. At the halfway point, the platoon entered a thick, murky shadow cast by higher surrounding hills. Darkness was only minutes away. On the Frontier, the night did not creep stealthily down; it descended with a total, all-enveloping rush.

Entering this gloom, 2 Sections split in half, passing either side of a spike-toothed crop of rock. A hundred feet in length, erosion had carved out cavities and bays that were ideal for concealment, benefiting from the closing twilight. Initially, the Pathan tribesmen who stormed from these hides fell soundlessly upon the three lead men of 2 Section who were passing on the north side of this feature. The first two were struck down with blade blows, hardly knowing they had been set upon. Tommy Gilbert was less fortunate; he had an instant's full sight of three bearded, bedraggled cloaked tribesmen surging towards him. In defence, Tommy hardly had time to raise his rifle before one had thrust a large, bladed knife into his intestines, cutting upwards, severing his webbed belt at the buckle. With the second attacker snatching his rifle away and the third stripping

the ammunition pouches from his body, Tommy
was left to collapse, screaming to the ground.

A few yards behind, Joey Payne had a fleeting
moment longer to react. Levelling his rifle at two
fearsome men in grimy, colourless turbans, he
flicked the cut-off plate of his Shorts Lee-
Enfield rifle open. Still, before he could cock his
bolt and feed a round into the chamber for
firing, one had swung a blow with his curved
talwar, striking Joey on his right shoulder. The
force of the impact knocked him to his knees,
the blade slicing a deep gash the length of his
upper arm. Then, with the right useless, he
released his left hand from the rifle stock, letting
it fall, to grapple with the second attacker, who
stabbed downwards at him with a knife.
Blocking the thrust with his forearm, the blade
tip deflected, piercing his flesh above the collar
bone. The tribesman's pungent body stink Joey
would only recall afterwards.

Benedict Lyall, 2 Section's last man leaving the
picket location, had not liked coming away so
late and, with an old soldier's intuition, had fixed
his bayonet to his rifle. At full tilt, he rounded a
blister of broken rock to come upon Payne
struggling under a Pathan bent on plunging a
knife into his chest. With Tommy Gilbert's
screams resounding throughout the hill's evening
calm, Benedict snapped a round into his
chamber, aimed it point blank and fired into the
face of a talwar-armed Pathan about to slash it

downwards onto Joey Payne's exposed neck. Without faltering, Benedict lunged forward and down. Joey, grappling for his life, had managed to roll atop of the attacker with the knife, a position which, except for Lyall's bullet, would have cost him his head, removed by a razor-sharp talwar. Instead, the man below him, ceasing to struggle, screamed in his face with pain and terror as Lyall's seventeen-inch bayonet blade sank into and through his breast.

"Up, Joey lad! Get up," cried Lyall silencing the Pathan's scream as he stamped a hob-nailed boot onto his mouth, wrenching the bayonet free. Payne, his right arm disabled, kicked with his boots, and pushed with his left hand at the tribesman Benedict had shot, who now lay collapsed across him.

War cries were being yelled all around them, echoing back from surrounding hills and out of valleys. The Pathans had sprung a silent ambush using swords and knives only. But, with Tommy Gilbert's scream and Benedict's rifle shot, there was no need to suppress their jubilation in the expectancy of committing more murder; they now loudly yelled their battle cries.

Benedict fired twice more at crazed wild men who tried to close on him, then reaching down with one hand, pulled Joey to his feet.

"My book!" cried Payne, making to recover his rifle.

"Leave it! Run!" shouted Lyall hauling the younger man away and behind him to gain space by swinging his rifle up and firing again at a figure skulking in close cover.

"Scamper, Joey! Scamper!" screamed the lance-corporal over his shoulder, backing towards Payne as he cocked his rifle bolt, feeding another round into the chamber.

Joey stumbled a few yards, then turned to make sure his mate was following. Lyall, firing his fifth and last round, turned to flee. The Shorts Lee-Enfield had a magazine which held ten games, but the spring could not be trusted, resulting in only five being loaded each time.

North, they ran along the side of the hill away from the road over boulders and squeezed between narrow rock gaps, their metal-soled boots clattering on the hard surfaces. Finally, after five minutes, Lyall called a halt to listen for pursuit and reload his rifle.

"I gotta go back, Benedict," said Payne in breathless gasps, pulling his bayonet from his scabbard as they sheltered back-to-back at the base of a large rock. "My bandook - I can't lose my bandook - not to those heathen bleeders."

"Kiss it goodbye, mate. By this time tomorrow, some tar-arse, hookworm-riddled Pathan will have bought himself a new wife with it," said Lyall, feeding a clip of five rounds into the magazine of his rifle. "

Joey sagged against the rock as his knees began to shake, a reaction brought about by shock. He was gripped in fear only minutes earlier as he fought for his life. Still, the emotion he felt now was anger at having lost his rifle and being taken so completely by surprise.

Tommy Gilbert was left alone and still screaming. He scrambled to his feet, clutching a mess of bloody, protruding intestines and stomach contents. He staggered aimlessly away, seeking help. Then, covering no more than thirty yards, he collapsed unconscious.

Lieutenant Bate, the rear man of 2 Section's left-hand half section, finding himself alarmed to real danger by Gilbert's scream and Lyall's rifle shot, could not halt himself until his downhill momentum had carried him another ten yards. Then, snatching his pistol from its leather holster, he stood looking at the cliff of ragged rock to his right.

"Down here, sir," called Sid Frith below him. "There's a way around here".

Hurrying past, Kyle ordered two other men nearby to follow him.

At the head of the platoon, Wilf Ridley grabbed at a rock to anchor himself.

"Stop! Fix bayonets!" he bellowed. "Back! Get back up."

Rounding the base of the obstructing rock formation, Bate could see no sign of his men who had come to that side of the rocks, nor so

much as a glimpse of those who had shouted
Pathan battle cries. Moving cautiously up
through the rocks, with Sid Frith keeping a wary
eye on the dark cave-like bays on their right,
Danny Short was the first to discover one of the
missing sections.

"Sir! Sir!" he called out, crouching over a body.
"It's Veevers, sir," he said as Kyle approached.
"Alive?" asked Kyle, kneeling to lift an eyelid of
a man with, among other wounds, a cutthroat.
Short, nervously watching out for any sign of
those who had done the brutal act, did not
answer.

"Sir!" hollered Gynger Langdon. "I've found
Mitchelhill."

"How is he?" Kyle called back, standing, one
hand stained with blood.

"He's gone, sir," came the reply. "Carved up like
something out of a butcher's window."

"But they were just in front of me - alive – just a
minute ago, they were alive," the officer's own
voice screamed within him.

"Mister Bate, sir."

Kyle turned to find Wilf Ridley leading the main
body of the platoon in a scrambling run back up
the hill.

"Spread out, lads, and keep a keen eye," he
ordered before joining his officer to stand
looking around, sucking in deep breaths.

"Veevers and Mitchelhill are dead, Sergeant
Ridley. Rifles and ammunition's gone, and

Corporal Lyall and one or two others from 2 Section seem to be missing." Kyle didn't give his sergeant this information as an intended situation briefing; it was blurted out to explain the horror around him.

"We'll have a sharpish look around for the missing, sir. But we can't linger about it. It's near dark. We must carry the dead and get down the road as fast as bleedin' monkeys." Ridley wasn't taking charge; he could see his young officer was struggling with the shock of losing men under his command and needed to be reminded of his duties to the rest.

"Right! Right, Sergeant Ridley!" responded Kyle. "You see to the bodies; I'll organize a search for the missing."

This search proved fruitless because two of the missing, Lyall and Payne, were nowhere nearby. Half a mile to the north, at the base of the hill, Benedict was tearing his shirt into strips to bandage Joey's injuries. These wounds were exposed to the bone and became more painful by the minute.

Tommy Gilbert lay undiscovered, temporarily insensible, and collapsed in a narrow gap between two rocks. Undiscovered, that is, by 6 Platoon, but not by the Pathan women who, on their men's victorious return to the villages, flocked out in a band, retracing their steps up into the hills to the scene of the earlier ambush. Dragging Gilbert to a suitable spot, they first stripped him naked before cutting away his genitals, then severing his fingers and toes; they entertained themselves by slicing strips of flesh from the soles of his feet. Mercifully his barbarous torture ended in drowning as the women took turns urinating in his mouth. Their final enjoyment was to expertly flay the skin intact from his body and carry it away with them in triumph as a trophy.

Joey Payne was lapsing into fits of unconsciousness induced by blood loss when he heard Gilbert's screams in a foggy state of unreality. Benedict Lyall, on the other hand, had no such relief and was only able to grip his rifle while he crouched on guard and cursed the harrowing screams that were echoing off the Khyber hills. The following day, the Queen had spent the night in a defensive position on the road and re-occupied the hills. B Company was sent up to where 6 Platoon had suffered their ambush and swept through the rocks scouring the ground for those who were missing. The butchered remains of Tommy Gilbert, wrapped in rubber ground sheets, were carried off for burial at Landi Kotal.

Before dawn, Benedict Lyall had helped a drowsy Joey Payne to his feet and guided him along the edge of a valley, finding a more defensible hiding place. Benedict knew that two British soldiers, with only one of them armed and lost in the Khyber, would merely be game for the local tribesmen to hunt down, kill, and rob. With this thought, he was reluctant to leave their hideout during daylight. However, Payne's wound kept bleeding, and by noon, he was on the brink of delirium.

"Come on, my old friend," Benedict encouraged Joey, swatting the flies off his wounds before assisting him up. He then took Joey's strong left arm, which was tightly holding his bayonet, and guided his mate along the edge of a valley. Disoriented, but choosing his path using the sun as a guide, Lyall maneuvered in the direction he hoped would lead to the road, staying undercover when he could. While taking respite below the edge of a dried, shallow nullah, he tried unsuccessfully to make Joey drink water from his canteen. The wounded man was parched, but every time his corporal offered the spout to his lips, he would reject it, spitting the water out. Despite his delirium, Joey's subconscious still made him refuse the contents of his canteen.

As Lyall readied to continue, he heard faint sounds from across the valley. He cautiously peered over the edge of the nullah and saw a line of pack animals crossing the valley entrance, a quarter mile away. Overwhelmed with relief and joy, he pulled Joey out of the nullah and began leading him in a clumsy run towards the pack train, guarded by soldiers in khaki uniforms.

"Come on, Joey lad, give it all you've got," Benedict encouraged through gritted teeth. "We're safe! Almost safe! Rescued by the bloody gunners, God love 'em!"

"On the caravan track, used by a mountain battery of artillery to march up the Khyber, an officer called for a halt. His men stopped walking, and from an adjoining valley, two men emerged. One was clutching a rifle, and the other was repeatedly falling and shouting at them in English. The lieutenant and two of his Punjabi Mussulmans' gunners intercepted the two fugitives, a hundred yards from the track, as they emerged from the dangerous country.

Benedict Lyall stood at attention with Payne slumping to the ground and saluted. When he explained who they were to the first officer, a second officer joined them with quick, energetic strides.

"Who do we have here, Bertie?" he asked, as he took a pipe from his mouth. He was a Major, the Battery Commander.

"Two infantry guys, sir. Survived an ambush and have been on the run," replied the lieutenant. "Hmm! Queen's Light Infantry, huh?" commented the Major, with a glance at the metal badge fixed to the cloth pugri on the side of Lyall's topee, which showed a fleur-de-lis and the letters QLI above a lightweight Infantry bugle.

"Your mate here, Corporal, he seems to have come out worse from the encounter," said the Major, kneeling to inspect Payne's wounds. Payne's body and uniform were encrusted with dried blood.

"He is in great shape compared with the two Pathan fellows who fancied their luck, sir," assured Lyall, tapping his blood-streaked bayonet."

"Good show," said the Major, scratching a cheek with the stem of his pipe. His eyes showed faint admiration before turning to give his junior officer a set of instructions. "Bertie, send one of your guys to fetch my horse and ensure this wounded fellow is mounted." Turning to Lyall, he said, "We set a cracking pace, but your Light Infantry; if you've still got your legs about you, we'll have you in Landi Kotal in just over an hour."

Payne was taken to the small hospital inside Landi Kotal fort. After his wounds were cleaned, he had an x-ray. This magical contraption, showering sparks every which way, showed his shoulder to be broken in three places. A week later, with his strength back and his wounds healing, Joey was sent south for special attention. First, to a military hospital at Rawalpindi, then high into the Darjeeling hills for therapeutic convalescence.

In the officers' mess that evening, Kyle Bate deliberately sat alone. He had repeated his story of the ambush dozens of times in the last twenty-four hours and was thoroughly sick of it. Time and time again, he blamed himself for not preventing it from happening. It was his fault for not choosing a different route beforehand. It was his fault for not deciding to remain on the hill overnight to be safer.

"Not drinking, Kyle?" The lieutenant looked up to see Captain McQuaid standing next to him, holding a glass in each hand - one with double whiskey, the other with a full tumbler of brandy.

"Oh, no, sir. Not in the mood," replied Kyle.

"Well, you should celebrate then," suggested the quartermaster, who was sitting on the chair opposite Kyle. "I had a conversation with that political officer. He told me that the insurgents didn't get away with it. It seems that in one of the village burial grounds, three more banners are flying to keep the evil spirits away from the graves of three new entries to paradise. It appears your Corporal Lyall evened up the score."

Bate, who was staring at the floor with dejection, looked up to find McQuaid offering him the glass.

CHAPTER 11

Beauty without virtue is a flower without perfume.
-French Proverb

Placing his pen next to the inkwell on his desk, Robin Cuimein leaned back in his chair, taking a break from the piles of correspondence and reports that incessantly demanded his attention yet were never fully cleared away. As June drew to its end and summer's oppressive atmosphere sucked the last bit of moisture from the Ranhar District before the monsoon's arrival, Hemlata ordered Madar, the bungalow's "tatti-wallah," to remove the khas-khas frames from the doors and windows. Part of Madar's job also included splashing cups of water on the outer rims, as the cooling, damp air no longer circulated through the room. This helped to prevent the room temperature from climbing too high, while it also got rid of the dank, musty smell.

The sub-district officer rose from his desk and strolled out onto the shaded veranda. He gazed at a patch of green grass that was tended to by Anil the mali, while the rest of the garden was a dust-laden wasteland with withered vegetation. Looking beyond his property's ridge towards the town of Chamblapur, Cuimein's eyes strained, but he spotted something unusual: an automobile kicking up a trail of dust had halted at the train station. Intrigued by the vehicle's arrival, Cuimein stood still, watching as they proceeded, turning towards his ridge.

As the car vanished into the barren land below, Cuimein was puzzled over the driver's choice of route. The road bypassing his bungalow led to nowhere significant— it was mainly villages and farmland. However, as a swirl of dust settled, the car roared through his front gate, harshly grinding the gravel beneath it. He had never seen such an automobile before— a touring car with an open top and rounded body. The driver, the only occupant, hopped out of the car. He was dressed in a topee, blouse, and jodhpurs and took off his goggles and muslin scarf that had protected his nose and mouth from the dust. His familiar features were now exposed.

"Collector," Princess Krishna called out, "you have a visitor. Come and greet me." As he approached her car, she asked, "What do you think of the motor?" Cuimein admired the boldness of the car, despite being surprised by her sudden arrival. Krishna explained that it belonged to Sahil and that she had borrowed it. When he asked how far she had driven, she nonchalantly replied that she had come from Pankaar, which was almost three hundred miles away. Cuimein suggested they move to the shade and asked Hemlata, the housekeeper, to bring them some drinks. Krishna noticed Hemlata's appealing figure and wrongly accused Cuimein of having her as his mistress. He denied the accusation and found the situation amusing, not understanding the reason for her sudden visit. Four months ago, they had a night of love in Udaigarh, but Krishna acted as if nothing had happened afterward, avoiding being alone with Cuimein to indulge in sensual pleasures.

"Are your family members doing well?" he asked, hoping to understand why the Princess had driven so far into British India. "Oh yes, everyone is fine. The Court has relocated to the summer palace on Mount Abu," she replied, "except for my father. He has remained at Pankaar. Matters of state have always been a priority for him, even over his own comfort and peace."

Hemlata, Cuimein's housekeeper, offered them a tray with large glasses of fruit juice. "You will like this, Princess. Mango and lime juice; it's quite refreshing," said the Collector. "Mmm, delicious," agreed Krishna, taking a sip. "And where do you get ice, Collector? In the summertime?"

"I've been afraid to ask," replied Cuimein with a mischievous expression on his face. "But, as you can see, Hemlata isn't just a decorative piece of furniture. I'm sure if asked, she could produce manna from heaven." Krishna took another sip of her drink and leaned back, savouring its fantastic taste.

"You have a menagerie in your ceiling, Collector," she commented calmly. Her eyes rested on the hessian cloth on the room's ceiling, which prevented flakes from falling. She saw something scurrying across its netting.

"Oh, it's nothing to worry about. Just small snakes, lizards, and the occasional bat," Cuimein dismissed. They both enjoyed their drinks in silence for a few seconds, while Krishna stretched out her legs fully.

"Your revenge was quite complete, you know," began the Englishman, his words prompted by long glances at the woman, knowing what rapturous delights lay hidden beneath her dust-coated clothing.

"I'm sorry?" she asked.

"The night you came to me at Udaigarh," he explained. "You allowed me entry to paradise, only to shun me later. Every night I lay awake hoping for you to return. When you left, I felt like Don Jose to your Carmen."

"I am not a harlot, Collector. I have only had two other lovers, both young. The first was in England," Krishna began softly, drawing up her legs and cradling the glass in both hands. She paused and locked gazes with him.

"You turned down the Maharaja's award in tribute to your brave leadership of his soldiers.

He holds you in the highest regard, as you know. You have done what he wished: to lead the Jaswara Legion into battle. I gave myself to you in payment for a Rajput State's debt of honour."

"Of the two offers, I will be eternally thankful that I had the courage to refuse the first one," Cuimein confessed truthfully, breaking the ensuing silence.

"Collector, I have a favour to ask," Krishna said, first looking at her glass, then up at him. "Would you like to have me as a house guest?"

"Yes! It would be my pleasure! But this is a sub-district officer's bungalow," Cuimein pointed out. "What you see is all I have. It's far from posh; I sleep there on a charpoy on the lawn at night."

"Then so shall I," replied Krishna, glancing to where he pointed.

"Is there a possibility of any hanky-panky between us?" asked Robin jokingly, hoping that there might be. "Because if so, I'm not sure how the servants would react."

"Hanky-panky!" Krishna laughed. "No, Collector, there won't be any hanky-panky."

"My bad," said Cuimein, continuing the joke before asking, "Will you stay long?"

"Maybe a few days. I have come because I need time to think. The Maharaja has proposed another suitor," replied the young woman, her tone becoming serious.

"A warrior?" asked Robin, matching her sombre tone.

"We have met. He's a nice boy," Krishna answered, her tone shifting. "He's the son of a Clan Chief."

Cuimein expected to hear more, but his dark, alluring, travel-soiled guest sat as if in a dream.

"Hemlata, we have a house guest. Princess Krishna will be staying," he informed his housekeeper as she came to refill their glasses. "Please arrange an early bath for her. Then we will have supper at about eight."

--oOo-

The following day, as was his routine, Cuimein woke up before dawn. As a sub-district officer, he had the responsibility of tending to his jurisdiction year-round. Krishna also woke up early to accompany him, despite Robin telling her that their time for entertaining her was limited. They had a light breakfast of coffee and scrambled eggs while Cuimein's syce saddled and prepared his two horses. His first task of the day was to settle a dispute between two farmers in a village five miles southeast. He would then travel two more miles to a town court building where he would handle minor litigations and affrays. Although Cuimein had the authority to pass small sentences and impose substantial fines, his powers were limited to judging. He could review the rulings of his tansildars, subordinate magistrates, but serious crimes like robbery or murder were handled by a Sessions Judge.

Krishna offered her car for the journey, but Cuimein declined as he preferred to travel on horseback. Horse riding gave him the ability to listen to the sounds of the land, observe the crops as they grew and ripened, and most importantly, made him accessible to the people. The junior members of the Indian Civil Service oversaw rural India. However, they were rarely highly regarded by those they served due to their backgrounds. Most were brought up to play fair and trust people at their word. They followed principles of dignity, honesty, and incorruptibility as they performed their roles. Yet, from the perspective of the villagers, who made up ninety percent of the population, they were the straw binding the clay bricks of their land.

Krishna witnessed this first-hand when they were a few miles into their journey. At a junction where they crossed a cart track, they were greeted by a barefoot farmer in a turban and loincloth. Cuimein returned his polite greetings in Urdu and continued to walk his horse. When the farmer asked about their destination and offered a shorter route, Cuimein stopped to sit and chat with him for a few minutes. He listened to the directions given and asked about the farmer's harvest. This seemingly idle chit-chat was a disguise for the real reason the Indian had intercepted the saheb.

The farmer had a concern, which Cuimein recognized when he offered directions. However, the farmer didn't explicitly state his problem. Taking the initiative, Cuimein addressed it. "My good friend," he began, "I can see you're troubled. Tell me, what is it?" Relieved, the farmer admitted to having a problem which he hoped the sahib could solve. He led Cuimein to his mango plantation, where a dry irrigation ditch was causing an issue. At first, Cuimein couldn't understand the problem and asked for more information. He learned that a neighbour had diverted the water flow from their shared supply, which was lifted from the well by a hide bag handled by oxen. Cuimein made a mental note to inform the tehsildar about the issue, and assured the farmer that his problem would be resolved. After their interaction, Cuimein and Krishna continued on their journey.

Dealing with such grievances had become routine for Cuimein, but he always treated them with sincerity and did his best to ensure they were resolved properly. As the Sub-District Officer and the Honoured Saheb, he knew that people relied on him for assistance.

After riding for another twenty minutes, they arrived at the site of Cuimein's first official business of the day. A group of men were waiting for him under a cypress tree. They were involved in a dispute over land ownership between two fields, and both parties had requested an earlier resolution so that a crop could be planted by the new owner. Cuimein had planned to deal with this issue during his tours after the monsoon but had arranged for a meeting that morning to settle the matter. Upon dismounting their horses, Cuimein was greeted first by the village headman, who lowered and folded his shading umbrella out of respect for the sub-district officer. Two men in baggy trousers took charge of the horses while a charpoy was set up for Cuimein to sit on, shaded from the sun by overhead branches. At this point, the headman introduced Cuimein to the patwari, who kept a record of land survey and ownership for every field, including who worked it and what crop it produced. This system ensured that there was no dispute over who was accountable for paying the land tax, a practice that the British continued from the Mogul Empire. The successful method of collecting taxes from peasant farmers, known as zamindari, was so effective that it was believed that the British would have invented it had it not already existed.

After examining the survey map of the disputed property and reading the land documents recorded in Sanskrit, Cuimein met the two parties in the dispute - two zamindars who owned adjoining fields. One zamindar employed a riot or cultivator to tend his fields, and this riot had begun planting on a small wedge of marshland that he reclaimed by building a bank around it. The second zamindar discovered this and believed the marshland to be his, which led to the complaint being brought to the village headman but eventually ended up on Cuimein's desk as the responsibility for land settlement fell under the 'Collector Saheb.'

After hearing the claims of ownership from the two zamindars and the riot, Cuimein requested to be taken to the property in question. Upon examining the surveyed map and documents recorded by the patwari, he concluded that the plot of reclaimed marshland was no larger than a good-sized room, and clearly fell within the boundary of the second zamindar's holdings. However, he decided that the first zamindar and the riot should be compensated for contributing to the expansion of the second zamindar's lands.

Next on Cuimein's agenda was to preside over a misconduct case. As he arrived at a humble township in his district, he was greeted respectfully by both Muslims and Hindus, with the Hindus showing their respect through a traditional hand gesture. On either side of the earth-stamped street, residents could be seen spinning their own cotton in support of Mahatma Gandhi's boycott of foreign-made cotton goods.

The court building, constructed from mud brick, was small and low-roofed. Due to the summer heat, the proceedings were to be held on the veranda. Gathered around the building were various groups: those with lawsuits to file or defend, individuals accused of petty crimes ready to prove their innocence and assembled witnesses. If more witnesses were needed, they could be recruited from under the tamarind tree situated in front of the court for a reasonable fee.

Cuimein's visits to the court building were infrequent, usually limited to checking records or inspecting the court. On this occasion, however, the magistrate was ill, and to alleviate the backlog of civil suits and petty crimes, Cuimein had decided to preside over the proceedings himself. He entered the building to confer with the court reader about the list of cases, while Krishna walked across the open square to a group of jack trees where a group of women were gathered.

Krishna exchanged namaste with the women and introduced herself. She explained that she was a house guest of the Saheb Collector and asked to join them in the shade. One of the women, a crone with blackened teeth, spoke up, teasingly referring to Krishna as a "Begum" and pointing out that a man who visits a widow in their street is not considered a house guest. Krishna replied jokingly by referring to herself as the "Honoured Saheb's strumpet," causing the women to erupt with laughter. She then took a seat among them.

Cuimein completed all the proceedings at eleven o'clock, as the day's temperature was nearing its peak. Krishna joined him at the horses, surprising him by holding his arm and gesturing towards the women, who once again burst into laughter. When Cuimein asked her about it, she promised to explain it to him one day, a mischievous twinkle in her eyes.

As they departed the town, Krishna asked Cuimein about the action he had taken in the Harilal Chopra case. Cuimein replied, "You mean the man who alleged that someone intentionally drove a bullock cart up and down his tomato patch? I dismissed the complaint because it seemed too incredible to be true. Furthermore, the bullock cart driver was merely passing through and had no intentions of causing such malicious harm."

"The Princess assured Cuimein that he had made the correct decision. When asked how she knew this, she explained that the farmer was away and the cart bullocks had wandered into the tomato fields to eat the tomatoes while the driver was having an affair with the farmer's wife, as the wife had told her.

Cuimein and Krishna spent the hot hours of the day sheltering in a government Post House before returning to Chamblapur to check the progress of the Jheel project. They returned to the bungalow to find Hemlata working doubly hard to provide two rounds of bath water. Cuimein realized the primitiveness of his domestic living style, with only a galvanized metal hip bath and a commode for sanitation. They had supper at eight, with Cuimein dressing up as it was his duty, followed by reading reports and correspondence. They enjoyed delightful conversation over coffee and brandy on the lawn until around eleven before returning to change before retiring. The servants arranged their beds on the lawn, ensuring they were draped with mosquito nets and raised in water saucers to deter ants, as it was impossible to sleep in the bungalow due to the heat.

Over the course of two weeks, Krishna established a pattern of staying with her host, accompanying him on his duties, and providing him with social companionship in the evenings. Cuimein was worried that Hemlata might react negatively to Krishna's presence, but this unease proved unfounded for two reasons. First, Krishna was a respectful guest who did not impose herself on the servants. Second, she won over Hemlata and her son David with her kindness, even driving David to school and helping him with his homework. Hemlata invited Krishna into the kitchen to show her how the food was prepared, an act of courtesy that Robin had only been able to achieve twice.

During a routine inspection of a police station and two schools, they encountered a young girl from an Untouchable community who was about to give birth. In a society that operated a harsh caste system, the Untouchables were considered unclean and only fit for the most menial tasks. Cuimein was unsure how to help, but Krishna took charge by asking him to cradle the girl's head in his lap. She then examined the girl and helped her through the difficult birth. In doing so, Krishna violated her caste and brought disgrace to herself in the eyes of all Hindus.

"She is very close. I can almost see the head," said Krishna as she took out a pocket handkerchief to place it to the side. She removed her topee and unwrapped a silk scarf that had been covering her neck for protection from the sun. Feeling the baby moving down, the young girl instinctively drew her knees up and forced her legs apart, overwhelmed with the sensation to push.

"Good job, little mother," encouraged Krishna as she rolled up the cuffs of her shirt sleeves. "Push! Push with all your might." This went on for three to four minutes, and the girl groaned in pain, gripping Cuimein while repeatedly straining. Finally, the head freed itself into the open.

Krishna encouraged the young mother, saying, "Great job, little girl, your child is coming. Now bear down! Bear down!" The baby's head turned to face one thigh, and Krishna wiped its nose and mouth with her handkerchief to clear away the fluid. The young mother pushed with all her might, and first, one shoulder and then the other came into view. Krishna grasped the upper portion of the baby and delivered the infant into the world, placing it on the scarf on the mother's abdomen. The new-born's lips turned from blue to pink and then opened to cry as it started to breathe.

"Robin, do you have a knife?" asked Krishna as she looked around. Cuimein fumbled in his pocket before pulling out a penknife. Krishna took the umbilical cord in the fingers of one hand, folded it over, and cut it at the bend. Then, she gently eased the placenta from the mother, tying a knot that attached to the baby. She cast the afterbirth aside.

"Be a proud, brave mother; it's a son," complimented Princess Krishna as she enveloped the baby in her silk scarf, handing him to the girl. "I'm so grateful, memsahib. You have been so kind," thanked the mother, weakly beginning to regain her senses.

Seeing several figures running from the hutted village's horse-drawn cart, Cuimein lifted the mother and the baby into his arms to carry them to the track. Enveloped in tearful praise from the youthful father and his family, Cuimein and Krishna watched as they returned to their village with joyous relief. Beside the track, a rill trickled from a large earth-banked water tank. Krishna rinsed the bloodstains from her hands.

"That was very brave of you," said Cuimein to Krishna.

"Delivering a baby is generally not a problem. I have seen it done many times in our state clinics," dismissed Krishna.

"I was not referring to the birth," replied Cuimein, his meaning veiled.

"Oh, you mean the violation of my caste?" asked Krishna as she raised her head, slowly and deliberately speaking.

Cuimein answered with a silent nod.

"I believe the loss of caste is very much a state of mind," she informed him, wiping her hands on the legs of her jodhpurs. "I see no need to forsake my soul because of it."

"Princess, you're the most remarkable woman I have ever known," said Robin, taking a long moment to reply.

"Collector!" exclaimed Krishna, bursting into laughter. "You English! An American would have swept me into his arms. A Frenchman would have seduced me with a velvet verse of romantic flattery. But you! You! Remarkable! Oh, Collector."

Abruptly, Krishna's amusement died away; perhaps his face had shown a hint of discomfort with her words. "Upon reflection," she continued with a tone of apology, "I have never been called remarkable before." As the landscape turned a mellow crimson, the Princess interrupted their return, halting beside a small lake. She dismounted and walked down to the stalls where chiraghs were sold. A Hindu shrine depicting Lakshmi, the goddess of fortune, was set back from the lake's edge. Chiraghs were clay saucers holding a cotton wick in oil, floated on the lake to reveal fortunes. To maintain buoyancy signified good luck, while sinking foretold ill fortune. Cuimein sat in his saddle, holding Krishna's horse as she crouched at the shore to launch her saucer. A warm breeze from behind her gently ushered the small flame past the cluster of shallow water lotus pads. Then his eyes were distracted by a flock of flamingos, blood red in the sunset, taking flight from the reeds on the far side of the lake. The saucer of light had sunk, and his companion was walking back.

Krishna had not given a reason for her stop to test the goodwill of the goddess Lakshmi, but he suspected why. "I have been your guest for too long, Collector," she told him, taking her horse's reins. "I will leave tomorrow."

"Before five the next day, she said goodbye to Hemlata at the foot of the veranda steps. From somewhere, David produced a garland of flowers, standing on tiptoe to place them around her neck. "Will you come again?" asked Robin as he saw her into the car. "I have enjoyed my holiday with you and this place, especially young

David. It was just the tonic I needed," she replied, avoiding his question. "You should come after the monsoon," he pressed, hoping for a positive response. "You've shown your appreciation of my visit," she replied, fingering the garland, still not answering. "I should be leaving something that reminds you of my stay." "You provided the district with a new baby. That surely is a gift enough," pointed out Cuimein, giving up on a definitive answer from her. "Besides," he continued, "I already have a token of yours, which I treasure."

Krishna took up the driver's seat of the car as he opened his cigarette case, carefully picking out a single stem of straw. "You left this under my bed in the tent the night you led me through the garden of delights," he said. The Princess looked and knew it must be the straw she had concealed behind her ear and dropped under the bed when he first laid her below the mosquito net. As a Rajput woman of noble birth, this traditional gesture of sleeping on nothing but a bed of straw was something she had retained since childhood. "Collector, I must go," she said. Ignoring his statement, she bid him farewell and held out her hand to shake his. "We'll meet again."

As the car sped out of the driveway, his heart was filled with loneliness. Before her arrival, he desired nothing; his job was all he needed. However, within a few seconds, he already missed her company during their rides, her presence across the dinner table, and their conversations after sunset on the lawn. Above all, he knew he would miss the mornings when she emerged from the charpoy, standing in the fading starlight, her nightdress providing little protection for the graceful form it embraced.

CHAPTER 12

No bending knee will call thee Caesar now.
-William Shakespeare

During the scorching summer months, it was a
tradition for the garrisons of the Northwest
Frontier to dispatch most of their troops to the
cooler northern hills. However, not all soldiers
were fortunate enough to take this break from
the sweltering heat of the Indus Plains, as this
was the Frontier. When one battalion departed
for their break, another company would take
over their stations to ensure their safety.
There was a small encampment outside
Peshawar, enclosed by a compound that was
typically manned by a whole regiment. However,
the Royal Norfolks had retreated to the
Himalayan Mountains to escape the hot season.
The encampment usually housed a thousand
men throughout the year, courtesy of the double
rows of brick-walled and iron-doored bunkers
that stored the garrison's war ammunition. A tall
double barbed wire fence enclosed the battalion
lines, with an even taller inner fence surrounding
the ammunition compound. A trench was dug
inside the outer fence, with squat, roofed
sandbag sangars at each corner for patrols. The

main entrance had a guardroom that overlooked the twin gates, and there was an additional gate at the entrance to the ammunition compound, which was also guarded.

On a muggy August evening, Lieutenant Hugo du Rand and a tall havaldar from his company arrived at the ammunition compound's gate. As the duty officer of the day, he was on his inspection tour after the lights-out signal was sounded.

After completing his probation with the 2nd Queen's Light Infantry, he joined his desired regiment, the 13th Frontier Force Rifles, after graduating from Sandhurst. His battalion, the 7th, was not composed of a single class, but consisted of companies that included different warrior classes and religious castes. For example, the 1st and 2nd Companies were Pathans from the Swat Valley tribes, whereas the 4th Company was composed of Sikhs from western Punjab, and the 3rd Company comprised Jats, who were farmers and herders from the southern banks of the Indus River. Despite his initial preference for one of the Pathan Companies, he considered himself fortunate to serve as an officer with the Jats by the end of his first year. He observed that the confirmed vegetarians, by religion, were dutiful, uncomplaining, loyal, and easy to command.

As the guard for the day, a member of his platoon opened the compound gate as their company and the Sikhs took turns guarding the camp. Meanwhile, the Pathans watched over their own lines in the Peshawar Military Cantonment located a few miles to the north. They then marched to the guard hut, where the corporal in charge had the off-duty guards formed outside, called them to attention, and saluted. After inspecting the guards and their hut, he and Havaldar Des Ram inspected the bunkers to ensure all were locked and secure. The constant monitoring of arms and ammunition was crucial because they were highly valued on the frontier. To the Border Pathan, a rifle was more valuable than wealth, as it was his means of survival, protection, and the tool he could use to kill his enemies and rob from them. Despite dismissing the possibility of an attack on the Peshawar garrison, the British were aware that the Pathan was a cunning thief. Therefore, two companies guarded the compound to deter him. Though the British believed an uprising could be forewarned by their Border political officers, they knew that assumptions were often not accurate on the border.

There were two borders on the North-West Frontier: one between India and Afghanistan, and a second, known as the Administrative Boundary, on the Indian side. Britain governed only up to this Administrative Boundary. Between these two borders, the Pathan tribes and clans lived much as they had for centuries.

In theory, Delhi exercised the rule of law over them, but in practice, they managed their own affairs and only complied with British directives when a brigade-sized column of troops visited. In recent months, the Amir had tried to introduce education for women on the Afghan side of the border. This action sparked outrage in a country that adheres to strict Muslim teachings, resulting in a rebellion in the Khost Valley. The Amir managed to control the situation by executing several of the ringleaders. However, the Fakir of Matun, along with his three sons and approximately twenty loyal followers, managed to escape across the border into tribal lands. He was a fanatical leader who sought to incite the clans to Jihad, a holy war against the Amir.

Initially, the Fakir failed to recruit many Pathans with his call to religious fervor. However, he changed his approach when he reached the homeland of the Afridi. He addressed his call to the women, who then pressured their men to prove their manhood by using their rifles and bloodying their knives. The Fakir also provided an incentive: explosives that he had brought from Afghanistan. He promised to amass rifles and ammunition with his explosives, and his force began to grow. By the time they crossed the Administrative Border, he had rallied over two thousand men.

Despite their large size, the hostile group wasn't discovered until they reached the outskirts of Peshawar. Sepoy Girdhala saw two Afghan traders outside the camp's main gate. He let them go when they claimed to have rich goods for sale only to British warriors. When they disappeared, they hurried towards the bazaar. Girdhala, who was initially uninterested, noticed a missing bundle from the packhorse as the party left. He alerted the Havaldar commander, suspecting the traders had left something behind. Looking towards the bazaar, he saw movements and a crowd of men rushing towards him. A blast knocked him back, and he struggled to recover as gunfire erupted from hidden riflemen. Inside the compound, Hugo du Rand and Des Ram were shocked by the sudden battle. They saw attackers outside the wire and the destruction of the outer gate. The guardroom was in chaos, with the guard commander motionless and the naik ordering his men to take positions around the guard hut. The gate sentry couldn't fire due to his weapon's ineffectiveness. The peaceful night had suddenly turned violent, with the anticipated enemy of loose wallahs replaced by tribal attackers.

The duty officer and the havaldar raced towards the guard hut, pistols drawn. du Rand fell in beside the naik, praising him for the quick deployment of the guard, while trying to formulate a plan to stall or repel the attack. The unarmed havaldar had thrown himself onto the landing of the guard hut, rolling to open the door and grab the gate sentry's rifle. At that moment, the two prowler guards who had been patrolling the bunkers joined them, increasing their strength to fourteen. The only one left out of the fighting was the tower sentry overseeing the ammunition bunkers.

As a second explosion disintegrated the inner gate, any thoughts of offensive action were immediately swept from the officer's mind. Before the dust had cleared, the tribesmen began infiltrating the camp, under the covering fire of others, through the breach. A handful of sepoys at the gate guardroom heroically refused to retreat. They were the main obstacle preventing the tribesmen from freely flooding through. However, their ability to resist was hampered by fire coming from several angles. As the tribesmen closed in through the destroyed gate, the sepoys were being forced to retreat and drag their wounded back into the guardroom. Observing this, du Rand ordered those around him to focus their fire on preventing the Pathans from rushing in and capturing the guardroom. By doing so, they became the immediate threat to the enemy and drew fire above them, kicking up splashes of sand and dust. The officer yelled in Urdu, instructing them to shoot only when they were certain of hitting a target, as each guard had been issued only twenty rounds.

The stranded sentry crawled back towards the guard hut, but he did not hear Hugo's warning to remain within the safer cover of the gate frame amidst the din of rifle fire. Net Ram, the naik, ran out of ammunition and cursed in frustration. He called out to his office to return to the guard hut and fetch more from the emergency supply kept in a locked metal box embedded in the guard hut floor. He flung himself up the steps, only to be shot dead in the doorway by a bullet through the back of his neck. Without hesitation, Des Ram scrambled across the ground, tumbling over the naik's body to reach the hut. Once inside, he dragged the dead Net Ram across the floor to the open box, as the key was chained around Net Ram's waist.

Hugo du Rand, keeping himself close to the ground, briefly lifted his head to monitor the enemy's growing dominance with bitter anger. They were brazenly closing in on the guardroom in front of him, some even shooting through the door and windows. More and more tribesmen who had initially hung back around the bazaar began sprinting towards the breached gates. Sentries stationed around the perimeter trench engaged them. However, their dozen or so rifles were nothing more than an annoyance to the tribesmen.

On giving an anxious glance toward Kanhaiya, Rand turned sick with outrage. The sepoy, motionless with wounds, was being used as target practice. In a fury, the officer, disregarding his own safety, charged headlong to the rescue of his sepoy. Emptying his pistol in wild ineffective, random shots, he reached the wounded sepoy unscathed by bullets that tore through the air around him. He felt a sting in his pistol arm when grasping the injured man's webbing shoulder strap. Dragging the sepoy to safety, du Rand suddenly felt nakedly exposed; he was a British officer, a Sardar saheb, and the killing of him would be an event recounted around future tribal campfires with boisterous delight for years to come. Now a second bullet found him, ripping through the corner of his mouth, peeling back a bloody leaf of flesh from his cheek. But still, he held fast to the sepoy, reaching last the fold of ground below the guard hut where most of the guards were in defence. In the previous yard of his rescue bid, he took a third, disabling bullet in the hip, which knocked him to the ground. Still, he refused to release his grip on Kanhaiya until both had been pulled to safety by others of the guard.

Despite the pain, du Rand pushed himself up, attempting to give orders, only to find his words garbled by a blood-filled mouth torn open at one corner. Finally, however, these orders were rendered superfluous, for, at that moment, the officer and his small detachment were thrust into the role of spectators.

Coming into view in the camp lines beyond the high bunker walls that first hid them was the battalion's Sikh company. In the lead, pistol in hand, shirt-sleeved and hatless, was the company commander, Major Hearsey. The Sikhs were a tall, handsome race, the men conscious of their appearance to the point of vanity, but this took second place for the moment. Flying from their beds to snatch up rifles, they rushed into battle turban-less, half-dressed and, in most cases, barefoot. Then, dashing to fire positions around the quartermaster's godowns, among the GS wagon park and below the camp water tower, they began bringing fire to bear on the tribesmen besieging the main gate guardroom.

The hill Pathan may have yet to sit on a battle appreciation lecture. He instinctively knew when to strike and when to run. In darts and bounds, the ragged, sandal-shod invaders from the tribal borderlands began flitting away. The semblance of an ordered withdrawal turned to a route as one, two. Then three Lewis guns, positioned in the perimeter trench, began firing burst after burst at anything that moved between the fence and the bazaar. Seeing their centuries-old enemy, the Pathan, in flight, there was no holding the Sikhs. Roaring their war cry, "Sat Sri Akal!" they swept forward, firing on the move, many with securing kangh combs lost, their long manes of black hair flowing behind them.

After retaking the main gate, the pursuit was extended to the bazaar, where several Hindu family shop owners had suffered looting and rape. However, for the rest of the night, the Jats and Sikhs prioritized defending the compound, confining themselves to double guards and platoon-sized patrols around the camp perimeter and the bazaar. The battalion suffered six wounded and five killed, while twenty-one bodies of the attackers were recovered.

The remaining raiders from the Tirah uplands had come for rifles and cartridges. Although their planned thievery was thwarted, they were now present in force, and Peshawar was rife with their other sources of booty.

--oOo--

Ten miles east of Peshawar, on the Grand Trunk Road, the 2nd Queen's Light Infantry was on their way back into the heart of Northern India. Having completed their year at Landi Kotal, they had left the Khyber three days ago and were now on the second leg of their night marches. However, this routine would only last part of the journey to their new station at Ravlapore in the United Provinces, forty miles northwest of Lucknow. By the end of the month, they would be overtaken by the monsoon, which would force them to march during the day, a change hardly regarded as a reward since they would spend most of the time soaked from rain.

At the head of the battalion were three men on horseback: the second-in-command, the adjutant, and the commanding officer, Lieutenant-Colonel Claude Gabson. In command of the 2nd QLI for over two years, his departure was only a few miles away. The morning halt for the battalion was to be at the garrison station of Nowshera. There, God willing, and with a bit of effort from the Indian railway system, he would be reunited with his wife. After his promotion to full colonel, following favourable reports on his command of the battalion during the disaster at Jhendara and his year at Landi Kotal, he and his wife planned to spend a month holidaying around the lakes and valleys of Kashmir before taking up his new posting at the staff college in Quetta.

Major Spears, the second-in-command, would lead the battalion to Ravlapore, where a new commanding officer awaited them. There were rumors among the companies that they would board a train at Nowshera for the rest of the journey. However, the soldiers didn't put much stock in this; most bets were on a long march.

Near midnight, the encompassing silence of the Grand Trunk Road, punctuated only by the dull rhythm of a thousand marching boots, was interrupted by the high-pitched blare of an automobile horn. The car raced past the marching troops, its headlamps illuminating the faces of the men as they watched it speed by. It skidded to a halt beside the colonel's party, causing their horses to shy away.

"Damn your bones, mister! Have some care for the horses," boomed Gabson, struggling with the reins to keep his horse under control.

The driver, the only occupant, and a young headquarters signals lieutenant, with an expression of alarm, dispensed with any thought of a salute. He stood up in the car and shouted, "Sir! The Afridi are up, Sir!"

A lesser man might have asked the young officer to explain his outburst, identify himself, his source of information, and then clarify what was expected of him.

Claude Gibson, without hesitation, turned to his second-in-command.

"Major Spears, turn the column about. I want Light Infantry bayonets in Peshawar before the sun rises."

--oOo-

By noon the following day, the 6th Platoon was in a static role protecting a track junction to the west of the city. Even though summer was almost over, over half the garrison was still away in the hills. With a town, a large military cantonment, and a Royal Air Force airfield to protect, no force was left to go on the offensive. The orders given to Kyle Bate for his platoon were to keep all marauding bands of Afridi out of the farm villages and city suburbs behind them. Therefore, positioning his rifle sections along a cart track facing west, Kyle held his Lewis gun section back in a cluster of trees where they could cover the track junction. All around were crop fields, the one to their south containing a high stand of maize. Beyond these fields were fruit orchards, where cultivation ended, and the land was broken and scarred with dry nullahs.

With the sun at its warmest, Kyle, from his platoon headquarters, a tree beside the track leading back into Peshawar, found himself about to be visited. Coming from the city, a party of soldiers leading mules were filing out of the baked mud brick village to his rear. Well before they arrived, Bates recognized them as their Dogras machine-gun platoon. Stepping onto the track, he waited for Subedar Dalip Nath to approach.

"Kyle, old man. You're not from A Company, perchance?" asked the Indian officer, the question posed uncertainly.

"Answered Dalip Nath, interrupting Lyall's thoughts. "Have you seen any signs of the enemy?"

Lyall shook his head. "Nothing yet, sir. Just trying to keep the lads on their toes."

The Subedar nodded in understanding. "It is a difficult task, but a necessary one. We cannot afford to let our guard down."

As they spoke, the men in the ditch began to stir, their eyes focusing on a point in the distance.

Lyall followed their gaze and saw a group of
riders approaching.
"Contact!" he shouted, drawing his rifle. The
other men followed suit as the enemy charged
towards them.
The battle was short but intense. Lyall's men
fought bravely, holding off the attackers until
reinforcements arrived. When it was all over,
they counted their losses - two men dead, three
wounded - and thanked their lucky stars that it
hadn't been worse.
"That was a close one," said Nath, shaking his
head.
Lyall agreed. "But we did our duty, and that's all
that matters."
They sat in silence for a while, watching as the
medics tended to the wounded and the rest of
the troops prepared to move out. It was a
reminder that, no matter how long they had
been in this godforsaken place, the danger was
always there, lurking just around the corner.
But as Lyall looked at his men, at the faces of
those who had survived yet another encounter
with death, he knew that they would keep going.
For themselves, for each other, for king and
country.
That was what it meant to be a soldier.
Lyall's head turned sharply back to Sid Frith. He
had removed the straw from his mouth and was
pointing with it towards the maize field to the
south of them. Approaching it from the nullahs

through the orchard at an oblique angle was a party of men in a loose formation, moving in a skulking manner from tree to tree. As the left-hand section, with the maize field obstructing the sight of the rest of the platoon, only he, Sid, Short, and Langdon could see these men making their way to the maize.

With their heads low, Lyall and Frith watched in silence until all the tall corn stalks were covered.

"They're Afridi and not afraid," Frith called in a low voice.

"Too true," agreed Lyall, continuing with an order to Sid: "Get back and find Mr. Bate; I'll keep an eye on those troublemakers in the corn."

Returning twenty minutes later, crawling on hands and knees, came Bate, Sergeant Ridley, and Subedar Dalip Nath.

"And are you sure they're Afridi?" Kyle questioned after Lyall confirmed that the infiltrators had not left the house.

"I'm dead sure, Sir. Each one of those foul-smelling men had a blue turban."

"Yes? Well... What should we do? What now?" the platoon commander voiced his thoughts.

"We could just go in and flush them out, sir," Sergeant Ridley suggested.

"No good, Sergeant Ridley. They would simply escape from the other side as we approached from one. And the field is too large to surround," the officer explained.

"Kyle, may I borrow your binoculars?" Nath asked, who had been scanning the fields to their north with a machine gunner's eye.

"Kyle, do you see that bank where the ground dips?" pointed out Subedar, handing back the glasses after confirming what he could barely make out with the naked eye. "Now, if you could spare me just thirty minutes, I could position two of my Vickers there, and if your men could push through the corn, my men would catch those mountain men as they broke cover."

"That's ruthless, bloody ruthless," Kyle complimented. "Let's do it."

"One point," warned the Subedar, "Make sure you don't come out beyond the maize yourselves. My gunners will be firing at everything on two legs that comes into view."

Sergeant Ridley was sent back to stay with the Lewis gun section while Kyle briefed the section commanders on his action plan. They then waited for the machine gunners to take up their positions. From the track, the rifle sections watched as the Dogra gunners, carrying their weapon parts and ammunition by hand, made a wide detour to approach the bank from the north. Using his binoculars to see the guns being assembled, Bate led his platoon down the track until they were abreast of the maize.

Kyle noted that it was a good hundred yards from the track across an open field, which could prove challenging to reach. The officers, facing the crop in an extended line, began the advance upon the central officer's signal. With bayonets fixed and rifles at the port, they stepped out onto the open ground. They knew that if the Pathan were on the eastern edge of the corn, it could become dangerous. Yet, Bate was banking on the theory that the tribesmen were using the maize as a hideout, waiting for darkness to sneak into the city. Safely reaching the crop, the line paused for a few moments. Then, as Kyle blew a long, loud blast on his whistle, they plunged in. Most entered with dry throats and damp bodies, signs of apprehension for possible injury or death. But they also felt a strong eagerness to confront the Pathan. These men had carried two of their injured mates off a Khyber hill, victims of these people, and had seen the gruesome remains of Tommy Gilbert. Navigating the corn stalks, which were eight feet tall and closely grown, was a challenge. The soldiers were forced to hold their rifles and bayonets vertically to not obstruct their passage. Their topees, wide on their heads, were either dragged off or allowed to fall away due to the nuisance they presented. They hadn't penetrated far when a cheer broke out. The sound of Vickers machine gun fire signalled that the plan was working. The tribesmen, alarmed by the whistle blast, were attempting to escape. Benedict Lyall had seen sixteen figures enter the cornfield, but now eleven were running like rabbits, dodging from tree to tree in a life-or-death hide and seek game with the Dogra machine guns.

Of the other five, three, seeing what awaited them should they follow the others through the orchard, turned south, remaining in the shelter of the maise. Two, crashing through the stalks, broke free of the crop and made their getaway. The third, losing direction, ran at an angle deeper into the field, causing him to cross in front of the platoon's two extreme left-hand men, Short and Langdon. Danny Short, hearing the noise as he forced his way through the corn stalks, stopped to bring his rifle down, going onto one knee, hoping to see more. What he did glimpse ten feet in front was a flash of dirty cloth.

"Gynger, get that bleeder!" he shouted to his mate after firing a shot he knew had missed, unable to swing his trapped rifle fast enough. Whipping his rifle down, Langdon fired instinctively as he suddenly found a bearded and scared, hawk-nosed face appearing through the barrier of stalks. The man dropped from Gynger's sight, but as the soldier followed through, a bullet disintegrating a corn husk passed under his left arm. Swiping with his rifle and bayonet at the growth in his way, he found the Pathan trying to crawl away. Working a fresh round into the chamber with his rifle bolt, he fired into the man's back. As the Pathan slumped face to the ground, Danny Short

crashed past Langdon to bury his bayonet
between the tribesman's shoulder blades.

"That's one for Tommy, you bastard!" cursed
Short between clamped teeth.

Of the two hesitating on the field's fringe, one,
young but brave, turned back into the corn. .
Crouching, he waited, vowing to kill a hated
infidel. But, if he was to die, he intended that his
niche in paradise would first be secured. The
man whose path he blocked was big Bert
Colling, a target that couldn't be missed, the
bullet shattering two ribs on his right side.

"I'm hit! Bugger me!" he cried, dropping to his
knees.

The Pathan, still in his teens, did not yet possess
a modern rifle; he was an old breech loading
single shot Snider with the barrel wired to a
homemade stock. Dropping the rifle, he sprang
forward, snatching a knife from its sheath at his
waist. Then, tearing at the stalks in his way,
trying to get at Colling, who had rolled onto one
side, he was charged down by Jock Cressy flying
at him from one side. Hearing Colling cry out,
he had turned to help and, with his useless rifle
in the air, released his grip to tackle the
tribesman bare-handed.

Tumbling to the ground, he took cuts on his left
shoulder and neck before Cressy could get hold
of the knife arm.

"Ye heathen bastard! I'll gut ye! I'll gut ye!"
screamed the Scotsman, smashing his fist into
the Pathan's grimy face.

Cressy didn't have the other's height, but his
years in the mines had given him powerful arms.
Rolling on top, he held the knife hand down
while his other gouged the tribesman's eyes.
Then, screaming, he clawed with his other hand
at Cressy's, blinding him. The Scotsman, tearing
out one eye, moved his hand to the throat and
squeezed. When Colling struggled to his feet and
retrieved his rifle to help, the young Pathan was
dead, his bid for paradise unfulfilled.

The last raider from the Hills to hesitate on the
crop edge decided to take his chances in the
orchard. Sprinting with all the speed his sandaled
feet could give; he ran headlong through the
fruit trees. But, unfortunately for him, he left it
too late. Behind him, Paani Waters, reaching the
boundary of the cornfield, threw himself down
into an aiming position. His bullet struck the
Pathan in the back, sending him to the ground,
his head flying back, his arms flung wide as he
sprawled onto the hard untilled earth with a
thump.

"His death marked the end of the joint
elimination of this doomed group of hillmen by
Dogra machine-gunners and British riflemen.
Dalip Nath only counted two of those who tried
to escape through the orchard, and possibly
three who managed to evade his Vickers. The

remaining members lay dead or severely wounded among the fruit trees. Over the following half hour, they were all killed, and the bodies were collected at a central point for counting. The first wounded tribesman they approached had tried to kill the closest soldier. By raising the stakes of this deadly game, they paid the price, with Bate ordering his men to finish them off with a bullet or bayonet.

Shortly afterward, in search of an explanation for the sustained use of machine-gun fire, Colonel Gabson arrived accompanied by two majors from the garrison headquarters staff.

"You were attacked, Bate?" the colonel asked from his saddle after silently counting the line of bodies.

"Well, not exactly, sir," replied Kyle, unsure whether to brag or apologize.

"I need a full written report by the evening," commanded Gabson, turning his horse towards Dalip Nath, who was leading his section of triumphant machine gunners to view the results of their work.

"Subedar, didn't I instruct you to join A Company?" the horseman asked sternly.

"Colonel, due to a navigational error on my part, it seems, as General Napier once said, 'peccavi,' I have Sind," answered Nath, quoting Napier's famous message after having unauthorisedly invaded and annexed the Kingdom of Sind for British rule.

"Indeed, you have, sir; indeed you have," replied the commanding officer, suppressing a chuckle. For another three days, the Afridi lurked around the city, searching for weak points that offered opportunities for looting. With the air force sending up search planes, the hillmen hid in the nullahs or with their friendly Pathan brethren who had long ago settled around the city. At night they would raid, some managed to evade the military guard around the walls and pillaged shops in the city's bazaar. Once a group or clan had gathered all it could carry, it would return to the hills. But by the fourth night, whether empty-handed or not, all had decided to leave. The arrival of reinforcements from Nowshera, Rawalpindi, and other garrisons gave them little choice. Upon returning to the Tiran, a tribal jirga was convened to assign blame for the raid's failure. The Fakir of Matun, who had promised to provide a plentiful supply of rifles and ammunition for their young men but failed to deliver, was unanimously blamed. He was consequently told by the tribal elders to leave and never return to the Afridi lands."
Embittered, the Fakir departed with his sons and followers. However, one son had died while attacking the ammunition camp gate. Due to this death and his humiliating loss of face, or 'izzat', he pledged to one day return. He vowed that the British would be made to pay.

CHAPTER 13

Let those love now who never loved before;
Let those who always loved, now love the more.
-Thomas Parnall

Joey Payne walked down the steep hill pathway with a standpipe and a stopcock key balanced over his shoulder, ready to start his morning work. At a small box frame set into the ground, a line of native water sellers was waiting for him to arrive.

"Jai ho!" he greeted everyone cheerfully.

"Jai ho! Saheb," they responded. Most of them were grinning.

Joey placed the stopcock key down and attached the standpipe to a connection inside the box frame. After securing it tightly, he picked up the stopcock key and switched the water supply on.

"OK, pal, let's fill you up," he beckoned the first man forward.

This native, like the others, had a moussaka, a goat leather water skin. He held the open neck under the tap as Payne turned it on. Joey then accepted the quartermaster's voucher slip that each man had purchased and tucked it into his pocket. For a month, he had been filling the natives' moussaka so they could sell the water as drinking water around the English bungalow households. The location was Razar, a hill station west of Darjeeling, one of many places where the British escaped to during the summer to avoid India's sweltering weather. Now it was October, and most families had returned to the plains as the monsoon season was wrapping up. Many had rushed back, but a few had stayed to avoid the torrential rain and the damp, unhealthy conditions brought by the monsoon.

Joey had been away from his battalion for nearly four months due to time spent in hospitals and recovery. He was tired of it and longed to return to his mates. The cut to his shoulder, a result of an attack in the Khyber, had healed without complications though it left a terrible scar. The broken shoulder bone had been the main concern, taking a long time to heal. After two months at Labong, a few miles away, the unit that had cared for him left, so he was transferred here. Now, he was scheduled for a check-up with an army doctor, who would hopefully declare him fit for duty and send him back to the 2nd Queen's.

After the last water seller had filled his mussak and left, balancing it over one hip, Joey turned the water off and removed the standpipe.

"Thank God, that's the last time I'll do this. The QM will have to assign someone else to this task tomorrow," Joey thought to himself.

The unit served as a permanent signals station. During the summer, it operated as a teaching school where Morse code, semaphore, and heliograph lessons were taught. Payne took instruction in all of these in his free time over the last month. Razar was a typical hill station where everything was either inclined or declined, with no naturally level areas. The parade ground, constructed by soldiers over many years, was long and narrow with a high bank wall on one side and a sheer drop of a hundred feet on the other. Bungalows didn't have roads, only footpaths. To move around the station most efficiently, it was best to climb the ridge to the miniature railway and catch a ride on the train. On his way to return the standpipe and stopcock key to the stores, Joey paused to watch a line of women tea pickers as they descended to the tea terraces. Each morning, they passed through carrying empty wooden tea boxes with rawhide straps, returning with them filled in the evening. An hour later, Payne, impeccably dressed in a starched uniform and polished boots, waited on the mission hospital veranda to be seen by an army doctor. Since the station didn't have its own hospital, it utilized the mission's facilities as needed. Every two weeks, an army doctor from Labong conducted surgery. Joey had failed twice to convince the medical officer that he was fit to return to the battalion. However, he was confident about passing the inspection today as he had been continually exercising his arm and shoulder, which was now pain-free, enabling him to perform any challenging physical manoeuvre. Being far from the signal station, Payne had yet to spend time at the mission, having only made two brief visits. It was primarily staffed by Indian or Anglo-Indian doctors and nurses, providing little opportunity for interaction at the standard soldier level. Therefore, he had not seen the blonde nurse who had come out of the bungalow to check on the comfort of two patients in wheelchairs until now. As she exchanged cheerful pleasantries with the two patients, her glance at Joey turned into a stare, her smile transforming into puzzlement. He watched her until she started to walk towards him, pretending not to notice. He was stunned when she addressed him by name.

"Hello, Joey?" Looking up at the nurse with a face shining like an English summer garden, Joey didn't recognize her at first, then suddenly, he became alert.

"Hello, miss," he answered her formally.

"What are you doing here?" she asked. "It's not miss; it's Lily. I'm only a student nurse."

"Oh, right-o then," he replied before explaining that he was waiting to see the army's Medical Officer.

"Oh, yes, your wounds," she said.

"You know about them?" asked Joey, surprised.

"Yes! My uncle wrote and told me," She replied.

"The Regimental Sergeant Major! He told you about me?" questioned the soldier, even more amazed.

Hunt peered at Robin over his spectacles and asked a question.

"Yes, sir. I haven't had any contact with him since," confirmed Cuimein earnestly.

"Oh, I always ask about you in my letters to him," she confessed. "After all, you saved my life." For several minutes, they continued to talk. Joey experienced feelings of polite respect for the young woman's uniform, and her nearness and charm invoked a fascination. Her figure was not hidden by the uniform, belted at the waist with a small yellow belt. She had a shapely body with a high, firm bosom. Her small, upturned nose was, to Joey, cute. Meanwhile, her pale blue eyes, almost grey, seemed a storage of merriment.

Along the veranda, an Indian nurse, also wearing a yellow belt, approached them. "Lily," she said in English, "Matron is asking for you."

"Oh! Sarita, thank you," responded the girl before introducing her to Payne. "Sarita, this is a friend from my uncle's regiment, Joey Payne."

"Very pleased to meet you," replied Sarita, inclining her head to give a faint Mona Lisa smile before turning back down the veranda. "Sarita and I are in the middle of our training together," explained Lily after Joey had responded to the girl's greeting.

"Look, I'm free for the rest of the morning – after seeing the doctor. What are the chances of having a cup of chai together?" asked Payne, desperate for more of the girl's company. (Chai is a Hindi word for tea.)

"I'm working all day, I'm afraid. I don't have any free time," Lily declined, showing disappointment as well.

"Lily! The Matron was insistent that you come right away," warned Sarita politely, having walked a few steps away.

"Yes! Right, I'm coming," answered Lily before proposing an alternative to the soldier: "We hold a small dance here every week. It's tomorrow night. Can you come?"

"I don't know about that; it all depends on the doctor," replied Payne, crestfallen.

"Well, I hope you can. I will keep an eye out for you," she called back, skipping with sidesteps after Sarita.

"It was delightful to see you again, cheerio!"

"Payne," called a Medical Corps corporal, his belt encircling a large belly. Then, standing in a doorway, he pointed over his shoulder. "In here."

"Well, Payne, what's the latest on this shoulder saga of yours?" asked a round-faced captain as he came out from behind his desk to examine the young soldier.

Joey, entering the office to stand at attention, made no effort to salute. Instead, he reached across with his left hand to stroke his right shoulder. "Grim, Sir! Absolutely grim. I must be having a relapse. It hurts something fierce."

Delhi, in October, was a city coming to life. Most Europeans from the business community, military, government departments, and shop owners had returned from the hills following the onset of the monsoon. Still, as the monsoon eased, families also begun to reappear. From the carriage seat of the tonga that was taking him to the Secretariat, Robin Cuimein took in the scene. The familiar activities cantered on familiar surroundings, which he remembered from his first arrival in the city two years earlier. It was a Tuesday morning, and responding to a summons, he had arrived from Chamblapur the day before, spending the night with his ICS colleagues at his old chummery.

Upon reaching the Secretariat, Cuimein made his way through the building to the undersecretary's outer office, where he waited to be shown in after his presence had been announced.

"Good morning, Cuimein, sit down," Hunt welcomed, coming from behind his desk to shake the younger man's hand before indicating he should take a chair.

"I believe nothing unpleasant occurred on the journey?" Hunt inquired in a courteous preliminary to their conversation, returning to sit behind his desk.

"Well, I left in quite a rush, sir. But other than that, nothing," Cuimein replied.

"Oh, that was unavoidable, I'm afraid," the under-secretary offered, giving the closest thing to an apology Robin would get before adding, "I take it that you are in the dark as to why you have been called?"

"Quiet, sir! It's a complete mystery to me," answered the sub-district officer truthfully.

"Yes," replied Hunt, drawing the word out as if pondering Cuimein's honesty. "Your acquaintance with Sir Antony Reimer, how well-rooted is it?"

"Sir Antony Reimer?" Robin responded, giving himself time to remember the name. "We met last February during a hunting weekend at the Maharaja of Jaswara's. He's the Regent there."

"And that's your only connection - a hunting weekend?" Hunt asked, peering at Robin over his spectacles.

"Yes, sir. I haven't had any contact with him since," Cuimein confirmed earnestly.

"Yes, sir," Cuimein affirmed. "We had a few engaging conversations. As I remember, he passionately believed in Britain's continuing involvement in India."

"Well, it seems like you have made a greater impression on him than he has on you," Hunt said.

"He forwarded a recommendation to the Viceroy for you to be considered for posting to the North-West Frontier," he said.

"I'm completely amazed, sir! I have no idea what could have prompted him to do that. However, it is most kind of him," admitted Robin. After saying that, he remembered mentioning to the Regent that he believed the North-West Frontier to be India's Achilles heel and that only the best men in government service should continue to be sent there.

"So, would you consider taking up a post there?" asked Hunt, looking straight at Cuimein.

"Yes, sir. I would love to. But I'm sure it would take more than one recommendation to convince the Viceroy that I am of the right material," Cuimein commented. The comment was made because it was common knowledge throughout the service that anyone picked for the Frontier was of exceptional quality and only selected after a successful personal interview with the Viceroy himself.

"Yes, you are right. That's why we forwarded the others on with it," replied Hunt off-handedly, picking up an interview memorandum from his desk. "Others? What others, sir?" asked Cuimein, startled in his chair.

"Mine for one. The First Secretary's another," answered Hunt in the same matter-of-fact tone, handing the memorandum to Cuimein. "You have an interview with the Viceroy in forty-five minutes."

Breathing deeply, Joey Payne ran onto the railway station platform, searching with bright, expectant eyes for the girl he was to meet. More of a halt than a station, the venue was made of plain concrete with no overhead shelter and a ticket office that was a simple hut. Finding only two middle-aged European women there before him, Joey slowed to a walk with a flutter of disappointment and approached the ticket hut to purchase two tickets. Hurrying through his morning detail with the water sellers, Joey had run from the quartermaster's store onto the ridge top and along it to this rail stops. Last night, Lily Richmond was down to work as the orderly night nurse at the mission, but even so, they had planned to go up the line for a picnic today. The train they were set to catch was a miniature one. Built many years ago, it was intentionally kept small to avoid encroaching too heavily on the limited flat ground available atop the ridge. Hearing a faint whistle down the line, Joey's heart skipped a beat. The train was approaching, and it would be over an hour before it would pass again on its return journey. He walked to the rear of the platform, scanning the path leading to the mission for any sign of Lily. As the train's shrill tooting grew louder, he anxiously alternated his gaze between the rail line and the mission pathway. Eventually, the train came into sight first, chugging toward the platform. Then, Lily appeared on the path, a straw sunhat in one hand, a picnic basket in the other, struggling to run up the hill.

Upon seeing her, Joey leapt down the stone steps and ran along the path to help her. "Crikey, Lily, you cut it close," he exclaimed, nearly laughing at the comical sight of her hurried efforts and his joy at her arrival. He took the basket from her and held her free hand in his, and together, they sprinted back to the platform. The train carriages were so tiny that none were enclosed, just a roof for shelter. The seats were arranged in two long rows, back-to-back, facing outwards. The couple threw themselves into two of these seats just as the toy steam engine began to pull away.

"We have Sarita to thank for this," Lily said, holding the picnic basket on her lap. "She kept me behind this morning to count the dhobi linen, and she prepared this for us." The ridge they were traveling along was not flat. Instead, it resembled the contour of a dragon's back; the rail line had to venture up, over, and down a series of dips and rises. As they climbed, the train slowed to a crawl, but once it crested the hill, it made a rapid descent that was so fast, Lily had to hold onto her hat to prevent it from being swept away by the wind.

Lily and Joey disembarked at the western rail terminus. If the train had a reason to continue further down to the plain, such as carrying passengers or freight, it would proceed from there. But since they didn't need to descend, the small engine and its carriages turned around and started their return journey along a track loop. The terminus was situated at the less popular end of the ridge, surrounded by just a few bungalows and the railway workers' makeshift huts. Lily and Joey soon left these structures behind as they followed a winding trail westward through the towering pines. After an hour's walk, the hillside began to slope down towards the north and west. Feeling fatigued from her night shift, Lily suggested they take a break. Nearly two weeks had passed since they had met on the mission veranda. After finishing his water duties, Joey made a daily trip to see Lily. He would report to the Quartermaster, request permission for a run, inquire about treatment for his shoulder from the hospital staff, or simply ask for time off. Since he was not on station strength and was excused from unit duties, his requests were usually granted. Once at the mission, he would wait for Lily to be free. If she was off duty, they would sit on the veranda and chat, or stroll around the grounds. In the evenings, they would sip tea in the small mission canteen, dance to the tunes of a wind-up gramophone, and had even attended the mission dance on two occasions. Every night, Joey had to sprint along the hilly footpaths in the dark to make it back in time for the bungalow's bed check.

Lily and Joey rested on the grass at the edge of a sloping glade, no larger than a back garden. The chirping and birdsong of blue jays, barbets, and finches filled the air from the pines and rhododendron bushes around them. The sweet scent of wild roses and the tepid rays of a warm, late October sun induced a sense of drowsiness in their limbs, causing them to doze off. A few minutes later, Lily woke up and exclaimed that Mount Everest was in view after the distant grey rain clouds had cleared. Joey also opened his eyes to see the dazzling white tip of the mountain.

Lily spoke about the picturesque view, something worth telling their grandchildren about, and then suggested they open their basket to eat. Joey turned his head to gaze at Lily's eyes, cheeks, lips, and long golden hair, which had kept him awake for many nights recently.

"What I would really like," Joey replied, moving to lay beside her as he touched the sleeve of her lilac patterned dress, "is a kiss." Lily responded with a cheeky smile, asking why she should give him a kiss. Pretending to be dismayed by her response, Joey retorted that it was for saving her life.

Lily laughed and stood up, stepping back and questioning whether he was expecting a reward for his actions. Joey replied that he would consider it a debt to be repaid. She refused to trade a kiss as a penalty for saving her life, but instead promised to give it as a gift in gratitude. She challenged him to come and claim it, throwing back his demand as she fled to the other side of the glade.

Joey was momentarily captivated by Lily's playful demeanour in the enchanting setting. He then chased after her, catching Lily and wrapping her in his arms. Joey asked if she was going to uphold her promise, to which she replied with a tight-lipped smile. He leaned in to kiss her, drawing out quivers of ecstasy with slow, lingering kisses. Lily, having never seriously embraced and kissed a man before, found Joey's actions stirring something within her. Although she did not recognize the feeling, it was nonetheless desire.

As her lips began to react to his, her arms, held at first at her sides, wrapped around the soldier. It seemed they clung together for minutes, neither making a move to release the other's lips. Then, finally, Joey broke the kiss, but only to move his lips to her ear.

"Lily, I love you," he whispered, a rush of hissed words.

"Oh, Joey! Oh, Joey!" she replied. This time it was she seeking his lips, but in doing so, her legs, trembling with newfound craving, gave out, collapsing her backwards and taking Joey with her.

Being on the ground did nothing to dampen their yearning for each other's embrace; if anything, it fuelled their growing lust. Joey's lips had now left Lily's and were hungrily kissing her cheeks and throat. Then, with eyes closed, her mind awash with desirous thoughts, she took one of his hands and placed it on a breast. Joey, beginning to squeeze the soft mound through the fabric of her dress, rushed his lips back to hers, which then began to utter little moans. Finally, with the stimulation of Joey's hand driving her to wanton abandonment, the young nurse unbuttoned the front of her dress to lift her bodice and replace Joey's hand on her now naked breast.

They lay kissing, stroking for half an hour, each advancing the other's inflamed passion. Then, finally, Lily, taking Joey's head in her hands to lift his lips from her breast, said: "Joey, make love to me".

Making love to a girl was not new to Payne. In the late summer months for the last two years of his farm life, he and his brother used to steal out at night across to adjacent farms where the London hop pickers could be found after work singing and dancing. So, when it came to learning about sex, there was no better teacher than a fun-loving East-end girl.

"Have you ever done it before?" he asked in answer.

"No!" replied Lily, shaking her head.

"Then I will not. I don't want to hurt you," he refused, in a tone heavy with compassion.

"Yes, Joey, please. It must happen sometime, and I want it to be with you," Lily's appeal bordered on begging.

"I can't, Lily. I love you too much to cause you pain," Joey replied.

"Please, Joey, don't refuse me," she whispered between kisses on his forehead. "Ever since you saved me from the bungalow at Jhendara, I've dreamed of making love with you. So please, don't disappoint me now, not now."

Joey looked into her eyes, seeing no sign of lust, only the innocent gaze of a virgin lover. Slowly, he reached below her dress and began stroking her thigh.

Lost in time, consumed in the tender passion of their lovemaking, they returned to the mission after dark, their picnic basket untouched. For an hour, they sheltered in the veranda's shadows, kissing and declaring their love before Joey raced back to the signal station before lights out.

The next day, he returned for his fortnightly appointment with the MO. Afterward, he searched the hospital for Lily and found her in a ward beside a patient's bed. A nurse and an older woman in a nursing uniform stood beside her.

"Yes, young man?" demanded the older woman.

"I've been passed fit," Joey told Lily, disregarding the woman.

"So, you're leaving?" Lily guessed; her eyes filled with helpless regret.

"Yes, today," he replied. For the first time since joining the army, he hated it.

"Young man, I don't allow unescorted private soldiers on my wards. So, you will have to--," the older woman began, her voice rising with each word. Oblivious to her, Joey cut her off with an impassioned plea to the young nurse.

"Being in the army, Lily, I can't marry until I'm a corporal. So, if I ask you to marry me, will you wait?" The couple, she nineteen and he twenty, were ten feet apart, with Lily holding paper forms in one hand. She dropped them, and her face lit up with joyful astonishment. She walked two steps towards Joey before flying into his arms. "Yes, Joey. Oh! Yes."

CHAPTER 14

There was two-an'thirty Sergeants,
There was Corp'rals forty-one,
There was just nine hundred rank an' file,
To swear to a touch o' sun.
-Rudyard Kipling

Company Sergeant Major Howard Little rose
from his desk and strolled onto the veranda of B
Company's office bungalow, seeking relief for
his back from the uncomfortable wooden seat of
his office chair. It was late in the morning on a
warm, sunny November day, with the battalion
lines exuding a calm atmosphere despite the
ongoing routine training and administrative
duties. Along the row of company orderly room
bungalows, only the commanding officer's stick
orderly could be seen, sitting outside the
adjutant's office in the battalion headquarters
bungalow. In front of Little, the square was
empty except for a group of junior NCOs being
drilled by RSM Richmond in one corner. Beyond
the deserted yard was the maidan, a dusty plain
dotted with trees where the companies practiced
minor tactics.

Little was a tall man with narrow shoulders and a
protruding waistline that gave him more of a

comical music-hall performer's appearance than that of a dashing soldier. His walk was more of a waddle. Seated or standing, he was not an impressive sight with his dark hair parted in the middle and a half-sized moustache with a quarter-inch gap at the centre. The ends of his moustache were waxed and twirled, making it look like two mice on the verge of mating. His idle viewing of the lines was interrupted by a buzzing sound. Looking up at the veranda's eaves, he spotted a hornet's nest, as large as a skull, constructed in one corner.

"Here, lad," Little called out to Paani Waters, who just happened to be passing by the veranda. "Take that down." Paani, halting to attention, glanced at Little and then towards the nest he was indicating. Not uttering a single word, he looked down at his feet, picked up a stone, and threw it at the nest. The nest crashed down only a foot away from Little's toes."

"Little, who was sprinting beside Waters towards the maidan, yelled out ten seconds later, "Why on earth did you do that?"

"Because you commanded me to, sir," Waters yelled back as he sped ahead.

"But I didn't mean that soon," Little retorted, gasping for breath.

From his observation point outside the adjutant's office, Joey Payne, the CO's orderly, witnessed everything and began to laugh uncontrollably. He hadn't experienced a moment of joy since returning from Razar, where he was held responsible for the loss of a rifle. Although the circumstances of the loss were known, being accountable for the rifle, it had to be accounted for. Unfortunately, Payne was the only survivor of the ambush, and the cost of the lost rifle had to be covered by the regiment. As lenient as possible, the CO fined Payne the exact cost of the rifle: four pounds, three shillings, and sixpence.

Despite it being a significant blow to his finances, costing nearly three weeks' wages, Joey took it in stride. He had set a goal to earn the rank of corporal so he and Lily Richmond could get married. If he was in the army, the only way to achieve this was to first earn the rank of corporal. In pursuit of this goal, he had forfeited most of his previously carefree lifestyle. Every spare moment was spent to improve himself as a soldier, studying manuals on drills, and duties of a junior NCO. His presence outside the adjutant's office was a result of this intense ambition. Every piece of kit he owned was cleaned, starched, or polished far beyond the accepted standard, and he was content with winning the honour of stickman. The new guard mounted seven men each morning, and during the inspection, the duty officer selected one to be the most smartly dressed and awarded him the stickman. This meant he did not have to go on guard, but instead became the CO's runner for the day and was dismissed at teatime.

For the British soldier stationed in India in the 1920s, hunger was a persistently dominating factor in his life, particularly for extra food, known as Connor. The food served in the cookhouse was as nutritious as could be expected, but there was never enough. It was doubly hard for the Queen's Light Infantry, as they did not qualify for county subsistence. There was a system at the time in which the parent county of a regiment contributed nine pence per man per day towards his rations. As the Queens did not have a parent county, they received none, hence their constant scavenging for extra food, or "buckshee Connor."

One evening before payday, Private Ken Hallin, Jock Cressy, Paani Waters, and Bert Colling were sitting in the platoon bungalow, talking while keeping themselves busy with small chores. Bert Colling asked Sid Frith, who had just come back from the dry canteen after buying ten Park Drive cigarettes, "Who's on tonight?" Frith responded, "A new bloke." Paani Waters, who was in the middle of darning a sock, asked, "How new?" This was of interest because some of the native staff in the canteen filled the tea mugs more than others. Hallin, who was unstitching his mattress biscuits and unravelling the coconut fibre that tended to pack down like clay, thought for a moment before asking Cressy, "Cressy, lad! You still got that suit you had made?"

"Yes. It's in my fit box," Cressy replied.

"Good!" said Hallin, pushing the coconut fibre back into the biscuit cover. "Dig it out. I'm taking you all to dinner."

A short time later, Hallin walked into the dry canteen wearing a white suit with white shoes and carrying a folded umbrella as a walking stick. He strolled through the room, giving a casual smile to everyone as he made his way to the service counter. Before he got there, however, he passed by a table where Cressy, Waters, and Colling were sitting.

"Good evening, sir," the three of them echoed, jumping up to attention.

"Ah, my good fellows. This is a fortunate meeting," Hallin replied.

There followed a brief conversation between Hallin and the three, in which they addressed Hallin as 'sir' no fewer than eighteen times. Turning to the counter, Hallin raised his umbrella and hailed the canteen attendant behind it.

"Yo, proprietor, a plate of your best fare."

"The young Indian, who had been watching the proceedings with interest, seemed not to understand.

"Char Saheb?" he asked, confused by Hallin's phrasing.

"No! Not before the main course, my good man," Hallin corrected, spreading his palms as he approached the counter. "Perhaps I could see the menu?"

"Menu, saheb," the native replied, looking puzzled before hesitantly pointing at a painted board behind him.

"Oh! It's on the wall. How provincial," remarked Hallin with a condescending smile, as if he hadn't seen such a setup since his last vacation in rural Spain.

Proceeding to order the entire contents of the menu board, he finished by turning to the other three and asking, "Dear friends, would you care to share something with me?"

"We'll have whatever you're having, sure," Cressy answered, practically bowing.

"Splendid," Hallin replied, turning to slap the counter. "Please make that three more of the same and bring it to my friends' table. Also, bring the bill. I don't carry money with me; I'll send my servant over in the morning."

The Indian's expression shifted from wonderment to faint suspicion for the first time. Observing this, Hallin's right hand darted across the counter, and he introduced himself to the man as Mister Kenneth Preston Hallin. He asked for the employee's name, and the nervous man introduced himself as Kallu Ram. Hallin expressed his pleasure, and they finished a second helping from the menu. As the others left, Sergeant Ridley entered the room and approached their table. He joked with Hallin, who replied that they were entitled to some gentlemanly dignity.

Typically, a regiment followed a routine cycle throughout the year, but towards the end of winter, the 2nd Queen's Light Infantry was allowed an unscheduled excursion. The soldiers spent their spare time playing sports, with football being the most popular. They supported their hometown teams back in the UK, and in India, the All-Indian Cup was a fiercely contested football tournament. Both British and Indian army regiments, as well as civilian organizations with registered football clubs, participated in this tournament. Surprisingly, the 2nd QLI was one of the two army teams to reach the final.

The battalion had quietly advanced through the competition, triumphing over every team in the knockout contest. Although the regiment was applauded for their successes, it was widely acknowledged that their winning streak might eventually end against one of the formidable civilian teams. In the quarterfinals, they faced off against the Bengal Railway team in an away game, and everyone assumed their journey would end there. However, they emerged victorious and progressed to the semi-finals, where they battled Sporting Howard at home. Despite no one giving them a chance, the entire garrison rallied behind them, and they emerged victorious once again. The commanding officer was overjoyed, and the garrison commander was so impressed that he arranged for the entire battalion to travel to Calcutta by rail to support the team in the final.

The team set up camp in a tented area on the maidan outside the walls of Fort William, the annual location of the final. The venue featured stands capable of accommodating up to ten thousand spectators. The Queen's opponents in the final were a rifle regiment stationed in Fort William. The rivalry between rifle regiments and Light Infantry was intense, both renowned for their sharp shooting and fast marching. Even the mere sight of each other often sparked conflict. Although Calcutta's brothel district was too expensive for soldiers, there were bars on the outskirts that sold beer at affordable prices. A couple of days before the final, Benedict Lyall and Joey Payne visited one of these bars to cool off. The bar was mostly filled with riflemen, and after taking a deep swig of beer, Benedict made a comment to a nearby table of them, "Getting a head-start on drowning your sorrows, are you?" One of the riflemen nearby asked, "Sorrows?" Benedict retorted, "Over losing the match." Joey knew what was coming. He had been through it before. Twice in Harwich, once in Aldershot, and twice again in Meerut – Benedict was ready to start a fight."

Another man at the table replied sarcastically, "You can think that if you want, but you'll find yourself in a sticky situation."

"Well, you may try your best, but we've seen the weak opponents you've defeated to get here. We aren't worried about meeting your group," Lyall argued.

"You'll see," another person at the table interjected, "in two days, your eleven posers will be drunk and out of commission."

"Yep, kicked out of this world for good," added another.

Lyall sarcastically complimented them, "Brave men, but you're in for a tough time."

"From the French light infantry?" the man closest to them mocked, referring to the fleur-de-lis on their Queen's badge. "I'm not scared of any French soldiers."

Benedict finished his drink, examining the unique pantaloons the rifleman wore. They were tightly fastened just below the knees, a departure from the typical khaki shorts. "I'm puzzled by those, but I suspect it's so no one will notice if you soil your pants."

The man closest to them lunged at Benedict, but he swiftly countered with a punch. Payne intervened, punching the second man in the jaw, which initiated a brawl. Tables were toppled, and everyone was engaged in a fist fight with bodies flying around. Though Lyall and Payne were cornered against the bar, they were assisted by Gynger Langdon and Danny Short.

"The four of them slowly retreated to the door, accompanied by three others from C Company. Despite the additional support, the group was still outnumbered four to one until six more men from their own 5 Platoon arrived. The fight continued, with more soldiers from both battalions joining in. The battle grew with every passing minute.

Soon, it was no longer a mere fight; it had escalated into a full-blown street battle spilling into alleys, shops, and side streets. Whistles echoed through the air as red caps started to arrive, effectively ending the struggle. A fight was one thing, but spending time in jail or under disciplinary action was a completely different matter. Like sheep before a wolf, the men began to scatter, hurriedly picking up the fallen topees strewn across the street. If they were lucky, they found a topee belonging to a notable regiment; if they were luckier still, it might even be their own.

The following day, Joey Payne, Sid Frith, Jeffrey Harrison, and Nash Slyfield decided to spend the morning as tourists, climbing up onto the ramparts of Fort William. Constructed two centuries ago, when Calcutta was a flourishing British power hub in India, the walls were impressively massive and robustly built. However, certain sections had fallen into disrepair over the years. Navigating around these parts, it took the group over an hour to walk the entire circumference of the fort. Along the way, Sid Frith discovered an old army order sheet from 1858, during the tail end of the mutiny. The sheet, secreted away in a niche, directed all troops to cease indiscriminate shooting of natives from the walls.

Upon their return to the tent lines, they found that both their battalion and the Rifles were confined to camp. Further skirmishes between the two units had been reported, a continuation of the previous day's fighting. This time, however, it had turned ugly; belt buckles had been wielded as weapons, resulting in several bloody wounds to heads and faces.

The following day, the cup final concluded in the worst possible manner. The Queens scored a goal in the first half and managed to maintain their lead for the remainder of the match. However, during injury time, the Rifles were awarded a penalty and managed to score, tying the match one-all. The match ended in a draw, necessitating a replay. But the GOC overruled this decision, refusing to tolerate the disgraceful sight of British soldiers battling each other in front of the native population of Calcutta. They were supposed to be the cornerstone of Pax Britannica, and such behaviour was wholly unacceptable."

"However, leaving the hostility between the two regiments unresolved could have led to an unpleasant situation. Consequently, the two commanding officers suggested a meeting with the General Officer Commanding (GOC) to settle the dispute and dissipate the animosity. The match was replayed behind closed doors on a football pitch located within the boundaries of Fort William, with only members of the two battalions present as spectators. The pitch was encircled by alternating rifle platoons, including the Queen's, and the men were instructed to intermingle. The teams were made up of battalion officers, none of whom were football players. The game commenced with the two commanding officers as goalkeepers, met with an eerie silence from the bewildered spectators. However, the game soon took a humorous turn as the unskilled officers amusingly fumbled around the field, causing the spectators to fall into fits of laughter. The match concluded when 2nd Lieutenant Andrew Flemington of the Queen's hit the ball from thirty yards out, tying the score at sixteen. The Indian referee then called time, effectively diffusing the tension that had overshadowed a football cup final held in as high regard in India as the FA Cup in England.

CHAPTER 15

Open the door of thy heart,
And open thy chamber door,
And my kisses shall teach thy lips.
The love that shall fade no more.
-Baynard Taylor

Awakening, Benedict Lyall reached under his pillow for his pocket watch, checking the time. It was half an hour before reveille, and he knew he had to get up. After washing and shaving, he strolled through the lines to the battalion stables where Lieutenant Bate's syce awaited him with two horses, one of which was saddled.

Before mounting the saddled horse and leading the second one, Benedict complimented the syce, saying "Shabash! Ashok." As he rode out of the lines, it was clear the horses belonged to Bate. The horse he rode was an Australian waler, used by Kyle on parades or to forget about on-field exercises, while the other was a smaller Arabian pony used for playing occasional polo matches.

Since the platoon commander was taking a six-month leave back in England during the summer, he paid Benedict ten rupees weekly to exercise his horses each morning and evening.

Riding around the edge of the cantonment at a walk, Benedict then took a half-circle path through a broad strip of cultivation, back out onto the maidan where he could give the horses a good run. Thanks to his work experience in Australia, Benedict had learned a lot about handling horses and truly enjoyed doing it. Moreover, the money earned from exercising the horses was easy and he would have done the job for nothing.

As he turned onto a farm cart track, Benedict noticed a girl on a bicycle near a metalled road that he had to cross. She was partially concealed by the tree trunks lining the roadside, observing the horses every morning as he passed by. This morning she grew bolder and stroked the polo pony's flank. Seeing this, Benedict halted his horse and asked, "You like horses?"

The girl, who was Eurasian, slim, almost petite in build, and very pretty, replied, "Oh yes, I think they are sweet." Wearing a topee and a light calf-length dress, she spoke English with only a hint of a chee-chee accent common among Anglo-Indians and English-speaking Indians.

Benedict laughed at her response and said, "Well, go on then. Give him a good pat. He likes that." The girl patted the horse's flank and then asked, "What's his name?"

"Dancer."

"Beautiful dancer," cooed the girl as she ran her hand along his shoulder. "Can you ride?" asked

Benedict, watching her stroke the horse's coat. "Oh no, I have never been on a horse," she replied apologetically. "Want to ride him?" asked the soldier. "Oh yes, please. I would love to," replied the girl, her face lighting up. "Alright! Tomorrow morning, I will bring him out all saddled up and ready to mount," confirmed Lyall. "Thank you, that's amazing," said the girl with a smile. "But don't come in this get-up. You need trousers or riding pants," shouted Benedict as he walked the horses off.

Her name was Sheela Mullan, the daughter of an Indian mother and an Irish railway official father. She lived with her family in the railway settlement adjoining the cantonment and worked in one of the railway administration offices, cycling there each morning. They would often meet at the track junction and ride out onto the maidan together. As the weeks went by, Sheela became more confident in the saddle, and one morning she asked Benedict to let her be more adventurous. This led to overconfidence on her part when she coaxed Dancer into a gallop, and Benedict had to race after her. He finally caught up with her as she fell from the horse.

Benedict was relieved that Sheela was okay, but he was also angry. "For God's sake, Sheela, why didn't you rein in when I shouted?" he exclaimed. "I'm sorry, Benedict. You have every right to be furious with me," replied Sheela weakly. Benedict then helped Sheela into the shade, and as she lay in his arms, he kissed her. "I better get you into the shade," he said, becoming embarrassed by his boldness.

Sheela stared silently, not saying a word. A person, Lyall, quickly scooped her up in his arms, carrying her to rest against the limb roots of a banyan tree. "Alright?" he asked. Sheela questioned him on why he kissed her, and Lyall struggled for words to express how he felt about her. Sheela then leaned in to kiss him, her eyes full of longing.

Hugo du Rand lay on a hillside, watching a tribesman with sheep and a rifle making his way towards him. He was with the South Waziristan Scouts, waiting for a notorious outlaw named Abdul Shamsi. Despite the unconfirmed intelligence report that Shamsi and his men were headed their way, Hugo cursed silently as the tribesman was not their target, and their patience in lying in ambush might be for nothing. Abdul Shamsi was a wanted criminal with a high price on his head, hiding out in the Mahsud lands under the protection of Wahid Anim, the chief of the Garuzi Khail Clan.

du Rand observed a group of nine herdsmen leading around two hundred sheep towards a water pool. He noticed the frontman unslung his rifle and prepared to use it, assuming that they had been spotted. However, du Rand then noticed the jemadar pointing in the opposite direction, indicating that there was another larger flock of sheep coming into the valley. The first group were Mahsuds, and the second were Wazirs, both tribes known for their lawlessness and treachery. While they were hated by those who had to deal with them, their only saving grace was their inward-focused hatred. They were un-neighbourly and dishonourable, but their own people were just as likely to be targets for their aggression.

The two herds were closing in on the water, neither giving way to the other. Knowing that the Mahsuds would reach the spring first, the leading Wazir shot and killed the front Mahsud with his rifle. For the next quarter of an hour, du Rand and the Scouts watched an intense gunfight between the two groups of herdsmen, culminating in the weaker Mahsuds fleeing the field, carrying their dead, wounded, and sheep. The victors then watered their sheep, ate lunch, and exchanged stories of the battle with triumphant laughter, while du Rand and the Scouts waited under the hot afternoon sun for two more hours.

During this wait, Hugo noticed a flock of geese flying southwards, indicating the imminent arrival of summer rains and the end of the hot weather. Almost a year earlier, Hugo had recovered from injuries and applied to join the Scouts. This wasn't because of dissatisfaction with his previous regiment, but due to financial constraints. Unlike Kyle Bate, Hugo didn't have a private income. The pay of a lieutenant wasn't enough to cover his expenses, and while he didn't live extravagantly, he still couldn't pay his bills or meet his duty costs. To avoid debt, he applied and was accepted into the Scouts, where he received a pay increase and was able to enjoy a more formal mess, which required fewer subsidies from its members.

The South Waziristan Scouts were established following the Third Afghanistan War of 1919, when their predecessors, the South Waziristan Militia, either mutinied or fled. The founder, Major Guy Russell, started in 1922 by enlisting a redundant force of the Mohmad Militia and recruiting volunteer tribesmen from the border tribes. However, no one from the Wazir or Mahsud tribes came forward.

du Rand joined the Scouts shortly after their new commandant, Major S.P. Williams, arrived. He met Williams during his joining interview, and Williams welcomed him, expressing the need for capable men like him on the Border.

During a patrol, the Scouts stayed hidden until Wazir herders had watered their stock and left. They then signalled each other to stand up, ready in case an ambush opportunity arose. The Scouts' most effective tactic was their rapid movement, known as gashing, used when on patrol or on the move. This allowed them to move swiftly through the broken border country and surprise adversaries when approaching objectives. If being pursued, they could outrun all but the fittest tribesmen. Du Rand and his Scouts were now gashing for home, the newly built Scout fort at Sararogha, located ten miles away on the Jandola Razmak road, for safety.

--oOo--

"Not again! I'm sick to death of these bloody beasts!" Jock Cressy exclaimed in frustration as he was forced to stop again to readjust the load of one of the battalion's baggage animals. They were on summer manoeuvres fifty miles northeast of Ravlapore, along with troops from other garrisons in the United Provinces, including Lucknow, Bareilly, and Cawnpore. These manoeuvres were scheduled to end just before the arrival of the monsoon, but this year the rains arrived early and had been pouring for the past eight days. As Lance-Corporal Joey Payne signalled for the group to halt, Jock vented his frustration at the native camel driver for his inability to secure the animals' loads and threatened him with severe consequences if it happened again. Unfortunately, this was a common occurrence on the journey, and the baggage escort detail was detested by all involved. Despite their slow pace and constantly shifting loads, a platoon was assigned to accompany the camels each day, arriving at the evening camp after everyone else with cold meals waiting for them.

Payne had hoped that his recent promotion would allow him to practice the drills and skills he had acquired in his junior NCO's cadre during the manoeuvres. However, these hopes were dashed when the rain began. The soldiers were perpetually wet and without fresh clothes, causing their enthusiasm for soldiering and field training to vanish rapidly. After spending a night in a leaky way station, infested with ticks, the CO announced that the GOC had cancelled the manoeuvres, and the troops were to return to their stations.

Sergeant-Major Little came around to assign a lance corporal from each platoon to lead a few volunteers to the cook wagon to collect a hot meal. Joey Payne had to fend off six platoon members to take four with him. However, they found themselves receiving only a piece of dry bread and a spring onion each. Nash Slyfield made a sarcastic comment about Little's sense of humour while picking up the onions.

The battalion trudged nineteen miles through waist-deep water, leaving their baggage and the contractor's char-wallahs behind. The char-wallahs had provided an excellent mobile canteen during the first week, but the monsoon seriously affected their ability to provide good service.

Upon reaching a raised road and consulting with the brigadier, the commanding officer gave the soldiers two options: either stay put or march through the night to their next destination, Ravlapore. The soldiers unanimously shouted to march on, and over nine hundred voices could be heard bellowing "March on! March on!"

After arriving at their posts, the following morning, the exhausted and soaked company awaited dismissal from Little. The rain showed no sign of stopping, and the officers were collapsing. "Right!" ended the CSM, "When I dismiss you, leave, strip off, towel yourselves down, then hurry to the cookhouse. I've ordered a hot meal for you."

"Damn! Another bloody spring onion?" came a voice from the soldiers.

"Sergeant Ridley! Find that man and put him under close arrest," Little ordered heatedly, leading to Nash Slyfield receiving seven days of restricted privileges. Nevertheless, the men returned to their bungalows, still weak with laughter.

Turning into the shaded lane leading up to the Saysha Mission, Hugo du Rand eased his foot off the throttle pedal, appreciating the brief reprieve from the sun's rays. It had been a long, hot journey from Kandao to Saysha in an open car, and now he reduced speed to savour the temporary shield from the sun. After parking his car, he walked towards Emily Sheffield's bungalow gate, sidestepping a few children who had scampered over at the unexpected arrival of a motor vehicle.

"Hugo!" called the doctor, dressed in white and greeting him with a wave from the clinic doorway. "Good of you to come. Make yourself comfortable on the veranda. I'll be right there." After a few minutes, she returned and said, "I'll just fetch a cup of tea," as she patted his arm lightly before heading into the bungalow. "Now tell me, what brings you here this time?" she asked upon her return, taking a seat beside him. "When was the last time you heard from Robin Cuimein?" asked Hugo, his facial expression hinting at a hidden secret. "Oh, a few months ago," replied the doctor, pausing momentarily to recall. "This came yesterday; I think you'll find it interesting." Du Rand handed her an opened letter. "From Robin! Hmm," Emily murmured to herself, glancing at the back of the envelope before reading the letter. She paused to thank her house servant as he placed a tea tray between them.

"Well, I'll be! District Officer! He's coming here as the District Officer!" Emily exclaimed. "That's wonderful news, isn't it?" Hugo declared, returning the letter. "Yes, indeed. I'm delighted for him. He'll make an excellent District Officer," Emily affirmed. "Oh, yes," Hugo concurred cautiously. "He'll make a first-class District Officer as long as he keeps the Border at arm's length." "And how about the Border, Hugo? Are you keeping it at arm's length?" Emily queried, pouring tea for both.

The officer grinned at her. This was du Rand's fourth visit to the mission since his enlistment in the scouts, and every time they found themselves arguing opposite viewpoints. Emily maintained that despite their raiding and killing tendencies, the Border tribesmen had redeeming qualities, while Hugo believed that the only good Pathan not in government service was a dead one.

"You know, I was on patrol the other day. I found myself talking to a young Afridi from Tirah who had just enlisted after completing his training. He couldn't resist telling me he had shot me in the mouth in Peshawar last year," du Rand began narrating a story in response to her question.

Emily studied the man sipping his tea, noticing the broad, ugly scar stretching from one corner of his mouth across his cheek. "Oh, come on, Lieutenant, you're lying," she voiced sceptically.

"Yes, I am," Hugo confessed, breaking into a chuckle. "Couldn't help myself. It was terribly naughty of me, but I had to try to win an argument with you somehow."

"Seriously though, Hugo, how is it?" Emily asked sincerely.

"Well, we're full steam ahead, building forts and posts like beavers. We just completed a new one at Kandao, north of Sararogha, on Razmak road. There's talk of re-occupying the old fort at Chashma. We patrol tribal land at least twice a week and search the villages where we can, but it's very much a case of hit and run. We hardly get any information about the nasty badmash chaps we would dearly like to apprehend," Hugo explained. (Badmash means scoundrel)

"Hugo, I've been on this Frontier for over thirty years," announced the doctor philosophically, picking up the teapot. "And the one thing I've learned is that nothing really changes. More tea?"

Leaving the platoon bungalow as the duty bugler sounded the 1400 hours defaulters' call, Benedict Lyall headed towards the lines. He passed the officers' mess where the battalion band was playing their last tune. It was Sunday, and after the church parade, they always played on the lawn for an hour or so, entertaining the officers and their ladies. Skirting the stables, he quickened his pace, hoping Sheela would be early. Rounding a corner of the track, he spotted her in the distance. She came into view between the bordering trees, and a relaxed run brought him to her. Sheela's innocent, angelic smile reached out to take hold of him long before they touched.

"Hello, Benedict," Sheela's voice sang as she took his hand.

"Sheela!" the corporal exclaimed just before their lips met. It was late October, and the couple had been riding and meeting together for six months. The monsoon had hindered them for much of July and August, cancelling their rides and restricting their evening walks. With Mr. Bate's return from England, riding was no longer possible. However, their evenings, now that the cool autumn weather had arrived, more than compensated for their lost days.

On Thursdays and Sundays, the army eased its grip, allowing Sheela and Benedict to walk hand-in-hand around the Indian village west of the cantonment. This village became their sanctuary, with the holy man under the peepul tree becoming their moral guide, the melancholic bullock tethered to the farmer's Persian water wheel becoming their creature, and even the elephant that passed by with bells tinkling from its harness feeling like it belonged to them.

In this village, Sheela guided Benedict, pointing out people and objects, explaining their identities and significance. The raw sugar bars in the market were known as 'gur.' The lavishly dressed young boy on the horse, led by drummers and flute players, was a groom on his way to his wedding. The rhythmic murmur heard when passing a house was a Muslim Sanskrit hymn from the Quran.

Through Sheela's eyes, Benedict started to appreciate the countryside's sights and sounds that he, as a soldier, had previously ignored. He admired the skill of the village potter as he formed his wares on a stone wheel spun by a stick, the smell of damp earth and ferns, the smoke hanging over the village in the evening, and the call of a cuckoo at the end of a rain shower. With Sheela by his side, everything took on a beautiful and meaningful form, even the scent of the villagers' lanterns, with their burning oil wicks floating in saucers, became another evening fragrance.

This afternoon was different as they were heading away from their village sanctuary towards the railway settlement. Sheela had repeatedly urged Benedict to meet her family, but he had always refused, unwilling to sacrifice their precious moments together. However, this afternoon he had finally agreed to meet them, and it was not because of another request from Sheela. At the entrance gate, a plaque on the wall read 'Dali-Bag.'

"'Dali-Bag' means 'Dolly's Garden.' My father named this bungalow after my mother," Sheela explained.

The bungalow was large, with a broad driveway and a spacious front garden. The recent rains had revived the grass, washing away the dust from the hot season, and leaving behind a lush, green lawn. Near the garden wall stood a row of palmyra palms, green parrots fluttering amongst the branches. Smaller guava trees lined the driveway, bearing pear-shaped fruits, Sheela informed him. At the corners of the veranda, shielded by wire mosquito nets, climbing plants thrived."

In the hall, Sheela introduced her mother, a woman with a ready smile, wearing an apple green sari and her hair lightly greying. She spoke excellent English, albeit with a pronounced Indian accent. As she was on her way to pick flowers from the front garden, she instructed Sheela to take Benedict to the back veranda to meet her father. However, instead of leading him straight there, Sheela, like a child, took him by the hand and started pulling him from room to room. Along the way, they encountered an older brother and a younger sister, pausing briefly in a central space within the bungalow.

"This is my mother's pooja room," she told him. "It fills our house with a pleasant aroma." Pooja means worship in English.

The room was filled with incense bowls, plants, and small shrubs like oleander, rose, jasmine, and hortensia. This was the source of the scent that had perfumed the air and filled Benedict's lungs from the moment he had entered the bungalow.

Her father, a slim man with reddish-blond hair and a wrinkled brow from too much Indian sun, folded a copy of the Calcutta Times as he rose to greet Benedict. For a while, the three of them conversed about the beauty of the house, Benedict's tenure in the army, and the weather. Then, Sheela excused herself to assist her mother in the garden, leaving Benedict to disclose the reason for his visit.

"Mr. Mullan, I apologize for us only meeting just now. I understand it may seem odd for a stranger to ask, but Sheela and I have been seeing each other for a while. It's been nothing inappropriate, simply enjoying one another's company. However, I would like to see more of her and thus, I am asking for your permission to marry her," said Lyall, clasping his hands together as he spoke."

"Benedict!" exclaimed Mullan, picking up a pipe from the table beside him but not yet filling or smoking it. "I suspected that was the reason for your visit. I'll be frank with you; you are the last person I would choose for Sheela."

Mullan paused to fill his pipe, then continued, looking directly at Lyall. "You've come to ask for my daughter's hand in marriage, but I presume you also plan to continue your service in the army?"

Lyall confirmed that he indeed planned to stay in the army.

Mullan then asked, "Do you truly love my daughter?"

Lyall affirmed his love, saying he couldn't stop thinking about her.

Mullan then inquired about Lyall's age, and upon learning he was 23, noted that he would qualify for the seven shillings marriage allowance. Lyall responded, "I haven't thought about that yet." Unfortunately, it was true as his mind was too preoccupied with romantic dreams to focus on the expenses of marriage in the barracks.

Now puffing his pipe and blowing smoke into the air, Mullan questioned Lyall, "Have you thought about what sort of life you're letting my daughter in for? Here with us in the railway community, she is Sheela Mullan, the Anglo-Indian girl. With you, in the lines and around the cantonment, she becomes a 'blackie-white', twelve annas to a rupee, a 'kutcha butcha.'" Benedict, who had in the past freely used those exact phrases to describe people of mixed race, clenched his fists in anger.

"I love her," was Lyall's only response.

"And she? Does Sheela return your love?" asked Mullan.

"I reckon," was Benedict's vague reply.

"Have you not asked Sheela or mentioned marriage?" inquired Mullan.

"I wanted permission from you first," said Lyall, shaking his head as he returned to sit on the edge of the chair.

Mullan, cupping his pipe in both hands on his lap, offered, "I will lay your doubts to rest on that matter. Over the last few months, Sheela has been like a flower in full blossom, brimming with happiness. All beginning with the meeting of you."

"But are you against me asking her to be my wife?" Lyall asked cautiously.

"Benedict, before I joined the railway, I was a gora-wallah, just like you in the Horse Artillery," explained Mullan. "I saw what the wives had to endure - poor food, substandard living conditions, and prolonged separations. Are you asking me to subject my daughter to that?" Benedict had no rebuttal and sank back into his chair.

"I can't provide you with an answer until I've spoken to Sheela's mother. Would you be able to stay for dinner?" Mullan invited.

"Yes, thank you," replied Benedict, wringing his hands nervously. His words were laden with emotion, and his tone was disheartened. In the backyard, a white monkey swung from a tree, scaring a crow into flight.

"Benedict," said Mullan, fingering his pipe, "when I speak to my wife, I will advocate for you. That's a promise."

CHAPTER 16

*An ambassador is an honest Man sent to lie
abroad for the Good of his country.*
-Sir Henry Wotton

The Madurai District in the North-West Frontier
was small, with approximately 35 miles
separating it from the Bannu District in the
north and Dera Ismail Khan in the south. Its
width varied between 25 and 30 miles, stretching
from the banks of the Indus River in the east to
the Administrative Border in the west. It took
Robin Cuimein the better part of three days by
rail, from Chamblapur to Rawalpindi, to reach
Janka, the main town in the Manduri District
where his headquarters was located. He then
traveled south along the east bank of the Indus,
crossing the river at Kalabagh, and finally took a
narrow-gauge railway to Janka along a second
line of track.

Upon arriving at the train station, Robin was
greeted by a tall Englishman in uniform, carrying
a leather swagger stick under one arm. He
introduced himself as Bernard Curis, the District
Superintendent of Police. Robin confirmed his
identity and exchanged pleasantries with Curis,
who politely inquired about his journey before
suggesting that Robin's baggage be attended to.
He then introduced Nazim Baksh, a middle-

aged, smartly dressed servant in a white uniform with a red turban, as Robin's butler and bungalow khitmagar who would handle his baggage.

"Grand!" replied Cuimein, turning to introduce the Indian woman and her son who had disembarked from the train and were standing modestly behind the district officer. "This is Hemlata Chawla, my housekeeper. She will oversee all domestic matters."

"So, you have brought your own housekeeper," said Curis as Hemlata led Nazim and his team of baggage carriers to the train's goods wagon. "Bullen, the chap you're replacing, was told you would arrive last week. He chose to leave yesterday, taking his wife and bearer with him. I'm sorry, old chum, but it's been left to me to get you settled into the job."

The superintendent's account of Bullen's departure was accurate. However, from what Curis shared, it seemed Cuimein was not yet fully informed. Cuimein and Bullen had exchanged several letters planning their handover and takeover, agreeing on dates and staffing arrangements. When Bullen informed him in this correspondence that he would be accompanied to his new district by his bearer, a Madrasi who had dedicated twenty years of service, Cuimein, without hesitation, asked

Hemlata to continue as his housekeeper on the Frontier.

Hemlata delayed her response, keeping Cuimein waiting for two days and held a council on the last evening at Harry Peterson's graveside. Bullen had not simply "left," as Curis put it. Cuimein's replacement, a young man recently arrived, was too unfamiliar with the procedures to be left on his own. This delay was why Cuimein and Bullen could not meet, a situation that was all too common in the service.

The baggage trunks and tea chests transferred from the train emitted a faint, aromatic scent, which came from neem and tobacco leaves placed among the clothing and household goods to protect them against white ants. Upon seeing them securely fastened onto a cart, Hemlata, her son, David, and Kazim took seats in a horse-drawn carriage. Following Cuimein, who had left earlier with Curis in his Austin Seven, they navigated through the town on busy streets filled with draft animals, horses, bullocks, and camels. Negotiating bazaars and market squares, they soon reached the city outskirts, transitioning from stone and mud-brick buildings to fields of apricot orchards.

Janka was positioned on a rim of land overlooking a ten-mile strip of fertile basin country between the Kurram and Indus Rivers. The district officer's bungalow was situated on the crown of a spur that ran off this high ground

down to the farmland below. Curis guided
Cuimein to the bungalow down a long drive
flanked by banks of apricot trees. Upon arrival,
Cuimein noticed that this bungalow greatly
differed from the familiar abode he had left
behind in Chamblapur. The head of the drive led
to a semi-circular complex of buildings, with the
stone and cement bungalow located to one side.
Behind the bungalow were the servants' quarters
and several godowns. The district officer's
official bungalow was centrally located among all
the residential buildings. The stables were
attached to the left of the residence, behind the
horse stalls. This flat-roofed structure was used
to house the district officer's 1922 Humber
touring car.

When Curis' car arrived, the servants and staff
began to gather in front of the two main
buildings. Cuimein dismissed those belonging to
the bungalow itself to meet them later in the
presence of Hemlata, so introductions to both
the saheb and the housekeeper could be made
simultaneously. On the office veranda, Curis
introduced the head babu or senior clerk to
Cuimein, a bent, white-haired Brahmin Hindu
who taught junior clerks and office servants.
After touring the building, Curis excused himself
due to pressing work matters, promising to
return the next day to provide Cuimein with a
comprehensive picture of Manduri's policing.

As Curis left, Hemlata and the luggage arrived, causing the bungalow servants to rush out and line the veranda front. After Cuimein had walked down the line, met, and exchanged words with each member, he introduced Hemlata to them as the bungalow's new khadma. Cuimein, having been shown around the bungalow's interior, stood on the back veranda, captivated by the view. He could see orchards and green crop fields watered by the Kurram, extending all the way to the Indus banks. Hearing a car horn, he moved to the bungalow's front and passed David, who was showing his mother the wonder of electric lighting. Upon reaching the front veranda, he noticed a woman exiting a Napier automobile. It was Emily Sheffield, who congratulated Robin on his appointment and waved a bottle of Cockburn's.

At four o'clock on a January day, the 6th Platoon was just waking from their afternoon nap when Bert Collin shouted a warning. Benny was out, and the men needed to prepare for sports before tea. They quickly put on their PT kits, hung mosquito nets, and pushed in their cot beds. Gynger Langdon even hung from the punkah frame. As tea and sandwiches were distributed to the hungry men, the char-wallah and Connor-wallah fled the room yelling in Urdu.

A four-foot peppermint green snake leisurely slithered along the bungalow floor. Almost everyone in the platoon had a pet, mainly dogs, but there were also parrots, monkeys, a couple of mongooses, and even a two-foot lizard and a chicken. Lance-Corporal Grif Griffiths, the Lewis gun section commander, kept a snake in a basket beside his bed and fed it with captured mice bought from the beastie boys, young native boys who did odd jobs and hung around the lines. No one was sure whether it was poisonous or not, and nobody was eager to find out. Amid boots and curses flying at it from all directions, Grif Griffiths scooped it into his arms to return it to the basket.

"Cor blimey, Grif! You thick-headed fool. Secure that dud before some unfortunate soul ends up in a casket," urged Sid Frith, descending from his cot. "Absolutely true! If that thing escapes at night, it'll throw many of us into a frenzy," added Paani Waters, swinging from the wall to change the record on the platoon's Meloto Table Grand gramophone.

While the platoon was enjoying a record, "Dark Eyes that Shine," it ended, and the disc kept spinning. It was replaced with Cicely Debenham's "Lonely Soldier," causing people to rush for the exit with groans of "not again." Joey Payne was seated on one of the spectator benches at the platoon's football pitch, unable to participate because he was just discharged from the hospital after recovering from a bout of malaria. It struck him on New Year's Day, right after the King's Proclamation Parade. He started shaking halfway through and couldn't recall participating in the march-past with the garrison command. He collapsed just before dismissal, and without hesitation, Howard Little had him rushed to the nearby military hospital.

The orderly who took his temperature looked at the thermometer and then disappeared. After a doctor came to his bedside and took his temperature again, Joey suddenly found himself being bathed in cold water. Once the delirium subsided, he was put on a diet of thin chicken soup, sipped from a spouted cup.

Despite anticipating an easy two weeks, Joey was never more relieved than the day he left because of the unpleasant experiences he had. Under his window was a security room for rabies-infected patients. Regrettably, the room wasn't soundproof, and one patient howled non-stop for the last three days of their life. On the evening before Joey's discharge, a patient suffering from syphilis and brain damage ran into the ward with a knife, causing mayhem. Fortunately, an Anglo-Indian civilian doctor intervened and disarmed the deranged patient.

As some men played football on the field, Benedict Lyall and his wife arrived. Married soldiers and their families usually attended these afternoon sports events, even if only as spectators. Benedict left to play football, leaving Sheela on her own. Just as Joey was about to invite Sheela over, Laura Ridley, the sergeant's wife, asked her to sit with her and her young daughters. Since the day Sheela married, Laura had been kind to her, even visiting to ensure she was settling into her new home. As Laura's two-and-a-half-year-old daughter climbed into Sheela's lap, Joey walked over to join them.

"Good afternoon, Mrs. Ridley," said Joey as he stopped by their bench. "May I join you?"

"Of course, Corporal Payne," she replied, adding, "not playing?"

"No, I'm still recovering from my recent illness," he answered, taking a seat next to Sheela.

"Have you heard from Lily?" She asked as the match began.

"Three letters last week when I left the hospital," he replied. It had been almost a year and a half since he and Lily met and fell in love. In that time, they had managed to meet only twice, once for two days during the 1924 Christmas holiday, and a year later, just a month ago, when she was able to spend five days with Joey. They could only be together for a few hours on the first Christmas. Because they decided to keep their intention to marry a secret, Joey couldn't visit her at the RSM's bungalow, so they had to limit their time together, meeting for walks up and down the cantonment Mall. Because it was not proper for someone from the ranks to court a member of the regimental sergeant major's household, they both feared that Lily's next Christmas holiday would be spent in secret meetings, just like the last one. But Benedict and Shecla's marriage changed all that. As a rule, the married bungalows were off-limits. However, at Christmas time, this rule was set aside by invitation, allowing Lily and Joey a base where they could meet, play cards, and listen to gramophone records with Sheela and Benedict, who were in on their plan to marry.

"Will she be able to visit again?" Sheela asked him.

"She believes not until the summer, after she finishes her student nursing training," Joey replied.

"Well, that's not too bad. We'll be in the hills by then," Sheela pointed out cheerfully.

"Yes, I know, but what about after that? As a nurse, she could go anywhere," Joey said in a downcast tone.

"Joey, don't be so negative. You'll soon be a full corporal like Benedict, and then you two can get married," Sheela said encouragingly.

The game ended just before 5 o'clock for tea. Benedict and Sheela said goodbye, while Joey remained on the benches, watching the couple walk hand in hand to their bungalow. "They are so lucky," he thought to himself sadly, wishing he and Lily could do the same.

As he returned to the platoon bungalow, he found Ramji, the tea seller, sitting on the veranda. Ramji was muttering the words of a lament. "What's wrong, Ramji?" Joey asked.

"Oh, Saheb, my heart is full of sadness for you and all the other soldiers in my splendid regiment," the Indian man replied sorrowfully.

"Why are you so sad for us, Ramji?" Joey asked, expecting a joke.

"Oh, Saheb, I just found out where you're being sent next," Ramji said as he continued to rock back and forth.

"You're pulling my leg, Ramji. Even the Colonel himself doesn't know where we're going next," Joey warned.

"On my children's heads, I promise I'm not lying. It's a horrible place, a terrible place," Ramji said with his hands in the air.

"What's the name of the place?" Joey asked sceptically.

"It's called Ishak. I'm so sorry, Saheb," Ramji replied with regret.

"Ishak? Where on earth is Ishak?" Joey repeated in confusion.

"We should go left at the signpost ahead, Robin," Hugo du Rand warned as they approached a T-junction.

"Right you are," replied Cuimein as he turned the wheel of his Humber car, just catching a glimpse of the name "Ishak" on the post sign. Driving north from Kandao towards Razmak, this post was a lone object on a stretch of desolate border road.

Since leaving just after breakfast, they had come across the occasional lorry driven by an enterprising tribesman. However, mostly, the traffic consisted of camels and horses. The road they were now on was like the one they had just left. It was paved, wide enough for two vehicles to pass, but newer. The army had constructed it in the last six months. It served as the main line of communication for a recently established military camp in the heart of the tribal territory. Since it was a "road open" day, they not only passed caravan traders from across the Afghan border, but Cuimein also had to keep well to his side of the road as a convoy of army supply vehicles went past.

There were three occupants in Cuimein's car: himself, Hugo, and a government-appointed official, Khan Amjad Taib Khan, the region's assistant political agent. Amjad was a Khattak Pathan in his late thirties. He lived in a village northwest of Saysha and administered his office from there. The day before, Cuimein had picked him up from his village. Together, they crossed the administrative border and spent the night with Hugo within the secured walls of the Scout fort at Kandao. The trio was on a mission that demanded a high level of tact and diplomacy. The Indian government was seeking a way to end the lawlessness of the border by promoting prosperity to civilize the Frontier. The key was road communication, which would liberate the tribes from their land-locked existence, introducing trade and commerce to isolated valleys and remote villages. However, the government's secondary motive for constructing a network of roads throughout the border was not for public knowledge. Some speculated that it was to provide the army with easy movement. The Pathan was traditionally a bandit. For centuries, he had lived in his barren hills, surviving from year to year on what his flocks and the sparse hill soil could provide. In contrast, on the plains below, farmers and merchants grew wealthy and prosperous on fertile land and ample trade.

The raiding that had been happening between the lean, hungry highland wolves, and plump lowland sheep long before the British arrived resulted in the formation of a doctrine within Pathan society that glorified theft and robbery. These were no longer crimes but considered crafts, with thieves being admired rather than arrested. However, those suffering from their theft on the plains saw it differently. Therefore, establishing a system of drivable roads would not only help to tame the wild Pathan but also expedite the authorities' response to chase and punish them.

The road they took led them to their destination, Ishak, a brigade-size camp situated on the edge of the Wazir tribal homeland. The camp was set up on a plateau and surrounded by low, bare, broken hills on three sides. The perimeter defence of the rectangular camp was a waist-high stone wall guarded by three tall banks of barbed wire. The uniform housing consisted of tents arranged in rows, as the camp had only been established six months earlier.

As they passed through the main gate, which had a partially completed stone-walled guardroom, Hugo directed Cuimein through the lines towards the wood-framed headquarters building. Upon exiting their car, the three visitors were greeted by a duty officer who handed them over to a uniformed man with white collar tabs. This man was Freddie, who led them to a side office where Taib Khan greeted him and shook his hand.

"Robin," Taib Khan introduced, "this is Freddie D'urban." Cuimein, the last to arrive at the office and the only one who hadn't met D'urban before, stepped forward with his hand outstretched. "How do you do, Freddie?" Cuimein said as he shook his hand. "I'm sorry we haven't met earlier than this, but I have read every report you wrote over the last two years."

Frederick D'urban was the area political officer whose job was to connect the tribes with the government. He was relocated from Kotkai to Ishak, a base established by the army to help the Rasmak garrison with some of its workload. His duty was to be available to the tribesmen, to hear their grievances, explanations, grumbles, and denials when there was an investigation of a crime. With British bayonets at his back, he had to enter the tribal country with a few local levies serving as guides and his hosts' word to observe the customs of hospitality.

Freddie D'urban may not have been a man who built empires, but he was the kind of man who maintained them.

Over coffee in his office, the four men discussed and agreed on their joint approach to the upcoming negotiations: convincing a thousand Wazir tribesmen that allowing a road to be built through their land up to the Afghan border would be a worthy investment. After paying a courtesy call on the brigade major and the garrison commander, the four walked to the main gate where they met their escort, a group of six levies from the nearest village. These men, known as khassadars, were hired by the army as road guards on bridges, and they were armed with their own rifles and not wearing any uniform.

After walking for two miles across the rocky and scrub-covered plateau, they arrived at the location for the day's debate. On the outskirts of a village that spanned the banks of a river where the water had trickled down to a yard across, they found a hollow where over a thousand tribesmen sat waiting in a semi-circle in front of seating for the government representatives. The edges of the semi-circle extended around them, almost touching, with a dirt-fouled carpet covering a plank.

After being welcomed by one of the more prominent clan chiefs with a greeting that began, "may you never be tired," and ended with "may you never be down on your luck," several variations later, the discussion began. D'urban clarified the purpose of the gathering and thanked everyone for their presence. Taib Khan laid out the government's points regarding their desire to build the road and how it would benefit the clans whose lands it would run through. Cuimein also pointed out that the shorter route through his district would attract more Powindahs for trade and barter from India and Persia.

However, the overall response to this proposal was a resounding "no deal." Many viewed their isolation as a form of protection, and for many others, a road marring their land would be a desecration. Despite the government's explanations, promises, and assurances, the tribesmen voiced their disapproval of the road project, shaking their rifles and shouting angrily from all sides.

Hugo du Rand played the role of a Scout observer, highly interested in the outcome as the area of operations would be more accessible if the road was built. He also had an excellent opportunity to scrutinize the opposition, identifying wanted men sheltering robbers and raiders under the guise of this truce.

During a brief silence, Robin Cuimein seized the opportunity to highlight another advantage of the road that had not yet been mentioned. "Of course, the road would attract a larger number of howdahs, meaning greater prospects for those inclined to loot," explained Cuimein, glancing up to study the skyline as if he had just noticed a cloud. His three colleagues reacted strongly to his comment. Hugo du Rand slowly turned his head to stare at the district office, his face a picture of stupefied bewilderment. D'urban was also staring, but his face had turned white from shocked horror. Taib Khan, however, sitting next to him, was struggling to suppress laughter. The tribesmen were initially stunned into silence, but then laughter erupted like a wave from the front of the assembly to the back as Cuimein's words were relayed through the crowd. Suddenly, the hillmen's mood changed; they began chanting, "Build! Build!" When Cuimein returned to the garrisoned cantonment, Amjad patted him on the back and said, "Brilliant move, Robin, old chap. Absolutely brilliant."

CHAPTER 17

When evil is advantageous,
He errs who does rightly.
-Pubilius Syrus

Upon the train's arrival at Sagar station, orders were issued throughout the carriages for everyone to disembark and assemble by companies in the goods yard. The battalion men who obeyed this command felt stiff from the long journey but were relieved that it was finally over. The 2nd Queen's Light Infantry was about to embark once again, this time for a year-long tour on the "grim" North-West Frontier.

Back in April, the battalion had left Ravlapore after completing a two-year tour and had marched up into the hills for the summer. The men travelled at night while their wives and families were sent ahead by rail. Once they reached the foothills, the marching took place during the day.

By August, the battalion bid farewell to their families, who were to remain in the hills while the men served on the Frontier. They boarded a train at Gonda, which took almost four days to travel in second class. Each compartment was crammed with six men, rifles, equipment, and packs. A porcelain slab in a booth served as their toilet, and meals were provided at station stops amidst swarming flies. Reading and letter-writing were the primary pastimes, except for the unscheduled stops where the men had to fend off the deformed, leprous beggars.

After marching out of town, the battalion settled in a tented camp surrounded by barbed wire. They still had over a hundred miles left to reach Ishak, and they had to cover this distance on foot. However, they first stopped for three days while they collected stores, draught animals, wagons, rations, and ammunition, and assigned responsibilities and positions for the march.

--oOo-

After an uncomfortable train journey, in which they slept fitfully, the men of the Queen's settled into their cots for the night in Sagar. However, Bert Colling, who was not a light sleeper, woke up in the middle of the night to find a local holding a knife to his throat. The thieves, completely naked and covered in cheetah fat to evade detection by dogs, stole everything they could from the 2nd Section's tent while the men were held at knifepoint. The next day, the embarrassed men had to search the town's bazaar in borrowed uniforms to buy back their stolen belongings.

The battalion's obstacle in reaching the Frontier was the Indus River. They spent an entire day crossing the river, with hired local river transport assisting them in embarking and disembarking. The animals and wagons posed a significant challenge, with horses and mules coaxed onto the craft, while the wagons were unloaded and boarded. The islands that extended each journey to four hours made the process even more tedious.

As they approached the Administrative Border, the battalion's movement orders became stricter. The rifle companies provided protection by advancing only along the main roads and occupying the high ground each morning. They moved in a stop-start manner, providing all-around protection and ensuring safe transit. While at their summer station in the hills, the 2nd Queen underwent another change in commanding officers. Everyone was keenly waiting to see how the new officer, Lieutenant-Colonel Darren Steinfeld, would perform on the Frontier. Steinfeld arrived in India in July, promoted and with no prior service in the country. He had to rely on the knowledge of others and was confident in doing so. After crossing the Indus, he picked up an officer and ten men of the South Waziristan Scouts as an escort. One of his first actions upon meeting the Scouts was to have their officer sit down in his tent for a chat over gin and ginger, requesting all there was to know about hill picketing.

Benedict Lyall was known for reserving his judgment of commanding officers for a longer time than most. This was due to the high standard set by his first commanding officer,

Lieutenant-Colonel Elstob of the 16th Battalion of the Manchester Regiment. At just fourteen years old, Benedict remembered him well, especially his inspiring leadership and posthumous Victoria Cross win in France in 1918, while defending the Manchester Regiment. Gabson, the new officer, barely met Benedict's standards, while the previous one fell out of favour. However, the commanding officer's wife still played a significant role in vetting applicants for marriage to men of junior ranks, as native women were mostly prohibited, and working-class white girls were rare in India. In this respect, she did not have a vast appointment book.

On the day arranged for Molly Palmer to meet Sheela Mullan, she arrived at the Dali-Bag bungalow on foot, insisting on being shown the gardens by Sheela and her mother before entering the house for refreshments. Two hours later, she left and stopped at the door to kiss Sheela. She said, "Sheela, my child, you are far too enchanting to become a soldier's wife. But I wish you and Corporal Lyall every happiness." Three weeks later, Sheela and Benedict were married in the Catholic church in the Railway Settlement, with Joey Payne as the best man. For Benedict, the departure to the Frontier was terrible. Love was an emotion he only vaguely remembered from his childhood, with hunger and cold being more prominent in his mind.

Leaving Sheela, who could fill him with elation with a feather-light touch or a single kiss, was heart-breaking. On the other hand, this move brought Joey Payne closer to the one he loved, giving him high hopes of meeting her. Now a qualified nurse, Lily had served a year's post-training probation at the first mission where she had begun work, called Saysha on the Frontier. Although he was concerned for her safety due to the proximity of lawless tribesmen, she repeatedly dispelled his worry in her letters and assured him that Saysha was an oasis of neutrality.

" Lily! What happened?" Sarita exclaimed, as Lily suddenly braked Emily Sheffield's Napier to a halt while on an errand to Gambila station to collect mail and freight packages for the mission. "

"Someone is lying in the nullah beside the stream," Lily replied after climbing out of the car.

The road to Saysha was still two miles away, running parallel with the nullah that passed the mission. As Lily glanced over a portion of the bank that had caved into the nullah bed, she caught a glimpse of a figure lying on the ground. Approaching the edge of the banking, Lily's suspicions were confirmed. Thereby the stream lay a man, and he was not just resting - his posture was all wrong. He was lying face down,

with one arm extended straight forward while
the other hung in the water.

"Sarita! Fetch the medical case from the car,"
requested Lily as Sarita joined her. "There's
something wrong; I'm going down."

"Wait," ordered Sarita, catching Lily's arm.
Moving towards the edge of the nullah, she
looked over to inspect the ground both
upstream and downstream before returning to
the car. She had a warning for her companion.
"Be careful, Lily. Don't touch him until I join
you."

To approach the figure, Lily descended the
cutting, wading through ankle-deep water, and
then climbed onto a foot-high bank. Standing
over the man, she thought he was a youthful
Pathan tribesman, almost like a boy. Whether he
was asleep or unconscious, his clothes were the
traditional dress of a frontier villager, consisting
of baggy shirt and trousers with a chadar shawl
wrapped around his body and chaplis, dwarf
palm fibre sandals. However, his turban was
missing, and there was dried blood the length of
one arm and on the back of his shaven head.
When Sarita arrived, Lily felt for a pulse on the
wrist of his uninjured arm. "It's fragile. If you
hold his head so that the cut doesn't collect dirt
from the ground, we'll roll him over and look at
that arm well," said Lily. As she pulled him onto
his back, the youth awakened and began
struggling weakly while crying out delirious

curses and threats. "Keep still, child of a hyena. We are here to attend to your wounds, so you may safely return to your village," warned Sarita, gripping his head to keep it still. Her words, spoken harshly, nonetheless worked, and the young tribesman fell silent and ceased struggling. "Oh, Sarita, he's opened the wound. It's beginning to bleed," exclaimed Lily, pushing up the shirt sleeve. Upon closer examination of the forearm, she realized it was a hole, a gunshot wound. "We should first bandage his injuries, then think about getting him to the Mission," advised Sarita, cradling his head in her lap. This was the Frontier, and she had seen many wounds while at the mission, and very few were not the result of a gun or knife.

After bandaging the injured youth, Sarita and Lily didn't dare move him themselves. They decided that Sarita would stay with the youth while Lily drove to the mission for help. However, before they could execute their plan, they were interrupted by the arrival of others. "Lily!" Sarita warned, "Don't try to go to the car." Lily, puzzled by her friend's request, looked first at Sarita, then in the direction Sarita was staring.

Walking toward them along the downstream bank was an armed Pathan man with his rifle slung across his back. He stopped where the stream crossed his path, about a hundred yards from them, placing him on the opposite bank.

"What should we do?" asked Lily.

"Call to him. Tell him we need help with an injured man," advised Sarita.

When Lily called out to the man in Pushtu, she received no reply; he seemed too focused on looking around. Then, he raised an arm, signalling ten more men who appeared to be rushing to join him. Two men on each side separated themselves, keeping their heads down and positioning themselves as sentries. It didn't take much for Lily to deduce their intentions. Joined by a second man, the first man began to wade across the stream toward them.

"Thank him for coming, Lily," Sarita prompted. "Tell him who we are. You can speak; he will pay more attention to you than me. And always remember to smile."

They were halfway to them when they were stopped by a whistle from one of the sentries on the road bank, who held up his hands as if he were steering a car. As soon as they began to advance again, Lily started thanking them profusely, beginning to regret, with every step they took, ever having noticed the injured boy. Both men were tall, intimidating figures with the cold, flinty stares of those devoid of humour. The first man had pale skin, grey eyes, and a light brown, almost reddish beard. The second, with dark skin and a black beard, had a wide scar running from his forehead over his right eye and down his cheek.

With a smile on her face and a nauseating feeling of unease, Lily explained to the two stern men what she wanted them to do for the young boy, who had once again lost consciousness.

"If you could carry this young man to our car, we will take him to our Mission, where his wounds will be cleaned and properly dressed," she told them.

"Mission hospital?" asked the first Pathan, looking up from the young boy's face, which was still cradled in Sarita's lap.

"Is it Mem Daktar Sheffield's?" asked the second man, using the native corruption of the word doctor, before Lily could answer the first query.

"Yes, it's our Mission. Daktar Sheffield's Mission hospital," Lily responded.

The first man turned around and gestured for two others to come forward. "There's no need to take this boy to the hospital; he's one of us. He fell into this ravine last night and we've been searching for him since. These are his cousins. We'll take him home to his village now," he told them.

Despite knowing that the wounds were at least three days old, Lily remained silent.

Two young, worried men arrived and one of them quietly called out, "Saleem, we're back," only to be sharply rebuked by the man with the scar.

All of them had slung rifles and were carrying chadars on their backs that were full. When one of the new men stripped off the injured youth's clothing to hand it to another, it clattered with the sound of metal. The injured youth was lifted and carried off piggyback.

Holding back the first two men from following, Lily took bandages and a small tin of ointment from the medical case. "Please take these," she said, "He needs to have his wounds re-dressed every two days." Lily was no longer smiling as she offered these items to the Pathan with grey eyes.

Without a word of thanks, he accepted the bandages and tin, stowing them in a pouch hanging at his hip.

"Badmash," Sarita said as the two young women stood together, watching the party of men move upstream. "Yes!" replied Lily, relieved to see them go. "Indeed, they are villains." They soon learned just how villainous these men were when Emily and Zahir Khan greeted them on the bungalow veranda.

"One with a brown beard and grey eyes, the other with a scar?" Emily asked upon hearing their story. "The one with the scar?" Zahir Khan drew a finger down the right side of his face. "Did it run like this?"

"Yes," confirmed Sarita. "And it was wide, too wide." Emily and Zahir exchanged a quick glance, both understanding the danger the women had unwittingly been in.

"You have been fortunate," Emily began, addressing the two women in a serious tone. "The man with grey eyes was Abdul Shamsi, the outlaw. He is from the Mohmand tribe, north of the Khyber. His ancestors were Greek settlers from Alexander the Great's army. For some reason, he was banished by his tribe and now has a bounty on his head for murder and robbery. He lives under the protection of hamsaya in the Kajuri Valley, deep in Mahsud lands. He sustains himself by raiding and giving a share of his spoils to the clan chief."

"And the one with the scar," added Zahir, "Firoz-un-Din, an Afghan of the Ghilzai tribe. He was a paid assassin but now raids with Shamsi."

"Should we inform the police?" Lily asked, "I'm quite certain they were carrying loot from a raid, and that boy was definitely shot in the arm."

"No," Emily replied. "At least not today. Perhaps tomorrow. You could have been hurt. But they left you unharmed for some reason, so I'm willing to keep quiet. He will be caught one day, but that day will not be today."

Standing beside each other, Lily and Sarita shared a look of both dismay and relief, their hands clasping tightly together.

CHAPTER 18

Folly is often more cruel In the consequence than malice Can be in the intent.
-Marquis of Halifax

In Ishak, the morning routine began with Reveille, which consistently took place at six o'clock throughout the year. The morning silence was broken by the sound of four simultaneous bugle calls, three for the infantry and one for the artillery. Instantly, the camp sprang to life, with men, bare to the waist, filing off to wash and shave. Tent walls were rolled up, and bedding and packs were neatly arranged outside in orderly rows. The duty platoon commenced their sweep around the camp perimeter, starting with a bayonet charge of the latrine, then working their way along the outer edge to discourage any potential threats. Contrary to safer Indian cantonments, men in Ishak were responsible for all menial tasks, including lifting, carrying, and moving things. The camp was situated in hostile territory, and even though the army was not at war, they operated on a war footing. As a result, there was no whole company muster parade. Instead, a significant call on manpower was required to secure the camp's boundaries and maintain daily operations. The camp was located adjacent to a flat strip of ground used by visiting aircraft as a landing field. A round, two-story stone-built sentry tower, enclosed in barbed wire, overlooked both the camp and landing strip, while two other towers manned by twenty men each, who were relieved every two days, stood to the north and east.

There were several Indian contractors at the camp, including char-wallahs and napi's. However, their numbers were significantly fewer compared to other stations due to the besieged cantonment. The camp was surrounded by wire entanglements, sentinel towers, and artillery gun emplacements, with 4.7-inch medium field guns pointing outward. The enemy, comprised of poorly armed tribesmen with a distinct smell, had previously managed to defeat armies and spread terror across the northwest Indian borders.

"Come on, guys, grab your stuff and come out here!" Joey Payne called to the remaining members of his section who were still in their tents after breakfast in late November. The sun was up, and the morning air was gradually warming, marking another "road open" day. The garrison was out on picket duty.

Platoon 6 formed two ranks on the dirt roadway outside their tent lines. Paani Waters was the last to arrive, having missed breakfast. He quickly finished up one of the egg wads from Connor-wallah. The platoon then sloped arms and formed a group of four before marching off as if on parade. However, their demeanor changed at the gate.

When ordered to fall out, the men fixed bayonets and split into two groups. Kyle Bate's group went left, towards a ridge south of the cantonment. Benedict Lyall's group, with Lyall acting as the platoon sergeant in Wilf Ridley's absence, went right towards the same ridge. Earlier that year, the road they crossed had been negotiated by Frederick D'urban with the Wazir Clans. However, construction had been slow, with just over three miles completed. This was due to the government's requirement that funds needed to be found from the province's average annual public works budget. Despite this, the locals were employed to work on it and were happy with the income it provided.

Advancing in open skirmish order towards the ridge, Benedict Lyall's picket, which included Joey Payne's 2nd Section and Grif Griffiths' Lewis-gun Section, began climbing the rocky slope. There were no large boulders to conceal ambushers, only shale-like rock. Few risks were taken as the sections made their way to the crest in dashes and spurts, always covering each other. The regular picket post was named Snowy Hook. It had its own permanent sangar, built by those who initially garrisoned Ishak. Its walls were four feet high and measured ten by fifteen yards wide, located on one edge of a cliff facing south. From this high point, the view north was open across the plateau to the camp two miles away, which stood out like a four-cornered island of tents. To the south, the land was a waste of broken, weather-eroded hills. To the east, the ridge they were on extended in line with the road for half a mile. Then, just where it began to drop away, another sangar was positioned, occupied by Mister Bate and the rest of Platoon 6. Snowy Hook was expected to keep a sharp lookout towards the west. The road crossed a river in this direction, passing a set of low hills on its left before winding out of sight towards the Afghan border. Although the road was unfinished, the Powindahs had started using what there was of it. Following old tracks and river courses, they would pick it up to the west of Ishak, resulting in the garrison providing picket posts along the route for their protection. Today, the 2nd Queens were tasked with securing the perimeter picket points overlooking the cantonment. Responsibility for the road was given to a battalion that had arrived just two weeks earlier, the 9th battalion, 15th Punjab Regiment. Benedict Lyall and his picket from Snowy Hook watched the new unit march out of the camp, passing down the road below them. Once across the river bridge, the first picket party peeled off across a space of rocky ground and then up to their hilltop post.

Benedict watched as they took their positions with issued binoculars. After studying the ground for any signs of suspicion, he slowly scanned to his right. Then, moving north, he spent a minute or so searching the village nestled on the riverbank amongst the flat-roofed houses and fortified towers for anything unusual. These towers were primarily built to protect each man in case he got caught up in a blood feud with his neighbour. They had narrow firing slits in the windows and round boulders on the roof edges to confuse snipers.

As the sun rose higher, the men settled in to wait out the day, some napping while others kept watch. There was no sign of Powindah activity along the road yet. However, unlike the kafilahs of the Khyber, these caravans never seemed to be in a hurry and seemed to appreciate the army's protective cover more.

"Hey, Jeffrey, those guys on Middlesex! What are they up to?" Nash Slyfield asked Jeffrey Harrison, who was resting against the sangar wall with his topee tilted over his eyes.

"Excuse me?" Harrison replied.

"Look! The picket! They've been tipped off," Slyfield explained. Harrison then looked out over the sangar, 700 yards away on the first hill where the Punjabs had occupied. The detachment there was moving off in the opposite direction, south, instead of towards the road.

"That's a really strange sight," Harrison commented. "We should let Benedict know."
"Corporal Lyall," he called, raising an arm to beckon the picket commander. "What's up?" he asked, crouching beside the two older soldiers. "I'm not in the mood to listen to any complaining."
"Those Punjabs over on Middlesex," began Slyfield, releasing his grip on the Lewis gun mounted on the sangar wall. "They're pushing their luck near the edge. What do you say?"
Benedict looked to the far hill, then cursed in disbelief. "Jesus! They've all gone crazy!"
In an urgent tone, he called Joey Payne. "Joey, quickly raise the Middlesex flag. Ask them what they're doing."
With the battalion's shortage of trained signallers, Payne acted as a replacement for the day. He put his rifle down and drew two wooden flags with his belt. He stood up and extended his arms like the hands of a clock, jerking them from one point of a circle to another, sending three identifying letters repeatedly. However, he had no luck signalling to an empty picket post.
"No good, Benedict. They've left," said Payne in frustration.
"What the hell…" voiced Lyall, unable to understand why the Punjabs had abandoned their hilltop.
"Joey, get to the camp. Tell them what happened," he ordered his friend. He then

turned to Lance-Corporal Griffiths, saying, "Griffiths, stick with Joey with a pencil and notepad. Garrison is going to be just as puzzled as us as to why those soldiers left their post. So, we'll be having a lot of communication going back and forth."

He was more than right. For the next fifteen minutes, Joey's arms were constantly in action, between reading messages from the camp, giving negative replies to heliograph flashes, and asking questions beyond answering.

"There they are," called out Ken Hallin, pointing at another hill, the next one over from the Punjabs' original picket.

"They're becoming quite puzzled! Really puzzled!" observed Jeffrey Harrison.

Benedict Lyall confirmed their presence through his binoculars and called out to Payne to inform the garrison that the missing picket was now on another hill, four hundred yards further south. The reply, of course, was, "Ask them why they moved." On contacting the wayward picket, they answered, "This looked like a better hill."

After sending that message to the garrison, the helio response came back instantly: "Tell those idiots to return to the assigned picket."

After Joey relayed the message in a more formal manner, the Punjab signaller began his response. Utilizing Benedict's binoculars, he spelled out the letters for Griffiths to write down: "W-I-L-L. New word. C-O-M-P... God! He's stopped one!"

Through the binoculars, Joey saw the semaphore signaller suddenly fall to the ground. As he spoke, there was a faint, but unmistakable report of a rifle shot. Lyall grabbed the binoculars back and focused them on the hill crest. The Punjabs had taken cover, with only movement around the signaler, where two men were crouched over him.

Grif Griffiths exclaimed, "Blow me, didn't take the nigs too long to spot them," and pushed away his pencil and notepaper to grab his rifle. Benedict, with binoculars fixed to his eyes, remained silent. Instead, he observed the Punjabs as more single shots rang out, looking for clues as to where the enemy was firing from. Scanning the surrounding hills, he saw no hint of the enemy's location, as the Pathan's dress blended seamlessly into the landscape. As he turned his binoculars back, he saw a Punjab take aim and fire. Benedict traced his line of sight, scrutinizing each boulder and shadow on a hillside to the east. He scanned back and forth, up and down, until he spotted a figure moving behind a rock, and that was all he needed.

"Joey, raise the guns. We need artillery fire. Send our recognition flag so the gunners know exactly who's calling for support."

Back at the cantonment, the on-duty fire control officer was enjoying a mug of tea when the telephone linking them with the signal post rang. "Right you are," he responded, glancing at the battery sergeant major and nodding towards the gun line.

The BSM turned around and yelled towards the battery tent lines. "Take your posts!" The gunners, who were on standby and relaxing in their tents, sprang into action. Tea mugs were spilled, letters were tossed onto beds, and playing cards were scattered as they rushed out to man their artillery pieces, which were only yards away. As soon as the fire control officer plotted where Benedict Lyall wanted the shells to land, using range and compass bearings on his map, he shouted down the gun line. "Number one gun!" The sergeant of the first gun raised his arm in readiness to receive his firing orders.

The first shell exploded short of the hill and to the side, but that was Benedict's intention. He planned to walk the artillery onto his target. To direct the first shot, he used Snowy Hook as the clock's centre, and now, using that shell as the clock's centre, he was ready to give the gunners a second target indication order. "Joey! Two hundred! Eleven o'clock!"

Payne stood atop the sangar wall to give the garrison signallers the best view of his flags. The second round landed higher on the hill, off target, but close enough for Benedict to confidently call out, "Two hundred yards, ten o'clock, fifty yards left, on target, five rounds of gunfire."

A thunderclap reverberated from the camp a minute later as six guns fired simultaneously. This was followed by whistled screams above the pickets as six shells arced in trajectory over their heads. The salvo of ammunition exploded in a broken line, throwing up dust, black smoke, and shattered rock around the hillside target area. As more shells rained down, the two sections on Snowy Hook reacted with whistles and shouts of exhilaration.

Benedict was not watching the explosions through his glasses; instead, he was more concerned about the Punjab picket's reaction to the artillery fire. Through disregard of standard Frontier drills, they had put themselves in a dangerous situation. Now, it was up to them to restore their pride by regrouping their small force. Men were seen leaving cover and dashing to a central point. Then, leaving a strong rear guard behind, a party slowly made its way down, some carrying others.

"Lyall called out to Joey Payne, "Add two hundred yards more! Repeat!" as he directed the fire higher up the hill, where he had seen a figure running. After the second barrage, there was a pause. The attacking enemy stayed hidden, and the Punjabs vanished from sight in the low ground. However, the standby company from the cantonment turned out on the road below Snowy Hook amidst the chaos caused by repeated bugle calls and shouting NCOs and hurried forward to provide support. Along this road, there were also fifty to sixty stationary camels belonging to a passing powindah. When the firing began, their handlers ran off to take cover, leaving the docile animals to lie down and wait for their masters' return.

After a pause of ten minutes, rifle fire resumed, muffled and with the source hidden. Nash Slyfield yelled to Benedict, "Down in the tangi," pointing at the riverbed. Two sepoys emerged stealthily from around a river bend, moving from one cover position to another, followed by a larger group carrying their dead or wounded. The Punjabs were trying to escape to the road along the riverbed rather than returning to their original hill picket. When they came into view, the rear-guard was seen falling back in bounds, with two rear men firing around the last bend before sprinting away.

They were being pursued, and even though Benedict Lyall couldn't see a specific target, he refused to just wait for one to appear. "Joey! Send new target, nine hundred, four o'clock, right two hundred," he shouted. Minutes later, he was directing artillery fire up and down the riverbed and around the bend, estimating the range to place several salvos in strategic locations.

Upon reaching the bridge, the commander of the standby company used Joey Payne's semaphore messages to deploy his platoons.

One platoon was sent down the river to join up with the Punjabs, while the other two covered bank to secure the river's flanks. The Punjabs and the first standby platoon then retreated through them to the bridge. At the bridge, a young English second lieutenant was nearly in tears, admitting blame for the disaster, while two Punjabi sepoys had their wounds attended to. Sadly, a third signaller was dead and was laid under the tarpaulin on the roadway.

With the threat of being shot apparently dealt with, the powindah drivers had returned to their camels and were moving again. As one Afghan led his beast past the scene, he loudly cleared his throat before spitting on the road beside the dead signaller."

As the sun began to set, spotting waterfowl flying low from the west became increasingly difficult. Robin Cuimein called out, "My bird!" as one flew in, reflecting off the water's surface. He fired his shotgun twice, missing both times before aiming and firing a third time. The duck crashed into the marsh with a broken wing.

"Good strike!" he complimented his shooting partner for the shot that brought the bird down. Princess Krishna politely suggested that the bird had given her a slightly better angle, which was why Cuimein missed. Cuimein chuckled and asked her not to insult him by making an excuse for his poor aim each time. Krishna replied with a mischievous grin, "So, you want me to call you a worthless shot, then, Collector?"

Cuimein nodded to the native handler to release his retriever dog as he turned. He watched as the animal bounded off through the reeds, then loaded two fresh cartridges into the chambers of his broken shotgun. The event was a shooting party organized by Amjad Taid Khan on marshland north of the village, fed by the waters of the Kurram River, and Christmas was only a few days away. Cuimein had wanted to organize a Christmas camp as a seasonal event, but social functions of that nature were not possible in the Frontier. Instead, he confined the festivities to rides, hunts, outings, and long dinner parties in the evenings. Invitations were sent to several friends in Delhi and other parts of northern India, but most declined for safer and closer offers. However, Cuimein was not upset, as he had made many friends in his eighteen months as a district officer who more than compensated for those unable to attend. Princess Krishna and her brother Sahil, who had made the journey to visit Cuimein shortly after he took office, were the only ones that mattered to him, and this was not their first visit. The day's shoot ended with the sound of a whistle blast and the sun just slipping out of sight below the distant hills. Shooters, handlers, and dogs then made their way towards the cluster of cars parked on a cart track skirting the fenland.

"Ah!" greeted Taid Khan, admiring the waterfowl shot by the dog handler's son. "You have taken a good bag, Robin."

"Not all by myself. Just most of the ducks and the larger geese," replied Cuimein modestly.

"Please don't lie to your host, Collector," retorted Krishna, nearly laughing. "Two of them are his, and the other seven were brought down by me."

After being served black coffee and brandy, the group stood around exchanging tales of difficult shots that either hit or missed. Most of the twenty guests left soon after, but Cuimein, Sahil, Krishna, Hugo du Rand, and Neil Osborne, the district deputy superintendent of police, Bernard Curis' second-in-command, remained as overnight guests of Taid Khan in his village. Ghorzandi, like most villages near the border, was surrounded by a wall. In past years, the gates were bolted after sunset, and the walls were patrolled. Nowadays, with the Frontier receding, one gate was always open and guarded by a watchman who slept in the entrance on a charpoy at night. As Taid Khan's two-car party slowed to pass through the gate, the grey, raw-boned ex-soldier guarding it straightened up to salute. The streets were narrow, although the village was large, with flat-roofed buildings, many of them two-story with balconies. Entering a square with a mosque flanking one complete side, Cuimein followed Taid Khan's car through a high mud brick-walled gateway.

Taid Khan's home was on the other side, a sizeable single-story house with a spacious, tree-planted front garden. To the rear of the house rose a relic of his forefathers, a square three-story tower. Telegraph wires leading into it indicated that the assistant political agent had transformed the building into his working offices. Stopping their cars, the bungalow's khitmagar hurried to open Taid Khan's door, giving a respectful bow. The chokidar, the bungalow watchman, opened the entrance of Cuimein's Humber for him before moving off to close the gate, for it was dark and time to latch up and begin his prowling.

After being shown to rooms where they could cleanse themselves using basins of warm water, the guests changed into fresh clothes and convened on the veranda for drinks. Taid Khan introduced his family, including his veiled wife who was dressed in tight trousers and a long silk chemise. As a devout Muslim, she stood behind her children and remained silent, but acknowledged the guests when her name was called. After a brief introduction, she left with her three children, leaving Taid Khan to entertain the guests alone.

Later that night, the group indulged in a supper of pilau and roast waterfowl, followed by spiced tea on the veranda. In the middle of their conversation, they were interrupted by a young man named Nasir Hatif, who urgently informed them of bandits in the village. Another man, Saleem Raza, reported that he had witnessed the murder of the gate watchman and saw the robbers running into the village.

Hugo du Rand and the others quickly devised a plan, suggesting that they notify the authorities via telegraph, but Amjad warned that the robbers may have already severed the lines. Despite this uncertainty, the group planned to contact help, with Robin and Neil given the task to reach the telegraph tower room.

Cuimein, acting as interpreter because Sahil and Krishna did not understand Pushtu, left them to accompany Osborn around the back of the bungalow. Armed with a lamp taken from one of the servants, they climbed up into the top tower room, only to find that Amjad was right; the line was dead.

Upon returning to the bungalow, they discovered the others arming themselves with hunting firearms from the storeroom. "I have sent Nasir Hatif to the mosque to sound the alarm," Amjad informed them. "It will take some time for armed men to assemble in any significant numbers. So, I suggest we strike for the bazaar before these villainous butchers do any more damage. Will you come, Robin?"

"I believe I should be offended that you asked," retorted Cuimein, moving to collect his shotgun, only to be stopped by Sahil, who was already armed. "Sahil," Cuimein started, his voice gravely serious, "as the heir to the throne, I bear responsibility for your safety."

"Robin, my host's house is under attack," the Rajput Prince responded. "Would you have me hide in a storage room?"

"As the five men filed out through the gate, held open by the watchman, a high alarm drum began sounding from the mosque. Just as the watchman prepared to swing the gate shut, another armed figure pushed past him. Krishna, with a cartridge belt draped across her dress and shoes kicked off for ease of movement, silently followed the men.

Despite it being night, the stars provided enough light to read print. Sticking to the sides of the houses, Amjad led the group down a street before guiding them through a narrow alleyway into another. Cuimein, the last man in the group, was watchful of the front, oblivious to what was unfolding behind him. As the street broadened, a woman's scream was heard, indicating their approach to the bazaar. The group pressed on, slower and more cautiously. As they passed between two low buildings facing each other across the flattened earth street, a turbaned figure on the roof of one building rose to aim at Cuimein's back. Before he could fire, a double shotgun blast sounded, and the figure fell forward. Simultaneously, a second figure on the opposite roof shot at the one who had first discharged the shotgun.

The five men in the street spun around, but only Sahil spotted the head and shoulders of the second rifleman on the roof opposite, who had just fired. With a flash of lightning, he pulled the trigger before the butt was in his shoulder. Then, recovering from the instinctive blink as he shot, the prince could no longer see the turbaned head. "On the roof," he called out. "I believe I hit one of the beggars."

Cuimein was accustomed to the chaos of battle, and this minor engagement was no exception. Pressed against a wall, with shots ringing out from behind, above, and within his party along the length of the street, he had no time to assess what had occurred before more rifle fire was directed up ahead. This was answered by the two frontmen, Hugo and Amjad. Dropping to the ground, they took turns firing their two barrels while the other reloaded.

It was darkest on the edges of the street, where the raiders were making the best use of it. Their only giveaway was the flashes of their rifles. Yet, even that was more than enough. The shotguns, firing number four pellets at ranges less than fifty yards, found a target with almost every blast. Not outright kills - they would have to be a lot closer for that. What they were doing was causing multiple wounds. They could have only brought a better close-quarter street fighting weapon by realizing it.

With resistance melting away before them, the five government men began leapfrogging into and through the bazaar until no enemy was shooting at them. Following up as far as the east gate, where the dead watchman still lay, it was clear the raiders had wasted no time escaping. Returning to the bazaar, they found it filling with armed villagers brandishing swords, jezails, muzzle-loading long-barrelled rifles and a few single-shot breech loaders. The Hindu traders were also out of their shops, terror-struck, most women wailing.

One man, who spoke rationally, told them that the gang had broken into the shops and family quarters. The gang killed one son in front of his father and tortured another man to death after blinding him, all to make them reveal where their money was hidden. Even though they were driven off, they didn't leave empty-handed, taking two money boxes of silver rupees and a captive Hindu girl.

Cuimein, burning with anger, declared that they must be captured before reaching the Administrative Boundary. As the district officer, he took charge and instructed Neil to stay with Amjad, organize the village militia to search the streets, and speak to traders to obtain a description of the gang. Osborne reminded Cuimein that they needed to warn the army and the nearest means of doing so was the police post at Barwand. Cuimein agreed to go with Hugo to warn the army.

The three hurried from the bazaar, retracing their steps back along the street. Nearing the scene where their engagement with the gang first began, they were met by a distraught Nasir Hatif who informed them that the Khan's guest had been shot. The village elder's son ran ahead of them, beckoning them to hurry.

Ahead, a small group of people showed Princess Krishna seemingly sitting with her back against a wall. She held a shotgun across her lap, and her dress was saturated with blood from a bullet wound to her upper chest below the right shoulder. Cuimein cried out in shock, dropping to his knees. Sahil threw himself beside Cuimein, taking his sister in his arms and wailing in anguish. The Englishman took hold of Krishna's head and tilted it back.

"She's unconscious!" he exclaimed. Due to his experience in the war, he had witnessed this reaction caused by gunshot wounds on numerous occasions and knew the reason behind it: blood loss. "Let's take her to the bungalow," he suggested.

Amjad's wife was waiting on the veranda, and upon seeing Krishna being carried, she instructed one of her female servants to bring towels and water. They laid her on a bed in one of the guest rooms, and Cuimein and Sahil stayed with her until the servant returned with the requested items. However, when the woman arrived, Amjad's wife ushered them out of the room, still adhering to her vow of silence.

Cuimein, his jacket tainted with Krishna's blood, punched one fist into his other palm and exclaimed, "What the hell was she doing there?" Meanwhile, Sahil, overwhelmed with distress, paced back and forth in the lounge.

"I need to get to Barwand to sound the alarm. Every minute is critical," Sahil insisted, emotionally affected by Princess Krishna's injury.

In response, Hugo du Rand reminded Cuimein of his primary obligation. "Robin, I have to go! Take the Humber. I'm sorry, but you'll have to go alone. I can't leave Krishna or Sahil. Not now," Cuimein replied, handing Hugo the car key.

As Hugo drove through the gate, Amjad returned, running across the garden, and asked about Princess Krishna's condition. Despite having a blood-stained sleeve from an injury, he ignored, Cuimein informed him that she needed a doctor, and Amjad went inside.

Upon his return, Amjad instructed them that Saysha must go to the hospital, and they should take his car, as it was the closest one to them, located just half an hour away.

Robin, accompanied by Sahil and holding Krishna in his arms, drove to the hospital through the night, with the stars illuminating the way in a beautiful purple hue, barely requiring headlights. Though the bandage wrapped around Krishna's wound was not neat, they had securely attached it.

Cuimein watched ahead for turnings that he would direct Sahil into, while holding the one person in the world that was more precious to him than life itself - Krishna. After spending two weeks with him at Chamblapur, Krishna returned to Jaswara and her suitor was rejected. Krishna's suitor was not considered suitable for marriage, as the Rajput was primarily pledged to the purity of the race. As an Englishman, Krishna's suitor could never be considered a suitable husband for a daughter of a royal house. Krishna's love for him remained concealed in his heart until now.

Cuimein urgently called Zahir Khan to Emily Sheffield's gate when they arrived at Saysha. Zahir Khan was waiting for them, and he was asked to bring the Mem Sahib Doctor since there was a woman who had been shot. He then instructed Cuimein to take Krishna to the medical room. They successfully brought Krishna to Emily Sheffield, who was surprised by Krishna's bravery. Sahil begged the doctor to save Krishna's life, and the doctor assured him that they would operate on her in the morning, when it was much safer. The doctor spoke to two nurses, Sarita, and Lily, instructing them to sterilize the instruments and prepare fresh bandages. She also asked for their help in removing the dressing from the princess's back. "And as for the two of you," Emily began, addressing the men, "clear out of here. Go across to the bungalow and help yourselves to some brandy." An hour passed before the doctor joined them. Both men rose from their chairs on the veranda, standing expectantly. "The bullet passed through," she started to explain, "it missed the lung, but the bones are broken, one shattered with fragments that must be removed. We will do that later this morning when we operate."

"How is she? Is she awake?" Sahil asked, unable to hold back his questions. "Thankfully, she's still unconscious. But it's the blood loss I'm concerned about more than anything," the doctor responded. Cuimein bluntly asked, "Will she recover?" "Once we're done with the operation, the fight to mend will be hers alone," replied Emily. "When can we see her?" Sahil asked. "Perhaps this evening, but until then, I don't want either of you within shouting distance of her," the doctor responded.

"In that case, I must get back," said Cuimein, "I've got to find out what news there is from the army." "I'll stay if you don't mind?" Sahil asked, turning to Emily, "only if it is agreeable with you, Doctor?" "Yes, of course, Prince Sahil, the bungalow is yours," Emily said, calling after

Cuimein as he hurried down the pathway. "Robin! The gang that attacked you at Ghorzandi; it was Shamsi." "How do you know?" Cuimein asked, stopping in his tracks. "One of our sweepers just came from the village. He said that Shamsi was seen crossing the road to the north at dusk yesterday."

"Emily," the district officer warned, his face showing a rage the doctor had never seen before, "if any of those curs show up here sporting shotgun wounds, I want to know. By god, I will make sure they feel the full extent of the law for this."

CHAPTER 19

If man come not to gather The roses where they stand,
They fade among their foliage;
They cannot seek his hand.
-William Cullen Bryant

During Christmas, Ishak, the brigade commander, attempted to decrease the number of garrison commitments and duties to foster a festive atmosphere. Regrettably, his efforts were largely in vain due to the Ghorzanid raid. His entire force was engaged in picketing and heavy road patrolling. However, there was some success as a Scout gasht apprehended six gang members attempting to cross the Rasmak road north of Kandao. Unfortunately, the captive Hindu girl was not with them, raising concerns that she had either been sold into slavery or killed across the Afghan border.

On December 27th, the garrison celebrated Christmas Day. Officers and senior NCOs woke the men with gun salutes and tea laced with rum. They later served them a Christmas dinner in dining tents adorned with blankets and cotton wool, and real butter on the tables.

After Proclamation Day on January 2nd, 1927, the garrison quickly resumed action with a deep operation within tribal territory. To assert their presence, the border garrisons conducted peaceful reconnaissance raids every two weeks into areas claimed by the tribesmen. Each regiment had a designated title when moving, such as Razcol for Razmak and Iscol for Ishak. These operations, lasting three to four days, were dangerous and demanding. Despite the British side maintaining peace, the Pathans viewed this as an opportunity to snipe or ambush the column. Nevertheless, the men were excited to leave the barbed wires behind and stretch their legs.

The infantry column always consisted of two battalions, leaving one behind to man the cantonment. The QLI and a battalion of Gurkhas composed the infantry, and they brought along a baggage train of animals that included horses, camels, and mules. The column's supply transport carried rations, fuel, tents, bedding, and ammunition. Though they may have appeared disorganized on the trek, each animal and load had a specific position in the column. The Artillery Pack Battery was unique as they transported dismantled artillery pieces between handlers and mules, sharing a strong bond of loyalty and mutual understanding.

The column utilized the leap-frogging picket system as their protective shield, departing from Ishak and following the unfinished road west towards the Afghan border. After three miles, they veered south across the country. Their mission was to reach a Mahsud village and administer punishment. Previously, a Scout gasht had been ambushed in the area, resulting in two injuries. Freddie D'urban identified the village men as the culprits and imposed a fine of fifty serviceable rifles. The village ignored the penalty, prompting the column to set off to prove that the Indian government would not tolerate disrespect.

The camping sites for the night had two priorities: proximity to water and defensibility. If necessary, the latter would take precedence over the former. Typically, a lieutenant would be responsible for selecting the site, and their decision was final. Ideally, the site would be in open country and square-shaped, with rocks assembled as sangars at each corner. The sides were fortified with a shallow trench or walls made from stones. The tent lines, gun lines, medical tent, cooking area, and animal lines were arranged in the centre of the site, where space was always at a premium.

Joey Payne stood guard with his section in one of the corners sangars, scrutinizing the camp and surrounding hills. Once the last of the two Scout gashts were safely inside, having provided a patrol screen for the column during the day, the final three pickets were signalled into the camp. As dusk fell, cooking fires were being put out. The men were using the remaining time to visit the latrine, and the brigadier's orders conference with all senior officers was concluding. Soon a bugle would sound, directing everyone to their positions on the camp perimeters for the stand-to alarm. After that, darkness would fall, ushering in another cold Frontier winter night. Following stand-down, Joey donned his knee-length woollen pullover from his pack. He then threads the rifle chain through a hole in his blanket, securing it to his wrist before settling against the sangar wall for a few hours of sleep until it was his turn for watch. Payne felt content being back on column duty, but he missed his friend Benedict, who was away on official leave visiting his wife, Sheela. She had chosen to stay with her parents in Ravlapore, instead of joining the other battalion wives in their hill station, primarily due to her pregnancy. She was due to give birth at the end of March.

Sharing in Benedict's joy over the news, Joey himself was suffering from a bout of depression. Despite Lily being in Saysha, merely sixty miles away - a short distance really, their dream of meeting had not yet materialized. This forced them to continue expressing their unwavering love for each other through cherished letters, reread countless times.

By mid-morning the following day, the Scouts had the offending village at their mercy. After placing pickets around it, the column moved in, encircling the entire area. Freddie D'urban offered the village headman a final opportunity to pay the outstanding fine. When payment was not forthcoming, the village was evacuated. A group of sappers was directed to plant explosive charges in ten selected houses. The detonation wires were then extended to a hillside where the villagers were assembled to witness the consequences of their blatant defiance of Indian government authority. Each chosen house was blown apart one after the other. In a gesture of courtesy, the village headman was invited to detonate the last building. Displaying the joyous anticipation typical of a Pathan tribesman's inherent love for destruction, he gripped the plunger handle and promptly reduced his house to rubble. However, the villagers did not display any outrage or sympathy. Instead, they erupted in laughter.

Kyle Bate, along with his platoon, was responsible for overseeing the villagers, but he did not partake in their laughter, and neither did many from his 6 Platoon. Instead, the lieutenant observed these poorly dressed people, roaring with laughter, his eyes filled with disdain. It was individuals like these who had killed his own men three years prior, mutilating their bodies in the Khyber Pass. He had overheard Freddie

D'urban referring to the tribesmen as 'his chaps' the night before, as if they were an opposing cricket team. Kyle silently scorned this friendly reference; he regarded them in only one way - as contemptible agents of death.

"Excellent, Your Highness, that is very good. Now let's try again, but this time a little higher," said the man overseeing Princess Krishna's effort as she again lifted her bent right arm. Despite concealing her pain behind a fixed expression, she persisted in her attempts. As her forearm reached the level of her brow, the man encouraged her to ignore the pain and focus on moving her arm above her head. The man coaching her was Douglas McDowell, a Eurasian and one of Emily Sheffield's colleagues. He was the closest thing to a surgeon that Saysha could offer and had performed surgery on her bullet wound.

Since the shooting incident two months ago, Princess Krishna spent a month in the hospital and was now recuperating with Robin Cuimein at his bungalow. Sahil was called home to explain their involvement in the raid, and a consultant surgeon had arrived to examine Krishna and assess future treatment. However, it turned out that what had already been done was sufficient, and Krishna's wound was healing. She only needed to stay in the hospital until she was well enough to travel.

One reason for Krishna's good recovery was due to the devoted care of Hemlata. She had arrived at the bungalow, sent by Cuimein in the Humber, and had been by Krishna's side ever since. She had taken on the role of caregiver, attending to Krishna's every need - feeding her, bathing her, and assisting the nurses and staff in changing bed linen. She had stayed by Krishna's bedside, ensuring that she received the best possible care during her recovery.

Her concern for Krishna's safe recovery was so great that she and Douglas McDowell had a dispute at one point. Two days after the operation, Krishna had a fever and occasionally experienced delirium. Hemlata, who had not slept, spent the entire time applying damp towels to Krishna's face and body. In the end, Hemlata was exhausted and felt that not enough was being done to protect the Princess's deteriorating condition. As a result, she confronted the Doctor. Although women usually regulate their emotions, Hemlata was so worried about Krishna's well-being that she argued with the Doctor and demanded more treatment. After a brief argument, he took her onto the veranda, where they sat for twenty minutes while McDowell calmed her down and assured her that there was nothing more, they could do but wait for the fever to break. Shortly after, it did, and McDowell spent more time at the Princess's bedside, often engaging in conversation with the two women.

"That's excellent! Excellent!" he congratulated. "Now rest."

Princess Krishna lowered her arm and sighed with relief.

"The arm," began the Doctor as she repositioned it back into a cloth sling hung around her neck, "keep it in that sling for at least another fortnight. At Saysha, bullet wounds are as common to us as broken limbs. I have seen how some body parts become useless when exercise is not performed during healing. So twice a day, you must work the arm and shoulder, not allowing them to stiffen."

As he spoke, McDowell was packing up his medical bag in preparation for returning to Saysha. He had visited Janka every other day to check on Krishna's recovery. This was his last visit; the next day, his patient would return to Jaswara."

Krishna expressed her gratitude and extended her left hand as she rose, saying, 'Thank you for everything you have done, Doctor. I couldn't have asked for a better physician. Because of your skills, I am fully recovering.' McDowell nodded briefly and took Krishna's hand, reminding her, 'And let's not forget the caring hands of Hemlata,' as he gestured towards the bungalow housekeeper waiting beside them. 'Yes, of course. Goodbye, Doctor,' Krishna replied. After leaving the veranda, McDowell was escorted to Emily Sheffield's Napier by Hemlata. They talked for twenty minutes or more, as they had done every day since his visits began.

Later that evening, Krishna asked Cuimein about finding a replacement housekeeper. He was genuinely confused by the question, to which Krishna giggled and said, 'Oh, Robin, you truly are an unromantic blind man. Haven't you wondered why Douglas McDowell has visited here so often?' Cuimein responded, 'To attend to you.' The Princess then explained, 'That's only part of it! My convalescence here provided him the added advantage of seeing Hemlata.'

Cuimein pondered the idea of the two together before saying, 'Well, if it progresses beyond flirtation, I wish them good luck.' Krishna then asked Cuimein if she had any admirers lurking around the palace. 'Indeed!' retorted the woman. 'I've had enough of suitors.'

Cuimein asked, 'Is it because the Maharaja has exhausted the list of candidates or because you have exceeded the suitable age for a bride?' There was a twinkle of mischief in his eyes. 'You rogue! If I were not familiar with your conversational mischief, I would be truly hurt by those suggestions,' countered Krishna. She gave the district officer a teasing smile before continuing, 'You say those things in jest, but they

are very close to the truth. I have become an embarrassment, almost a shame upon the house.'
Cuimein asked, 'Then why don't you get married? Has the list really dried up?'
Krishna did not answer for a moment. Then she tilted her head back and spoke to the stars.
'When I was a girl, before going to England, I daydreamed of the prince I would marry. But instead, my family confined me in purdah because I was rebellious and would not marry their chosen husband. And then, a handsome young man rescued me on a satin black stallion.'"
"And where did your prince carry you off to?" Cuimein asked good-naturedly.
"To a castle," Krishna replied, ending her fantasy tale in a matter-of-fact tone before lowering her head again.
"I'm pretty sure we all had such fantasies at a young age," Cuimein consoled. "I must admit, in my youthful mind, I often rescued the odd damsel in distress from perilous situations."
"Unfortunately, Collector, real life is not that simple," Krishna replied.
"So, have you given up on your Prince Charming then?" Cuimein teased with a smile.
"I still harbour the hope that perhaps one day someone will come," Krishna said, her eyes lifting to meet Cuimein's, a whimsical air about her. "What do you think? If given the choice, would you come?"

Cuimein was amid formulating his sarcastic reply when a broad shaft of light from the bungalow lit up the lawn. David, on an errand for his mother, switched on a light for visibility and returned to the cookhouse with food wrapped in muslin for the next day's meal. Krishna, standing, announced she was retiring for the night due to her long train journey the next day. This spared Cuimein having to answer her question.

As Krishna exited, the district officer remained behind to smoke one last cigarette and reflect on their conversation. He inwardly thanked David for his timely interruption. Cuimein had been grappling with a personal conflict, challenging his own convictions, desires, common sense, and moral courage. After weeks of inner conflict, he made the only decision he could live with for the rest of his life. He had almost confessed to Krishna a feeling that extended beyond simple fondness.

Cuimein kept his destination a secret and applied for a week's leave. Despite the brief amount of time, he explained in a letter to Sir Antony Reimer, the Regent of Jaswara, that his proposed visit was not intended to be a social event.

A group of men waited among the rocks above a valley for the entire day. As the blue smoke rose from the evening cooking fires in the houses, they prepared to descend from the hills to the village below in the calm spring twilight. The location was Afghanistan, east of the Maraha River, opposite the North Waziristan Border of India.

All sixteen men were clothed in Afghan attire and carried rifles, however, two were not Afghans, betrayed by their unfamiliar gait. Upon reaching the valley floor at nightfall, they crossed crop fields and passed large stacks of chopped straw. They were invited to wash their hands at the mullah's house, where they were welcomed by a servant in the courtyard. Three of them were escorted inside to meet the mullah, who acknowledged one as a warrior of the Faith, identifying him as the gaunt, bony-faced Afghan with a scruffy, pepper-grey beard and perpetually narrowed eyes, known as the Fakir of Matun. After introducing his sons and the village headman, the Fakir introduced the two men accompanying him as friends of the Faith, who had travelled from the distant west. These two Europeans, one blond and the other dark, reciprocated with flawless Muslim etiquette. Once the formalities between the guests and the host were concluded, the mullah guided everyone to a room filled with cushions and rugs, where food was set out before them.

Upon finishing their meal, the visitors were led through the village to the council ground. Oil lamps surrounded the village square of flattened earth, infusing the stagnant air with a foul odour of burning oil. The recently arrived group sat beneath a holly oak tree, facing those who were already assembled. The oil lamps cast more shadows than light, and fifty or more men waited for the discussion to commence. Afghani Border tribesmen, Zadrans, Tannis, Ghilzais, Durranis, and others represented various tribes and influential clans. The first to speak was the mullah, expressing local concerns about the British and their road construction, which could attract Indian merchants and settlers to their border. From there, the influence of the detested British Christians, Sikhs, and Hindu idol worshippers could potentially infiltrate their lands from across the Frontier. Setting the agenda for this jirgah by stoking fears and magnifying rumours, the mullah yielded the floor to the Fakir, who stood to address the assembly. His posture was hunched as he raised his arms in the air, his patchwork dilaq cloak billowing out. "God is great!" he exclaimed loudly. "Know me, brothers. I am the Fakir of Matun. God is great!"

"God is great!" echoed his audience.

"Warriors of the hills," he began, "Mighty Allah has sent me here on a mission. Soon the hated firangi will push their roads up to the border, leaving your valleys and villages open to invasion from the infidel moneylenders and those who burn the souls of their dead-on fiery pyres. They must not be allowed to cross and befoul your lands." *(firangi- A foreigner, mainly a British or a white person)*

"The talk of the roads across the Border is that they're going to provide the powindahs with a shorter route, not bring the dark-skinned Hindu to our hills," called a voice from the semicircle of listeners.

"Yes! And when has a white-faced firangi ever kept his word? Remember how he comes, awal roti, bad soti," replied the Fakir, seizing on this. *(awal roti, bad soti- First bread and then the stick)* What followed was a wrangling debate that echoed around the square in the best Pathan tradition, everyone talking at once, arguing and questioning each other, the delegation below the tree exercising no control but simply adding to the exchanges of opinions and dialogue.

At last, a voice from the shadows asked a question that again allowed the Fakir to gain centre stage. "If there is a danger to our lands from outside, why has the Amir not signalled an alarm?"

"Amir!" scoffed the Fakir, spitting onto the soil at his feet. "When has Kabul cared about what happens in these hills. They only think of themselves, their women, the warmth of their fires, and their bellies. Nothing more. Look not to them for an ally."

"The firangi have many guns, many soldiers. If we are to push them away from our border, what is to stop them from returning repeatedly?" asked someone, visualising the escalation of events sparked by a sizeable cross-border raid.

"Once beaten, the firangi will not be back," replied the Fakir raising a finger, his voice adopting an insidious tone. "In the lands beyond the great Indus, the people are crying out to be rid of the white faces. Soon with the help of others, they will rebel, slit the foreigners' throats, and scatter their bones to the jackals. Then their March to our Borders will be finished, and the firangi will be gone forever!"

"Who are these 'others'?" cried a sceptic. "And what is the greatness of their power that they will defeat the Firangi's armies?"

"They'll be given the same power as we have been," replied the Fakir. His words thundered off the surrounding walls as he turned to take two large pouches held out to him by the Europeans. Then, holding them up, he spilt their gleaming contents to the ground. "Russian gold! For you. And with it and the blessing of Almighty Allah, we'll strike the enemy with a fatal blow. For I, the Fakir of Matun, declare jihad, a holy war upon the Firangi. Now, brothers! Now is the time for Azrael, the angel of death, to visit their beds."

These pledges and statements, intended to incite, would, in the weeks to come, prove false. Throughout the nineteenth century, with designs on India, Russia continually sent agents and instigators to make mischief along its Afghan border. With the replacement of the Tsarist government by Lenin's Bolshevik regime, this had, for a time, ceased. But now, in the last year, this expansionist policy has experienced a rebirth. In search of provocateurs to further their cause, the Fakir of Matun was found, in hiding, with a price on his head, in caves in the Kotanni Mountains. What made this hunted old man accept the mantle of the religious crusader was not the inducement of gold nor their fairy tales of Punjab about to explode in rebellion and the Mahatma Gandhi movement soon to overthrow the British Indian government. The gold meant nothing, and the words he knew were lies, but to someone embittered and raging for revenge against those who had killed his son, it was like a gift from the Prophet himself.

At the sight of gold coins cast at their feet, any scepticism among the gathering of tribal chiefs was brushed aside. In heady outbursts of emotional fervour, they leapt to their feet.

"I have a thousand men sworn to follow!"

"Five hundred men await your call!"

"On your command, two thousand rifles will spring to your side!"

"From Sir Antony Reimer's Regency headquarters to the State Winter Palace was a pleasant ten-minute drive through the northern outskirts of Udaigarh. It was March, late spring in Jaswara, and the morning was well into the day's full heat. Off the roadway, flowers and blossoming shrubs displayed their final splendor before the summer heat arrived to turn them to dust.

The passenger in Sir Antony's car, being driven to the Winter Palace, observed them as he passed. Nonetheless, Robin Cuimein's eyes and ears registered neither sight nor sound, his mind in turmoil, apprehensive that his mission to Jaswara would end in disappointment. He had arrived by train earlier and went directly to the Regency, where he announced the purpose of his visit to Sir Antony. After listening, Sir Antony neither disapproved nor tried to dissuade him. However, he thoroughly outlined every insurmountable obstacle between him and a successful conclusion to his mission.

Upon turning into the palace grounds, the gate guard saluted to the familiar car as it drove past. Blue peacocks on the field lawn watched the car while squirrels darted between trees. The palace, when initially constructed, was a fort, which under Mogul rule, was expanded and refurbished in Persian and Turkish styles. As a result, its color was a dazzling mix of white and pink, highlighting towers, domes, and windowed turrets, all connected by balconies and enclosed decorative stone verandas.

After thanking and dismissing Sir Antony's chauffeur at the main courtyard entrance, Cuimein was met by the palace majordomo. "The Dewan is expecting you, Cuimein saheb. If you will follow me, please," he said, bowing before leading the way.

While the upper floors of the palace were designated as bedrooms, apartments and leisure rooms, the lower floor was allocated for reception rooms, function halls and offices. The majordomo knocked on one of these office doors and announced the arrival of the district officer upon being allowed to enter.

Krishna's father dismissed his chief secretary and left his desk to greet Cuimein in a large office with a high ceiling, where the walls were adorned with century-old frescoes, and the windows filtered the sun's rays through a lattice framework. "It is always a pleasure to see you again, Robin," the Dewan welcomed, extending his hand to the Englishman. "And I cherish each visit, Your Highness," replied Cuimein, inclining his head as he shook the prime minister's hand. Narain Singh was also thinner and taller than his older brother, the Maharaja, and his upswept cleft beard was less grey.

"Sir Antony's telephone message indicated that you requested a formal audience, but not too formal, I hope?" ventured the Dewan, as he escorted Cuimein across the room and motioned him to sit in one of the six lounge chairs arranged around a low, carved wooden table. "Yes, Your Highness. The nature of my visit is formal. I am not here officially as a servant of the Indian Civil Service, but on my own accord," started Cuimein, sitting upright with his white topee on one arm. "Firstly, I must offer my sincerest apologies for placing your daughter under my charge in such a location and circumstances that nearly resulted in her death."

"Robin," the prime minister replied, "as Princess Krishna's father, I am deeply touched that you have travelled to Jaswara to deliver such a heartfelt declaration. However, Prince Sahil made it clear that my daughter's eagerness for the encounter significantly contributed to her near-fatal shooting. You cannot be held accountable for that."

Cuimein insisted that the responsibility for the danger was his alone. The Dewan reminded him that his own district police had reported that Princess Krishna had killed a raider who was about to shoot Cuimein, and that the prince had shot another raider, allegedly the one who had wounded the princess. Although the situation was a near tragedy, the princess was safe and recovering, and she had not dishonoured the Royal House of Jaswara.

Cuimein still felt undeserving of the Dewan's leniency, but the prime minister urged him to let go of his guilt. Neither of his children blamed Cuimein in the slightest.

Cuimein then made a request he knew he shouldn't ask, but one that wouldn't leave him until he asked. He respectfully asked for permission to marry Princess Krishna. The prime minister was surprised but managed to conceal any emotion. He stood and faced the window with his hands clasped behind his back. "Robin, you're not a foreigner unfamiliar with our customs, traditions, and codes," corrected the Dewan.

"I am well aware of them, sir," confirmed Cuimein. "That's why I feel so pained and anguished. I realize that by asking to marry your daughter, I have insulted you and the Royal family. I beg your forgiveness, but I cannot restrain my love for her any longer."

The Dewan asked, "And what about my daughter? Does she share your feelings?"

"In all honesty, your Highness, I do not know," answered Cuimein truthfully. "We are not lovers, and I have never confessed my love to her or anyone else. She treats me with sisterly fondness."

"Despite this, do you believe she would agree to be your wife?" questioned the Rajput noble.

"That is the dilemma I face, sir. Only by asking will I know. And then, one way or another, my torment will end," replied Cuimein, trying to keep his emotions in check.

"Robin, do you understand our Rajput tradition of retaining the purity of our bloodline?" asked the Dewan.

"Yes, sir, I am familiar with it," Cuimein responded.

"In our Royal Houses, we prefer our daughters to marry commoners rather than impure princes of other states. This is a tradition that has never been broken," explained Narain Singh, turning to look at Cuimein intently.

"Your Highness, I am in love with your daughter," Cuimein declared, providing his only counter.

"Robin," said the speaker, "despite being Krishna's father, I am appointed as the officiator of affairs of State. The Maharaja handles court matters and is responsible for selecting suitable marriage matches for heirs to the dynastic line. The Maharaja will decide whom Princess Krishna should marry."

"To date, Princess Krishna has refused all suitors, Sir," Cuimein reminded the prime minister, hoping to justify his petition.

"That is an undeniable fact, Robin," the prime minister agreed. "But do you possess acceptable credentials? For example, are you of suitable Aryan blood, and is your horoscope in harmony? Are you the son of a Rajput Clan?"

Cuimein's resolution faltered, knowing that Narain Singh did not expect a response, and he lowered his gaze to the chair seat opposite him. For a few moments, the two men remained silent, Cuimein feeling dejected and the prime minister studying the handsome Englishman who would forever be a part of Jaswara's history.

"Robin!" The Dewan's voice interrupted their silence, sounding tender. "There is a garden below these windows. Wait there, and refreshments will be brought to you. I will then meet with the Maharaja. He will make a decision on this issue."

Cuimein complied, but as he opened the door to leave, he was stopped by the prime minister. "Robin, you must realize that there will be no dowry. If the Maharaja grants your request, Princess Krishna will come to you penniless. All her jewellery is the property of the State," the prime minister reminded him.

"Your Highness, having her is beyond value to me. If I had the wealth, I would pay the State a king's ransom for her," Cuimein replied.

Upon entering the Maharaja's apartment, the prime minister found him seated at his desk.

"Ah, my brother!" the Maharaja greeted him.

"The issue of Princess Krishna's unmarried status has come up again."

The Maharaja's expression showed mild confusion.

"I must inform you that a suitor has proposed for her hand in marriage," the Dewan stated matter-of-factly. The Maharaja's expression quickly shifted to one of displeasure, angered those preliminary discussions had not been held.

"He is here right now, awaiting an answer," his brother further informed him. The Maharaja straightened in his chair, his fists clenching, as fury began to build in his eyes. "And he is an Englishman," Narain Singh concluded, watching with concealed amusement as the Maharaja rose from his chair, appearing as though a volcano about to erupt.

"Father, did you want to see me?" Princess Krishna asked as she opened the Dewan's office door. She was wearing a European-patterned sky-blue muslin dress, with a white silk sling supporting her right arm. She stood holding the door handle, waiting for a response.

"Yes, my daughter! Come in!" the prime minister confirmed. "I regret to say, but once again, the topic of your marriage has come up," her father declared, placing his writing pen down.

"Marriage!" she retorted, halting in her steps. "I thought we were done with the suitor selection process for me."

"It's not a matter to be ignored," the Dewan responded. "You are a Princess. You have already exceeded the usual age for marriage by ten years. Others might feel embarrassed; you, however, seem to revel in it, but now it must stop. And just for your information, we did not pick him; he chose you."

"He chose me!" Krishna exclaimed. "And the Maharaja agreed to this?"

"With reservations - yes," her father replied. "He's poor and lives far away."

"Ha!" the Princess snorted. "And who is this beggar who expects me to share in his poverty?"

"See for yourself, daughter," the Dewan suggested, pointing to a window. "He's in the garden below, awaiting your response."

"Here?" Her voice escalated to almost a shout. "He has the audacity to come here - expecting an immediate answer? What's the name of this audacious man?"

"Look for yourself," her father advised again, picking up his pen to feign writing.

Torn between curiosity and the temptation to storm out of the room, curiosity prevailed over pride. As she sauntered hesitantly towards the window, the Dewan looked up to observe his daughter. Reaching the window, she raised herself on tiptoes to peek through the lattice. Below, an Englishman sat on a terrace wall with a white topee beside him. A servant had just offered him a drink from a tray, which he accepted and placed untouched on the wall. Watching his daughter's face transition from indignant anger to astonished joy remained one of Narain Singh's most pleasurable moments in life.

"It's Robin! It's Robin!" she cried out, turning around to exclaim: "He came!"

As the Dewan left his desk, Krishna ran towards him to embrace him.

"Oh, father, thank you!" she sobbed, her tears of happiness cascading down her cheeks.

"Thank your uncle, my daughter," said her father, hugging his daughter and stroking her hair as she rested her head against his shoulder. "But in agreeing to your marriage, he has stipulated that you will not have the sanction of a royal wedding."

"It is of no great importance," she replied through her tears. "As long as Robin and I are together, that is all I care about."

"Then go and tell him," said her father, gently pulling away from her. "He is suffering terribly, waiting to hear the Maharaja's decision."

The princess did not rush to the terraced garden. Instead, she bathed her reddened eyes in cool water and waited for a servant to collect a flowered garland.

On the terrace, Cuimein was waiting like a man in a trance. He alternated between sitting against a low wall and pacing back and forth, barely aware of his actions. Unnoticed by him, the garden was full of natural beauty and sweet scents. At the fountain, a clump of maidenhair fern grew surrounded by red and orange blossoms. Above patches of purple heliotrope, blue convolvulus climbed up to the balconies. The imperial standard flew high above him on the palace's tallest point, where a flock of white doves soared in wheeling circles.

"Collector! I will not forgive you for this. I had to learn of your presence here from the servants." Emerging from his worried depths, Cuimein found the last person he wanted to see approaching him through the garden. In her left hand, Princess Krishna carried a garland of flowers.

"I beg your pardon, Princess, but I had to finalize a point of business with your father," Cuimein explained.

"Your visit is a surprise," Krishna played innocently, determined to set the terms for him. "Did you inform anyone that you were coming here?"

"Oh, no. I didn't have time to send a telegram before leaving," Cuimein lied, quickly changing the subject. "And your injury? I hope there are no complications."

"None! The exercises are proving their worth. Soon I'll be able to dispense with the sling," Krishna assured.

As their conversation continued, Cuimein found his concentration slipping. He sat back down on the wall and repeatedly glanced towards the palace entrance, hoping to be summoned.

"Do you love me, Robin?" The sudden, frank question caught the Englishman completely off guard.

"Oh, Jesus! You certainly know how to put someone on the spot," replied Cuimein, buying himself a few moments to think before answering her question.

"Do you?" She repeated.

"Yes," he admitted. "I've been secretly in love with you for some time."

"Since when? When did you fall in love with me? That one night we made love?" Krishna waited in silence for his response.

"No, the evening in the field after you delivered the Harijan baby, when I called you 'remarkable,' and you laughed at the word," replied Robin, his eyes staring straight into hers, his voice soft and sincere.

"Am I still remarkable, Robin?"

"Yes, even more so," Cuimein replied, aware that he shouldn't confess his suppressed feelings to Krishna at this moment. Her proximity was making it difficult for him to restrain himself.

"Then why did you never tell me of this love?" She asked.

"Damn it, Princess. You know why. It would have been pointless. You are a princess of a royal house of Rajputana, and your customs prohibit any form of shared infatuation between us," Cuimein burst out in anger. He pushed himself from the wall and walked a few steps away. Realizing he had let the conversation spiral out of control, he responded bluntly to prevent any further questions from the woman he loved deeply, which could jeopardize the negotiations at the palace. "I love you," Krishna confessed with the innocent grace of a regal maiden. The Englishman was unable to respond, his mind a whirlwind of relief, joy, and impending sorrow. "Robin, ask me to marry you. Now! Please!" Krishna's request was calm, but her eyes pleaded. "No!" Robin rejected, his anger returning. "I won't steal you! I won't." Krishna stood silent, watching the man of high principles whose love she had reciprocated for a long time. For her, it had started on the first day they met.

""I never asked you to steal me, Robin," Krishna replied with amusement. "But should you consider it, no one here would stop you. Not even the palace guard. Apprehend Chitor Cuimein? They're more likely to give our elopement a royal escort to the borders of British India." Once again, the Englishman was rendered silent.

"Ask me, Robin. It's important. Please, ask me?" pleaded the dark, alluring beauty before him, who he yearned to marry so desperately.

"My darling, will you marry me?" he heard his own voice say. In response, Krishna stepped forward and draped a garland of flowers around his neck with her left hand. "Do you know what I've done?" she asked. Cuimein, understanding the significance of the marriage garland, looked up from the ring of flowers on his chest. "You've accepted me."

"Yes, my love," Krishna said with a faint triumphant smile. "I have accepted you." Cuimein responded solemnly, "It is of no consequence. Regardless of what we may feel for each other, I will not disrespect the courtesies and friendship your family has shown me by taking you as my wife without the Maharaja's permission. I can't do it. I just can't!"

"But he has given it, Robin," the Princess announced, filled with pride at Cuimein's chivalrous stance.

"What? He's given his permission?" repeated the Englishman, staring in surprise at the woman, his expression momentarily showing anger. "And you knew this? You let me fret this entire time, even though you knew everything?"

Then, as he fully comprehended what she had said, his face softened in relief. He stepped forward, gathered her in his arms, and kissed her cheeks and neck. "You are a troublemaker," he teased. "I've been in agony waiting for that news."

"I'm sorry, Robin," she apologized. "But I couldn't come to you as a gift. It had to be a pledge between us, one bonded by mutual love." They gently sought each other's lips, savouring the desire this aroused, recalling a night of unbridled passion.

"Remember when I told you I would marry none but a warrior, Collector?" his Rajput Princess whispered as their lips parted. "And it's a warrior I have won."

CHAPTER 20

Death is the black camel that
kneels before every door.
-Indian Proverb

Pausing momentarily in her writing, Lily Richmond looked up to check on a woman who was sleeping in the bed just a few steps away. The woman, Eleanor Ratcliffe, was suffering from a recurrence of malaria fever and was resting peacefully for the first time that day. Lily could see Eleanor's face through the mosquito net, which was pale but dry. Earlier in the day, Eleanor's face had been glistening from outbreaks of sweating. Eleanor's husband, Oliver, was the District Excise Assistant Commissioner but was unfortunately called away to Peshawar. As the family were close friends of Emily Sheffield, Lily had offered to come from Saysha to Janka to help nurse Eleanor through this bout of illness until she was satisfactorily recovered.

Although it was nearing midnight, Lily was using no artificial light to work by. The brilliance of an April full moon provided more than enough illumination by which to read and write. Lily had just finished writing a letter to Joey Payne and had just begun writing another one to her aunt

Harriet. As she was asking about her two cousins, Peter, and Simon, who were both now enlisted in the 2nd QLI's corps of bulges, Lily was interrupted by sounds and movements on the veranda. The family dog, a black Labrador, had just slunk in a cowed manner past the veranda door, with its neck fur raised and giving a muted growl.

Leaving her writing, Lily stepped out onto the veranda to investigate. Outside the bungalow, looking left and right, she could neither see nor hear anything suspicious. The night was quiet, the garden still, and no shadows moved in the surrounding apricot orchards. The servants' quarters and stables were peaceful and now there was no sign of the dog. Assuring herself that all was well, as a routine precaution, Lily walked down the veranda to check on the family's only child, Tracy, their five-year-old daughter. From the veranda window, the nurse saw with alarm that the child's bed was empty, and the mosquito net pushed back.

Catching her breath, Lily rushed to the nearest door and stopped in the central hallway with a sigh of relief. Tracy, with her brown hair hanging down the back of her white nightdress, stood barefoot at the lounge doorway, looking in. As Lily's heartbeat steadied, she approached the girl, intending to put her back to bed. But before reaching the girl, Tracy slowly walked into the lounge, as if to explore.

"Tracy! What is it, sweetie? A bad dream? Is that what-?" Lily whispered as she reached out to catch hold of her, then abruptly froze in her tracks.

The room was large and extensively furnished, which should have provided darkened areas. However, with the spotlight beam of a full North Indian moon flooding through the windows, this was not the case. The three men in the room made no attempt to conceal themselves - not because there was nowhere to hide in this light - but rather because they were unafraid. Two stood beside a gun cabinet where rifles and a shotgun were secured by a lock and chain, and the third was ten feet back from the hall doorway to one side of Lily. All three, except for turbans and loincloths, were naked and holding knives.

"Salaam," said Lily, clapping Tracy's shoulders and drawing the girl close against her dressing gown.

"If you have business with the household, you must return tomorrow. Everyone is asleep as of now." Despite knowing that they were men focused on theft, the nurse felt the need to say something. It didn't matter that she didn't receive a response because what was important was that she was able to speak to them and remain calm. By speaking in English, she could lessen the chance of reminding the robbers of their previous encounter with her. One of the men standing near the gun cabinet was Abdul Shamsi, and the man next to her with the recognizable facial scar was Firoz-un-Din.

In response to their discovery, Shamsi lifted his knife, staring at Firoz-un-Din, and gestured towards the hall doorway. Alerting Lily that he was there, Firoz-un-Din indicated for her to remain quiet by putting a finger to his lips. He then moved to one side of the doorway, blocking the exit for the two Europeans.

Tracy turned to the nurse and asked, "Who are they, Lily?"

"They are the men your father sent to collect his rifles," whispered Lily, offering comfort. "Now, let's stay quiet until they finish. Then we can both go back to bed."

As the two men at the gun cabinet returned to the business of stealing, Lily, with an arm across Tracy's chest, held the girl tight against her. Then, patting the child's shoulder with her other hand to soothe doubt, Lily, a captive viewer, watched the two Pathan robbers as they worked. In dressing-gown and sandalled slippers, with her blond hair hanging long down her back, she believed for the moment that the gang did not, as yet remember her.

For what seemed a long time, with the room's air beginning to taint with the foul odour of the men's body stench, the woman and child waited.

Once Tracy looked up to whisper Lily's name, only to receive a soft hush from the nurse.

"Lily! What is this? Who are they?" demanded a voice behind. It was Eleanor Ratcliffe. In her nightdress, on bare feet, still suffering from fever and distraught at awakening to find intruders in her house, she began raving in a loud voice. Then she shouted at the two men by the gun cabinet: "You! Get away from there. Get away!" Her head spinning around, Lily had no time to warn her shocked and sick patient to remain silent. However, with sickening horror, she could only witness Firoz-un-Din pounce from behind to draw his knife across Eleanor's throat. As the woman dropped to the floor, her eyes, opened wide, were now slowly closing, a flood of blood gushing from her slit throat.

Keeping Tracy's face away from the sight, Lily backed off to the nearest wall.

"Mommy! Mommy!" cried the girl, fighting against Lily's hands and trying to turn to her mother.

"It's alright, Tracy. Your mother can't talk; she's fainted. Be still and be quiet," whispered Lily, gripping the girl tightly and holding her head so she couldn't see her mother collapse on the stone floor, her face lying in a rapidly expanding pool of blood.

Now fearful for their safety, Lily watched and listened warily to the gang members as they reacted to this ominous escalation of their night's robbery.

"The servants will have heard. They'll raise the alarm," warned Firoz-un-Din.

"Yes, we must leave the rifles," agreed Shamsi, joining Firoz-un-Din to stand over Eleanor Ratcliffe's body.

Before saying more, he looked towards Lily and Tracy, his cold predatory eyes assessing their value, loath to depart empty-handed. "Take the woman hostage and kill the child."

"No!" cried Lily, clutching Tracy even closer to her. "Don't kill the child. Her father has money. He will pay richly for her safe return. Take both of us. I will see that she does not cause you any delay."

Momentarily surprised by Lily's outburst in Pushtu, the three outlaws stared at her in silence, broken only by Shamsi gesturing with a flick of his knife towards the veranda door. "Take both of them."

As Firoz-un-Din and the third villain moved towards them, Lily lifted Tracy into her arms.

"Now, Tracy, we have to go with these men. We will return to your mother and father, so please don't worry. And it is very important that you stay quiet and don't cry out."

"I don't want to, Lily. I want to stay! I want to stay!" pleaded the young girl.

"Shush, Tracy! Shush, my love. We must go. We must," said Lily in a light but firm voice as she responded to the push by Firoz-un-Din towards the veranda door.

Crossing the garden, they were joined by a fourth figure who took up the rear. At the surrounding wall, Tracy was handed over by two men, while Lily was bundled over with hands, the backs of which were slick with cheetah fat. Through the orchards they ran, Lily struggling to carry Tracy, her sandal slippers threatening to fly off at every step. Then, before crossing one of the district's main roads, a halt was made in the cover of a clump of barberry bushes. A fifth gang member awaited them, guarding the others' clothing and rifles.

As they donned their garb, Lily, biting at the lower fabric of her dressing gown, tore off strips of cloth to tie her sandals more securely to her feet. She bound Tracy's bare feet using the same material as protection should she be forced by fatigue to release the girl to the ground.

Reaching the bushes, Lily was breathless, her arms aching terribly from carrying the girl, but it was a pain she was prepared to suffer if her mind and flesh could endure it, for she believed that the gang members would kill her with neither compassion nor pity should Tracy become a hindrance.

Lily, who was comparatively new to the Frontier, had learned that the Pathan, despite his lawless and piratical habits, held sacredly to a fundamental humanitarian code that prevented intentionally killing women or children. However, the ruthless Abdul Shamsi and his gang disregarded these ethics when they coldly took Eleanor Ratcliffe's life. Armed with this knowledge, Lily knew that she and Tracy had to keep up with the gang during their flight back to the safety of the tribal territories to survive. Shortly after, a man standing over her kicked her on the thigh and ordered her to rise, signalling that they had to leave quickly.

The following day, Robin Cuimein was sorting through telegrams and reports at his desk when his chief clerk informed him that the Superintendent of Police urgently wished to speak with him on the phone. Meanwhile, Cuimein had also received a telegram from Delhi congratulating him on his wedding and requesting an invitation to the wedding procession with an elephant ride. After Halting his car in the Ratcliffe's drive, Cuimein sought out Bernard Curis to discuss the matter of urgency. He found Curis on the rear veranda overseeing the search of the garden and orchard by his uniformed men.

"Bernard," Cuimein called, alerting the policeman to his arrival. "Good morning, sir," greeted Curis. He turned towards Cuimein with his hands clasped behind his back and a leather-bound swagger stick tucked under one arm. "No sign of the child and nurse. My boys are out beating about the brush, but we've turned up not so much as a footprint." "Thank God. Then there's a chance they could still be alive," replied Cuimein. "Yes," agreed Curis. "But if so, they're undoubtedly kidnapped." "By whom?" asked Cuimein. "It's difficult to say," replied Curis, shrugging his shoulders while turning to lead the district office into the lounge. "The servants discovered the body at first light. According to them, nothing has been taken, although the gun cabinet looks to have been tampered with." Cuimein examined the cabinet lock and joined Curis, who stood beside a pool of blood that had not yet been cleaned up. "I guess they were caught in the act by Eleanor," said Curis. "Then, one way or the other, this led to them abandoning robbery for kidnapping." "Poor Eleanor," commented Cuimein earnestly, for he had been a dinner guest here on two occasions. "There was no struggle," went on Curis. "Her throat was cut cleanly. She must have fainted because of the shock, then died of asphyxiation." "Who? Who?" demanded Cuimein in frustrated anger, his voice echoing off the room's walls. "Curis offered, 'If they are from the hills, they'll be skulking back that way now.'

Cuimein asked Bernard, 'What actions have you taken so far?' He put aside his personal grief and assumed his role as the district officer.

Bernard replied, 'If the murder and possible kidnapping were committed by tribesmen beyond the Administrative Boundary, their interception would be a matter for our border posts and the army. Neil Osborne is attending to that side of things. If, however, criminals from within the district committed this, our informants will soon give us news of that.'

Cuimein pressed, 'Can you think of anything else which could be done now? I must get this news off to Peshawar. But, first, I want to inform the Chief Commissioner that we're doing everything possible to find and rescue Miss Richmond and the child.'

Curis suggested, 'You could ask for an aeroplane. Some of those RAF bods up in their machines are worth a regiment of cavalry on the ground.'

Cuimein replied, 'Right! I will demand them. I'll be in my office at the bungalow for the rest of the morning. If anything, new develops, telephone or send a messenger.'

The police superintendent spoke up as Cuimein stepped out onto the veranda, 'Oh, sir. I have taken one other action. I have sent a local person who's worked for us before into the town to find out what the bazaar gossip is. I've found that the lower you go, the better the information.'"

--oOo--

Once a week at Ishak, just before the guard dismounted, the khassadars' levies who watched over bridges and other critical points on the new road would present themselves at the garrison for payment of their wages. They were not allowed into the camp armed and had to leave their rifles at the guardroom. The guard lance-corporal was responsible for checking them in. Joey Payne took the last tribesman's rifle and returned a numbered tin disc while Bert Colling helped him collect the rifles. Bert pointed out that the khassadars' rifles had symbols signifying the number of killings each had done. Payne cautioned Bert not to tell the tribesmen that they smelled bad, attributing the odour to the number of beads and notches on their rifles. He also noted how poorly the khassadars maintained their guns and marveled at the fact that the bullets even discharged properly.

Sergeant Harry Evans, the guard commander from the previous night, interrupted their conversation. He informed Payne that the RSM wanted to see him urgently. Payne asked if he could go after the dismissal parade, but the sergeant insisted he go immediately.

Payne found RSM Richmond standing alone, a short distance from the battalion orderly room tent. He halted to attention and asked if the RSM had summoned him.

"Yes, Corporal Payne," the RSM replied in a sombre, almost melancholy tone, a departure from his usual crisp and forthright responses.

"It's not about you. It's about your colleague, Corporal Lyall," he continued. "With the Padre on leave, the Commanding Officer wants a close friend nearby when he speaks to him. Come with me, and I'll explain as we walk."

As they fell into step, they marched through the lines of tents and across the football pitch towards the camp's low boundary wall. Lieutenant-Colonel Steinfeld and an adjutant were waiting for them, but not for the RSM and Corporal Payne. Sergeant Major Little arrived soon after as an escort for Benedict Lyall. Both stopped to attention and saluted as they approached. The colonel returned their salutes and dismissed Sergeant-Major Little with a, "Thank you, Sergeant-Major, that will be all." After nodding to the adjutant, the colonel left, taking Jake Richmond with him.

"Stand easy, Corporal Lyall," said Colonel Steinfeld, walking up to address him. "I've asked to see you here because I have a difficult task to perform, one that cannot be dealt with in a normal orderly room parade."

"Yes, sir," acknowledged Lyall as the Commanding Officer paused.

"We have just received a signal from Ravlapore Garrison Headquarters," began the colonel, his voice formal, his eyes looking away. "Your wife gave birth to a daughter yesterday morning."

"A daughter, sir," replied Benedict with a smile, his shoulders rising as he stood up straight. "Thank you very much, sir. That's great news. Simply great."

"Corporal Lyall," Steinfeld continued, looking him in the eyes. "I'm sorry to inform you that tragically, your wife died during childbirth."

"Sir?" Benedict uttered, his face registering shocked dismay.

"I'm sorry, Corporal Lyall," said the Colonel.

"No, sir. It's not possible. She can't be dead, sir," Benedict pleaded, his voice rising in appeal.

"There's no doubt," replied the Colonel. "As soon as the signal came in, I had the adjutant verify it. Unfortunately, the confirmation of your wife's death has just arrived - I'm sorry."

"Sir...Sir..." the Corporal repeated, trying to think of something to say to change this nightmare and allow his wife to remain alive."

"You must be willing to see your daughter," interrupted the Colonel. "At the first opportunity on compassionate grounds, I'll ensure you are sent away on leave."

With nothing more to be said, the commanding officer walked away, passing Joey who sprang to attention and saluted.

"Watch over him, Corporal Payne," he ordered, returning the salute. "Talk to him if he wishes, but don't leave him alone."

"Yes, sir," replied Joey, his saluting arm dropping limp to his side before he slowly walked towards Lyall.

When the RSM told him of Sheela's death, he went numb. His mind was engulfed with sorrow for Benedict. Only now was he beginning to struggle out of the shock and attempting to think of words of condolence that could in some way lessen the impact this appalling tragedy was having on his friend.

"Benedict, I'm sorry," was all he could think to say.

Lyall did not reply and stood as if rooted to the ground, his head down, looking first at one point of the ground, then another. Then turning to Payne, his hands came up as clenched fists.

"She's not dead, Joey. She can't be dead."

The sight of Benedict desperate to believe that the death of his wife was untrue was pitiful for Payne, who had served with him for over five years. In that time, Payne had seen Benedict laugh at peril and show bravery in the face of death. However, this was not the man he knew. Benedict was reduced to a pathetic, child-like cry for help, his face distorted in pain and anguish. Payne didn't wish to destroy his friend's attempt at self-delusion, so he agreed with him that there was a chance the message was wrong.

Lyall clung to the hope that the news of his wife's death was an error but was filled with anguish. He loved her deeply, and they were happy together. Joey knew that nothing he could say would lessen Benedict's pain. As Benedict's mind was filled with memories of their mutual love, joy, and laughter that would never be repeated, another emotion began to take hold - anger. He raised his fists and raged against the Almighty for the unjust act. The anger subsided, and Benedict blamed himself for his wife's death;

he believed that he gave her the illness, and if they hadn't met, and if he had just ridden past, she would still be alive.

"No, Benedict," Joey protested. "It's never your fault." He found himself watching as Benedict fell to his knees and began to cry. Joey knew there was nothing to do but wait for his friend to let it out. Benedict cried even as the buglers in the lines behind them began playing "assembly." After five minutes, Joey turned as someone called his name. It was Lance-Corporal Sid Frith, who had been recently promoted.

"Joey! Sergeant Ridley sent us. He says you need to hurry over to the RSM," Frith said, breathing heavily.

"Okay," Joey replied. "But keep an eye on Benedict. He's having a tough time."

"Sure. What's going on?" Frith asked.

"His wife just died," Joey answered.

"Damn," Frith said. He then explained that the bugle calls were due to a kidnapping of an English woman and a child.

For the second time in an hour, Joey found himself reporting to the RSM for an undisclosed reason. Outside the battalion headquarters tent, Richmond was preparing for a rapid deployment, armed with a rifle and a pack on his back. The adjutant was giving him instructions, and preparations for the deployment were in full swing. As Joey waited at attention, Richmond approached him. He seemed composed, but his eyes betrayed a hidden fear.

"The kidnapped woman," he said, his voice tense. "We have gone out on a mission to intercept the gang. They have taken Lily, lad."

Throughout the months that turned into years, Joey and Lily managed to keep their love for each other alive. His Regimental Sergeant Major had never given any indication of knowing about their relationship, treating him like any other junior NCO in the battalion. However, in this moment, he hinted that he knew about the infatuation between Joey and his niece.

After being dismissed by Richmond, Joey rushed back to his tent, collecting his pack, ammunition, webbing, and rifle before joining 6 Platoon on the roadway. Overcome with worry and fear for Lily, he didn't notice Benedict Lyall joining him at the head of 1 Section until he spoke.

"Don't worry about Lily, Joey lad," said Lyall, wiping away tears from his cheeks. "We'll bring her back."

--oOo--

On the third morning after the kidnapping, Robin Cuimein led a convoy of three cars and a lorry containing a squad of frontier constabulary down the tree-lined lane leading to the Saysha Mission in his Humber. Once again, he was coming to seek Emily Sheffield's assistance to resolve a crisis.

On the first day after the crime, Bernard Curis' sources acquired enough scraps of bazaar hearsay and cross-confirmation of strong rumours to confidently point at Abdul Shamsi and his gang as the culprits responsible. However, identification and apprehension were two different challenges. The country between Janka and the Administrative Border was full of nullahs and broken hills, providing ample hiding places for a handful of skilled men. Upon discovery of Eleanor Ratcliffe's body, the police and army dispatched patrols to block the gang's escape by fanning out across the district. Although this was more of a drill than a barrier, as the police were limited to roads and villages, the army had only a regiment of Indian Lancers whose horses were unsuitable for searching through nullahs and rugged hills.

With the arrival of a flight of "Ninaks", two-seater DH 9A biplanes from Peshawar, Cuimein moved the headquarters for the search operations from Janka to the police post in Barwand. The post was located on the district's main road from the border to Indu's crossings and its primary function was to provide secure storage for powindah traders' rifles, which were forbidden to travel armed into India. Using the road outside as an airstrip, Cuimein remained there for two days to set up a command post and organize the erection of accommodation tents, a refuelling point, and facilities for providing meals for the staff and those involved in searching.

Raids resulting in robbery, kidnapping, and murder were a daily occurrence throughout the North-West Frontier, but only once before had a victim been British. Therefore, the government reacted vigorously to prevent the crime from becoming a trend. Every soldier, scout, policeman, and khassadar was sent on the hunt for the kidnappers after Sir Horatio Bolton, the Chief Commissioner of the North-West Frontier Province, sent his deputy, Victor Edwardes, to take charge of the rescue operation.

While waiting hopefully for news of a successful interception, Edwardes called a meeting of civil and military personnel to formulate a plan to extract Lily and Tracy from the heart of Mahsud tribal lands, should it become necessary. By dawn on the third morning, no sighting had been reported, and Edwardes had to assume the kidnappers and their victims were deep across the Administrative Boundary. Therefore, he ordered the agreed-upon plan to be implemented.

When Emily Sheffield stepped onto her bungalow veranda, she saw three men entering her gate. Two were old friends, Robin Cuimein and Neil Osborne, and the third was a man she had only met the day before when Robin had collected her and taken her to meet him. He had asked her to play a significant role in the plan to rescue Lily and the child. "Good morning, Deputy Commissioner," she said, leaving her veranda to greet them.

"Good morning, Doctor Sheffield," Victor Edwardes replied, tipping his topee. "I expect you have come to ask me to make that little trip?" Emily anticipated.

"Regrettably, Doctor, I don't see any other choice," Edwardes apologized. "With no news of the gang's whereabouts, we can only speculate that Shamsi and his band of thugs have eluded our patrols and escaped to his hideout in the Kajuri."

"No need for regret. I make the journey willingly," replied Emily. "When do we leave?"

"Right now," was Edwardes' answer."

"Then, may I have a hand? I have some medical supplies and a bag containing fresh clothes for Miss Richmond and the child," the doctor explained.

"I will be accompanying you, Emily. But first, I'll ensure it's put in our car," offered Neil Osborne.

"Emily, I have to wish you luck now and leave," Cuimein excused himself. "I have to pick up Amjad at Ghorzandi soon, and it would be impolite to keep him waiting."

"Of course, Robin. You go ahead," replied the woman, offering her hand. "And good luck to you and Amjad. Between us, we should see a happy ending to this disgraceful business."

After a hurried lunch with Taib Khan at his village, he and Cuimein drove the forty miles to Kandao in just over an hour. Hugo du Rand awaited them with a group of forty men. They would relieve the Scout garrison at Chashnal, close to the Afghan Border, and act as escorts for the two government officials.

At the deputy commissioner's conference, Amjad had volunteered to go into Mahsud territory and negotiate for the release of the two captives. For Cuimein's part, it was suggested that someone familiar to Lily and Tracy should be as close as possible to where it was suspected they were being held - someone with authority who could make quick and impactful decisions. Cuimein was deemed the perfect fit for this role. Though the journey to Chashma was challenging for him, he kept pace with the rest of the group and arrived just before nightfall. He stayed there to await the next steps while Amjad headed southwards into Mahsud lands.

Of those Cuimein had left behind at the Saysha Mission, Victor Edwardes had departed immediately after him to set up his operations headquarters at the South Waziristan Scouts HQ in Jandola, under the escort of the frontier constabulary. Emily and Neil Osborne followed shortly after, but to a different destination - Sararogha, another Scout post on the Razmak road south of Kandao.

Here, Emily was to join a second expedition led by Mullah Mohammad Shareef, a highly respected religious figure in that sector of the Border, to negotiate the release of the captives. Emily was invited to join him and his party as someone whom both Lily and Tracy knew and trusted. She was likely the only foreigner who could enter the Kajuri Valley and survive, given that she was a woman who spoke Pushtu and was the Doctor. Mahsud men and women had walked for miles to receive medical attention at her mission hospital.

As planned, the mullah was delayed due to the need to gather a strong party of loyal followers who would guide them safely into a notorious Mahsud stronghold. He arrived in the early morning, driven through the gate by Major Noel Lomas, the Political Agent. Emily and Neil Osborne watched as their thirty-strong escort continued to emerge from a solid rubber-wheeled Ford truck, raggedly dressed and grinning Border cutthroats.

"Lomas apologized for our lateness, saying that he had to tour the villages to rouse the men from their beds. Emily and the mullah were introduced by Lomas, and although they hadn't met before, they both were familiar with each other's reputation. Mohammad Shareef advised Doctor Sheffield to discard his hat for their trip, explaining that it was a symbol of the despised foreigners in the Kajuri. Emily accepted Zahir

Khan's shawl in exchange for her favourite headgear. While waiting for their horses to be saddled, Neil Osborne watched as Zahir Khan reminded each of the escorts of their mission's top priority: returning the doctor safely. He emphasized the consequences of failure to do so by drawing his hand in a cutting motion across his throat."

CHAPTER 21

When dealing with the insane,
the best method is to pretend to be sane.
-Hermann Hesse

Realizing that the ground was sloping
downwards again, Lily Richmond raised her eyes
to look ahead. Before her, the three men in front
were following a goat track down into a long,
broad valley through which a river flowed, with
green cultivation on its banks. From their high
vantage point, crossing a saddle of ground
between two hills, Lily could see several villages
scattered along the length of the valley. Then,
resignedly, she lowered her head to stare with
pain-dulled eyes at the pathway at her feet. The
valley held no significance for her; it was just like
all the rest. Beyond it were more mountains,
with even more valleys to cross. For three nights
and a day now, she had been walking, most of
the time carrying Tracy on her back.
On the first day, they had hidden in the hill
caves overlooking a section of the Bannu-Pezu
Road. From this vantage point, they watched the
pursuing cavalry and normal road traffic pass by.
At dusk, Lily and Tracy were woken and, with
the band sticking to the hills, they set off to walk
through the night. At dawn, after crossing the
Administrative Border, they rested throughout

the day hidden in the shelter of a friendly house. Then, as the sun set, their movements hidden by the darkness, they travelled west into the fading twilight. After the hours of the night, with the sky beginning to lighten behind them, there was no stopping this time. They were in a safe country now, with no need to hide, so they trekked on without pausing to sleep or even rest for a few hours.

Despite the extra demand on her stamina, Lily never complained or whimpered for rest. She was too far gone to voice a protest. The first night was tiring for her, constantly out of breath, tripping over while simultaneously reassuring Tracy that all was well. Since Tracy's feet were only wrapped in cloth, Lily had carried the young girl on her back for most of the night. Those hours were arduous enough, but worse was to come. At the start of the second night, Lily's limbs had stiffened, making all effort at walking painful. It wasn't until after an hour that this left her, only to be replaced by excruciating agony as she strained with all her willpower to keep pace with the men.

Unaware of the danger of becoming a burden, Tracy soon showed signs of weariness with the journey, repeatedly questioning Lily about why they had to do it and asking to be taken home. Finally, when Lily's legs felt like they would give out, she had to put the girl on the ground to walk. Tracy did so for a short distance, then sat down, saying she had to rest. Snatching her up before anyone had seen this, Lily hoisted the girl onto her back and carried her there for the remainder of the night.

At the village the following day, Lily, bundled into a hut, collapsed on the dirt floor, her arms and legs trembling uncontrollably, her body racked with searing pain. By the late afternoon, after a long sleep that began with a faint into unconsciousness, her mind, if not her body, had benefited from the rest. Pleading for a decent set of footwear, she was given a worn pair of dwarf palm sandals. She fastened her own to Tracy's feet using strips of cloth. She was also given a tattered and dirty chadar, which Lily tied around her shoulders, offering Tracy a sling to sit in while clinging to her back.

Descending into a new valley, Lily had been walking continuously for twenty hours with only brief stops. Unbeknownst to her, she had covered eighty miles since her kidnapping. Despite her incredible feat, her pain was excruciating, feeling as if every muscle in her body was being torn apart. Exhaustion blurred her vision, and the sweat pouring into her eyes caused her senses to verge on hallucination. As they passed through a village, the local children followed Lily and her kidnappers, pointing, and smiling in wonder at her blonde hair. However, Lily hardly noticed, keeping her eyes fixed on the trail ahead. Suddenly, the man she was following pushed her against a pile of stones, bringing her to an abrupt stop. Tracy, who had been carried on Lily's back, awoke, and wanted to be let down. Lily looked up to see why they had stopped and saw Abdul Shamsi and Firoz-un-Din engaged in a conversation with three men at a house entrance on the edge of the village. One of the men approached Lily and demanded to know if she was the Saysha woman, using the name the gang had given her. Lily replied that she was Miss Lily Richmond, a nurse employed at the Saysha Mission. Despite her exhaustion and disorientation, she stood tall and gave a straightforward answer, wearing a filthy torn dressing-gown and nightdress, her face covered in sweat and dirt, and every nerve in her body emitting pain.

"Is this child from Janka?" he asked, pressing her for identification validation. "This is Tracy Ratcliffe, and her home is Janka, from where we were both kidnapped," confirmed Lily in a tired yet frank voice. The tribesman's questions were answered, and he went back to arguing with the gang leaders. The argument ended when one of the younger men was sent into the village. Firoz-un-Din then called on the three men watching over the captives. With a shove from one of them, Lily took Tracy's hand and followed another into the entrance of the house. They first entered a courtyard and were led to the tower building. They climbed stone steps to a room on the first level, which had no windows except for three narrow rifle slits. One of the slits threw a thin shaft of light from the setting sun and revealed the room to be bear with a stone floor. Later, one of the young men provided wool rugs for the two hostages to sleep on. They were grubby and foul-smelling but still an improvement from the stone flooring. After sunset, a young girl brought them a flask of water and a dish of meat mixed with rice which they shared. She stayed to watch the strangers in the corner, seemingly intrigued by them. The native girl returned to them with a ripened pomegranate, which she produced from beneath her robes. They ate the fruit in two portions. Lily asked the girl the name of the village to discover where they were being held. The girl was hesitant to speak at first, but eventually revealed that the village was Lakkar in the Kajuri Valley. She was the daughter of the village headman, Mahmud Na'im Shan. This was his house, and he and two of his sons were the first people she had seen. With the gang occupying the ground floor, Shah was providing shelter for both them and the captives until Abdul Shamsi either negotiated ransom terms or took them away for sale into slavery across the Afghan border. Lily kept this chilling disclosure to herself and instead told Tracy that they would no longer be walking for the time being. Tracy responded with delight and cuddled into Lily's arms. They slept until dawn on the evil-smelling rugs with a soiled chadar for covering.

--oOo--

Few outsiders were permitted to enter the Kajuri Valley, a stronghold of the Mahsud clan known as Garuzi Khail. The clan had a tradition of maintaining their isolation, and traders were not allowed to enter the valley. The Garuzi Khail either bought what they needed from elsewhere or stole it. There was a tale of a French Jesuit priest who ventured into the valley to seek Muslim converts and was given to the women to be skinned alive. On the fourth day of the kidnapping, Taid Khan looked down upon the Kajuri Valley at dawn, watching the smoke rise from the villages below. As a government official, he had never been to the valley before, and the scene was unfamiliar to him. However, he had a letter of safe conduct from Mullah Mohammad Shareef to Mullah Qari Kashid, the lead Garuzi Khail mullah in the valley, which he hoped would grant him entry. As the first ray of sunlight appeared, Amjad listened to the disjointed, overlapping chorus of village mullahs calling their followers to prayer. When full daylight arrived, he set off on his journey into the valley unarmed. He met a goat herder with his son on the way, and after exchanging greetings, he explained that he was an emissary of Mullah Mohammad Shareef bearing a letter for Mullah Qari Kashid. The herder allowed

Amjad to see his letter but couldn't comprehend the Sanskrit symbols on it. Amjad was then escorted to the village of Lakkar by the herder's son, passing the headman's house where Lily and Tracy were having breakfast.

Qari Kashid greeted Taid Khan in a cordial and friendly manner, demonstrating the traditional hospitality of the Frontier. However, he concealed his discomfort at the unexpected arrival of Amjad, a paid firangi servant. Before even reading the letter, he understood the purpose of Amjad's visit. News of the kidnapping of two white women had already reached Kajuri, a day before Shamsi's return. Kashid put the letter aside and Amjad told him that Mullah Shareef had requested his help in rescuing the two kidnapped English women. Kashid questioned how he was supposed to achieve this and Amjad suggested calling a council of the Clan, to caution them about the risks of cooperating with the kidnappers. Kashid found the idea ridiculous and questioned whether any Kajuri men would participate in such a crime. Amjad responded sympathetically but fearfully that there were men who would, if allowed, trigger an invasion by the British that could expel them from the Kajuri forever. Kashid strongly denied this and asked what would be gained by kidnapping English women. Amjad then suggested that Abdul Shamsi was responsible, but Kashid lied, claiming Shamsi was not present.

"But if he returns with those English captives, he must be convinced to release them unharmed," urged Taid Khan. "He is not Mahsud. We are not the ones who gave him a knife or a rifle," replied the Mullah, as if absolving himself of responsibility for Shamsi's actions. "The talk on the border is that Abdul Shamsi and his followers have captured an English woman and girl," said Amjad formally. "If this is true, they should be brought here for protection under your shelter. If the British come looking for them, they may punish everyone. That is why I ask for a jirgah, to warn that Shamsi must not return with the stolen goods and should instead face the hangman's noose." "The affairs of Abdul Shamsi are his own," pointed out the Mullah, using the traditional Pathan escape clause to deny responsibility for his actions. This claim of non-involvement would be considered an insult anywhere else, but it had to be accepted here because these brigands genuinely believe in it. Taid Khan knew the situation was dire and tricky because Lily and Tracy were Shamsi's captives, to be sold for profit. Ransom would be ideal, but if that was not an option, others would pay to take the hostages off his hands. To save them, Amjad had to keep Shamsi on the Indian side of the border. If the gang crossed into Afghanistan, recovering the captives would be slim. To prevent this, Amjad had to convince the

Garuzi Khail that Shamsi and his men posed a threat to the valley, forcing them to turn against Shamsi and release his captives unharmed.

"I am simply an emissary on behalf of Mullah Mohammad Shareef," Taid Khan said, subtly pressuring the Mullah with the letter in his hand. "He has expressed his intention to journey here to the Kajuri himself. The first questions he will ask are about the assistance provided and the progress made in the release of the kidnapped British." The Mullah confirmed that Mullah Shareef planned to come but stated that decisions about Abdul Shamsi and the calling of a jirgah must be made by Clan Chief Wahid Anim. Taid Khan appealed to the Mullah, emphasizing the rewards that awaited those who provide support when called upon, to use his influence to help the situation and gain favor with Mullah Shareef and the British. Their discussion took place in an anteroom of the Mullah's house. He promised to ensure that the clan chief was made aware of their wishes and left Amjad in the care of one of his sons. Amjad was served breakfast of tea, a boiled egg, and fresh black bread, and he waited through the morning and into the afternoon before being taken to the village council area in the heart of the settlement.

The attendance could have been better, with only a few hundred people at most. Unfortunately, the only influential figure was

Mullah Kashid. Several sub-clan chiefs were present, but like everyone else, they were merely there to listen to the government outsider. This lackluster response was due to the Frontier tradition of not taking sides until the victor was clear. Additionally, Amjad was unaware that the gang had relocated their captives to a different location upon learning of Taid Khan's presence in the village. The gang was distrustful of everyone, determined to retain bargaining control of their prisoners. Taid Khan appealed to the gathering for over two hours, continually pointing out the folly of Abdul Shamsi's actions. However, ill-tempered men dressed in rags and tatters rebutted that raiding was a legitimate source of income. For Amjad, this was a difficult argument to counter. It was not until Wahid Anim arrived that the government made a breakthrough. The clan chief did not say much, but his presence drew others who watched and listened.

At one point, Amjad turned to look behind him at the spectators standing near the buildings at the edge of the council area. He spotted a man with a heavily scarred face who was half-hidden against a wall. "Firoz-un-Din! Come forward and represent your gang," he called out. "Or should I assume that you are so ashamed of your actions that you have to leave it to the warriors of the Garuzi Khail to defend you?" Firoz-un-Din stood with glaring eyes, neither retreating nor accepting the invitation. The silence was broken by the single clap of a hand. The clan chief beckoned Firoz-un-Din to join the jirgah with a single hand gesture. Over the next hour, Firoz-un-Din and Taid Khan engaged in a series of questions and answers, with the Mahsuds, who had not once admitted to knowing the gang's whereabouts, happily joining in. Amjad attempted to tactfully ascertain the location and health of the two English captives without threatening the kidnappers, fearing they would flee with their hostages. He only overstepped his boundaries once. Finally, Firoz-un-Din proposed a ransom of a hundred thousand rupees. In response, the assistant political agent quoted a Pushtu parable that ridiculed Firoz-un-Din's demand. The parable was about a camel that desired to be a handsome prince.

Before any offense could be taken, a tribesman hastily approached Wahid Anim and whispered in his ear. The clan chief, a thin man with a focused expression, stood up and dismissed the jirgah with a wave of his hand. He had received information that Mullah Mohammad Shareef had brought another English woman with him and had entered the valley. During their journey across Mahsud tribal territory, women dressed in smocks over broad skirts and brightly patched trousers approached Emily Sheffield on horseback at each village, asking, "Daktar! Daktar! What is the news of your Saysha woman and the child?" It was not only that east of the Administrative Border who considered the abduction of English women unacceptable. As they entered the Kajuri Valley, the women who welcomed them did not ask for news; they declared that the woman and child were safe in Abdul Shamsi's custody. Met by a young mullah, the son of Qari Kashid, Mullah Shareef's party was led to his home where the Garuzi Khail mullah greeted them warmly. However, Emily, being a foreign woman who prayed in Christian temples, was not welcomed into the Mullah's home. Instead, she was taken to the village headman's son's house and accommodated in the chauk room, a room reserved for village business and housing travellers. She was not offered the tower where Lily and Tracy had been earlier that morning.

Negotiations between government representatives and the kidnappers were delayed by nightfall, despite several hours of activity. Wahid Anim, sub-chiefs, and clan elders arrived at Mullah Kashid's house to pay their respects to Mohammad Shareef. During this visit, Shareef insisted on calling a full clan jirgah in the morning and suggested that they keep an eye on the gang's quarters for any signs of escape. The clan chief complied with these requests yet remained indecisive. Later that night, Taid Khan visited Emily to discuss the day's events and next day's plans. The doctor gave Khan packages of clothes for Lily and Tracy, hoping he could deliver them. In their room, Lily sang to Tracy, using water from a saucer to clean Tracy's face. A gang member guarded the door, and Lily was surprised to awake and find two bundles of clothes, including her own clothes and shoes. The jirgah held the next morning was much more significant than the previous day's meeting, with attendees filling the council area and spilling onto nearby rooftops. Taid Khan was the first to speak, echoing much of his previous statements and adding fresh news from Mohammad Shareef. He informed Abdul Shamsi and Firoz-un-Din that two gang members who had visited their homes were seized during a Scout patrol raid on their village. Shamsi responded by shaking his fist in the air, asserting that this news was insignificant because the English women were to be ransomed, not traded. This sparked murmurs of agreement from the crowd, some even expressing support by criticizing Britain's border encroachments. Eventually, Mohammad Shareef rose to speak, quieting the crowd after they had rambled on for some time. Even though he was short and unimpressive physically, his religious standing on the border demanded the audience's respect. Shareef was the Mullah Mohammad Shareef of the Akoras, who had raided British India in his youth. He earned the distinguished privilege of wearing the robes of a mullah after becoming a disciple of

Mullah Karbogha from the village of Karbogha. Shareef's insatiable thirst for knowledge, coupled with his impressive oratory skills, made him a respected scholar of the Quran and Islamic teachings. As a result, he became a prominent figure on the Frontier, primarily in settling disputes among the quarreling border tribes and clans.

"Mahsuds of the Garuzi Khail," he began, his voice echoing to the rooftops. "It is written in the Holy Koran that the beginning of wisdom is the fear of the Lord. However, brothers, it seems that there are those here who are neither wise nor afraid of Allah's wrath." Allowing time for his words to take root in the minds of those present, the Mullah slowly raised an arm to point accusingly at the gang leader. "Abdul Shamsi, you and your followers have broken Muslim law. You have degraded the teachings of the Prophet. You slew a woman. By committing this single act, you have spat upon the Holy Koran." With those opening sentences, Mullah Shareef undermined any local support the gang may have had. In the Kajuri, raiding was a supplement to everyone's means; each had a vested interest in the results of this consultation could set a precedent for future pickings. However, as the Mullah had so dramatically made clear, the topic under discussion was no longer one of settling the question of a kidnapping taboo but of breaking Islamic law. For Wahid Anim, the outcome was no longer in doubt. As Abdul Shamsi struggled to justify the murder of Eleanor Ratcliffe, the clan chief whispered instructions to one of his lieutenants. Minutes later, he arrived at the house where Lily and Tracy were being held, giving the two gang members on guard instructions to move their captives. However, facing twenty armed men pressing in at the lieutenant's back, they had little option but to comply.

Lily and Tracy were taken to a smaller place nearby, which was a village guest house, instead of Mahmud N'im Shah's house. Lily noticed that they had been transferred to a new prison cell and their captors were also new. At the same time, the kidnappers who were at the jirgah were quarrelling among themselves due to the hostility they faced from all sides. Eventually, Taid Khan proposed terms of release, and after wrangling for an additional hour, an amicable solution was reached that spared each side's izzat and loss of face. The terms were written down as a message to Robin Cuimein, delivered through one of Mullah Shareef's escorts to Chashma, and verified by the son of Mullah Qari Kashid through a relay of heliograph signals from Chashma to Ishak. Emily Sheffield complied with her host's request to remain unseen inside his house due to being an English woman and unveiled. However, she had a stream of visitors seeking treatment for injuries or diseases as word spread about the doctor's presence. During her makeshift surgery, one of Mohammad Shareef's men arrived and led her to a nearby house guarded by other members of the Mullah's escort. Lily was inside combing a young girl's hair with a small fork of wood, unaware of Emily's presence at the doorway.

"The next time you gallivant about the countryside, Lily Richmond, I will not come this far to collect you again," the doctor chided in a stern voice. Startled, the young nurse looked around but saw only a figure in a coat standing in the doorway. Nevertheless, she couldn't help but smile with joy upon hearing the voice, which was unmistakable. "Emily! Oh, Emily!" exclaimed Lily as she rushed towards the older woman and embraced her tightly with relief and gratitude.

CHAPTER 22

Where cheetal are plentiful there is no tiger,
Where tigers are plentiful there is no cheetal.
-Indian Proverb

The flag hung limp against its staff two miles
away, making it impossible to distinguish its
colours from the Chashma Scout post walls.
However, to Lily Richmond, the British Union
Flag was the most beautiful sight in the world.
She looked at it from a ridge crest, the last
obstacle before reaching safety, under the
protection of her rescuers. As she walked
alongside the horse carrying Emily's medical kit,
she asked Tracy, the little girl riding the horse,
whether she could see the fort. Tracy replied
tiredly, wondering if her father would be there.
Lily informed her that he wouldn't be there, but
perhaps tomorrow. Once terms were agreed
upon, the two captives were released quickly,
and Lily had spent the previous day assisting
Emily with her surgery. When messengers
returned from Chashma late at night with the
news that the exchange deal was acceptable, they
left at dawn to pass the valley perimeter and
head to Chashma. Chashma was a small fort that
had been abandoned in 1919, located in the
centre of a broad, barren gravel plain, and was
recently reoccupied by the Scouts as a forward

picket before the construction of a new road. Upon nearing the fort, they were greeted by British soldiers who raised their hats in the air, and a party emerged to greet them, including Major Robin Cuimein and Hugo du Rand in his Scout uniform. The Mullah, Mohammad Shareef, leading on horseback, pulled up as Cuimein held up an outstretched hand and expressed his gratitude.

Amid a flurry of greetings, introductions, and congratulations, the rescue party passed through the fort's gateway, where more English soldiers cheered. Emily Sheffield entered and repeatedly nodded to the troops in acknowledgment, occasionally raising her arm. Young Tracy sat on her horse, puzzled by the noisy reception. On the other hand, Lily was overcome with embarrassment due to her appearance. She had been captive for almost a week and hadn't been able to bathe; her hair was tangled and dirty, and her body felt gritty with accumulated grime. The interior of the fort, which was over a hundred yards square, was empty in the centre except for the flagstaff and a sunken ammunition bunker. The only buildings, offices, and living quarters were against the rear wall. Neatly arranged rows of soldiers' packs and bedding rolls lined the other three sides. Major Hartnell halted Lily on the veranda and showed her and the women to quarters given up by Hugo du Rand. A lean man with a thin, sharp-edged face, he spoke politely, but briskly. "Miss Richmond, somehow we have avoided meeting until now, but until recently, I was the battalion's Adjutant and worked closely with your uncle, the Regimental Sergeant Major." It wasn't until then did Lily realize why some soldiers seemed familiar. She glanced at the flash and badge on the Major's topee. It was a Light Infantry bugle on a green and gold background, the Queen's Light Infantry. "The battalion passed this way on the column, but it was withdrawn after learning of your delicate situation in the Kajuri Valley. Only my Company remained behind to support the Scouts if assistance was needed. In anticipation of your release in this direction, your uncle left you a letter in my care," he continued. "Oh, this is wonderful, Major Hartnell, thank you," said Lily, as the Major drew a letter from his breast pocket and handed it to her. "Oh, Major, which company is this?" she asked a moment later as he walked off to re-join the Mullah, Taid Khan, and Robin Cuimein. "B Company. Why?" asked Hartnell, mildly mystified at the question." "Thank you so much, Major Hartnell," Lily said gratefully, clutching her uncle's letter. She scanned the soldiers who were scurrying away in response to the midday meal call from the company bugler. Not spotting the man she was searching for; the nurse directed her attention to the letter. Perched right at the entrance, she had just begun reading when she was interrupted by a question.

"All safe, then?" Joey inquired. "Oh yes, Joey, safe! All safe," Lily answered, her face gleaming with joy as she lifted her gaze to the soldier standing at the far end of the veranda, a rifle slung over his shoulder.

"I'm truly sorry I didn't arrive earlier," Payne admitted as he approached. "Joey, I've missed you immensely. Throughout my captivity, I thought about you, concerned that you were worrying about me," Lily confessed.

"You can't fathom how anxious I was," Joey admitted, moving towards her while remaining vigilant of any possible intruders. "Please don't come too close, Joey. I'm dirty and I stink," Lily warned.

"I don't care," Joey retorted, quickly assessing his surroundings before removing his rifle from his shoulder and propping it against the wall. "I'm going to kiss you."

"No, Joey! Don't!" Lily pleaded weakly, but she didn't resist as he enveloped her in his arms and their lips met.

"Young man! You'd better be Joey Payne, or I'll find a good reason to discipline that girl you're smooching," Emily Sheffield threatened, appearing in the doorway. Startled, Joey withdrew from Lily, but she turned to Emily and smiled. "Yes, Emily. Finally, this is my sweetheart."

"Well, I'm pleased to meet you, Joey, even though you intend to whisk away the best nurse I've ever had," the doctor replied, offering her hand to Joey. "I'm about to fetch something for Tracy's bath, and possibly for Lily as well. If you intend to continue your dalliance, I suggest you retreat indoors." Joey declined her advice and stepped back to retrieve his rifle.

"Come back later, Joey," Lily suggested, hesitant to let go of the soldier's hand. "After I've bathed, we can sit out here and converse. I'm confident that won't get you in trouble. And bring Benedict; I'm curious about how Sheela is managing her pregnancy."

"Lily," Payne said, retaking her hand, his expression suddenly grave. "Sheela passed away giving birth to a girl." "Oh, Jesus!" Lily exclaimed, her face turning pale. "But is the baby, okay?" Joey tried to cushion the blow with the news that Sheela's family was looking after the infant.

"Oh my God!" Lily shrieked, her eyes darting around. "Where is Benedict?" The mullah and his escort party were not in Chashma for long. They had fulfilled their mission of delivering the two English women and the baby safely to the fort. However, before departing, they had congregated for their noon prayer. As Lily dashed from the veranda in search of Benedict, she spotted him walking with two other soldiers.

On seeing her, Benedict halted, allowing the soldiers to continue their way.

"Benedict! Oh, Benedict! I've just learned about Sheela. I'm so sorry," Lily sobbed, her voice filled with sorrow.

"I appreciate you saying that, Lily, my love. If she's listening, she'll be much obliged," said Benedict, his voice gentle but tinged with sadness. Across the fort, the Mullah raised his arms and praised Allah. Lily couldn't hold back her emotions and wept as Benedict comforted her. "Don't cry, Lily," he said, putting an arm around her. "She may be gone, but she left a part of herself behind. I have a daughter now, and her name will be Sheela." As they embraced, the Islamic worshippers knelt to the ground, foreheads touching the earth and rifles beside them, chanting Quran-i-Sherif verses in praise of Allah.

--oOo--

At sunset, half an hour before dusk, B Company's bugler blew retreat. The men stood at attention as the fort flag was lowered around the inner wall, where the British soldiers stored their equipment and slept. After this daily ritual, the men checked their rifles and ammunition pouches. In Chashma, the flag-lowering ceremony also served as a warning to stand as the two times of day most favourable for a surprise attack were first and last light. While the forty permanent members of the Scouts garrison

429

took up their usual positions at the main gate and in the fort's four-square corner towers, two platoons of the Queen's stationed themselves along the wall's parapet. The other two platoons remained in reserve in the compound below. On the Indus plains, April's temperature was already uncomfortably high, unlike here in the border hills. To the north, snow could be seen on the crest of Pir Ghal, the region's tallest mountain and considered sacred by the Pathan. Regardless, it was still hot, and the cooling of the evening air was a relief. Taking full advantage of it, Emily, Lily, and Tracy sat on chairs provided by the officers on the veranda as the post stood. Although thrilled to be under the army's protection, the women were not yet out of danger.

As a Scout post with limited personnel, the fort did not have a radio transmitter. Therefore, Chashma's only means of communication with the rest of India was through a heliograph to Ishak. However, due to the distance and terrain, the relay point for this communication was a fortified tower constructed on a hill twelve miles away. This tower was heavily guarded by Scouts and overlooked the current end of the new road. This relay system enabled the news of Emily and the kidnap victims' safe arrival at Chashma to be reported to Ishak shortly after they entered the gate. Unfortunately, Ishak informed the group that they would have to wait at Chashma for a few days as most of the garrison was away, supporting Rascol to the north. B Company, though nearly 160 strong, was not sufficient to escort the group safely through hostile tribal territory. As night fell, the troops stood down from their alert and resumed their routine. Robin Cuimein welcomed the ladies and ensured that they were settling in comfortably. Emily expressed her gratitude to Hugo for providing them with a hip bath.

"We are very fortunate here as well," explained Cuimein. "The water supply is pumped up from the river at the bottom of the tangi. It's a temperamental apparatus that's forever breaking down, and even when it's working, it provides an insufficient supply for the number of people here at present." "So, our stay here until collected by the Ishak Column will be modest," Emily remarked philosophically. "Most certainly, the scarcity of victuals alone will see to that. The fort is not stocked with luxuries," confirmed the district officer. During the brief conversation, Cuimein observed Tracy, who had experienced a terrible ordeal as a child, witnessing her mother's ruthless murder and subsequent abduction by the most barbarous of border cut-throats. "Well, young lady, it seems your adventure will be extended for a bit longer," said Cuimein, attempting to engage Tracy in the conversation as she appeared solemn and distant. Sitting next to Lily, his words had the opposite effect on

Tracy who withdrew further without responding to his comment. "How is Princess Krishna, Mister Cuimein?" asked Lily, shifting the focus away from Tracy and onto herself as she comforted the child. "She has fully recovered now, something she attributes to the care she received at your mission," replied Robin. "And you're getting married," said Lily with genuine delight. "That's fantastic, absolutely fantastic. I am so excited." With the subject of Cuimein's impending marriage introduced, he found himself answering questions about the wedding arrangements at the Janka Anglican chapel, tactfully omitting the fact that he and Krishna had already participated in a private ceremony. On the last evening of his visit to Jaswara, he proposed to Krishna, but the palace guards persuaded him to attend a celebration instead. The soldiers of the Jaswara legion had just received news that Chitor Cuimein was going to marry a daughter of the royal household. They gave him a horse and escorted him to a secluded village outside the winter capital. Once there, he was surrounded by joyful people, musicians playing flutes and drums, and garlands of flowers were placed around his neck. Lal Singh, his servant in France, whispered that Prince Sahil had arranged everything himself since he was excluded from the ceremony by the Maharaja. Cuimein was led into a room where a veiled figure sat, and he willingly submitted to the rites of a Hindu marriage when he realized that the veiled figure was the serene and beautiful Princess Krishna. Later, Emily explained to Robin that Tracy had been silent during their company meeting because she had an early start and a long journey from Kajuri, which caused her to fall asleep leaning on Lily.

"She's still recovering from the shock of everything, but as you can see, she turns to Lily for comfort and protection," said Cuimein. He put out his cigarette, intentionally pausing before continuing, "Emily, Hugo has procured a bottle of Madeira from a secret source. He and the other officers were hoping you would join them for a celebratory drink. However, we cannot extend the invitation to Miss Richmond, as she is the Regimental Sergeant Major's niece. It would be impolite to entertain her without his knowledge, it's not snobbery on their part."

"They should be celebrating that girl, not acting like uptight aristocrats," replied the doctor, pointing into the room behind her. "It's more about Mess protocol than rudeness," Cuimein defended politely. "Shall I tell them you're too tired to attend?" "Yes, you may," Emily immediately replied. But then, on second thought, she changed her mind. "No! Wait! I will come. I have a favour to ask Major Hartnell, and if he wants my company that badly, he better grant it." Emily was gone for only an hour. Shortly after her return, Joey Payne reported for duty. "Excuse me, Doctor," he began, "this part of the fort is off-limits. But the Sergeant-Major says I'm supposed to report to you." "Yes, Joey, that's correct," confirmed Emily, taking Lily's arm. "I've convinced your Major that Lily, after her imprisonment, deserves the freedom to walk around the fort. And you are to act as her escort."

"Emily, you're a terrible liar," Lily rebuked, kissing the doctor's cheek. "Thank you."

"Joey, don't hang back like that. Walk beside me," Lily coaxed as the couple crossed the fort compound.

"It's best not to right now, pet. I'm supposed to be your escort, not some Casanova parading his lady around. Besides, all my friends are watching us," the lance-corporal answered, aware of his good fortune in being in the girl's company and afraid of appearing to abuse his position.

"Oh, come on," replied Lily, making a silly face. Lily led them up the stone steps to a wide parapet. Below, the soldiers of B Company who were not on duty were lounging in their sleeping areas around the foot of the wall, smoking, chatting in hushed tones, and playing cards in small groups. Oil lamps were hung around the interior, providing only token lighting during this period of the month.

"The moon and stars are so bright, it's like the sky is lit up with electric lights," observed Lily.

"Lily, don't go too close to the edge," warned Joey, catching her arm to pull her back from looking beyond the wall.

"Oh, I forget sometimes how dangerous it can be out here. The Frontier is so quiet and peaceful at night," said Lily as she turned to walk down the broad parapet. As they walked, they encountered a Scout sentry coming from the opposite direction. There was a marked contrast between Joey's metal-shoed boots and the silent footsteps of the Scout, who wore palm-sandals.

"Hello there," greeted Lily as they passed.

"Hey!" replied the bearded Scout, giving Lily a sharp look of surprise.

"You take care," said Payne.

"Pardon?" asked Lily, unfamiliar with the barrack-room slang.

"Speak the language," he clarified.

"I know enough to get by. But I told you this in my letters. Don't you read anything I write, Joey Payne?" Lily asked, pouting, and moving closer to grab the soldier's arms. He sprang back a pace and nervously glanced around, causing the chain to snap onto his wrist and rifle.

"Goodness," chuckled Lily. "I wasn't going to seduce you."

"Lily, you know I'm crazy about you. But I won't get caught hanging around the RSM's niece in the open like this. Look, we're on stage," Joey said, twirling a finger at the stars and moon to emphasize his concern. Without responding, Lily began walking backward and sidestepping toward a nearby, large corner sentry turret.

"Lily! I'm told I'm getting my second stripe next month," Joey said. "Do you still fancy marrying? Because I want to put the notice in as soon as that tape's on my arm."

Moonlight cast a shadow on one side of the block-like turret. Lily backed into it, drawing the soldier with her.

"You're good for a giggle sometimes, Joey," Lily teased, this time wrapping her arms around his waist to prevent his escape. "Of course, I still want to marry you. I want to fall asleep at night wrapped in your arms and wake in the morning still being held. I want to have our children, a family, OUR family. Yes, Joey, I want to be your wife. I want to be your wi--" Lily's words were cut off as she kissed Joey and squeezed herself tight against him. There was no resistance; instead, Joey's caution was swept away by a rising flood of passion that made him curse the rifle chain restricting his embrace. As they kissed, the naik of the Scout guard called out, and the sentries began to answer in Pushtu that all was well.

"Joey whispered to Lily that the battalion would leave Ishak in July and their next posting would be Ferozepore. He asked her to wait for him to tie things up so they could get married.

However, Joey suddenly became tense and ordered Lily to call the sergeant of the guard.

Confused, Lily called out in Pushtu, and the sentry responded, asking what was wrong. Joey pointed to a distant range of hills where a dull, yellowish light was blinking on and off. Payne realized it was a heliograph message from the relay post at Khwaja Kalan and quickly went to the fort's heliograph signalling apparatus to acknowledge the message.

Looking through a sighting aperture, he tried to adjust two dials simultaneously, but his rifle chain hindered him. "Here, Lily, hold onto my rifle while I line the mirrors up," he said while handing his rifle to her. "Joey, is this a heliograph? At night?" the nurse questioned him as she took his rifle. "It's a Lunagraph. We use moonlight," replied Payne, concentrating on the moonlight's reflection caught by the heliograph mirrors. "What's going on, Miss Richmond?" Hugo du Rand asked, arriving just yards ahead of his havaldar. "There's a signal from Khwaja Kalan, sir," Payne spoke before Lily could answer. "Is it important?" the Scout officer asked sharply. "I was only able to receive a portion of it before they stopped transmitting, sir," Joey said, standing at attention. "It read - attacked by hostiles. Inside wire." "That's all?" pressed the Scout officer. "Yes, sir. That's all. I was just about to acknowledge," confirmed Joey, "Shall I continue?" "Yes, continue. And ask them to repeat their message," directed du Rand, turning to call into the fort. "Major Hartnell, sir."

By the time Cliff Hartnell had responded to this summons, most of the queens were standing in curious clusters, observing the drama unfolding around the heliograph frame. Along with the Major, Kyle Bate, Sergeant-Major Little, and Giles Kingston, the young second-lieutenant commanding 7 Platoon, had also arrived. "And you haven't had any further communication with Khwaja Kalan, is that correct?" Hartnell asked Joey Payne after being told why he was summoned. "Yes, sir," was Joey's brief reply. The Major, with his hands clasped behind his back, was silently staring westward when a red flash appeared. "I say!" exclaimed young Kingston loudly. "Quiet," ordered Hartnell, his hands moving quickly to his sides. Then, after several seconds, a muffled explosion was heard. "Corporal Payne, that flash. Can you sight a bearing to it with the helio?" Hartnell asked." "Joey ceased bending to take a look and immediately straightened up. "Directly in line with Khwaja Kalan, sir," he reported. "Mr. Kingston, have your platoon guard for the rest of the night. They'll take double shifts," said Hartnell, addressing the officer. "And Sergeant-Major, inform the Company that they are to sleep in their webbing." After an uneventful night, the fort was peaceful at dawn, but the loss of contact with Khwaja Kalan left the soldiers uneasy. The morning routine began with a party sent down to the pump shed for water, supported by the 6th Platoon. Joey remained with the other signallers to watch for any communication attempt from Khwaja Kalan but detected none. As the fort was effectively isolated, the number of sentries on the walls was doubled, with Major Hartnell conducting inspections twice that day. As the senior officer, he took command upon the arrival of B Company, with Hugo serving as his deputy. Joey informed Major Hartnell that there was still no word from Khwaja Kalan, and the Major speculated that they were likely still recovering from the previous night's events.

"Certainly, sir," responded Hugo confidently. Everyone in the fort knew that Khwaja Kalan had been attacked the previous night and contact with them was lost after the explosion, leaving them to guess what had transpired. Despite this, the officers agreed to show neither doubt nor fear, as Hartnell reiterated during his morning briefing: "When in doubt, put on a brave face." Maintaining an air of nonchalance, the Major stepped up to the stone battlement of the wall, pushed back his topee, and raised a pair of binoculars to his eyes. As he scanned the foreground and the hills to the East, those around him remained silent. Suddenly, the silence was broken by the whistling rush of air and a thud, followed by a single distant popping sound. Hartnell was thrown backward, and Hugo and Joey rushed to his aid. Sergeant-Major

Little shouted, "Stand by the guard!" and off-duty soldiers seized their rifles and equipment. Hugo called for Dr. Sheffield's assistance, but Hartnell was already dead. Emily confirmed this, revealing a large wound in the Major's chest. Du Rand explained that it was likely caused by a jezzail, a long-barreled musket fired from the nearby hills by tribesmen who knew the fort's range precisely. Hugo suggested informing the men of the incident, to which Cuimein agreed, as everyone present was in shock.

"Sergeant-Major, assemble the Company. I need to address the soldiers and send a party up here with a blanket to wrap the Major in," Kyle responded, turning to Little. Before any of this could take place, a sentry warned of an incoming aircraft. A Bristol F2B single-seater biplane flew in, dropped a small package while flying low, and circled the fort. The officers gathered in an office to examine the package's contents, which turned out to be three sheets of paper. After determining who was in command, Bate began to read the papers which conveyed news of destruction, aggression, and orders to evacuate from the Area Divisional Commander.

""Cuimein validated the order from his headquarters at Dera Ismail Khan," Gabson fumed after handing back the signed duplicate copy, "What does he think this is? A stroll through Richmond Park? We have women, a child, and sick men in the medical room." For fifteen minutes, Bate led a discussion to weigh the advantages and disadvantages of obeying or defying the order. However, the debate ended when the plane returned, delivering another message hidden in a glove, supporting the divisional commander's evacuation order. The note read: "Lashkar is spotted approaching the border, with four to five thousand troops. They should be arriving at your doorstep by first light tomorrow." Upon the arrival of reinforcements, the brigadier bellowed, "Evacuate? The order came by plane this morning," to which Steinfeld calmly responded, "I forwarded a copy to Chashma for delivery by pilot. I suspect Peshawar, perhaps even Delhi, pressured the Division to order the post's abandonment." "Oh God!" Gabson exclaimed, "Do those desk jockeys realize what they've done? It's going to be utter chaos!" Gabson, being a British army officer promoted to brigade rank, had no right to command troops in India. However, he was asked to head a commission studying the feasibility of closing down Ishak and moving the garrison to Wana before leaving the country. Upon arriving at Ishak, Steinfeld briefed him on the events leading up to the evacuation order, including the release of the captives, their move to Chashma, and the attack and destruction of Khwaja Kalan.

"The Brigadier was called north to support Rascol because the Fakir of Matun and his force of Afghan tribesmen were threatening to cross the border towards Mir Khan Khail. However, the Fakir landed south, catching them off guard. Gabson, confused by the evacuation order, turned away to watch the Seaforth Highlanders march in. The Brigadier asked Colonel Steinfeld which direction he would take if leaving the Chashma Fort, to which Steinfeld replied that it was hard to guess, but they were the nearest haven. The Brigadier noted that the enemy is under orders to emerge and will need their support. The garrison's strength included drivers, handlers, cooks, signallers, and other various staff, as well as three companies with machine guns under Colonel Kinsley and Colonel Steinfeld's battalion."

"Yes, yes," Gabson pondered thoughtfully. "Well, I don't think Division would approve of me firing on the column with the garrison only weakly defended. So, we won't tell them." Taking a deep breath while straightening his shoulders, the brigadier began to brief his officers for the next day's operation.

"Gentlemen! We'll march at the crack of dawn. The force will comprise Colonel Steinfeld and his entire battalion, Major Alison and his Pack Battery will be greatly needed, and Colonel MacKenzie with his Highlanders. Will they be fit for another slog?"

"You will not hold them back, Brigadier," forcefully replied to Colin MacKenzie, the commanding officer of the Seaforth's. A tall, powerfully built man with blond copper hair, he spoke with a broad highland accent. In addition to being the colonel of a British battalion, MacKenzie was also the Laird of Kilcoy. "Colonel Kinsley," continued Gabson, without any hint of apology, "I will leave the defence of Ishak in your hands, your gunners, and those odds and ends." Kinsley, a slight man with a thin black moustache, nodded in response. "No doubt we will cope, sir."

CHAPTER 23

*Ef you take a sword an' dror it, An' go stick a
feller thru,
Guv'ment ain't to answer for it, God'll send the
bill to you.*
-James Russell Lowell

As the sun set, the upper walls of Chashma saw
only regular activity, with sentries patrolling and
reporting that all was well. However, the
situation was different in the compound below.
The Queen and the Scouts were occupied with
various tasks, speaking quietly, and giving
commands. They distributed ammunition, tore
blankets into strips to bind boots, refilled water
bottles, and dug a pit to bury packs, bedding
rolls, and extra gear. Men from each platoon
were cleaning and priming hand grenades.
Soldiers with mining experience, including Jock
Cressy, were creating an exit hole through the
stonework. Meanwhile, in the ammunition
bunker, Robin Cuimein used his wartime
experience to devise a delayed initiation device
to destroy surplus ammunition.
The decision to evacuate was not immediately
accepted. Kyle Bate, Robin Cuimein, Hugo du
Rand, and Ahmed Wakil spent two hours
debating the feasibility of staying or leaving.
Leaving meant facing the enemy's sniping and

ambushes, but staying would mean a siege with no food and limited water supply. Moreover, they were surrounded by tribesmen on the hills. They decided to attempt to escape at night, hoping to reach Ishak safely.

Before their evening meal, generously served in double portions, Kyle held a briefing. In attendance were the Scouts, Queen's officers, and sergeants, CSM Little, B Company's Quartermaster Sergeant Ian Heydrich, Robin Cuimein, and Emily Sheffield. As Bate explained the escape plan, Emily watched him with a mixture of amusement and admiration. She wondered how this stern King's officer, confidently delegating potentially life-and-death tasks, could be the same young man who pursued maidens on the ship from England like an adolescent puppy. The plan was simple, provided they could slip away undetected. After midnight, the Scouts, led by Ahmed Wakil, would exit through the hole in the north wall and secure an assembly point. The company's main body would then follow, escorted by Platoons 5, 7, and 8 along with the company headquarters personnel, the sick, and the fort's sweepers. The last to leave would be Platoon 6, now under the command of Sergeant Ridley, who would act as the rear guard under Hugo du Rand's charge until Robin Cuimein set his devices in the ammunition bunker.

Major Hartnell's death was concealed by burying his body against the fort wall without any ceremony or firing party. His body was laid on the ground at sunset, and the bugler blew retreat. If possible, the body would be recovered and reburied with appropriate honours later. Just before ten o'clock, Kyle and Hugo du Rand toured the fort to check on the preparations for leaving. They first visited the area where his men were breaking through the wall. They found them working by the light of a single kerosene lamp, their bodies glistening with sweat. When asked if they were on schedule for midnight, CQMS Heydrich replied that they were, having had to coax building stones out one at a time to avoid noise. The final stop was the ammunition bunker, where Robin Cuimein had just finished setting up his improvised incendiary device. Kyle jokingly praised Cuimein's creativity. The plan was to use two candles placed upright among a pile of kerosene-soaked rags to destroy the surplus ammunition.

The final inspection was carried out on the platoons themselves. The company commander went from one to the other, verifying with the officers and NCOs that everyone understood their role in the withdrawal, and everything was ready. As he moved among them, the men fell silent not due to his presence, but due to the sweet, lilting tones and haunting melody of the lullaby that Lily Richmond sang to Tracy

Ratcliffe as she cradled the child in her arms. With the night being warm and moonlit, the men listened to Lily's tender lyrics and reminisced about their homes, other nights, and other girls who sang. When the song ended, the silence lingered, only broken by a single voice with a noticeable lump in his throat asking, "Can you sing it again, miss?" Despite feeling embarrassed, Lily obliged. Meanwhile, Bert Colling and Paani Waters were bickering as they navigated their way out of the exit tunnel. Joey Payne, positioned at the pit's edge, ordered them to quiet down as he was guiding his section out of the fort. The 2nd sections, the last to leave, were being taken down one by one from their sentry posts on the walls. Moments prior, Robin Cuimein had reported that the candles were lit, and the bunker door was bolted and locked. Currently, he was waiting on the orderly-room veranda while Hugo du Rand and Wilf Ridley, their boots wrapped in blanket strips, moved quietly across the fort's presently empty compound yard. Before departing, the scout officer surveyed the walls of the command post he was about to abandon. If the tribesmen outside didn't hear the sentries respond at one o'clock, they would become suspicious. By two o'clock, they would be certain something was amiss. Nevertheless, they could buy some valuable time if the Pathans hesitated in their pursuit to loot the fort. Emerging through the short tunnel, Joey Payne found Benedict Lyall crouched over the exit. Lyall's 1st section was providing the guard on that side of the wall. The last two to exit were Hugo du Rand and Wilf Ridley, with Ridley covering the rear while du Rand moved to the front of the waiting platoon. Unexpectedly, du Rand found one of his scouts there. The plan had changed slightly: the scouts, on their way to take up a position around the pump shed, had noticed movement nearby. It could have been a nocturnal animal, but no risks could be taken. Guiding his men, Ahmed Wakil relocated the assembly point further north along the bed of the tangi.

The Takht Toi river flowed from the Afghan mountains, past Chashma to the southeast, before eventually merging with the larger Baddr Toi. At this point in the tangi, the sides were not as steep as in other places. However, the 6th Platoon still had to watch their footing as they single-filed down a goat trail. The tangi was almost a quarter of a mile wide, with the eastern side illuminated by moonlight. The platoon had to take a roundabout path to reach the riverbed, a journey which took almost half an hour. Everyone had shed non-essential equipment, carrying only what was necessary for speed and mobility.

The pace was slow as they maneuvered through the canyon, careful to stay on the dark side of the tangi. The canyon sides eventually narrowed, forcing them to wade through ankle-deep water. With the risk of flooding during the summer rains, the route could be treacherous. After an hour, the canyon widened, and the sides became less steep.

Here, the Scouts led the platoon up a precarious track, guiding the garrison out of the tangi to the east. By first heading north, they added an extra four miles to their journey to Ishak, which made escape inevitable. They faced a twenty-mile cross-country dash, at one point, arcing five miles north of Khwaja Kalan. Just as the last members of the 6th Platoon reached the crest of the tangi, a muffled explosion echoed from the direction of Chashma.

Nash Slyfield whispered to Jeffrey Harrison, "That's stirred up the hornet's nest now, Jeffrey." As he shifted his Lewis gun to his other shoulder, Bate checked his pocket watch and turned to Robin Cuimein, "Congratulations. Your time fuse is a bit dodgy, but it's right on time." Cuimein replied, "Yes, simple and effective. But they'll be after us now." Tracy asked, "What was that, Mr. Heydrich?" "That was a little surprise we left back at the fort, Tracy. And call me Ditchy, as I've asked you to," replied the quartermaster sergeant.

Ian Heydrich, a sturdy, bull-necked man with bandy legs, carried the girl on his shoulders. Through the night, they marched without stopping, supporting the sick and injured. They followed seldom-used paths and avoided villages. By sunrise, Bate's command had covered ten more miles and were on track to reach Ishak well before noon.

In the morning light, they passed through a desolate landscape of low eroded hills, their boulders bleached white by the sun. With the aid of daylight, their marching pace increased. Hugo du Rand's Scouts, still leading, began to pick up the pace, but the slowness of those following held them back.

Behind the Scouts was the 2nd Lieutenant Nigel Tillis's 5th Platoon, followed by Bate and his HQ element, CSM Little, the women, Robin Cuimein, the sick, and sweepers. The 7th and 8th Platoons were next, with the 6th Platoon taking up the rear. This formation was not ideal for moving through tribal territory in broad daylight; there was no picket protection, and they were moving too slowly. No one felt this more keenly than Kyle, knowing he had no alternative. He and his command had exhausted all their strategies. From this point forward, fate would be their only guide.

Crossing a low ridge, they followed a trail descending into a broad basin littered with boulders. While climbing up the other side, 6 Platoon was halfway to the crest when a rifle shot rang out, narrowly missing Benedict Lyall, who was at the back of the column. He quickly sought cover behind some large rocks and asked his section if they could identify the shooter. China Yeoman, who was closest to him, responded that there was nothing in sight. Despite having the rising sun at their backs, the platoon could not spot the shooter who had blended into the surroundings, a tactic they had seen the Pathans use many times before. However, the sniper might have had difficulty aiming precisely due to the sun's glare. Wilf Ridley ordered the platoon to pull back, hopping from one protective rock to another, avoiding the trail. As they broke cover, they came under fire from multiple shooters hidden in the distant ridge. Joey Payne kept an eye out for puffs of smoke, indicative of the shooter's location, and managed to return fire on one occasion. Meanwhile, the air filled with the sounds of gunfire and ricocheting bullets.

Their shot was a rare occurrence from 6 Platoon, who were more focused on moving from cover to cover and leaving the return fire to 8 Platoon. After overseeing his men's movement over the ridge, their platoon commander, 2nd Lieutenant Matthew Laffan, deployed two sections to provide covering fire for 6 Platoon. Wilf Ridley and Benedict Lyall were the last ones to reach the safety of the crest where they found Kyle Bate waiting with orders. "Sergeant Ridley, place your platoon on this ridge as the rear guard," Bate instructed, pointing across a shallow valley to another ridge half a mile to the north. "The rest of us will be heading for that feature there. When you hear the bugler sound the withdrawal, I want you to join us immediately. Is that clear?" "Yes, sir," responded the sergeant, turning to shout at his platoon, his voice ragged from lack of breath. "We are to hold here - as the rear guard - take up firing positions on the crest - Corporal Griffiths - position your Lewis Section on the trail - 1 Section to their right - 2 Section on the left - 3 Section back in reserve - Now move quickly!"

As Bate joined 8 Platoon in hurrying after the rest of the company, Ridley's men spread out along the ridge, taking up positions and unwrapping their boots of the now unnecessary blanket strips. "Who is that limping with Mister Laffan's crew?" Jeffrey Harrison asked Nash Slyfield. With the Lewis-gun team settling into the shelter of a rock, Harrison had turned on his side to remove a spare ammunition pan from his haversack and spotted a man limping away with 8 Platoon. "Arthur Tagg," Nash replied after a quick glance. "He's from Sid's section. Seems like he took a bullet in the leg." "He won't be too pleased about that," Harrison commented, placing the pan beside the gun. "Cressy! I'm feeling unwell," Charlie Robey confessed to Jock Cressy, who was sharing the other side of his boulder. "Don't worry about it. You're not the only one feeling that way; we all are. You're not any different," the Scotsman reassured the young soldier, who was only a few months out from Blighty. "Corporal Lyall, is anything happening on this end?"

Benedict looked around and saw Wilf Ridley crouching low as he approached from behind. Since they had taken their position, no further shots were fired. The far ridge looked peaceful and serene in the morning sunlight. "Anything happening, Sarge?" asked Wilf. "Well, tell your men to stay alert," warned the sergeant as he moved off to check the other side. On the opposite side of the trail, Joey Payne told Wilf that he didn't see anything either. Although it was six hundred yards away, the angle of the sunlight made it look closer. Joey looked back and saw that there was no recognizable formation in the main body of the company. The scouts provided a broken line as an advance guard, while the rest followed in a flock. "This is most unwelcome," said Wilf as he watched the enemy's ridge closely. "Unwelcome?" asked Joey. "Silence, Corporal Payne. The pills over there were shooting at us. I don't feel comfortable when they are not in my sights," replied Wilf. "Gaffer has almost reached the hill, Sergeant," pointed out the lance corporal, turning to look at the company. "Aye. Good," replied Wilf, quickly glancing before returning his focus to the enemy's ridge. "Sergeant Ridley!" shouted Sid Frith, alerting everyone. Running to his reserve section, the sergeant saw that a body of tribesmen, approximately a hundred strong, were crossing over to the same ridge that the company was targeting. "I only just spotted them, Sergeant," said Frith. "Corporal Griffiths, can you see any movement across the basin?" called Wilf, still watching the group of men in the distance. "Not a twitch, Sergeant," came the reply. "I knew it. I bloody knew it," stormed Wilf. "Right, everyone! Get yourselves ready now. We are changing grounds."

With the scouts having secured the crown of the new ridge, Lieutenant Bate stopped just below the crest. CSM Little and the company bugler, Kip Donn, also halted beside him. Raising his binoculars, the officer looked back at the rear-guard platoon. He recognized Sergeant Ridley because he always held his rifle across his chest. But Ridley was not looking towards the enemy or the company, but towards the northwest. Kyle looked towards the northwest but could not see what Ridley was observing due to the angle. Returning his gaze to the sergeant and snapping his binoculars back to his eyes, he barked, "Sergeant! The withdrawal. Quickly! Right, young Donn. Good and loud now!" Little passed on the order to the bugler to sound the bugle notes, which were five minutes earlier than he had intended. 5 Platoon was up and securing the far lip of the ridge, along with his HQ element and the non-combatants all catching their breath behind him. However, 7 and 8

Platoons were still struggling up the slope. Kyle watched as the bugle call was heard, and suddenly Sergeant Ridley sprang into motion, shouting orders and waving an arm. The Lewis Section was the first to leave its position, followed closely by the two on the flanks. The reserve section was the last to get off, but none dallied as they were departing at a dead run. "Sir, it is Mister Kingston," CSM Little informed Kyle, indicating the arrival of 7 Platoon. "Well done, Kingston. We're forming a defensive square until joined by 6 Platoon," he informed the younger officer. "I want your men on the western side of the box, down the ridge." "Hugo du Rand warned Kyle, 'We don't want to get caught static. Are you planning on staying here? My Scouts are nervous and don't want to be stuck in one location.' The OC assured Hugo that they weren't staying long and would leave as soon as the rear guard caught up. Hugo agreed to inform the others and was about to leave when Bate stopped him and asked who they were dealing with. Hugo replied that they were in the heart of Wazir holdings, and the tribesmen in the area were hostile and dangerous. While they talked, Kyle kept watch on 6 Platoon's flight, periodically checking the ridge they had left for any renewed hostility. As they reached the valley floor, shots were fired at them, and Kyle quickly sent a bugler to inform Mister Kingston to watch their front. The tribesmen had turned and were now heading towards the company position, making it impossible for the platoon to rejoin the company without running into danger."

With their hearts pounding wildly, the soldiers ran downhill, each one searching for the best route over or around the unstable and rocky surface that threatened to trip them up with every step. Despite the danger to their footing, they still glanced anxiously over their left shoulders. The bugle recall sounded, and 6 Platoon was about eight hundred yards away from the band of Pathans scrambling eastwards along the ridge. However, the distance rapidly decreased as the soldiers matched the tribesmen's steps and headed towards them on an intercepting course.

 Ridley's men were able to pull ahead with their downhill momentum, but it didn't make much of a difference as the angle narrowed, making them a target from the light infantry platoon. The first attempt to shoot at them was made by a young Wazir with a single shot Martini-Henry, but his shot missed and hit a rock, causing stone chippings to pepper one of the Lewis Section members. Ridley yelled for his men to stay nimble and not give the enemy a sitting target. They ran across the valley bottom, stumbling and losing their topees while trying to regain their footing. Nash Slyfield struggled to keep up with his Lewis gun, with others from the rifle sections overtaking him. They then began a tiring and deadly climb up the ridge. Graham Garvie from Benedict Lyall's 1 Section was the first to be hit, with a bullet passing through his shoulder blade and shattering the bone in his right forearm.

"Jesus!" he cried out through clenched teeth while falling forward.

"Graham, run with it!" exhorted Spud Murphy, pulling his mate to his feet.

Sprawling sideways, 2 Section's Spider Webb rose to his knees, clutching his throat, blood gushing between his fingers, his windpipe severed. Struggling to breathe, Jock Cressy and Charlie Robey dragged him to his feet.

"Get off yer shanks, Spider lad. Or the scuts will have yer liver," beseeched Cressy, slinging his rifle over his shoulder to grab Webb's.

The tribesmen were halted now; they had come as far along the ridge as they dared. Then, finding firing positions noticed by the British already on the ridge, they settled down to picking off 6 Platoon.

Keeping covering, dodging from rock to rock, pausing only long enough to fire snap shots, Ridley's platoon fought its way upwards. The distance between the two groups halfway up the hill was about three hundred yards; beyond that, the range would begin to extend again. It was at this point that the worst of the casualties were suffered.

Frank Quinn from the Lewis Section was flung to the ground with a bullet that struck his side, splintering two ribs. As Paddy Lynch of 1 Section bent to help him up, Eric Moody from 3 Section stopped beside them to return the fire. On taking aim, a bullet struck his rifle, deflecting into his chest. Goody Goodwin, also of 3 Section, seeing him collapse, picked him up to balance him across his shoulders, both men's topees spilling to the ground. The way Moody collapsed with his eyes open, sightlessly staring, Goodwin was sure the man was dead. Despite this, he endangered his own life by taking on his mate's extra weight, for this was the Frontier and dead or alive, no one was to be left to the vile mercy of the Pathan.

Another now being carried was Spider Webb. He had died while Cressy and Robey laboured to drag him up the hill. With Robey carrying three rifles, the Scotsman, under the weight of Webb, was pulling and clawing his way to the ridge summit.

Ducking from rock to rock, trying to defend themselves with hastily aimed snapshots, 6 Platoon doggedly battled their way in an oblique, upwards withdrawal. As the bulk of the platoon reached the same height on the ridge as their enemy, the tribesmen, rather than come out from around their cover and expose themselves to the rifle sights of the men of the company already on the ridge top, instead concentrated their fire on the platoon's stragglers.

Chalkie Gray of 2 Section, the platoon's resident comic, who was forever doing Charlie Chaplin impersonations, fell among the rocks with a bullet through his knee.

"Don't give up now, Chalkie," Joey Payne encouraged, crouching behind a rock to fire a shot. After ejecting the spent cartridge, he looked back at Gray, who twice attempted to stand, only to collapse both times. Finally, Payne reached down with his right hand, pulling the wounded man into an upright position. Losing his topee in the process, he lifted Gray onto his shoulders.

Sid Frith's men, being at the very back, were now the focal point of all the Pathan's fire. The Pathans were now bravely shunning their cover to get a better aim at the last of the fleeing British. While dashing across an exposed gap between two large rocks, Stan Findlay was hit above the hip, causing him to spin onto the ground. Tom O'Hanlon and Sandy Saunders rushed forward, gripping Findlay, and dragging him back under heavy fire. O'Hanlon was grazed by a bullet on the back of his neck. Nash Slyfield, who had crossed just before, caught his breath alongside Jeffrey Harrison. Seeing the others trapped on the far side of the gap, he courageously un-slung his Lewis gun, mounting it on a boulder, and began firing bursts at the

Pathans, who were gleefully engaged in their murderous acts.

Wilf Ridley, along with Sid Frith, the very last man, arrived at the scene breathless and wild-eyed. The sergeant yelled at them to pick up Findlay and hurry before he lost his patience. Thanks to Slyfield's relentless shooting, the Pathans' fire had weakened. O'Hanlon and Saunders carried Findlay across the gap, but he cried out in pain as his injured leg hit the stones. Once safely behind cover, O'Hanlon mentioned his gratitude that it was not his head that was injured. The gun team was ordered to move on, and they climbed higher to where Lyall and his section were stationed, now above the Pathans and sniping at them. Lily was urged by Emily Sheffield to stay put rather than investigate the shooting. Shortly after, Garvie, Quinn, Cressy, and Webb's body arrived, all injured or worse. Emily examined them one by one, shaking her head in despair.

"Are they dead, Ditchy?" asked Tracy, who was tucked up between two rocks, watching as the doctor searched for any signs of life in the two soldiers lying nearby. "Yes, Tracy, they are. Good King's men who have done their duty," replied the CQMS as he picked up the child and moved her away from the corpses. Lily stopped bandaging Graham Garvie's arm as Chalkie Gray cried out in pain. Joey Payne had been carrying him, but his knee wound had worsened due to the movement. "Don't worry, love. We held our own," Joey said, patting Tim Cressy's shoulder and urging him to return to the platoon. Willy Sale offered to help Tom with his neck wound, but O'Hanlon, who was also injured, pushed him away, more concerned about rejoining his section. "Well done, Sergeant Ridley," praised Bate as the last soldier, Wilf, made it to the defensive box. "How many are dead, sir?" asked Ridley. "Maybe one or two," replied the officer. "Lucky, sir. You recalled us when you did. We could have lost the whole platoon," Ridley gasped for breath. "Join your platoon. We're moving off soon. You'll be the reserve force," commanded Kyle. As 6 Platoon fought their way up the ridge, Bate decided to continue their march along its summit. The ridge was higher than the surrounding land, giving them a tactical advantage. The ridge also ran for four miles, pointing out into a plain where they'd have to descend to reach the Faizu river. The Faizu was at the bottom of a steep tangi, with only one crossing point, beyond where their ridge met the plain.

Kyle and Hugo du Rand planned to walk their force east in a defensive posture, which was not a common tactic in military manuals, but was necessary given the unique situation at the North-West Frontier. They were a small force and the hostile Pathan tribesmen could attack them from any direction at any time. B Company and Hugo du Rand's Scouts Platoon had to fight their way out of enemy territory, carrying the wounded and the dead. Benedict Lyall's 1 Section assisted in carrying the wounded, while the sweepers carried the dead, despite their fear. The district officer provided reassurance and leadership for the non-combatants. Kip Donn gave the signal to advance, and the Scouts led on a narrow front, while the other platoons covered the flanks. Giles Kingston's 7 Platoon had the dangerous task of bringing up the rear, and they were already under fire from tribesmen on the west ridge.

"Bate and his command made significant progress for a quarter of a mile, even though it was challenging to maintain control. Everyone strived to keep pace so that there were no gaps or bunching, and they covered the ground slowly but surely. Then, Sergeant Henry Groocock of the 8th Platoon, called for Kyle. "Here, sir," said Matthew Laffan, the platoon commander, standing on a rock on the southern rim of the ridge, looking back towards the feature they had left for the one they were currently on. "What is it, Matthew?" asked Kyle, as he climbed up beside him. The 2nd lieutenant pointed to the far ridge and simply said, "There." Raising his glasses, the OC focused on the far ridge, spotting hundreds of raggedly dressed Pathan tribesmen moving down the track they had followed from the river throughout most of the night.

Bate, we need to pick up the pace. We must move faster than this," said Kingston, as his forces were about to face an increased number of enemies. He sought out the officer most likely to feel the brunt of the assault first. "It's challenging to move any quicker, sir," replied the 7th Platoon commander, who was crouched behind rocky cover, directing his sections with shouted orders and whistles. "The enemies are sniping at us from all angles, and it's impossible to break away cleanly. So, we've had to fall back in stages, section by section." "Whether you like it or not, Kingston, you have to speed up. The tribesmen we left behind have arrived in numbers and will be upon you soon. Unfortunately, I can't spare any extra men to reinforce you. However, I will have 5th and 8th Lewis Sections switched to your flanks, under your command." Bate ducked away, leaving the young 2nd lieutenant to handle the fighting withdrawal. Meanwhile, he ordered the regrouping of the two Lewis guns. His small command cell, including CSM Little and Donn, followed behind them. The 1st and 3rd Sections of the 7th Platoon rose to dodge and weave another bound to the rear. Like a caterpillar, this small defensive island moved westward along the ridge. In an hour, they retreated a mile, reaching the boundary of the plain. The crown of the ridge from which they were stubbornly withdrawing was not conducive to rapid manoeuvres. The terrain was jagged and led to injuries for those who attempted to cross it. Due to the area's jumbled terrain, there was ample cover for both sides.

When Giles Kingston's men tried to fall back to keep the enemy at bay, the tribesmen attempted to strike them. However, this moment of vulnerability worked both ways, and the Queen's men also had deadly shots. They would spend hours each week practicing their musketry skills to earn an extra nine pence a day. Despite the 7th Platoon taking four casualties, including one dead and three wounded, they continued to withdraw while carrying their injured comrades. Bate checked on the casualties and discussed the challenges they faced with Emily Sheffield. With some severe injuries, they had to be carried to the rear, which was painful and time-consuming. As the Pathan firing increased, they realized they were in Kingston's hands and had everything in the shop window except for the 6th Platoon. The sight of an RAF two-seater biplane flying overhead lifted their spirits, but they would have preferred another platoon at that moment.

CHAPTER 24

We aren't no thin red 'eroes, Nor we aren't no blackguards too,
But single men in barracks, Most remarkable like you.
-Rudyard Kipling

The post at Khwaja Kalan was a large, two-storey tower surrounded by barbed wire. The small garrison that occupied it defended themselves from the upper storey. When attacked, they sealed the only entrance by bolting shut an iron trapdoor, which, enclosed in thick stone walls, theoretically made them impregnable against the tribesmen's small arms. The only way the tower could be taken was with artillery or explosives. The Fakir of Matun had no field gun but still possessed explosives.

Just before Lily Richmond and Tracy were kidnapped, he had selected Chashma as the objective of his attack on British India. By taking this garrison outpost, he believed the Wazir and Mahsud tribes would not hesitate in flocking to his banner. First, though, he had to lure away the bulk of the force at Ishak. This he did by calling for the Afghan tribes to gather with their arms on the border, northwest of Razmak, prompting that garrison to call for immediate aid from

Ishak. Word of the column moving out was sent by one of Fakir's sons, who then attacked Khwaja Kalan with the help of local tribesmen, severing communications between Ishak and Chashma.

The sight to those in Brigadier Gabson's command who had never seen the Pathan's handiwork was sickening: the explosion blast to the tower had ripped away a quarter of its wall. The defenders' bodies were lying over a wide area around the tower, all mutilated. Some, it was apparent, had been tortured to death. The British officer's corpse was found inside the tower, his skin pegged out on the ground at its entrance.

Observing this grisly sight, the brigadier turned to the man at his side: "Tell me, D'urban. You are attuned to the workings of these creatures' minds. Just what justification do they make to you when explaining acts of bestiality such as this?"

"Sir, the Pathan sees no evil in this barbarism," the political officer answered. "They're like children playing with sharpened toys."

"Children!" Gabson replied, snapping the word off. "Well, I believe then, it's time we purged the nursery."

Departing from Ishak at first light, it was now mid-morning. With the column securing the destroyed post with picket positions on the high points, the recovery of the bodies had begun on

466

the evening before the brigadier informed Dera Ishal Khan of his arrival at Ishak and his assumption of command of the garrison. He confirmed that Chashma had received its evacuation order and updated the local situation report. He also added his intention to bring a force to Khwaja Kalan the following day to recover the scouts' bodies.

While most of the Queen's Light Infantry were positioned on picket, a company of the Seaforth Highlanders took care of collecting the dead. With the mules of the column resting, free of their loads, each body was wrapped in a blanket and placed on stretchers in neat rows.

"Aircraft, sir," Captain Qunell of the garrison artillery regiment, whom Gabson had borrowed as his brigade major for the appointment, alerted.

In his message from the previous evening, he had requested observation aircraft to scout out the area around Ishak and to keep track of the evacuating garrison from Chashma. Accordingly, the plane was ordered to first land at Ishak, where Lieutenant Colonel Kinsley was under orders from Gabson to instruct the airmen. As soon as they located B Company, they were to find his column and inform him of its whereabouts.

"As it swooped low over the damaged tower, a small object was flung from the 'Ninak'. Upon retrieving this leather pouch, a Seaforth corporal hurried to hand it to Captain Qunell.

"Message, sir," said the corporal, taking a sheet of paper from the pouch to hand to the brigadier.

As Gabson read the note, the principal officers of the column stood silently around him.

"They've found the Chashma garrison," he announced.

Looking up from the paper with a foreboding look in his eyes, he said, "They're five to six miles north of us, being engaged by a force of Pathans and apparently fighting for their lives." He handed the message back to his acting brigade major and without preliminary discussion, Gabson set his command in motion: "Gentlemen! Get the pack animals loaded. We're going north," he ordered, extending his arm towards a gap in the hills.

--oOo--

Robin Cuimein dropped to his knees and let Spider Webb's body slide from his shoulders onto the ground. The rising number of enemies attacking the British had caused their casualties to increase. Six soldiers were dead, and twice that number were seriously wounded. Everyone pitched in at the aid post when the wounded needed to be moved. The walking wounded, like Arthur Tagg and Graham Garvie, helped each other move away from danger. Cuimein moved among the sweepers, giving them words of encouragement. Stray bullets flew from the west, so everyone had to crawl or crouch to avoid being hit. Cuimein made his way to the center of the aid post to see if he could assist Emily Sheffield. The area for the wounded had expanded, and they had to spread out to avoid being an easy target. Emily was working hard to save the life of a young soldier who had been shot in the side of the face and was choking on his blood. Cuimein praised Emily for her hard work and offered to help. Their conversation was interrupted by Wilf Ridley, who informed Cuimein of one of Hugo's men who had just arrived but couldn't speak due to exhaustion. Due to a lack of time, Cuimein quickly asked the Scout in Pushtu why he had come. "Mister du Rand sent him to find the OC to ask for reinforcements," translated the district officer. "He is with Mister Kingston at the moment, sir," Ridley pointed out. "Well, you and I better go and see what the crisis is," Cuimein decided, waving the Scout into the lead. "Corporal Lyall," the sergeant shouted. "Look after the Platoon for a minute or two. I am just off with Mister Cuimein to do a spot of reconnoitring." As they approached the Scout's advance line, the two Englishmen became aware for the first time that the Scouts had halted and were exchanging shots with an enemy blocking the company's withdrawal. They found Hugo waiting in shelter next to a crag of rock, pistol in hand. "Some of the beggars have gotten around us. They are holed up in a pile of rocks right in our path. My chaps are Scouts, not trained for assaulting. I wanted some of Mister Bate's Queen to storm the position," he informed them. "Well, it's certain we aren't going anywhere until that group is dislodged," Cuimein agreed, quickly assessing the tribesmen's strong point with a battle-trained Royal Engineer officer's eye. "Kyle is busy fighting at the other end. We can't afford to waste time seeking a decision from him. So, I suggest you use Sergeant Ridley's Platoon to dislodge those devils while I find Mister Bate and inform him why we are deploying his reserve." "Right you are, Robin," complied du Rand, patting Wilf Ridley on the shoulder. "Sergeant, get your platoon up here fast. Time is not on our side."

"Alright, platoon, grab your fighting gear and follow me!" Ridley shouted, turning towards the aid post. "Mr. du Rand is in trouble up ahead and we've been tasked with helping him out." As they passed through the aid post, Cuimein quickly equipped himself with Spider Webb's ammunition pouches and picked up a rifle from Arthur Tagg.

During his early days in the Great War, Cuimein had adopted the practice of arming himself with a rifle as he went to find Bate on the front line, having arrived in Chashma unarmed. After Major Hartnell's death, he took possession of the officer's pistol. Upon reaching Kyle, the district officer approved of Cuimein's preparedness. Due to a loss of control in movement, the position now held by the British stretched over three hundred yards, resulting in gaps on the flanks. Kyle was striving to close these gaps by accelerating 7 Platoon's withdrawal. Bate had dispatched Jeffrey Gurrin and Henry Groocock to take charge of their detached Lewis Sections to help ease Giles Kingston's burden.

Before Cuimein's arrival, Bate had just briefed the two sergeants on their expected roles during the next phase of the withdrawal. "Donn! Go tell Mr. Kingston to retract his men. The Lewis guns on the flanks will cover," Bate ordered. The company commander then turned back to Cuimein, providing instructions on how to manage the ensuing events.

"Robin! Go back and provide any assistance Hugo may need. He must keep our route along this ridge open. I need to stay here with Kingston, but I need you to take charge of the wounded. Let the Quartermaster know that you're in charge of the aid post," Bate instructed. As he gave these orders, two soldiers dragged a wounded casualty towards them. "Take him to the aid post now," Lieutenant Cuimein ordered, understanding the importance of providing medical attention to those on the firing line. "I'll do that, Kyle," he declared, assuming responsibility for the wounded.

With the district officer returning to the aid post, carrying the weight of the dead soldier on his shoulders, Bate tried to join CSM Little behind a rock, but a bullet hit his pistol holster on his hip. Little rushed to his aid, and fortunately, the bullet only glanced off the pistol in its holster, preventing serious injury. Despite being wounded and dazed, Bate didn't want his men to think he was disabled, so he asked Little to help him up.

Meanwhile, Cuimein placed the dead soldier next to another one who had been shot in the face and unsuccessfully saved by Emily. Back with the Scouts, Hugo had already begun the platoon attack and pointed out to Ahmed Wakil the enemy soldiers crawling forward through the broken rocks.

As the Scouts moved towards the Pathan stronghold, they faced a hundred and fifty yards of rocky terrain before encountering stony ground with no cover. The tribesmen occupied a small natural rock fort in the center of the ridge, blocking their way. During the attack, Colling and Waters exchanged taunts, but their section commander, Joey Payne, silenced them and ordered them to focus on the enemy.

Meanwhile, the sweepers were recovering water bottles from the dead soldiers to quench the thirst of some of the wounded men.

du Rand's plan of attack was straightforward: to creep close enough to throw grenades, then engage the enemy in hand-to-hand combat. To keep the enemy's heads down while the three rifle sections navigated through the rocky terrain, the Lewis Section was dispatched to the right-hand rim of the ridge from where they could provide covering fire. The other three sections navigated through the rocks along three separate routes. Benedict Lyall led his 1 Section on the right, du Rand led Joey Payne's 2 Section in the centre, and Sergeant Ridley took charge of Sid Frith's 3 Section on the left.

It was close to midday, with the sun blazing hot and the stone surfaces scorching. Crawling on all fours and slipping from rock to rock in the heat was exhausting, causing the men to sweat and gasp for breath. Then, at the halfway point, automatic gunfire began to erupt in short bursts from their right.

"Good old Nash," Danny Short hissed through clenched teeth.

Reaching the edge of their protective rock entanglement, the three sections spread themselves out in a disjointed line which, at some points, was two deep. The strength of the 6 Platoon upon leaving Chashma had been forty all ranks. However, due to casualties, wounded, and the detachment of the Lewis Section for support, the actual assault force was reduced to twenty-six. This number also included Hugo du Rand and Arthur Tagg, who was back with 3 Section, although he was limping badly from a bullet wound in his thigh. Unbeknownst to them, the enemy they faced was a band of about twenty, only half armed with rifles. They were all young and focused on the prize of a rifle or the killing of an infidel to guarantee their entry into paradise.

By staying low, the Platoon had managed to approach within forty yards – a good throw for a cricket arm. Accepting a grenade from Joey Payne, Hugo du Rand tested the range. He pulled the pin and waited for the next burst of Lewis fire before hurling it towards the enemy's rocky bastion. As his upper body was momentarily exposed for the throw, a bullet whizzed past his arm. The grenade, just reaching the near edge, struck a large rock and was deflected to the side and down. The explosion, which sounded like a loud cough, sent up a shower of stones in a cloud of grey smoke. For a brief period, silence followed; this was perhaps something the tribesmen had not expected. "Get ready to attack, Platoon!" shouted du Rand, aware they had no time for a game of cat and mouse. "When I give the signal, 2 Section will throw grenades, and 1 and 3 will provide cover fire. Then on my command, charge! We attack. Get ready."

As 1 and 3 Sections removed the cut-off plates from their rifles to free the magazine rounds, 2 Section reached into their haversacks for grenades.

"Get ready to throw," du Rand yelled, prompting nine pins to be pulled. "Ready, set, go! Up!"

As arms that were reaching back flung forward and up, men on the right and left took aim and fired. Only eight grenades arched through the air; however, the ninth slipped from Ken Hallin's grip as he fell backwards, crumpling among the rocks, a bullet through his forehead. When it went off, the grenade blew away most of his right shoulder. Of the others, three landed short, but five sailed into the fringe of the enemy's defence, all exploding over two seconds.

"Now, Queens! Charge!" hollered Hugo du Rand springing to his feet, the arm that held his revolver plunging forward in a high sweep. Responding to the call, 6 Platoon bolted up, bayonets reflecting flashes of light from the high noon sun. With stomachs knotted, throats dry and choked, their minds blanked to everything except the pile of rocks before them; screaming curses, they flew over the ground hurdling boulders and zigzagging around larger rocks. Finally, Benedict Lyall rose, bellowing a barrack room quip used when expressing dissatisfaction: "Roll on the boat!"

Picked up by others, it was roared as a battle cry. Forty yards at a run was a great distance if you threw yourself across it at an armed enemy. 6 Platoon, on launching themselves into the assault, had no supporting fire from the Lewis-gun or the Scouts, the risk of hitting their own side being too chancy. Their one hope of success in this attack was in the swiftness of their rush, enabling them to fall upon these tribal killers before they could be cut down.

With twenty yards to go, Jack Fenton from 3 Section saw one of the enemies, a dirty cloth on a swarthy head, aiming a rifle at him. The instant he saw the rifle fired, he felt the bullet strike his chest, killing him. Another fatally hit was 1 section's Chris Perry, shot through the heart. His mate beside him, Jim Lockie, also went down, doubled over with a bullet in the stomach. Sandy Saunders of 3 Section spun to the ground after taking a shot in his upper right arm. Falling behind, gamely struggling with a stiff-legged limp, Arthur Tagg took a bullet through his left lung that also shattered his spine. Then, giving a last cry, "Roll on the bloody bo---" he collapsed to the ground, dying.

Then with relief and thirst for revenge, they stormed into the island-like feature, hunting the Pathans through a maze of narrow passages and across room-size spaces. Joey Payne, stopping himself on the shoulder of a bend, stole a quick look around it, ducking his head back as a rifle was fired at him from only a few feet away. Snapping a shot back, he leapt after the raggedly dressed youth who had turned to flee. Feeding a fresh round into his rifle chamber, he shot the tribesman in the back as he tried to escape down a stone-enclosed alleyway. Then, spinning around as his name was shouted out and a shot fired, he found behind him Gynger Langdon thrusting forward at a tribesman who had rushed out of concealment to his rear, intent on cutting the section commander down with a *talwar*. Wounding him in the back, Langdon silenced his screams with two forceful bayonet jabs into his side ribs as he floundered on the ground. Pressing through a narrow gap, Jock Cressy, without warning, came face to face with three tribesmen armed with knives and a *talwar*. Firing point blanks at one another with a scream, his face twisted in a snarl, lunged at him with a knife. Blocking the plunging blade arm by pushing his rifle crossways in front of himself, the third Wazir swung his *talwar*, severing the Scotsman's left hand at the wrist. As the arrow fell to the ground, Charlie Robey shot this tribesman through the mouth. To free himself of the second, Cressy kicked out before he could use his knife, forcing the Pathan to stumble back. Then still gripping his rifle with his right hand, he drew it back, driving the bayonet into the native's torso, carrying forward to pin him to the ground. He forced the bayonet down three more times, using it like a stake.

"Finish him, Charlie lad. Finish him," called out the Scotsman to Robey, who had not noticed the first tribesman that Cressy had shot and only wounded, stumbling away in a bid to escape.

"Jesus Christ, Jock!" exclaimed Robey after shooting the tribesman twice in the back.

"Stop ye greetin' mun. And git ma lace oot'a ma boot." Then, sitting, gripping the base of the stump of his left arm with his right hand to stem the gush of blood, he stuck a foot towards the young English soldier.

Benedict Lyall entering the rocky complex at a point where moments earlier he had seen a Wazir firing, found it abandoned. Taking a grenade from the haversack hanging on his hip, he pulled the pin and threw it deep into the enemy position. Even as the grenade, its fused detonator sounding with a pop, was still curving through the air, the corporal resumed his pursuit.

Others were also doing the same, for some tribesmen were lying in ambush, around corners and tucked away in hides. The Pathan had the advantage of knowing every twist and turn in this labyrinth, so the Queens were re-dressing their lack of ground knowledge by bombing their way through. Paani Waters, when preparing the Platoon's grenades at Chashma, had primed one with a three-second fuse, which he now carried in one hand with the pin out.

"Paani, get rid of that damn Mills bomb," urged Bert Colling. "If you drop the bloody thing, we'll both end up dead meat."

"Shut up," retorted Waters. "Just watch. I'm not about to be sliced open by some native's tin sword."

With Waters in the lead, the two men were cautiously stalking along a natural tunnel with openings every ten feet. Suddenly at one of these junctions, the muzzle of a rifle appeared, pointing towards them.

"Paani!" shouted Colling, the first to spot it, striking the other man's hat as he levelled his rifle and fired.

With the bullet ricocheting away, Paani, who had just caught a glimpse of the rifle barrel as it was withdrawn, ran forward to throw his grenade into the alcove the tribesman, frightened, had retreated into. The two soldiers found a bloody heap of flesh and tattered cloth following the explosion. A young Wazir, trapped in this confined space with only one exit, had picked up the short-fused grenade to throw back when it exploded, blowing away most of his arm.

Hearing pistol shots on the opposite side of a high hedge of boulders, Benedict Lyall and China Yeoman spun with levelled rifles towards an entrance in it. Bursting from these only feet away, two youthful Pathans, armed with bloodstained *talwars*, flung themselves at the soldiers without hesitation. Yeoman, the nearer, fired his rifle from the hip at one, raising his sword blade to strike, also plunging his bayonet into the tribesman's chest; as the *talwar* slashed into his shoulder and left forearm, Yeoman was also selected as the target by the second tribesman. With his right arm high, poised to decapitate the Englishman, his section commander drove his bayonet into the tribesman's rib cage, turning Wazir's cry of triumph into a scream of agony. Carrying on with the momentum of his thrust Lyall shoved his victim to the ground.

"Feel that you filthy heathen?" taunted Benedict without pity. "That's pure English steel you are tasting."

"Good show! Bloody good show, Corporal Lyall," congratulated Hugo du Rand, appearing through the same gap used by the tribesmen. "Come on now, follow me. We must drive them all out."

"They just killed Murray," announced Wilf Ridley, closely trailing behind the officer. They maneuvered through the rocky entanglement, strategically moving from one dangerous point to another until they finally broke free into the open on the east side of the stronghold. Lying on the ground before them were three Pathan bodies. Robin Cuimein led six Scouts to one flank when the Platoon entered the position, successfully shooting down three of the seven who tried to escape. Older, wiser tribesmen would have fled as soon as the 6th Platoon began their assault. However, the younger ones stayed far too long, driven by the desire for guns, glory, and a reputation.

"Hugo! We need to relocate the aid post. Perhaps you could bring your Scouts forward and join this Platoon here. In the meantime, I'll take the Lewis Section and start transporting the wounded," Cuimein suggested, approaching with a rifle in one hand.

"All right! Go ahead. I'll gather all the wounded here," responded du Rand.

Wilf Ridley retraced his path through the captured position, looking for dead and wounded. He ran into Jock Cressy who was on his way back to the Platoon.

"Young man, you need medical attention. Head to the aid post," instructed the sergeant, quickly assessing the bloodied stump of Cressy's limb, the bleeding halted by a makeshift bootlace tourniquet.

Twenty-six men had answered Hugo du Rand's call to charge, but only seventeen remained standing on the far side of the assault position. Six were dead, and three were wounded.

"Oh my God, Cressy! Oh my God!" Lily exclaimed in shock upon seeing that Cressy had lost a hand. She didn't know many of the companies' names, but Cressy was one whom Joey had introduced.

"Don't fret, Lily lass. It's just a flipper. I still have the other," Cressy calmed her.

As the nurse began to bandage the severed wrist, Pete Hollinghurst approached Cressy, asking, "Is there anything you need, Cressy?"

"Yes, Cooky, could you fetch me a bootlace?" replied Cressy, extending a leg towards him.

With Robin Cuimein's return, the aid post began relocating again. He brought Corporal Griffiths' men with him and directed them to carry the wounded down the ridge. He also dispatched the sweepers, who followed behind with some of the dead. However, even combined, the two groups couldn't transfer the number of dead and wounded surrounding the doctor and her medical team. With casualties steadily increasing, those assigned to the task would need to make two or three trips.

Insisting that Emily accompany the first group, as her professional skills were needed by the wounded from the 6th Platoon, the district officer resumed his search for the company commander.

"How many are dead?" Kyle asked, hearing Cuimein's report of the 6th Platoon's successful attack.

"Four or five, maybe more. I didn't wait for the casualty count."

"Damn, Robin! Damn!" cursed Bate punching a fist onto a thigh, one side of his face encrusted with dried blood.

The two men were hunched in the cover of a rock, the fire just forward of them sluggish but steady. Both sides were conserving ammunition, but the tribesmen's shots made it dangerous to move about upright along the ridge.

"This is turning out to be too costly," went on the officer, his voice filled with frustrated anger, "if we can't break off contact, we'll have no choice but to stand and fight. Go back, Robin. Find Hugo. Tell him we will take up a defence on the end of the ridge. We will decide our next step from there."

"Right, Quartermaster. I will clear it up here. " Get off to where we are being re-established and take charge until I arrive," ordered Cuimein, returning to the aid post to find all the wounded and most of the dead taken away.

"Right, sir," replied Heydrich, turning to collect Tracy. Sitting alone behind a protective rock, she was waiting for the CQMS. With Lily committed to the wounded, the young child now entrusted herself to Heydrich, refusing all other escorts, only moving on when he did.

"Here we go again, Miss Ratcliffe," declared the burly Quartermaster, lifting her to shoo the girl before him like a mother hen would one of her chicks. "Hurry now, we've no time to waste around another..."

A bullet striking Heydrich on the back of his head pitched him face forward onto the stony ground, his topee landing at the girl's heels. Jock Cressy, after the completion of his bandaging by Lily, was just slinging his rifle across his back when he saw the quartermaster fall. The aid post was almost cleared; Lily had gathered up her bandages and dressings, and with Roy Lockwood, one of the signallers was hurrying to see to the carrying off Stan Findlay by two of 6 Platoon's Lewis Section. His hip wound would not stop bleeding, and he was screaming from the pain of being moved.

"Oh, Ditchy! Get up!"

When Cressy reached Tracy, he found her tugging at one of Heydrich's hands with both of hers. The heart-breaking sight of the young child trying to lift the fallen man stirred a deep sense of pity in the Scotsman's heart.

"The Quartermaster isn't going to get up just now, young girl," said Cressy, wrapping his armless left arm around the girl's waist while picking up Heydrich's rifle with his right. "You need to come with me. You can't stay here. He wouldn't want that."

Knowing that his words offered little solace, Cressy held Tracy tight with his crippled limb while she clung to his neck. As he carried her away, Tracy continued to stare at the body of the fallen Quartermaster, sobbing tears of grief onto the soldier's shoulder and heartbreakingly crying out, "Ditchy! Ditchy!"

After alerting Cuimein that Heydrich was dead, confirmed by a glance at the rupee-sized exit hole in the Quartermaster's forehead, Cressy quickly whisked Tracy away from the scene. As they passed through the enemy position that he and 6th Platoon had captured earlier, he noticed that the platoon had, in turn, taken up its defence.

"This will break those bleeders' hearts," called out Sid Frith as the Scotsman, with Tracy still in his arms, made his way through. Sid was smashing the rifles of the dead tribesmen one by one against a rock.

In deploying his men, Wilf Ridley organized them in a defensive line on the western edge of the captured rocky redoubt. He placed the strongest, the Lewis Section, in the middle, with 2 Section, who had only lost four men, on their left. Lastly, 1 and 3, down to nine men between them, he stationed together on the right. Then, they waited.

They were joined by Cuimein, who relayed Bate's orders to Hugo du Rand. The Platoon listened as the sounds of shooting grew closer, while the rest of the company retreated. The first to be seen was 8 and 5 Platoons, who were retreating while guarding against attacks from the flanks. Then, they saw Kyle and his party rushing through the rocks, halting at the edge of the stones where 6 Platoon had started its attack half an hour earlier.

"Over here, sir," Wilf Ridley called, waving his topee to the officer.

"Well done, Sergeant Ridley," Bate complimented, arriving in a rush. "You've chosen your location well. You're going to need the advantage. I need you and your men to oversee the company's retreat and hold this position until I call you back with two loud whistle blasts."

"We will do that, sir," Ridley promised. "Good, good," said the commanding officer, turning to Cuimein. "Bob, is Hugo aware of the situation?" The district officer confirmed this and then described the difficulties encountered during the relocation of the aid post, mentioning Heydrich's death. Before he could finish, a shout from Donn interrupted him.

"7 Platoon, sir."

"Right, Sergeant Ridley, we must leave you to it. Now remember, two whistle blasts and back you come." While speaking, Bate braced himself with both hands on a boulder, watching 7 Platoon's retreating group darting back among the rocks. Then, he left with a suitable luck squeeze to the sergeant's shoulder, taking Cuimein with him. 7 Platoon, for the first time, was falling back at a rolling gait, able to break contact; they were keeping themselves marginally ahead of the pursuing Pathan. Interspersed with rifle shots and the occasional burst of Lewis fire, they leap-frogged to, then through 6 Platoon's position. First, the injured: two walking wounded, one with a bloody arm, and a second limping with an equally bloody leg. One man, dead, was being carried between two others. Close on their heels came the remainder of the sections. Thinned by the loss of deceased and wounded, they doubled back, stopping only to cover their mates. Faces streaked with sweat, uniforms patched with dark sweat stains, eyes had taken on the hunted look of animals at bay.

As 7 Platoon passed through the 6th's position, gallows humour and jokes were exchanged, along with some sincere advice. "Just give 'em a short burst, Nash. Don't waste lead on these wicked men," offered Doug Culverwell, the Lewis gunner of 7 Platoon, to Slyfield.

"Sergeant Harry Evans, Ridley's counterpart, warned Wilf to tell his boys to keep their heads down. Giles Kingston, the inexperienced and overwhelmed platoon commander, advised Ridley not to let any of his men become isolated. After he departed, the soldiers caught fleeting glimpses of movement between the rocks in front of the platoon. They pressed themselves into the rocks, peering through their rifle sights for any signs of the enemy. The hill men, a united force of bloodthirsty Mahsuds and Wazirs, shared a common hatred for the British and an eagerness to kill for rifles and loot. Danny Short, positioned back-to-back with Gynger Langdon, noticed a hand inching around a rock from his angle on the right. He removed his bayonet to avoid revealing his position and aimed at the hand. When the owner's head, black-bearded and hawk-nosed, came into

Short's line of sight, he pulled the trigger and relayed to his mate that he had hit his mark. The target instantly vanished, leaving the rock-stained red."

The opening shot triggered a series of sniping exchanges that lasted for ten minutes, resulting in only one casualty for 6 Platoon: Charlie Robey, who was shot through the cheek. After hearing two long whistle blasts from their rear, Joey Payne tied a bandage over his wound. Ridley shouted for the platoon to prepare for withdrawal. At his command, Griffiths, Slyfield, and Harrison left immediately with the Lewis gun while everyone else prepared to throw a grenade. Ridley aimed to prevent any retaliation from the enemy by throwing grenades, causing them to seek cover. Gray cursed the Ninak aircraft that circled above them, helpless to aid. Quinn, grimacing in pain from his side wound, replied that Gray wouldn't be so eager to join the fight if he was the one in the aircraft. Both men were at the aid post, Gray having been shot in the knee and needing to be carried. Despite his rib injury, Quinn used puttees from the dead to bind Gray's other leg to the injured one. Gray asked Quinn for a cigarette, to which Quinn handed him a pack of Park Drives.

"I'd smoke your sock if you rolled paper around it," Gray replied, his eyes closing as he battled another wave of pain. Wounded soldiers lay scattered around them. Members of 7 Platoon sifted through the belongings of the deceased for additional ammunition and grenades. Lily paused from bandaging a newly arrived wounded soldier to reassure Tracy that everything would be okay. She noticed that Cressy was taking care of Tracy. When Lily asked Tracy if she had someone to look after her, Cressy indicated that Ditchy was no longer available. Lily tried comforting Tracy, wiping away her tears and assuring her that Jock would take care of her. However, Tracy refused to acknowledge Jock's name and clung to him. Meanwhile, 6 Platoon returned and received new orders from Kyle. Robin Cuimein was directed to move his people again, using Sergeant Ridley's men to transport the wounded first. Hugo du Rand dispatched his scouts to find a suitable location for Robin's aid post and scout the area for potential fighting.

"Up you come, Chalkie lad," declared Bert Colling, gripping Gray's upper body. Then, Gynger Langdon took his other side, while Paani Waters and Danny Short took his legs. Together, they lifted him to sit on a rifle held by Colling and Langdon. Waters and Short kept his bound legs off the ground with another rifle as they carried him off to the end of the ridge, with Gray cursing in pain. When Joey Payne and Charlie Robey arrived to move Stan Findlay, Lily informed them that he was already dead. Payne still insisted on taking him and complimented Lily on her work. However, Lily was clearly affected by the death and felt ashamed, asking Payne and Robey to leave her to finish up. She ran over to Emily Sheffield, who was attending to Gerry Pearton and Tom May, and asked Pearton why he hadn't gone with the others. He replied that he was waiting for his mate, and Lily offered to help him by putting his arm in a sling. She rummaged through the pack she now carries with her everywhere.

"Here, young man, put your finger on this," Emily said as she tied a bandage around May's leg, indicating a knot she was fastening. Bullets whizzed through the air as the enemy followed 6 Platoon and advanced to hidden firing positions. One bullet ricocheted from a rock, humming briefly before it crashed into the area of the aid post. The impact made May gasp, "Oh God!" Emily, who was leaning over May, was pushed as she attempted to finish tying the knot. Her hands failed to respond, and she eventually collapsed onto May's legs. A soldier cried out, "Jesus! Doctor!" May struggled to lay Emily flat and called for help. Hearing this, Lily cried out "Emily!" and threw herself beside Emily's crumpled form. "I'm fine Lily. I just had my breath taken away, that's all," replied Emily weakly.

"Where are you, Emily? Hurry! Where?" asked the panicked nurse. "It's in the back, dear," the older woman responded gently. Pearton and May quickly joined Lily in helping Emily onto her side as gently as possible. Lily found a thumb-sized entrance wound on one side of Emily's back, between her hip and lower ribcage. There was no sign of an exit wound, and blood was seeping through her blouse. "You'll be alright, Emily. I won't let you die. I won't!" Lily promised, her voice shaky from shock and fear. Emily responded in a hushed voice, "Lily, child, haven't you learned anything? You're ignoring the first rule of nursing. Never show your emotions to the patient." Tom May held Emily in a sitting position while Lily quickly applied dressings to the wound to halt the bleeding, securing them with a tight bandage around her waist. "Lily, tell Douglas he is to take on supervisory duties for all our Missions. I recommended him to our London board last year as my replacement. They accepted, but I've neglected to tell him," Emily whispered. "I won't do it, Emily. You'll tell him yourself," Lily replied, regaining control over her emotions. Benedict Lyall and several others from 6 Platoon arrived to remove the dead, shocked to find Lily still at the scene. "Oh, Benedict! Thank God," said Lily, finishing up the bandaging. "It's Doctor Sheffield. She's been injured. We need to carry her." "I'll do that," said Robin Cuimein, taking charge of the situation. "May and Pearton, escort Miss Richmond to the new aid post," he ordered.

"I would rather stay with the Doctor, Mr. Cuimein," the young woman protested. "You are the Doctor now, Lily. Now get down to the aid post where you are needed," he replied. Upon discovering Emily injured within the group, his anger was unleashed against the nurse. He loudly objected to her suffering because of some Pathan's senseless pursuit of loot. As the three departed, Cuimein slung his rifle across his back. "I will carry the Doctor, Corporal. You stay nearby," he requested of Benedict as he bent down to lift the woman into his arms. "I am going to lift you, Emily. It might be painful, so brace yourself."

"Robin Zahir Khan," the Doctor declared, her hand tightly gripping his shoulder to emphasize her words. "Tell him there is to be no badi. I will not tolerate a blood feud instigated in my name."

"There will be no need for that. You are far too tough a bird," Cuimein responded, stepping off with her in his arms. As the last ones to leave the old aid post, they navigated through the shattered rocks and occasional scrub bushes. Upon reaching the new aid post, Cuimein gently placed Emily behind the shelter of a boulder situated just over the ridge, which descended to the plain 500 feet below. Leaving the Doctor in the care of Willy Sale, one of the cooks, he began to check on the other wounded and their current positions. The deceased and injured were shielded by the ridge top, well outside the line of fire.

The Scouts had formed a screening line just in front of the rim, while Sergeant Ridley was positioning the 6th Platoon in a defensive semicircle below and to the sides of the aid post. Looking eastwards, Cuimein could spot the Faizu Tangi that ran from southwest to northeast, etching a deep scar into the plain. Its edges were sharp lines everywhere except one spot where a few hundred yards in diameter of crumbled banking showed its only crossing point for several miles. Just beyond the crossing was a cluster of fragmented hills, a forward guard to much larger ones further back.

Drawn to the top of the ridge by a surge in gunfire, Cuimein joined Hugo du Rand. They watched as Kyle led the rest of the company back. Then, with the 7th Platoon moving backwards in overlapping dashes, the 5th and 8th Platoons started to move inward ensuring no one was left behind, everyone returning in a single line. Carrying or pulling their wounded, the three platoons moved through the Scouts, finding cover just below the ridge line.

"Bate needed more time to issue his defensive orders, but was interrupted by Abdullah Tarzi, the Scout havaldar who shouted in Pushtu. "He says more enemies are coming. A lot more enemies," translated du Rand. With Kyle leading, the officers scrambled over and around rocks and boulders, following the havaldar to the northern side of the ridge top where they could see where the plain and escarpment met. Two miles away, they saw a mass of figures flooding onto the plain from the hill slopes. "It's Fakir's army. Four, possibly five thousand, and they'll be on us in thirty minutes," Bate confirmed as he studied the scene through his binoculars. Lowering the glasses, he turned to survey the ridge. "Well, we won't be able to hold them here. We'll surely be overrun," he said, his gaze sweeping across the plain where he spotted the only piece of ground where they might stand a chance. "The crossing, it's our only hope. Robin, get back to the aid post. Use Sergeant Ridley's men and your sweepers to move the wounded off this ridge. We'll have to leave the dead." "But sir," protested Howard Little. "I know, Sergeant-Major! It's an order I regret giving, but one I must," shouted the OC, interrupting his CSM. Lowering his voice, he turned to du Rand: "Hugo, I must ask you and your Scouts to hold this ridge top until the rest of us have reached the plain. Hopefully, I'm only asking you for ten minutes. Can you manage?"

"Ten minutes? Yes. But I wouldn't bet on much more," replied du Rand as he reloaded his revolver.

"Right, gentlemen, return to your platoons and let's get to that damn crossing," Bate commanded, focusing his attention on his three platoon officers.

Setting the aid post in motion, Cuimein went to collect Emily Sheffield."

"I think she might be dead, sir. She's not come round since ya left," pronounced Sale hesitantly, shaking his head.

"Well, Mrs Sheffield," declared Cuimein grittily, picking the woman up in his arms, her head and limbs flopping back limply, "alive or dead, I'm not going to leave you here."

Hugo stationed himself in the centre of his thin line of scouts as B Company raced away. The fire was hotter as the Wazirs and Mahsuds closed along the ridge. Soon they would begin to spread around the flanks and finding them unprotected could very quickly cut off their line of retreat. As for the time allotted, the officer needed to consult his watch - he looked instead to the base of the ridge. Although five hundred feet tall, the distance to the plain was about six hundred yards. So only when the first man reached the bottom of the ridge would he order his command to retreat?

Looking toward a cry, he saw one of his men holding his face. In a crouching run, the officer responded to help. Finding him with a bullet wound that had shattered a cheekbone and torn away part of an ear, he told the Scout to hold the damage tight with one hand to stanch the bleeding, then dispatched him after the aid post.

On returning to his position, he glanced once again to the plain. He was rewarded with the sight of several figures emerging onto it. Signalling for his men to fall back, Hugo stood in a half stoop to see they were all obeying. To his left, everyone was bounding away downhill. Then, pivoting to the right, he found they were doing the same. He was about to flee when a bullet struck the side of his waist, destroying one kidney and severing his lower spine.

Still gripping his pistol, the officer fought to regain his feet but found all he could do was push or pull himself the ground. Alone and facing a grisly death at the hands of brutal tribesman, Hugo struggled to drag himself up into a sitting position against a rock. A man knelt at his side as searing pain collapsed him onto his back.

"Saheb, you are injured," said Abdullah Tarzi.
"I have no legs, Havaldar. I'm unable to walk," replied the officer.
"I'll carry you," offered the Scout senior NCO.
"No! Go! Save yourself!" ordered du Rand.
The Scout, making no attempt to answer, remained to kneel next to his office. Then, lifting his eyes towards the enemy, he tensed, assuming a vigilant stance. Before joining the South Waziristan Scouts, Tarzi, an Afridi, had served on the Frontier with the Guides and knew well what du Rand's fate would be.

"For God's sake, man, I'm crippled. You cannot save me. Now. Go! Go!" beseeched du Rand, pounding a fist on the ground.

"Saheb, I have eaten at the King's salt for fifteen years. And now I am ready to die." The Scout's words were spoken as if reciting an oath.

Despite the pain, Hugo rose on his elbows, determined that the man beside him should not throw his life away needlessly.

"Havaldar Tarzi. I order you to re-join your Platoon. Jemadar Wakil will need your help. Now leave me. That is an order". Delivering this final command, Lieutenant Hugo du Rand placed the muzzle of his pistol to his template and squeezed the trigger.

CHAPTER 25

But search the land of living men,
Where will thou find their like again?
-Sir Walter Scott

"Damn it, man, do you have any sense? Get out of the way!"

The soldier, who had crouched down in Claude Gabson's path to adjust a loose puttee, quickly stood up and moved out of his way, stammering an apology. Then, with the column stopped within the tight space of a narrow nullah, the brigadier had to push his way through the mass of men and mules.

"Brigadier, sir, up there," Major Stephen Stanley, the Queen's D Company commander, directed, pointing up to a ledge on the side of a hill that towered over the nullah. Standing there, with binoculars raised, was Colonel Steinfeld. With Alan Qunell, his acting brigade major, following him, Gabson began to climb up to join the Queen's commander.

The time was nearing one o'clock in the afternoon, and the column had been marching from Khwaja Kalan for almost three hours. With no clear route to guide them, the queue had set off on an uncertain course to the north. They were only given an actual direction to follow when the aircraft returned to circle repeatedly,

498

far off in the distance. Using this as their guide, the column, setting up pickets as they went, continued across the country.

For the last hour, they had been following a valley that had narrowed to become a tight, high-walled nullah, almost a miniature tangi.

"What have we got, Darren?" Gabson asked sharply, having reached the ledge, and breathing heavily from his exertion. For some time now, they had been driven forward by the sound of small arms fire and exploding grenades.

"There, on the hill feature, sir," Steinfeld pointed out. He then raised his binoculars, and the brigadier scanned what was to them a hilltop. He saw figures, some carrying others, making their way down the rock-tangled slope.

"Yes, Darren. Those are your people," Gabson announced. From the hill, the gunfire continued without pause. "There are still a number of them on the hill crest. The Company seems to be executing a fighting withdrawal."

Having reached the embattled Company, with their rescue imminent, the brigadier turned his attention to the ground. This terrain would dictate his strategy. The nullah where his troops were waiting, led into the Faizu Tangi, the eastern entrance to the crossing.

At the mouth of the nullah was a wide bowl that extended on both sides of the tangi. Near the rim, the rock had crumbled away, allowing a crossing down a centuries-old camel path. The path twisted and turned for a hundred feet to an ankle-deep stream, then led up the other side. On both sides of the tangi, the bowl was mostly level ground composed of loose rock and sandy soil, interrupted by patches of wild rose bushes. Gabson was about to give orders to his junior commanders, all assembled on the ledge, when his brigade major interrupted him:

"Sir! Look there."

All eyes turned to where Qunell was pointing on the plain northwest of the hill.

"Well, well. Well, well," Gabson muttered to himself after lowering his binoculars. "So, the Fakir of Matun, you've returned."

"Right, gentlemen, things are looking up. Our priority is to safely retrieve the Chashma garrison from the enemy. I intend to accomplish this," the column commander declared forcefully. Gabson emphasized his words by punching his fist towards a hill a mile away across the plain. He then gave his battle orders. "Colonel Steinfeld, have your machine-gun platoon set up on the edge of the tangi. They should remain concealed. We want to surprise our enemy, the Fakir. The machine gunners' target is the approaching rabble, and they are to open fire only when I wave my topee. I'll be waiting on the other side of the tangi to start our attack. Major Alison, can you bring your guns into action where the machine guns will be? Your target is the top of that hill, and your signal to open fire will be the same as the machine guns'. Is that clear?"

Upon receiving confirmation, Gabson instructed Darren Steinfeld to lead the companies across the tangi and hide them in the bowl. He ordered Colonel MacKenzie to remain and safeguard their exit. However, MacKenzie objected, asking to join the battle. After considering the situation, Gabson commanded Steinfeld to take the Seaforth's Company under his command and form an extended line as the left forward company. He also directed Major Stanley of the Queen's to follow the Seaforths and take the position as the right forward company."

After receiving the command to advance, the Highlanders and Light Infantry rushed out of the nullah, encouraged by the NCOs' shouts and bellows. They sprinted across the level half-bowl and down into the tangi, merging along the way. Major Alison's Mountain battery closely followed once the nullah entrance was clear. Each pack battery gun, carried on eight mules, was led out of the nullah's tricky terrain, before turning right and breaking into a trot. Upon reaching the spot where the gun line was to be formed, the command was given to halt. The Punjabi Mussulman gunners quickly disassembled the guns from the mules and assembled them into six 3.7-inch howitzers, complete with stores, ammunition, and crew at their posts, awaiting the command to fire.

On the other side of the tangi, Seaforth and Queens infantry companies spread out into extended lines. They knelt shoulder to shoulder and fixed bayonets, as the basin was too narrow for each man to spread out to a tactical distance. Major MacRaith asked Fitzgerald to play "Blue Bonnets over the Border" before they began their advance, alerting the enemy of their arrival. B Company, located three-quarters of a mile in front of Gabson, was being rejoined by the Scouts platoon. Bate's platoons, having caught up, were mixed in among the wounded and disentangled themselves. Kyle's force formed a line, protecting the wounded, with 7 Platoon leading as the advance guard. The Scouts were sent to the left as they arrived, with 6 Platoon on the right, and 5 and 8 in the center. The Company's marching pace was determined by the speed the wounded could manage. Twenty-four wounded were aided at the post, five needed to be carried, and three sick were guided along by walking wounded. Graham Garvie helped a Scout suffering from sand-fly fever, while Pearton and Saunders steered two malaria sufferers in the correct direction. Chalkie Gray was carried by four sweepers, while another two sweepers assisted a soldier in piggyback fashion. The wounded helped each other; Frank Quinn, shot in the ribs, gave Tom May a shoulder to lean on as he limped on his one good leg. China Yeoman, despite a heavily bandaged left arm and shoulder, used his right arm to assist four others in carrying a man shot in the hip.

Jock Cressy, with Tracy clinging to his neck, approached Robin Cuimein to ask, "Sir, if you understand my meaning, may I have your pistol, please?" Cuimein, his arms aching from carrying Emily Sheffield, glanced at the Scotsman and then at Tracy, before agreeing, "Here, take it," and returning his gaze forward. Cressy, the shock of losing his hand wearing off and now in excruciating pain, held the young girl tightly with his armless stump as he took the pistol from Cuimein's holster.

The pain was a common factor among all the wounded. Ideally, each one should have been resting, with most needing urgent surgical treatment. Despite continuing to bleed from torn flesh and experiencing further damage from shattered bone grating within injured limbs and torsos, those who could, did not hesitate to extend a helping hand to their less mobile comrades."

The Company, in its retreat, thanks to the Scouts' rear-guard, had for the moment broken off close contact with the enemy. The majority of those now on the ridge had paused in their pursuit to strip and mutilate the bodies of the Queen's death. Others, though, were engaging in long-range sniping, with their bullets kicking up strike splashes of sand and dust, missiles that were by no means harmless. A corporal from 5 Platoon was killed by one; his body is now dragged along by two of his section.

"Bugger me!" cried Nash Slyfield, collapsing to the ground, a bullet wound in his right ankle.

"Get 'im up, Jeffrey," ordered Grif Griffiths, recovering the Lewis gun.

"God! Don't much fancy ending it all here," stated Slyfield, grimacing with pain as he reached to feel his ankle.

"So who gave you a licence to live?" gibed Harrison, through teeth clenched on his unlit pipe, as he reversed his rifle to jab the bayonet into the ground. Then, heaving his gunner up onto his shoulders and plucking out the rifle, he carried him off towards the other wounded, retreating with the aid post.

Kyle was focused on the redeployment of his platoons, leaving the organization of the Scouts, who were re-joining in small groups and individually, to Ahmed Wakil. It wasn't until he noticed one man significantly behind the others that he realized Hugo was missing. While retreating with his command, Bate, walking backward, shaded his eyes with his hand as he slowed down. The man, who was holding a rifle but was blurred in the midday sun glare, was unidentifiable for a moment. The officer then suddenly stopped; this last man had a beard.

His abrupt halt confused the soldiers nearest him, causing some to stumble. Little, always at the lieutenant's side, turned on them angrily: "Keep moving. Stop now, and it's over for all of us." Then, turning to Kip Donn, the Sergeant-Major waved him away so the three wouldn't provide a larger target for those on the ridge. The solitary figure maintained a steady run, approaching at a quick pace.

"It's the Scout sergeant, sir," Donn called out, pausing on one knee, his sharp eyes noticing the stripes.

The man came to a halt in front of Bate, standing silently with his chest heaving from deep breaths.

"Mister du Rand?" asked Kyle, with a stern look on his face.

In response, the Scout NCO silently pulled a pistol from his belt and handed it to the officer. Kyle took the weapon, gripping it around the chamber and holding it in his palm without saying a word.

"Rejoin your platoon, Havaldar," ordered Bate, who remained standing after the man had left, staring at the revolver.

"We're losing touch with the Company, sir," warned Little, speaking urgently.

Kyle, showing no sign of having heard, continued to stare at the pistol.

"You must see to us now, sir," the CSM stated, approaching the officer's side as he spoke. "The men are looking to you to get us out of this difficult situation." "Alright, Sergeant-Major," Kyle responded, glancing briefly at the crest of the ridge before turning to run with the other two. They were halfway to the crossing now, and as they distanced themselves from the ridge escarpment, more of Fakir's army came into view. The Fakir had anticipated twenty thousand men, but only had a potential force of five thousand. He had promised guns and gold that never materialized and had to rely on cunning deceit and trickery to convince his followers to join him. With Chashma now under his control, the Fakir needed captured rifles and British bodies to persuade sceptics that he was invincible. B Company executed a fierce withdrawal for five hours, suffering severe casualties but maintaining high morale. Now facing the broad, dense pack of murderous Afghan tribesmen, a stand had to be made with only rifles, ammunition, a bag of flour, dates, and a flask of water. The vast lashkar advanced towards the outnumbered British, but instead of being intimidated, they countered the enemy's triumphant cries with challenges and threats, reminiscent of their forefathers at Agincourt, Rorke's Drift, and Mons.

"Get closer, you flea-ridden bastard, so I can put lead in your traps!" Paani Waters bellowed. "Come on! I'm aiming to shove this up your arse!" Gynger Langdon yelled, hoisting a bayoneted rifle above his head. Defiance was thrown at the Afghan horde from every corner of the line. Then, with adrenaline pumping, hats lost, faces streaked with sweat, throats parched with thirst, and some with bloodied bandages from recent wounds, they retreated step by step, casting aside fear, eager only for the chance to seek revenge for their lost comrades. Joey Payne, fearing not for himself but for Lily, turned around to look for her. But when he saw Jeffrey Harrison carrying Nash Slyfield towards the group of wounded, she had rushed to them. She was removing the gunner's boot as they continued to walk. "Benedict!" Joey called to his mate at his side, turning back to face the enemy. "If we get cornered, and I don't make it, don't let them take Lily alive." Behind the basin at the crossing, the Queen's two rear companies were almost across and formed to the rear of D Company and the Highlanders. "Mister Richmond," Darren Steinfeld called to his RSM, who was waiting in the company with his adjutant ten yards to the rear. "Give Major Stanley my compliments. Tell him I've sent you to accompany him in the attack. I have no use for you here." "Very good, sir," replied Richmond, who had been enduring the torment of hell's flames, forced to listen to the firing, aware that his niece was somewhere amidst the chaos. As the RSM left at a run, Brigadier

Gabson gave the order to advance. "Colonel, you may proceed when ready.""

As the order was given, the Queen's and Seaforth's, the two lead companies, scrambled up the bank and pushed towards the flanks, forming an extended line. One of the Harijan sweepers, who was carrying a wounded comrade on his back and walking in step with Robin Cuimein, was the first to see the advancing troops. He shouted in joyous surprise, "Saheb! Gora-wallahs!" (Gora-wallah is a term used in the Indian subcontinent to refer to a white person). The district officer, who was focused on keeping his legs moving while holding onto Emily, looked towards the tangi half a mile away and saw a regimented line of troops advancing towards them. 7 Platoon began to cheer when they heard the Scottish bagpipe music drifting towards them across the barren ground.

On the ledge across the tangi, Freddie D'urban watched as Claude Gabson reached the top rim of the basin behind the two lead companies and waved his topee back and forth above his head. The political officer observed the troops on the plain in front of him, admiring the first line of three hundred evenly spaced men, their rifles held at the port, stepping out to Highland music. He shook his head and said to Colonel MacKenzie in a mildly perplexed voice, "It may be conventional, sir, but the Brigadier is breaking every Frontier rule for engagement ever laid down." Colonel MacKenzie replied, "Oh, yes, but it's a grand sight," and his head rose as his shoulders fell back.

B Company's rear-guard line was excited and wildly hurling curses at the Fakir army. They were impervious to 7 Platoon's cheering until they heard a blast followed by a whistling rush of air above their heads and an explosion halfway up the ridge. Then they found their voices again and joined 7 Platoon in their jubilation. The stern expressions the men had moments before were now replaced with delight as they screamed into each other's faces.

"Flamin' Jesus! It's the Column! The bastards have come for us!" shouted Benedict Lyall to Joey as he spotted a line of troops advancing towards them. Despite the loud cheering, the sound of machine gun fire just above their heads made it clear that the troops were firing at Fakir's army. Moreover, a second artillery shell had been fired and landed out of sight over the ridge. The fire control officer was pleased with the shot and moments later dispatched a salvo of six shells that exploded where the Mahsud and Wazir had earlier been mutilating the Queen's death. Bate urged his men to keep withdrawing, hoping to extract them from danger and avoid any further loss of life.

As they withdrew, the ridge was being bombarded by the 3.7-inch howitzers, causing showers of rock and stone to erupt. Hostile fire from the ridge had been eliminated, and the tribesmen were beginning to make their getaway around the sides of the ridge slope. Fakir's army had disregarded their own Border code of fighting by charging headlong across the featureless plain, leaving themselves out of cover. The Queen's Dogras machine-gunners mercilessly fired burst after burst into the Afghans' packed ranks. The Vickers machine gun had a well-spread beaten zone at twenty-five hundred yards, causing rounds to fall like rain with devastating effect.

In the initial moments, the eight Vickers machines guns began firing, and men started falling down dead or injured, the Pathans' first instinct was to seek cover. However, this approach proved ineffective as the bullets kept showering on them. Gradually, they began fleeing in groups of ten, twenty, and eventually hundreds. Some sought protection behind the ridge escarpment and others tried to cross the plain. Regardless, the Dogras' machine gunners pursued them until they were either hidden behind rocks or out of range. The Chashma garrison and the forward relieving companies were ecstatic to reunite. The sight of the Seaforths, dressed in kilts with stag head badges on their topees and a piper playing, brought Tim Cressy close to tears. "Lily, thank God you're safe," he exclaimed. Lily, who was still tending to

Slyfield's injured ankle, saw that the person who had gripped her arm was RSM Richmond. "Oh, Uncle Jake!" she gasped, falling into his embrace. "Come along, I will take you back," he proposed to Lily, which sounded more like a command. "No! I have wounded here," Lily, the nurse, refused and distanced herself from the man. "Miss Richmond has done a splendid job, sir," Slyfield intervened, leaning on Harrison's shoulders. "A stretcher party is on the way. I'll go and hurry them along," declared the RSM, pausing to look around at the injured. Once the first line of Highlanders and Queens had moved beyond his line of men, Kyle greeted the commanders of the relieving force. "Bate, where is Major Hartnell?" Darren Steinfeld asked as he approached the lieutenant. "He was killed yesterday at Chashma, sir," Kyle replied, saluting his Colonel and Brigadier Gabson. "Who has been in command?" inquired Gabson. "I have, sir," responded Bate. Gabson only grunted before giving Steinfeld a series of orders.

"Colonel, stop your men. Turn them around. This is as far as we need to go. We will return to the crossing."

"Sir!" Kyle interjected, his voice void of emotion but the intention was clear, "I've had to leave almost twenty dead on the ridge. One of them is Lieutenant du Rand."

"I'm sorry, Bate," Gabson replied, surveying the artillery-ridden ridge top and the plain littered with bodies. "Right now, my concern is for the living. We will return for your dead. I promise, but not today." As D Company was halted and ordered to return, one soldier shouted out to Tom O'Hanlon, "We saved your skin there, lad." "Saved us? You clumsy idiots got here too soon, had them right where we wanted," retorted O'Hanlon, his shirt stained with blood from his neck wound. As both the rescuers and rescued retreated, a platoon of Seaforths arrived with stretchers to collect the wounded. The Queen's and Seaforths' medical officers also joined. "She's weak, but she has a heartbeat. She's alive," the Queen's medical officer stated after examining Emily Sheffield with a stethoscope. "Thank God!" exclaimed Lily Richmond, holding Emily's hand and walking beside the stretcher carried by four men. Once everyone was safely across the tangi, Gabson ordered a retreat towards Khwaja Kalan and the road back to Ishak. He was determined to save the evacuating Chashma garrison from a massacre. As for defeating Fakir's army, that would be a matter for another day. From its vantage point above Fakir and his followers, the aircraft observing B Company's fight had to depart due to low fuel. It was soon replaced by two other aircraft, which lingered over the crossing area long after the column had retreated. They reported that between 110-130 tribesmen's bodies lay on the plain alone, providing a casualty estimate of 400 when considering the wounded. No matter how vehemently Fakir demanded they pursue, they wouldn't. The two attacking groups, Wazir, Mahsud, and Afghans, preferred to remain hidden until it was safe enough to return and loot each other's dead. Despite carrying casualties, the retreating column managed to make good time. While the rest of the infantry shielded their movements by picketing, B Company took on the task of carrying stretchers. They arrived at Khwaja Kalan within only two hours and unexpectedly encountered reinforcements. Later that morning, the other two battalions in Claude Gabson's brigade, the 6th Battalion of the 10th Baluch Regiment and the 7th Battalion of the 12th Frontier Force Regiment, reached Ishak. Colonel Kinsley set them to picket the road to Khwaja Kalan without allowing them any rest. Both battalions were experienced Frontier units and had secured the route two hours before the column's return to the road head. Anticipating the needs of the wounded, Kinsley sent five motor lorries typically used for collecting supplies. Gabson had the seriously injured placed on board and the vehicles were dispatched on the return journey to Ishak. In one truck, Emily Sheffield lay with her head in Lily Richmond's lap while Robin Cuimein crouched over her to ensure her wound did not meet the floor. B Company led the column, and the vehicles began to pass them with Lily sitting next to the open tailboard. The men of B Company cheered and waved at her, and she acknowledged their greetings before frantically waving and calling out for Joey. Payne, bareheaded and carrying his rifle slung over one shoulder, marched alongside Benedict Lyall. He also called out for Lily, waving back before disappearing. Cuimein's main reason for traveling with the wounded was his concern for Emily, but he also needed to report the details and outcome of the border incident to Peshawar. As the senior Indian Civil Servant involved, Sir Horatio would expect a full report as soon as possible. However, upon their arrival at Ishak and halting in front of the hospital bungalow, they found Victor Edwardes, Noel Lomas, and Taid Khan waiting for them. Cuimein assured Edwardes that Emily had willingly joined the rescue party and that his self-blame was unfounded.

When Emily was laid down, Lily was by her side checking the bandage for any additional bleeding. As she was examining, a figure knelt beside her, and she mistook him for one of the sweepers. However, she realized her mistake when a large hand reached out to hold Emily's hand. "Daktar, is she alive?" Zahir Khan asked, holding Emily's battered topee in his other hand. "Oh, Zahir Khan," Lily replied with relief, resting her head on his arm. "I don't know, at the moment, I just don't know." Without any delay, the Queen's medical officer went down on one knee on the other side of the stretcher. He lifted one of Emily's eyelids, quickly checked her eye, and then addressed Lily, "Miss Richmond, I know you must be tired, but we have several others who need surgery, and I can't heavily rely on my claw-fingered orderlies during a major operation. A trained nurse would be invaluable. Would you agree to assist?" "Is there somewhere I can wash up and change into something other than this?" Lily asked, standing to point at her blood-soaked dress. Cuimein withdrew with Edwardes, Lomas, and Taid Khan to the headquarters building, occupying the vacant office of Freddie D'urban. The district officer spent the next hour recounting what led up to and occurred during the retreat from Chashma. Upon hearing about Tracy and Lily's rescue party arriving at Chashma, Edwardes set out from Jandola with Oliver Ratcliffe, Tracy's father, to Sararogha. They met up with Noel Lomas, Zahir Khan, and Taid Khan, who had arrived in the night with Mullah Mohammad Shareef and his men. Upon learning about the evacuation order issued without Edwardes' knowledge, arrangements were made to accompany the Baluchis and Frontier Force Regiment to Ishak.

Soon after the district officer delivered his report verbally, their attention was drawn to the main gate by the sound of approaching music. The Queen's band had gone to greet the returning column, leading it into the camp. At the entrance, the group stopped on one side of the road to play as the line passed. Their platoons depleted, the Scouts just behind, and B Company marched in with Bate at their head, led by Claude Gabson from the front. Rifles sloped, arms swinging shoulder-high, they entered Ishak. They were dirty, stained with sweat, some bandaged, many without hats, but all in step with the band's music as it played "Daughter of the Regiment." By day's end, the Company had finally fallen out, and the tip of the sun's red glow had just dipped below the horizon. In respect for those absent, Platoon 6 quietly entered their tents. There were no shouts of boisterous relief, curses, complaints, or the dumping of kit, only solemn, deliberate movements. When they spoke, it was in hushed tones.

"You better get across to the hospital and have that face seen to," Joey Payne suggested. "Later. Those linseed lancers have enough on their plates at the minute," Charlie Robey replied. Joey left it at that, casting his gaze around his section tent. Everyone was sitting or standing near their beds, four of which were empty. Spider Webb and Ken Hallin were dead, and Chalkie Gray and Jock Cressy were at the hospital. Of the section, only six remained. Benedict's had the same count: two dead, two injured. The Lewis Section fared best, with only two wounded. Sid Frith's 3 Section suffered the most losses: five dead, one wounded, or two if you count Tom O'Hanlon. It was customary for the belongings of the deceased to be sold within the platoon. The items were passed around and resold, the proceeds of which would be sent to the deceased's next of kin in England or elsewhere. With so many losses in the Company, this would have been a difficult task, but the sales were conducted with the entire battalion's support. After the entire military force, now based at Ishak, had returned within its perimeter wire, Brigadier Gabson held an orders conference for all senior officers. The aim was to return to the recent battle area the next day to honour his promise to Bate and collect the dead of B Company. However, the 45-minute briefing on how this would be conducted and who would be involved was a waste of time. At dawn the next day, as the lead company of the Buluch Battalion was forming at the main gate to prepare to line the road to Khwaja Kalan, a train of camels was seen turning towards the encampment. Each camel carried the recovered bodies of Hugo du Rand and those from B Company who had died the previous day. They were secured on either side of the camel, wrapped in sacks. Local tribesmen led the camels, denying any involvement in the fighting. They claimed that bringing the bodies to the camp was an act of sincere compassion, and the standing bounty for doing so was of minor importance to them.

Early in the morning, scouting aircraft discovered that the invaders had retreated to Chashma. They occupied it for two days before dispersing on the second night in tribal and clan parties back across the border. The Wazir and Mahsud were left alone to await the arrival of British punishment columns. The Fakir himself was one of the first to leave. He blamed everyone but himself for the bloody defeat. He blamed the Russians for not providing the gold he needed to supply his army. He blamed the Afghan tribesmen who abstained from joining him. He blamed the hesitant clans of Waziristan for not rising. He slunk away to become a fugitive once more, with a price on his head.

Returning to his tent after visiting the men's lines, Kyle Bate sat on the edge of his bed and closed his eyes with a heavy sigh. He had been functioning in a continuous state of stress for most of the past twenty-four hours, and only now was the tension beginning to dissipate. He picked up Hugo du Rand's pistol that he had left on a chair and held it in his hands, reflecting on the unfairness of fate.

Kyle had joined the army seeking adventure but was unsure if he would stay for the entire course. On the other hand, Hugo always aspired to be a career officer and serve in his father's regiment.

At Sandhurst, he worked diligently and graduated within the top ten percent of his class. Kyle, however, was more interested in girls and weekends in London, resulting in him graduating in the middle of his class. Hugo undoubtedly deserved to climb to a high rank within the King's uniform. "Hugo! Christ, Hugo," Kyle whispered, clutching his friend's piston to his chest before falling asleep.

It was almost midnight when Lily finally left the hospital's medical room where most of the wounded had been operated on. The Queen's Doctor had instructed Lily to rest after she had stitched up Frank Quinn's wound. With Quinn being the last critical casualty to be attended to, Lily exited the room and entered the hospital ward. There were only eight beds, which was inadequate for the number of minor battle casualties, not to mention the catastrophe that had just transpired. They managed this problem by annexing a nearby tent.

Lily removed her apron to reveal her outfit, a pair of baggy men's trousers and a loosely fitting shirt, given to her by one of the orderlies. She placed it on a chair and walked over to Emily Sheffield's bed, whom she had earlier assisted in removing a bullet from her back. Throughout the evening, many people visited to check on the doctor, but Lily assured them all that she was in a satisfactory condition and didn't permit anyone to see her. Claude Gabson was one of the last to check on her and left grumbling under his breath.

As Lily stepped onto the veranda, she began to feel the full extent of her exhaustion. Her limbs ached and her eyes burned. Zahir Khan sat at one end of the doorway, maintaining a watchful eye with his knees pulled up and arms crossed. Lily reassured him that she was safe and urged him to rest, as she had recovered from her previous ordeal. Another soldier sat on the veranda, his head resting against a narrow stone pillar. She discovered him fast asleep when she approached and woke him by addressing him as Private Joseph Payne. The soldier embraced her and professed his love for her.

In a different setting, Katherine Harper, a night nurse at St. Thomas's ward, exclaimed "Oh, sugar!" when she realized she was behind schedule for her hourly rounds. She had been engrossed in writing a letter to her boyfriend and had lost track of time. As she hurriedly checked on her patients, she found one missing from his bed. She located him four beds away, removing the drip tube from his arm. As she chided him, Katherine was surprised by his statuesque pose. The nurse placed her hand on Joey's neck, below his ear, to check for a pulse. She was alarmed to find his skin cool to the touch. It was then she noticed Payne's hand clutching the hand of the man in the bed beside him. Katherine quickly left the room to fetch Doctor Gerald Page.

Upon his arrival, she informed him that it was the two elderly gentlemen who were assaulted in the tube station. The doctor checked both men's chests with his stethoscope and found they had both passed away. He also noticed the men's hands were tightly interlocked and made a jest that one must have owed the other a drink. Katherine chastised him for his inappropriate comment, reminding him of the sufferings and pain the two old gentlemen had endured. Accepting her criticism, Dr. Page arranged for the deceased to be moved."

After re-buttoning Joey Payne's pajama front, the young nurse stepped back to wish the two men well in their afterlife. "Good luck to both of you. It probably won't be paradise, but I hope you find peace wherever you are now." These were touching words from someone who wasn't obligated to express them. However, she was wrong. They were in paradise. Benedict was once again under the cooling shade of the banyan tree, with his face held in the feather-light fingertips of a beautiful Eurasian maiden as she drew his lips to hers. And Joey was in a sunny glade high in the Himalayan foothills, asleep in the arms of the girl he had fallen in love with and married. They were watched over by a distant, noble mountain that had watched over them once before and was preparing to do so again for all eternity.

\-   **The End -**

BY THE SAME AUTHOR

NOVEL
That's My Love Story
The Society in Opposition to Everything
Kaikkea vastustava seura

SHORT STORY
Where the Pandemic Started

NONFICTION
Nature God
Human Behavior on the Internet
Conceptualizing and Measuring Human Anxiety
on the Internet
Quote Me Everyday
Gags and Extracts
Nothing shakes the smiling heart
Why Nepal Fails

POETRY
A Very First Book of Poems: Heartbreak...
109 Quotes, 07 Poems and a Song of despair...
20 Love Poems and the Economy Crisis
25 Sexy Poems

Yet another Book of Poems
Happening: Poems
I Am Dead Man Alive
You Can
An Aphrodisiac
The Warrior
Obscurity
The Vandana & Other Poems
Warrior of Light
Adventus
One-liners
The Lacetier: a collection of poems, quotes, and arts

CHILDREN ILLUSTRATED BOOK
Pinky and Winky